The roof squealed, the sound high-pitched and long and desperate. Maddie instantly looked up, sensed Rivlin Kilpatrick do the same. A half-dozen muddy rivulets cascaded down, carrying bits of dried grass away from the widening slivers of light above. The squealing deepened into a shivering groan and then a bone-numbing rumble. The horses whinnied in panic. The planks parted. The rivulets gushed, thick and black. Above the noise of the collapsing roof, Maddie heard Rivlin swear. He moved with breathtaking speed, pulling her into his arms and tumbling both of them into the nearest corner.

She clung to him, keenly aware of the mass of sinew and heat wrapped around her, shielding her from the mountain of falling debris. Protected, she half-heard the crashing come to its end. It was beyond her realm of concern. Rivlin had pinned her upright into the shelter of the corner, holding her there, pressed hard against her, his breath quick and warm against her temple, his heart hammering hard against her breast.

He eased his shoulders back and brushed wet tendrils of hair from the side of her face. "Maddie?"

She looked up into dark, searching eyes. Her throat tightened. She couldn't breathe, but it didn't matter.

"Are you all right, Maddie?"

No. I want you to kiss me.

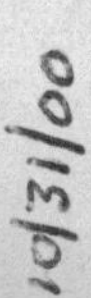

Leslie LaFoy

MADDIE'S JUSTICE

Bantam Books

New York Toronto London Sydney Auckland

MADDIE'S JUSTICE
A Bantam Fanfare Book / September 2000

FANFARE and the portrayal of a boxed "ff" are trademarks
of Bantam Books, a division of Random House, Inc.

ISBN 0-553-58045-0

Published simultaneously in the United States and Canada

Bantam Books are published by Bantam Books, a division of Random House, Inc. Its trademark, consisting of the words "Bantam Books" and the portrayal of a rooster, is Registered in U.S. Patent and Trademark Office and in other countries. Marca Registrada. Bantam Books, 1540 Broadway, New York, New York 10036.

PRINTED IN THE UNITED STATES OF AMERICA
OPM 10 9 8 7 6 5 4 3 2 1

For Marti J
who has always believed

Prologue

13 August 1871
Cincinnati, Ohio

Rivlin Kilpatrick stood in the corner of his mother's drawing room and watched his family and their friends celebrate the birth of yet another Kilpatrick grandchild. He knew the people in attendance, had grown up with most of them. He had once belonged among them, had something in common with them. But then he'd gone off to do his duty and fight for General Grant in the war and everything had changed. He had changed. He had left as a boy of seventeen and become a man in a world far distant from drawing rooms, fancy clothes, and polite society. He no longer fit in this place, among these people, or in the kind of life they led. Rather than face the painful truth of it day after day, he'd left. And then returned again, this time the dutiful son taking up the reins from his late father's hands. It had been a mistake.

But then, he mused, tossing whiskey down his

throat, if there was one thing he did exceedingly well, it was make mistakes. He could be counted on for that. He could also be counted on for taking damn near forever to see the error in his judgment and then taking yet another eternity to do what he should have done in the first place.

It had only taken him six months this time, though, and that was a record for swiftness. He could only think that it had something to do with managing to live—against all odds—to the ripe old age of twenty-five. If he ever reached thirty, he might actually be capable of good judgment. If it ever happened, he'd write his mother to tell her of the rare accomplishment, trusting her to share the uncommon and unexpected news with his six older siblings. They'd all be astounded. And, with any luck at all, their exclamations would be just as joyously exuberant as their outraged squealing was going to be when they discovered that he'd slipped from their clutches again.

With a tight smile Rivlin set his empty glass on the tray of a passing servant and left the room. He paused at the table in the foyer to remove the telegram from the Marshal's Service from the breast pocket of his dress coat. He carefully placed it on the silver tray then went upstairs to change his clothes and the course of his life.

13 August 1871
Oklahoma Territory

MADDIE RUTLEDGE STEPPED from the one-room schoolhouse and shaded her eyes against the glare of the late-morning sun. The heat rose from the parched earth in shimmering, undulating waves. Maddie peered through the rippling curtain, trying to see down the trail that led into the woods. It was so unlike Lucy to be late. If it had been any of her other Cherokee students Maddie wouldn't have worried, but Lucy Three Trees religiously abided by white concepts of time. Something was wrong. Maddie could feel it in her bones.

The dark shape of a single horse and a black carriage separated from the tree line and came toward her through the heat. Maddie recognized the vehicle and knew that Mrs. Stewart, Tahlequah's self-appointed Maven of Right and Proper, was coming to conduct her monthly surprise classroom inspection. Any other time Maddie would have been annoyed by her presence. Today, however, she saw the woman's arrival as a welcome blessing.

Ten minutes later, with Mrs. Stewart enthroned at the front of the classroom, Maddie strode to the line of horses picketed in the shade of the school building. Hers was an ancient steed, saved from death by her insistence that the animal could ably serve her simple riding needs. Pausing at the saddlebags, Maddie removed her battered felt hat and holstered revolver with a wry smile. The good Christian women who had raised her in the Iowa orphanage would be appalled by both articles, she thought. The hat they would eventually, but grudgingly, accept as being a frontier adaptation necessary to protect her skin from the harsh sunlight.

But the gun . . . The good women would never, ever accept a six-shooter. Guns were the devil's tools, an evil that corrupted the heart and hand of the person holding it. Of course they didn't have western diamondback rattlesnakes in Iowa and, having never been confronted by six feet of coiled, deadly poison, the good women would never understand that sometimes snakes had to die from a cause other than old age. That was a fact of life in the territory and one Maddie had quickly learned on her arrival two years before.

Appropriately armed and shaded, Maddie swung up into the saddle and set off toward the Three Trees' cabin, her mind working through the possibilities. Lucy was almost ten, an only child, and since her mother's death last winter, the woman of the house. Her father was frequently absent, visiting friends and relations in neighboring settlements. Lucy could be ill and suffering alone. Or she could have had an accident and been unable to get herself to the mission for help. Or . . . Maddie jerked upright. Eight Cherokee girls had been brutally raped and beaten to death over the course of the last six months. She didn't want to think that Lucy could be the ninth.

Maddie pushed her aged horse as fast as her conscience would allow, assuring herself that there could well be a thousand other reasons why Lucy hadn't come to school that morning. The mental fortification was fairly successful until the trail entered the tree line. As she forced herself down the narrow trail to the tiny clearing that held Lucy Three Trees's dilapidated, one-room cabin, her hands trembled on the reins and the hairs on the back of her neck prickled.

The sound of an equine snort stopped her own animal short. Maddie's mind clicked through the implications even as she swung down from the saddle. Lucy didn't own a horse. She walked to and from the schoolhouse every day. None of Lucy's friends owned horses either. They were all just as dirt poor as she was. Leaving her mount at the side of the cabin, Maddie strode to the corner and cautiously peered around it.

Her heart slammed into her throat. She recognized the big sorrel. It belonged to Caleb Foley, the son of the head Indian agent. And the whispers said that it was Caleb. . . .

Maddie dashed round the corner, a cry strangling in her throat at the sight of the splintered cabin door. Her only thoughts those of saving Lucy, she scrambled over the debris and through the opening.

In the darkness of the tiny cabin Maddie caught terrifying bits of the reality . . . Lucy cowering naked in the farthest corner, her face streaked with tears, her long dark hair tangled and bloody, a half-dressed Caleb turning away from the girl to swing the fireplace poker in another direction. Maddie gasped and instinctively stumbled back and out of his reach. He bellowed and came after her. Lucy cried softly.

Inescapable truth and a strange sense of calm flowed over Maddie as Caleb Foley bore down on her. *Sometimes snakes had to die.*

Chapter One

October 1873
Fort Larned, Kansas

Dust motes danced in the stream of afternoon light. Only half-listening to her fellow prisoner's labored efforts to read, Maddie gazed into the light angling through the slats of the attic window. There had been a time in her life when she hadn't given light and dust motes a passing thought. Then, in the first months of her sentence, they had become the only gentle link to the world beyond the attic cell. The color and slant of the light marked the season and the time of day. The motes told her of the weather enjoyed by those whose lives were still their own. She had marked the passage of nineteen months, one week, and three days by the motes. And then Rosie and Myra had been shoved through the door to share her confinement and she hadn't depended so much on the dusty light to keep her sanity anchored. Now she watched the motes dance because they were a pretty distraction.

". . . our lives, our fortunes, our sac-red honor."

The mispronunciation caught Maddie's attention and she pointed to the text. "Look at this word again, Rosie," she softly corrected.

Barely fifteen, and a full twelve years Maddie's junior, Rosie still had the natural curiosity of a child. She knit her brows and leaned closer to the page. "Oh! Say-cred!" she cried a moment later. She looked up and smiled. "Sorry, Maddie."

Maddie gently brushed a lock of chestnut hair out of Rosie's line of vision. "There's no need to apologize. Everyone stumbles over a word from time to time."

"Ohmigod! Maddie! Rose!" Myra exclaimed from the tiny northern window of their shared room. "You got to come look at this!"

Rose vaulted to her feet and bounded through the maze of their cots to join Myra at the window. Maddie slipped a bookmark into the text, closed it, and then rose to follow.

"Da-mn," Rosie offered on an appreciative sigh. "That gelding has to be sixteen hands if he's one. And broad in the chest, too. What conformation! I could get a fortune for him." She snorted before adding, "The one bein' led ain't nothin' special, though. Just your run-of-the-mill stringer."

"To hell with the horses," Myra countered. "Look at the man. You want to talk about conformation. My, my, my. I could eat him right up. Maddie, you need to come look. Honest. It isn't gonna hurt your virtue none to peek."

Leave it to Rosie, the horse thief, to notice the animals, Maddie thought as she reached the window.

And Myra, the middle-aged prostitute, to notice the man. What was a teacher supposed to notice from the height of three stories? Intellect and degree of education were somewhat difficult to judge from a distance. Rosie stepped back to allow Maddie room to peer through the slats.

Rosie, as always, was right about the horses. The roan gelding the man rode was clearly an animal of quality breeding and the other, a sorrel mare, nothing special by any standard of measurement. And the man . . . His shoulders were as broad, maybe even more so, as his mount's chest. He sat in the saddle with ease and comfort and command—as though he had been born in it. A wide-brimmed felt hat that had once been gray cast his face in shadow. "He is rather nicely proportioned," Maddie offered. Both Rosie and Myra nodded. Maddie smiled.

"Honey," Myra drawled, "that's a fair piece beyond nice. That's the muscle an' sinew dreams are made of. Oh Lord, what I wouldn't give for just a few minutes alone with that one."

Rosie poked her head around the edge of the little window and looked through the opening again. As the man reined in his horse and swung down, Rosie whispered, "Well, criminey. No wonder he's got such a huge horse. Any shorter an animal an' his feet would drag the ground."

In Maddie's experience there were two kinds of men: those that looked like they had dressed by crawling through a dirty laundry basket or those that looked like they'd spent hours primping before a mirror with a frazzled valet at their beck and call.

This man was decidedly different. He was dressed in what amounted to the civilian uniform of the West: pointy-toed leather boots with a substantial heel, faded denim dungarees, light blue cambric shirt, red bandana knotted around his neck, and a vest of scarred brown leather. It was how he wore the clothing that marked him as being apart from other men—with an intriguing mix of both precision and nonchalance that suggested he knew how to dress like a proper gentleman but couldn't be bothered with it.

"He looks like a lawman," Maddie observed, watching the way the stranger tilted his head to sweep the compound with his shadowed gaze. "Cautious. Gun belt slung low and tied off."

"Well," Myra cooed, "for him I'd be willing to set aside my differences with the law."

Rosie nodded. "You keep him busy an' I'll see to nippin' the horse. Split with you sixty-thirty."

"It's sixty-forty," Maddie corrected, watching the man tie his mount to the hitching post below their vantage point. "The total has to be one hundred."

"Sixty-forty?" Myra countered, stepping back, her hands going to her ample hips. "That's hardly fair!"

"Sixty-forty is too fair. You'd be havin' the pleasure of makin' his acquaintance while I was riskin' my neck."

"And it would be a pleasure," Myra admitted with a knowing smile. "Know how you can tell, Maddie?"

Maddie winced. "I really don't want to know," she replied pleasantly. "But thank you for offering to tell me."

The stranger strode toward the building below and out of their sight.

"We made a deal and Rose and I have been holding up our end," Myra said, turning away from the window. Rosie nodded as Myra went on. "We've been letting you teach us how to read and write. It's only right for you to take another lesson in what we know."

The finer points of horse thievery and prostitution. Agreeing to the exchange of expertise had seemed like such a good and noble idea at the time. "True enough," Maddie admitted, regretting her honorable tendencies. "All right, Myra. How can you tell he'd be a pleasure?"

RIVLIN PAUSED IN THE SHADOW of the porch and studied the room through the open doorway. The central guard room was the same as to be found at any one of the forts scattered throughout the West—rough-hewn wooden floor, walls, and ceiling. Aside from the haze of grime, the windows were bare. A wide door of iron bars occupied the far wall and between it and the front door sat the obligatory battered desk. The guardsman assigned to the watch slumbered in the chair behind it, his feet on the desk, his body sprawled over the chair, his hat over his face. Everything, man included, was coated with a fine patina of dust. Rivlin pulled his hat brim lower and crossed the threshold. The room reverberated with the sound of his footsteps, prompting the man behind the desk to lift his hat from his face and cast a doleful look Rivlin's way.

"What can I do for ya?" the man asked, not bothering to remove his heels from the desktop.

Rivlin Kilpatrick reached inside his vest and withdrew the thrice-folded court order, saying, "United States Marshal. I have orders to escort one of your prisoners to a courtroom in Leavenworth." He handed the official documents to the guard. "I'd appreciate being done with the transfer and on my way as soon as possible."

"How appreciative might you be?" the man asked, tapping the paperwork on his outstretched leg.

Rivlin's smile was tight. "So appreciative I might forget to file charges against you for soliciting a bribe."

"Just funnin' ya," the man said defensively, easing his feet off the desk.

"Yeah. Fetch my prisoner."

The guardsman glanced at the paper, tossed it on the desk, and used both hands to leverage himself out of the chair. "Might take a minute or two," he supplied, taking a set of wrist irons and a ring of keys from the desk drawer. "This one always makes it a fight."

Rivlin watched in silence as the man opened the iron door and shuffled up the dark stairs beyond. The door stood open and Rivlin slowly shook his head. Proof—as though he needed it—that every lax-brained man in America had somehow found his way to the frontier. One corner of his mouth quirked up in a wry smile as he considered, not for the first time, what that observation implied about himself.

He set the musing aside. He knew the general nature of the task ahead of him. The report had been, as usual, short and blunt. His prisoner had been convicted of first-degree murder two years ago in the Oklahoma Territory. As per the law, the prisoner had been transported to Kansas to serve his sentence at the cost of twenty-five cents per day to the American people. The reason why he hadn't been incarcerated at Fort Leavenworth hadn't been mentioned in the report, but then that detail would have been considered irrelevant to the current task of transport. Rivlin had been at his job long enough that he could well guess the particulars that hadn't been mentioned but *were* relevant—the man was a killer and hadn't been imprisoned long enough to have had his attitude tempered. It was going to be a long, hard ride to Leavenworth.

A thud and a low oath came from the stairwell. Rivlin instinctively placed his hand on the butt of his revolver. Another hard thud, then another. A string of curses followed. And then the guard half-rolled, half-slid down the wooden steps to land in an unceremonious heap at the bottom.

The dust was still rising around him when a flash of blue flew over him and came to a skittering halt between the man and Rivlin. Long dark hair in a single thick braid. Ringlets curling around a small oval face. Wide, impossibly blue eyes. A shirt torn open to reveal creamy white swells. Manacled hands. Rivlin silently swore. "Are you M. M. Rutledge?"

She looked him up and down, her appraisal as quick as his own had been and just as thorough. She didn't answer, but instead straightened her shoulders and lifted her chin. The manacles bound her hands before her, allowing her to reach up to jerk her shirt closed. The iron rod between the cuffs prevented her from fastening the buttons that remained. He could see that she had pride and more than the average amount of poise. He also suspected that under the grime she possessed a bit of prettiness as well. Rivlin clenched his teeth. Damn if he'd ever once thought to call a prisoner pretty.

"She's a cold-hearted, murderin' little bitch."

Rivlin looked at the guard struggling to his feet. The man's nose had been mashed flat; blood poured over his mouth and dripped from his chin. Given the state of Rutledge's clothing and the guard's face,

Rivlin could well imagine what had transpired on the stairs. "Whatever she is," Rivlin said evenly, "move to touch my prisoner again and I'll kill you. Sign the transfer papers."

Maddie considered the lawman again—for a lawman he certainly was, all six feet and however many inches of him. His shoulders were even broader than they'd looked from her third-story vantage. And where before the height and his hat brim had kept her from seeing his face, she could clearly see it now—hard-chiseled features, sun-burnished skin, dark strands of hair, a day's growth of stubble. It was his eyes that told her the most about about him, though. Dark brown, flecked with slivers of gold, they missed nothing. In them she saw the light of keen intelligence and a cool steadiness that spoke of lethal willingness and ability.

The guard clawed his way to his feet and stumbled to his desk. Maddie half-turned and took a step back so that she placed both men in her line of sight. The lawman stood silently, keeping his hand on the butt of his gun while the guard found a pen and an ink pot, then scribbled his name across the bottom of the last page. Shoving the paper across the desk, he warned, "Don't turn your back on her."

One corner of the lawman's mouth quirked upward. "Where's the property room?" he asked.

"Across the quad." The guard fixed Maddie with a murderous glare before adding, "Middle building."

"I'll have the key to her irons," the lawman said, extending his left hand. When the key had been surrendered, he shoved it into his pants pocket and nodded curtly, saying, "Much obliged for all your help."

His voice was low and measured and with a roll

of distant thunder lying beneath every word. The lawman turned to face her and Maddie's heart skipped a beat. When he stepped forward, it took everything in her not to retreat. He was a good head taller than she was, at least a hundred pounds heavier. If she had to fight him, the odds were she would lose. Maddie tried to ignore her hammering heart. It was too late to feign a gentle demeanor. Maddie saw no recourse but to stand openly ready to meet his challenge.

His right hand shifted away from his gun butt, but it was with his left that he took the bar between her cuffs. Without so much as a word, he turned and pulled her along in his wake. She went because she had no other choice, but she refused to make it easy for him. Angling her shoulders back and dragging her booted heels over the plank floor, her resistance succeeded in making the massive muscles in his shoulder and arm bunch, in making him tighten his grip on the bar. The effort didn't seem to tax him, though, and in that Maddie was sorely disappointed.

"I don't have to be dragged along like a pack animal," she said through clenched teeth. "I can see where we're going and I'm perfectly capable of getting there under my own power."

At the edge of the porch, he stopped and slowly turned around to face her again. "Don't try to run, Rutledge."

Maddie looked around the hard-packed yard, around the high stockade, before looking back at him. She arched a brow. "Where would I go, lawman? And how far do you think I'd get?"

After a long moment, he released his hold on her manacles and stepped to the side. With an abbreviated gesture he indicated the buildings on the opposite side of the yard. "After you . . . ma'am."

She heard the hesitation he employed before the courtesy title and knew that he fully intended it to be an insult. The son of a bitch actually thought verbal slaps had the power to wound her. Maddie offered him a condescending smile and stepped out of the porch shadow. The first rays of sunlight to hit her shoulders in almost two years nearly knocked her to her knees. The brilliance of the light was blinding and, only three paces along, she was forced to lift her arms and shade her eyes.

Leading the horses, Rivlin walked slightly behind and to the left of his prisoner, watching her intently. Her boots were too big, forcing her to drag her feet as she walked. If she did get loose, she'd be easy to track. Unless she discarded the boots, of course, and attempted to make her way barefooted.

As was his habit in every prisoner transport, Rivlin assessed her as best he could, trying to decide how far she might have the ability to get before he caught up with her. She wore faded denim dungarees that, like her boots, were several sizes too large for her. She wore no belt—no prisoner being allowed the means of hanging either himself or another—and he suspected that it was only her barely tucked-in shirt that kept the waist of the pants from sliding down over her hips. The shirt was too big for her as well, the cuffs having been rolled back several times just to bring the sleeves to her wrists. Almost tall—he guessed maybe five-six—and fine boned. From what he could tell there wasn't an ounce of spare flesh on her.

She definitely wasn't a meek kitten-type woman. He'd seen with his own eyes that Rutledge had the wherewithal to bloody a guard's face and knock him down a flight of stairs. And from what he could tell, she wasn't any snarling wildcat either. That, of course, didn't mean she wasn't a force to be reckoned with. Her sex notwithstanding, she carried herself in much the same way that professional gunfighters did.

He mentally figured the distance to Leavenworth. At least a dozen hard riding days lay ahead of him. Maybe more, depending on how much strength and grit the Rutledge woman had in her. He couldn't push her too hard. She had to be able to walk into a courtroom when he got her there or there wasn't any point in making the damn trip in the first place. Sweet Christ, a female prisoner. Of all the god-awful assignments he'd ever been handed, this one ranked at the top of the heap. As if the logistics of prisoner transport weren't goddamn difficult enough in and of themselves.

She marched into the quartermaster's office ahead of him, the hollow sound of her boots on wood ending his internal grumbling. Her arms fell to her sides as much as the manacles permitted and for a half-second her shoulders slumped forward in apparent relief. She quickly squared them and then looked back over her shoulder as though to be sure he was still there. He cocked a brow in silent assurance and her lips thinned in response. Rivlin dropped the reins over the hitching rail and followed.

"Well, as I live and breathe," drawled an all-too-familiar voice from behind the counter, "Cap'n Rivlin Kilpatrick."

Rivlin swore under his breath. First a female prisoner and now having to deal with one of the lowest forms of life the U.S. military had ever stuffed into a uniform.

"Been a mighty long stretch, sir. What's it been? Nigh on five years since we was garrisoned at Leavenworth?"

"About that long, Murphy," he answered tightly. "We'll have Rutledge's personal effects." *If you haven't stolen them all by now.*

Rivlin Kilpatrick, Maddie silently repeated. *Captain. Leavenworth.* The latter two facts told her a great deal. Kilpatrick had a military background and his rank said he'd either distinguished himself in service or paid for his commission. As for paying for his commission . . . Something about him suggested that it wasn't likely. The former possibility didn't seem too far-fetched, though. Judging by the look of him, he was just old enough to have served in the late War Between the States. Being stationed at Leavenworth meant he'd served on the Union side. Not that she would have guessed him to be a Johnny Reb anyway. His voice didn't have the soft edges typical of southerners, his behavior none of the southern civility.

Maddie glanced between the two men. Murphy was running his finger down the columns of a ledger and flipping from one page to the next, oblivious to the hardness in Kilpatrick's eyes. Kilpatrick didn't like Murphy at all. Even a blind man would notice. The air practically hummed with tension.

"Heard you didn't like being back East and was hooked up with the marshals these days," Murphy said without looking up. "You transportin' our prisoner somewhere?"

Maddie dropped her gaze to the floor in an effort to conceal her interest in the answer. No one ever told prisoners anything. You were simply to obey a command to move, the whys and wherefores not at all important as far as your compliance was concerned.

"Yep."

Maddie squirmed in frustration. Did Marshal

Kilpatrick have to pay a nickel for every word he uttered?

"Will you be bringin' her back?" Murphy asked.

"My orders are to deliver her. What's done with her after that isn't my concern or responsibility."

Maddie mentally shrugged. There was nothing she could do to alter the course ahead of her. She'd sealed her fate the instant she'd pulled the trigger. Where she went and what happened to her didn't matter. It never had.

Murphy's finger stopped and he mouthed a number before turning and heading into the line of shelves behind the counter.

"Here you go," he said a moment later, coming forward with a tattered cardboard box. He opened it, identifying each item as he laid it on the counter. "One hat, one coat, one pair of moccasins an' one of them there Injun medicine bags. That'd be all of it." He turned the ledger around, dabbed a pen in an inkwell and held it out to Maddie, saying, "Make your mark in the book, Rutledge."

"I had a pocket watch when I came here," she said. "You put it in the box. I watched you."

"You must be rememberin' someplace else," he replied blandly. "The book don't show a pocket watch. Make your mark."

It was gone, stolen; Reverend Winters's pocket watch, the one remembrance she had of the only good years in her life. Her chest tightened but, refusing to let these men see her cry, she snatched the pen from Murphy's hand and signed her full name, Madeline Marie Rutledge, complete with artistic flourishes—because she could and because for some unfathomable reason she wanted Murphy and Kilpatrick to know she wasn't illiterate. If either of them noticed her ability, he gave no sign of it.

Kilpatrick took her coat and hat from the counter. Murphy flopped the ledger closed and leaned his elbows on the counter.

"See you around, Cap'n?"

"Never know."

Maddie snatched up the medicine pouch, dropped the long leather thong over her head and tucked it beneath her shirt front. Then she scooped the moccasins off the counter and headed out the door. At the edge of the porch she sat down, yanked the heavy leather boots off her feet and pitched them as far as she could. She didn't care what Marshal Rivlin Kilpatrick thought of her willful disregard for property belonging to and provided by the great State of Kansas. If he wanted to give those damn boots respect, he could fetch them and cart them around as she had for the last two years. She'd actually had dreams about slipping her feet into the comfort of her moccasins and she wasn't about to settle for clutching them to her bosom as she rode off to God only knew where.

Rivlin watched her struggle to get her hands close enough together to effectively tie the lacings of the knee high moccasins. Good judgment told him to insist that she put the government-issued boots back on her feet. The childlike yearning on her face, however, prodded his sense of compassion. It had to be hell being a prisoner, having every facet of your life controlled by others. What did it matter to him what footgear she wore? If he ever had to track her, the moccasins would leave a distinctive enough trail to follow. And it was a sure bet that she wouldn't discard them; he'd seen the almost worshipful look in her eyes when Murphy had pulled them from the box. Rivlin tossed the coat and hat down on the porch beside her and then stepped around to face her. She looked up, her eyes sparking with unspoken challenge as she continued to fumble with the laces.

"I'll tie them for you," he said gruffly, easing down onto one knee, never taking his gaze from hers. "But the instant you move to smash my face with those irons, Rutledge, I'll knock you into next week. Understood?"

She assessed him, then slowly nodded and pulled her hands back, tucking them deep into the curve of her lap. When he'd finished the task, she said quietly, "I really did have a gold-plated pocket watch when I was brought here."

"Yeah, well," Rivlin answered, grasping her upper arm and hauling her to her feet, "it doesn't surprise me that it's gone now." He retrieved her coat and hat, settling the latter firmly onto her head as he added, "Murphy's fingers have always been sticky. I've never trusted him any further than I could throw him." He indicated the horses with a jerk of his thumb.

She studied the sorrel and then drew a deep breath. "Where are you taking me?"

"Leavenworth."

"Why?" she pressed.

"You're to testify at a trial," he answered, taking her by the arm again and guiding her between the animals.

"Testify about what?" she asked warily.

Either she was a very good actress or she truly had no idea what the federal prosecutors expected of her. "I'm given orders and I follow them without question," he said.

"And I'm to do the same, correct?" she asked resentfully.

"It seems to me that you're in no position to do

anything but what you're told," he replied matter-of-factly. "Do you need a leg up?"

She jerked her arm from his grasp and reached for the saddle horn. "Only when it's a cold day in hell, Marshal," she said, slipping her foot into the stirrup and swinging up.

Her right foot grazed the flank and before Rivlin could open his mouth to warn her, the horse threw Rutledge off its back, and she plowed a short, shallow furrow in the dirt with her backside.

Rivlin caught the reins and brought the animal back under control, then stepped forward, extending his hand to help his prisoner rise. She glared up at him, twisted her shoulders away, and climbed to her feet without his assistance.

"She spent some time as a military packhorse," Rivlin supplied, heading to his own mount. "She's touchy about her flanks."

His prisoner muttered under her breath, gave him another hard look, and managed to climb into the saddle without making the animal dance out from under her. Rivlin tilted his head so that the shadow of his hat brim concealed his smile as he snagged the lead on her horse and headed toward the gates.

Chapter Two

SHE DIDN'T HAVE ANYTHING to do but sit and think. The marshal held her mount on a short lead, forcing her to ride beside him on the left. *Leaving his gun hand free,* she noted. *As usual.* He was far more cautious than the marshal who had brought her to Fort Larned. William Hodges hadn't considered her the least bit dangerous. Maddie smiled ruefully. Hodges had been right; she hadn't been all that dangerous. Then. Hodges had been the one to teach her the necessity of it.

Her gaze slid to this marshal. Was he of the same ilk as Hodges? God help her if he was. Kilpatrick was taller and broader than Hodges. But then this marshal had yet to look at her in the same way Hodges had. She'd known from the moment Hodges had set eyes on her what he wanted. He'd looked right through her clothes. It had taken him all of a day's ride to make his first attempt to rape her.

Maddie shut the ugly memory away and deliberately brought another to her mind.

Myra . . . Rosie . . . When she'd turned in the saddle at the gates and lifted her hands in farewell, they'd poked strips of cloth through the window slats and fluttered them—had kept fluttering them until the gates had closed behind her and blocked them from her sight. Maddie had known in that moment it would be the last she ever saw of the two women who had become her only friends. She forced herself to swallow, stiffen her back, and put that memory away as well. It wouldn't do to let Marshal Kilpatrick think she was the least bit weak or vulnerable. If you looked like easy prey, acted like easy prey, then odds were you'd end up being prey—easy or otherwise.

"What does the M. M. stand for?"

She didn't look at him, but considered the tone of his voice. It was much gentler than it had been back at the fort. Maddie wondered why the change as she answered, "Madeline Marie. I'm called Maddie."

"Were you named for a favorite family member?"

And then she understood what he was about. "Are you worried about your back, Marshal?"

He smiled thinly, but otherwise didn't seem concerned about her having discovered the reason for his questions. "Always do, ma'am. It's a necessity of the occupation."

"I can well imagine," she countered dryly. "It seems to me that marshals must make enemies by the hour and the cartload."

He shrugged. "I can think of a few men I'd rather not have to deal with again any time soon. And you, Maddie Rutledge? Do you have any enemies I should know about?"

"It's not my enemies that concern you, Marshal," she observed. "It's my friends."

"No family to speak of, huh?"

"I didn't say that," she retorted easily, appreciating his tenacity, but not willing to let him know just how right he was. She was better off if he was uncertain and wondering, if his attention was focused on the possibility of his hide being ambushed. The more occupied his thoughts were in that direction, the less likely they would be on ambushing her. "I've got scads of brothers and cousins and uncles."

He offered her a low, rumbling sound in response, something between a grunt of acceptance and a snort of disbelief. "How'd you end up down in the Oklahoma Territory?"

"I came out of Iowa as a teacher."

"Most schoolmarms don't end up in prison."

"I'll have to take your word for it," Maddie replied.

"What went wrong?"

She chuckled quietly. "Everything."

"That covers a lot of ground." His gaze slid to hers and his brow inched upward. "Would you care to be more specific?"

"No, I wouldn't," she answered, irritated by his inquisition. "You're going to have to find some other way to pass the time on this jaunt, Marshal Kilpatrick. I'm not about to entertain you with the tales of my wanton and wicked life. If you want a dime novel story, then you're either going to have to buy one or make one up yourself."

He studied her openly, his eyes moving slowly over her face and then down the length of her body. She watched for the telltale flicker of lust in his eyes. His gaze came back to meet hers, still somber and blandly appraising.

"What is it that you're looking to see?" Maddie demanded, feeling oddly angry at having apparently failed to meet whatever expectation he harbored.

"I'm trying to decide when you need to stop for the day," he explained. "I figure you probably haven't had much opportunity to ride of late and that the effort's got to be tiring."

Part of her thought he was being genuinely compassionate. Another part of her suspected subterfuge in the proffered kindness; there always was. "Don't stop on my account," Maddie ground out, focusing her attention on the trail. "If you want to ride straight through, I'm not going to complain."

"There's a natural spring about a mile ahead," he said as though she hadn't spoken. "It's got a pool deep enough for bathing if you're of a mind to do that."

Bathing? Oh dear God, to have a bath . . . And then the moment of joyous prospect came to a shattering end. First fear and then anger shot through her veins. Experience had taught her that neither was a safe emotion to display. Blandly, she asked, "Is that your roundabout and exceedingly polite way of saying you find me odiferously offensive?"

"Odiferously offensive?" he repeated with a wide grin that creased the corners of his eyes. "Can't say that I've ever heard that one."

"Then permit me to put it in terms you might have encountered before," she said, struggling to control her anger. "Are you saying that I smell bad?"

The smile faded from his face. "Didn't say that at all, ma'am," he replied gently. "And I didn't mean to imply it, either."

She turned her face away, but not before Rivlin saw the shimmer of tears in her eyes. Her shoulders were squared, her back ramrod straight, and her small hands fisted as she stared out over the land to the north of them. Rivlin frowned and went back to watching the trail through the space between Cabo's ears. Madeline Marie Rutledge was without doubt the oddest woman who'd ever crossed his path. One minute she'd bristle with indignation and the next she'd quietly demur to his control. And when she opened her mouth to speak he was just as likely to get an earful of scathing sarcasm as he was a genteel response. As far as he could tell, there was no logical way to predict which it would be.

He wondered if Rutledge herself knew how she was going to react before she did. If she didn't, it went a long way toward explaining how an Iowa schoolteacher had ended up committing a murder. She'd probably been just as surprised as the poor son of a bitch she'd killed. He'd probably stopped by the schoolhouse and asked her to dinner thinking he'd take pity on her, being a spinster and all. And for his attempted kindness, she'd beaten him to death with a slate board.

Rivlin strongly suspected, however, that the truth wasn't anywhere near the image he'd conjured in his mind. It was quite reasonable to assume that Maddie Rutledge's sharper edges and erratic behavior had come after whatever had prompted her to commit murder. Prison changed men and seldom for the better; it would undoubtedly have even deeper effects on women.

Not that any of it was his problem, he reminded himself. He was simply the lawman who had been assigned the task of getting her to a trial. He didn't have to understand her. Hell, he just had to tolerate her as best he could and get her there in good enough shape to walk and talk with the federal prosecutors.

As long as her unpredictability didn't get in the way of his duty, then Maddie Marie Rutledge could be as odd as she damn well pleased.

Still, he admitted, as the site of their evening camp came into view, there was something about her that niggled his curiosity, something that didn't have a thing to do with her behavior. He didn't have any real sense of what it might be, but with twelve days stretching before him, the chances were pretty good that he'd have some fair idea by the time he handed her over.

And that, he decided, reining in Cabo, was all the thought he was going to give the matter for the time being. There was camp to make, food to prepare, and the matter of getting the prickly Miss Rutledge cleaned up a mite. With any luck, the dunking would improve her general disposition.

He swung down off his mount and ducked under Cabo's neck, intending to help his prisoner down. She didn't give him the chance, but instead kicked her feet from the stirrups, swung her right leg over, and slid down the side. Her feet landed squarely under her, but her legs refused to hold her weight.

Rivlin, too far away to reach her in time, winced as she crumpled into the dust at the horse's side. "You might want to wait a day or two before you try those fancy dismounts," he said, helping her to her feet.

She swayed and then widened her stance in an effort to steady herself, her gaze focused on the center of his chest. And then she slowly and very deliberately lifted her face to look up at him.

His pulse quickened as he gazed into china-blue eyes. The fabric of her shirt might as well have been gauze for all the barrier it served between his hands and her skin. He wondered what it would be like to brush his palms along the length of her arms, to bend down and kiss her. She blinked and drew a shaky breath.

"Thank you." It was the merest whisper, a sound so soft that it barely reached his ears. "Please let go of me."

The simple, gently stated request had the effect of icy water. Rivlin immediately let her go, stepping back and only barely keeping an apology from tumbling off his tongue. "You might have a sit down while I unsaddle the horses and make camp," he said brusquely. "Then we'll see to that bath if you're of a mind to have one."

She nodded and walked toward the shade cast by the stand of cottonwoods. Rivlin watched her from the corner of his eye as he loosened Cabo's girth strap. Maddie Rutledge was flat-out exhausted from no more than two hours of riding. Life in a cell had apparently taken its toll. The trip was going to be hard on her. Which made it easier on him in a way; she wasn't going to have the strength to escape.

He was acutely aware of her gaze following him as he worked. She said nothing and didn't so much as move a muscle, and he found himself wondering how many women could bring themselves to exercise that much self-discipline for that long a stretch. Precious damn few, he decided. And the silence was so unnatural it was downright spooky.

"Are you always so quiet?" he heard himself ask.

She hesitated, then touched her tongue to her lip and replied, "I don't know that I have much to say to you. It's not as though we're sharing company at a church social."

"True enough. But we've got the better part of

two weeks to pass together and the days are going to get mighty long if we watch them pass in silence."

She seemed to consider the prospect and then shrugged. "The cottonwoods are still leaved. Fall's late this year."

Rivlin silently groaned and reminded himself that he'd been the one to prod her into conversation. There was nothing to do but offer his own inane contribution to the damn parlor talk. "It's been the longest, hottest summer I can remember."

"You should have spent it locked up in an attic with tiny windows. It's felt like a whole year in hell."

He knew he had no reason to feel so much as a twinge of regret for the misery of her experience, but he did anyway. "Well, it's on its last legs," he offered in meager consolation. "The nights are cooling and it won't be long before the days follow suit."

"Do you think it will be a hard winter?"

God, what had he been thinking to encourage this torturous exchange? Escaping such polite conversation had been one of the reasons he'd come back West. Unbuckling his saddlebag, he retrieved his cake of soap as he answered, "The woolly caterpillars seem to think it will be. But I haven't seen that many geese moving south yet, so it's hard to tell."

He'd no sooner turned to face her with the soap in hand than she came to her feet. The effort was soundless and so smooth that he wondered just how exhausted she really was. Her gaze flicked from him to the spring on their right and then back. Wariness darkened her eyes and she pressed her lips together tightly.

"The pool looks a mite lower than usual," he offered, puzzled by her response to the obvious fact that the time of her bathing was at hand. "It's been a long time since we had any rain to speak of and the underground spring's likely seeing the shortage."

She nodded, but didn't say anything. Rivlin stared at the pool of water and scowled. Just exactly how in the hell was he supposed to balance his responsibility and her modesty? Damnation. Escorting male prisoners was a helluva lot simpler in some respects.

"You've never escorted a female prisoner, have you?" she asked, as though reading his thoughts.

Rivlin shrugged and ambled toward the edge of the water, motioning for her to proceed him and saying, "There aren't that many of you."

She complied and, without looking back at him, said, "And so you've never found yourself having to deal with the peculiarities of it."

"No, ma'am, I haven't." A sudden realization brought him a half-smile and a sense of relief. "But since you've obviously been down the road, I assume you have some idea of how the . . . peculiarities . . . are handled?"

She stopped and very slowly turned to face him. Cool defiance showed in her eyes. "Not the least bit honorably."

His gut tightened as he understood all she'd left unspoken. "I gather that your last keeper wasn't the first to get your irons laid across his face?"

"No, he wasn't," she answered, her voice quiet, but with an edge to it that hinted at steely resolve. "It took ugly experience to teach me how to swing hard enough to make a difference. The last marshal to escort me had fewer reservations than you seem to have."

"Christ," he said softly, shoving his hat back on his head. The report hadn't mentioned the details of her previous transfer. "Who was it?" he asked, suspecting the answer he'd get. "Hodges?"

"I gather you know him?"

Yeah, he knew the sleazy son of a bitch. Hodges not only gave the Marshal Service a bad name, but generally tainted the reputation of the whole male sex. No wonder Maddie Rutledge was wary at the sight of soap and the prospect of stripping out of her clothes for a bath. And if she thought this trip was going to be like the one she'd taken with Hodges. . . . Christ Almighty, no wonder she'd been prickly as a cactus and skittish as a colt in a thunderstorm. Rivlin met Maddie Rutledge's gaze.

"Ma'am," he said slowly, choosing his words carefully, "I've never had an unwilling woman. I've never found it necessary and have never been interested in seeing what it might be like. I'm not about to put you on your back unless you want to be there and you can take that promise to the bank. Now, I'm willing to consider any suggestions you might have for accomplishing your bathing while preserving what we can of your modesty in light of my needing to keep you under control."

She studied him long and hard, the battle between the fear of experience and the wanting to trust plain for him to see. The stiffness of her shoulders eased a bit and she shifted her weight onto one leg. The wariness in her eyes softened just a tad, patinaed by what he thought might be a touch of mischief. "You could just walk away and trust me."

"Sorry," he replied honestly. "I wish I could, but I can't . . . seeing as how we're of such short acquaintanceship and all that."

She smiled—the first honest-to-God real and unguarded expression that he'd seen from her. It made her look so much younger, so much softer. Again

Rivlin's gut tightened, but this time the reaction was a purely male response to feminine charm. He quickly looked away, knowing that her fragile sense of trust wouldn't survive even a glimpse of his appreciation. "Got any other ideas?" he asked, rubbing the back of his neck.

She sighed, but her voice was more buoyant than he'd yet heard it when she answered, "Honestly, I don't know what to suggest. I haven't had a single bath in the last two years that didn't begin with leering and end with a full-out struggle. Privacy isn't something accorded to female prisoners."

Yeah, he could easily believe that. "How about if I stand here with my back turned while you bathe?"

Her laugh was musical and light and oddly warming. "Marshal, I don't trust you any more than you trust me . . . seeing as how we're of such short acquaintanceship and all that."

"Well," he countered, "unless you can come up with something better, it seems to be the only way we have to go. How badly do you want to scrub away the grit of Fort Larned?"

She looked back and forth between him and the water, her brows knitted and her lips pursed. "How about this?" she finally ventured. "You turn your back while I get undressed and into the water. I'll call out and then you can take my clothes and go back to camp. I'm not going to run off stark naked. When I'm done, we'll reverse the process."

Rivlin gave her a quirked smile. "And what's to prevent you from laying your irons across the back of my head the instant my back's turned and before you take off so much as one stitch?"

Her grin was wide and her eyes sparkled. "The

idea has some merit, doesn't it? I can't tell you how sorry I am that you thought of it, too."

He decided in that instant that there was lot more to Maddie Rutledge than he'd guessed. "Maybe we should forget this whole bathing thing," he drawled.

She sobered and looked at him with childlike earnestness. "I'd really like to have a bath, Marshal. If you'll let me have one, I'll promise not to try to escape. I'll swear it on a stack of Bibles if you've got them."

He didn't, but her willingness was enough to move him to a degree of minimal trust. "Here's what we're going to do, Miss Rutledge," he said, fishing in his pocket for the key to her manacles. "I'm going to take your government-issued weapon away from you before I turn my back. We'll play out the rest of it as you've suggested."

She held out her hands and allowed him to remove the heavy iron contraption. "Thank you," she whispered as he handed her the cake of soap.

There was something about her way of thanking him that he found unnerving. Turning his back on her and crossing his arms over his chest, he cautioned, "The edge drops off fast and the water's deep. Be mindful of it."

"I can swim."

He listened to the rustle of her movements, mentally marking the removal of each article of her clothing and prepared to whirl around if he heard the slightest pause that would indicate she intended to go back on her promise. Then there came the splash of water and a quick gasp. It was quickly followed by a sigh—a sigh more deeply blissful and satisfied than any he'd ever heard from a woman. His loins instantly tightened and he swore under his breath. Taking a blind step backward, he found her clothing where she'd discarded it, snatched it up, and then strode quickly back to camp.

Maddie watched him go, marveling at the first piece of good fortune she'd had in such a long time. Marshal Rivlin Kilpatrick appeared to have a streak of gentleman in him that ran fairly deep. She'd watched his face when she'd alluded to Hodges and what he'd tried to do to her. Kilpatrick had been disgusted and maybe even a bit angry. That had been the first real sign she'd had that maybe he deserved a little of her trust. The breadth of his gentlemanly character had been revealed as she'd stripped out of her clothes. He hadn't so much as half-turned to catch a peek. And when he'd backed up to retrieve her clothes . . . Maddie smiled. Something about that gesture had been rather boyishly sweet.

She let the soap float before her as she untied the short piece of leather binding the end of her braid. Holding it with her teeth, she undid her hair and then laid back in the water, reveling in the first real luxury she'd been allowed since she'd been arrested. Whatever else could be said of Marshal Rivlin Kilpatrick, she had to admit that the man knew the surest way to a woman's heart.

Which was exactly what Myra had said about him. Maddie reached for the soap, remembering the other observations Myra had thought necessary to share. In Myra's considered and experienced opinion, the marshal could have his pick of any woman he wanted. Maddie lathered her hair and conceded that Myra was probably right. Rivlin Kilpatrick was undeniably handsome and, as Rosie would have put it, beautifully conformed.

As for Myra's opinions concerning the marshal's abilities as a lover. . . . Maddie dropped the soap back into the water and scrubbed at her scalp, reminding herself that Myra had a tendency to wax colorfully poetic from time to time. Rivlin Kilpatrick might indeed be able to make the stars burn brighter and the world spin crazily, but she had absolutely no intention of determining the truth of it for herself, Myra's parting encouragement notwithstanding.

How to fight hadn't been the only lesson she'd learned from William Hodges and the host of others who had tried to live up to his example. And while Rivlin Kilpatrick seemed a better man on the whole, he was, when all was said and done, still a man. She wasn't about to trust him *that* much.

CHAPTER THREE

"ARE YOU STILL over there?"

Maddie treaded water and looked through the stand of trees at the camp. Kilpatrick had built a fire and then announced that he was coming down to the spring to fetch water for cooking. She needn't have bothered hiding behind a clump of grass at the water's edge; she'd watched him dunk the pail and he hadn't so much as stolen a glance her way. Now he sat beside the fire, his back toward her. "Yes, Marshal," she answered. "I am. Is my time up?"

"Take as long as you like," he called back. "Supper's simmering and it'll be a while yet. I just wanted to make sure you hadn't run off. Call me when you're ready to have your clothes back."

Truth be told, she was chilled to the bone and her fingertips were beginning to look more than a little wrinkled. She didn't want to leave the pool, but if she stayed much longer she'd either shrivel up completely or cramp and drown. It was the latter prospect that led her to call, "I suppose a woman can stand only so much heaven, Marshal. If you'd be so kind. . . ."

He came down to the water's edge, his eyes still carefully averted, and placed her clothes, neatly folded, on a patch of grass. Then he turned and took two steps back toward camp before stopping and folding his arms across his chest.

Maddie considered his back as she walked out of the water and took up her shirt. Wide shoulders tapered to a narrow waist and lean hips. His clothes hung on him fairly loosely, but weren't so baggy as to completely hide the hard lines of his frame. And where his crossed arms pulled his shirt taut across his shoulders, she could see the distinct outlines of corded muscle.

Her gaze dropped down to her shirt front. "You sewed on new buttons," she said, incredulously fingering the three black buttons that been added to what had remained of the white ones.

He shrugged. "The sun gets pretty bright and you're fair-skinned. Are you about done there?" he asked. "The stew needs to be stirred."

Maddie buttoned her trousers and picked her moccasins up off the grass. "You know, Kilpatrick," she said walking around him, "I just might write President Grant and tell him what a fine man he's got marshaling for him."

"Do and I'll deny it all," he countered with a quirked grin.

Smiling did wonders to his face. The hard lines lost their edges and the crinkles at the corners of his eyes deepened. The gold flecks in his eyes brightened. He had wonderfully straight white teeth and a dimple just to the left corner of his mouth. "Well, then just between us," she ventured, thinking that if he could be charming, she could do the same. "Thank you for the bath, Marshal. And for being such a gentleman about it. I appreciate both very much."

He touched the brim of his hat. "Any time, ma'am."

When he gestured toward the camp, she complied, feeling like a wholly new person in her clothing. Her pants, as always, shifted on her hips as she walked and she caught the waistband to hike them up again.

"Have you always worn men's clothes?" Kilpatrick asked from behind her.

Maddie considered the question, knowing she could give him a simple lie or the complex truth. In the end she decided that he'd earned honesty. She sat down beside the fire as she answered, "Actually, I always wore skirts until my trip to Fort Larned. My dress was . . . destroyed along the way and Hodges dredged up enough decency to loan me a set of his clothes. I immediately saw the advantage of trousers and I haven't worn anything else since."

"I imagine it would be a lot easier to ride in pants than it would be in a skirt."

"Yes, it is," she agreed, unrolling the considerable extra length of her pant legs. "Not that I've done any riding between those days and this one. But I discovered that pants are a kind of barrier in that they're a lot harder to get past than a skirt. It takes a man more time and effort and gives me a fighting chance to defend myself."

Rivlin stared down at her, amazed by the way she so frankly approached the subject yet managed to so carefully avoid using the word *rape*. Yep, her attempts to be demure and compliant were nothing more than facades. The honest and real Maddie Rutledge had a good measure of steel in her backbone and a healthy sense of self-preservation.

"You wouldn't happen to have a knife, would you, Kilpatrick?"

His brow shot up. "Which one of us are you planning to stab?"

She smiled. "I'd like to cut the extra fabric off my pant legs. It chafes under my moccasins."

"Get up," he instructed, crossing to his saddlebag. Then, with his knife in hand, he pointed to the fallen cottonwood against which he'd rolled out their blankets. "You're going to stand up there," he explained. "And you're going to balance your weight on one foot while I cut the fabric from the other leg. Understood?"

"You forgot to mention knocking me into next week if I try to kick you," she observed, stepping up onto the log.

"I figured you remembered the threat well enough that I didn't need to mention it again."

She turned around to face him, her eyes level with his own and somber. "I'm not going to try to run on you, Kilpatrick."

"Nice try, Rutledge," he offered. "But one of the first lessons learned in prison is how to play the confidence game with any and all."

"That's assuming you're locked up with people who have some inkling of how it's done," she instantly countered. "I've spent the last four months with a fifteen-year-old horse thief and a forty-year-old prostitute. What I've learned doesn't have anything to do with confidence games. If it becomes necessary to steal a horse during the course of our journey, I'll be glad to put Rosie's lessons into practice for you. As for the necessity of prostitution . . . You're on your own, Marshal."

He considered her, his eyes sparkling with amusement. Then he seemed to think better of giving voice to whatever thought had so entertained him and the light in his eyes went out. "I can't envision having to face either circumstance," he said flatly.

Maddie chuckled dryly. "What you envision and what you actually get are often two different things, Kilpatrick. Life takes odd turns sometimes and usually when you least expect it."

He made a quick, small gesture with his shoulders and chin that said he had no choice but to admit that she was right. The handle of the knife rotating in his hand, he half-smiled and drawled, "Just out of curiosity, Rutledge . . . Why do you expect me to believe you wouldn't escape if given the chance?"

Because I have nowhere to go. Maddie pasted a smile on her face. "How many men do you suppose are out there who'd sew buttons on my shirt for me?"

He swore softly and shook his head. "Stand still or you'll get your ankle slashed."

Maddie did as he bid, looking off into the cottonwoods rather than surrender to the temptation of watching the muscles in his shoulders flex as he worked. She shifted her balance when he tugged at her left pant leg. His fingers brushed over her skin and her breath caught. She stopped breathing when he paused and then lifted the fabric to see what lay beneath.

"The last fellow who shortened your pants for you get a bit carried away?" he asked, trailing a fingertip over the scars encircling her left ankle. "Looks to be two of them, one on top of the other."

Maddie chewed the inside of her lip. He was tracing the scars with the pad of his thumb as though he could make them go away with a gentle touch. She watched him, her heart swelling and knowing that if she didn't say something now it would impossible in another moment. "I was ten, I think," she said, using memories to distract herself. "We ate only twice a day at the orphanage, in the morning and then again at night. The stretch in between got long sometimes. Especially for the little ones and for those who had just come to live with us. I couldn't bear to hear them cry and so I'd sneak into the kitchen and steal them bits of whatever I could find." He looked up at her sharply and she smiled ruefully and with a shrug added, "I got caught. My punishment was three days in the cellar, chained. I didn't know enough to just sit there and wait it out."

"Jesus."

There was disbelief and anger and sadness in his eyes. She smiled to ease his turmoil. "It didn't reform me, in case you're wondering."

"The second scar," he prompted. "How did you get the second one?"

Not wanting to see him troubled by what was in the past and couldn't be undone, she explained lightly, "The second time was when I was arrested. It was a ball and chain. And the chain was short, so I couldn't pick up the ball and carry it. I had to drag it everywhere, even into court. It made a mess of my stockings."

Rivlin stared up at her. How in hell's name could she so blithely talk about being hurt so badly?

"It's all right," she said softly. "They don't hurt."

But they had and he knew it. Jesus. He busied

himself with the task of cutting away the fabric and when he was done, she thanked him and asked for permission to climb down off the log. He granted it by pointing at the fire in silent command. She went without a word, sat, pulled on her moccasins, and laced them up. She finger-combed her hair and as she braided it, her gaze fell on the bedrolls and the manacles he'd tossed onto one. Noting the direction of her attention and knowing she was wondering if he intended to put the irons back on her, he thrust a bowl of steaming stew in her direction, saying, "After you eat. Before we bed down for the night. And be careful with the bowl, it'll get hot quick."

Maddie accepted the food, the pronouncement, and the warning with a nod and tight smile. The first spoonful of stew effectively scattered her unpleasant thoughts. Full of little chunks of meat and vegetables, it was satisfying in a way she'd forgotten food could be. A moan of appreciation escaped her, followed by a sigh of what came close to being contentment. Kilpatrick scowled into his bowl.

"This is quite tasty, far better than anything I had while at Fort Larned." She was about to comment on cooking being another of his domestic virtues, but the look he cast her said it wouldn't be appreciated and so she kept it to herself. They passed the meal in silence, the only sound that of their spoons against the metal pans. When she'd all but licked the bowl clean, Kilpatrick took it from her. Her thanks brought his brows together and compressed his lips into a thin line.

Setting their bowls and spoons beside the fire-blackened cook pot, he reached for the manacles, saying, "I'm going to cuff you to the saddle horn while I go down to the spring to wash up. Which hand would you prefer to have free?"

"I don't think it really matters," she admitted. "I don't have anything to do but sit here." She held out her left arm and the marshal clamped her into the irons with quick, smooth motions. Then without another word, he picked up the dishes, snagged his saddlebags, and walked toward the spring.

Maddie watched him go, remembering how Myra had described his walk, not a swagger, but still a way that spoke of confidence, of knowing how to use his body to his best advantage. That had been the key to Myra's assertion that it would be a pleasure to bed him. Myra claimed that the marshal was one of the few men into whom God had instilled a special kind of physical awareness. Myra was convinced—on sight alone—that the marshal considered it a point of pride to give as much pleasure as he took. Maddie shook her head and smiled, remembering how Myra had wailed at the unfairness of life when Patterson had opened the door and announced that Maddie was being transferred. And in the time it had taken for Patterson to get the manacles around Maddie's wrists, Myra had thought to hastily review the more salient points of the instruction she'd been giving Maddie for the past four months. The most important to Myra's way of thinking had been to remind Maddie that being a willing partner was a very different experience than being a forced one and that if the opportunity for discovering that truth happened to come along, Maddie would be a fool for passing it up.

"Poor Myra," Maddie whispered. "She'd give anything to be in my shoes." Maddie looked to the west and the last mauve traces of the day, back toward Fort Larned. "I wish it were you, Myra. I really do. And I'm sorry that all your lessons and hopes are going to go for nothing."

The clank of metal drew her gaze toward the spring. Kilpatrick walked back into the meager circle of light cast by the dying fire, the saddlebags slung over his shoulder, the pots in one hand and his hat in the other. Even in the dim light Maddie could see that he'd shaved his face and washed his hair. His shirt collar was wet and the shoulders of his vest were sprinkled with the droplets that still fell from the ends of his hair. It was longish—as though he hadn't had the time to visit a barber in the last month or two. It fell around his face in a haphazard way that suggested it was seldom if ever tamed by a brush or the pomades that fashionable men used. Maddie decided that the style of it suited him well. She couldn't even begin to imagine him in a suit and tie, his hair carefully parted and slicked down.

He draped the saddlebags over the log and set the pans beside them, then reached into his pants pocket and brought out the key to the manacles. Without a word he unlocked them and freed her hands. Maddie murmured her thanks.

"If you'd be so kind as to stand up, turn around, and put your hands behind your back," he said gruffly.

Maddie climbed to her feet, but couldn't allow herself to obey any further. Being compliant had its advantages only so far. She held out her hands and calmly replied, "The only way I allow myself to be cuffed is with my hands in front. Behind me and I don't stand a chance. I'm willing to trust you a ways, Kilpatrick, but not that far."

He met her gaze squarely. "Trust runs both ways, Rutledge. If I cuff them in the front, I'd be giving you the chance to bash my brains in while I sleep, saddle a horse, and ride off."

"Has anyone ever mentioned that you're a

deeply suspicious man?" she countered, arching a brow.

"There's a reason you're a federal prisoner."

"Be that as it may, Marshal, I'm not going to let you cuff my hands behind me without a fight. Better now than when I can't defend myself."

He considered her wrists and then carefully placed the cuff around her right one. Then, before she knew what he intended, he cuffed the other ring around his left. "Satisfied?" he asked with a half-smile.

She was for the moment, but she hadn't had enough time to see where the unique solution would lead. "I'm reserving judgment," she admitted, eyeing the manacles binding her to him.

"We'll drag our bedrolls a bit closer so neither one of us wakes up with stiff shoulders." A ripple of fear crawled down her back. He must have sensed it because in that moment he added, "I meant what I said about not forcing you, Rutledge. This arrangement is purely for the sake of practicality."

She believed him. The acceptance produced a physical sensation, comforting and relaxing, Maddie decided, rather like drinking a cup of warm milk in the middle of a cold night. They wordlessly closed the distance between their bedrolls and managed to get themselves stretched along the length of their respective blankets without undue awkwardness. Their hands lay in the hard-packed earth between the edges of their bedding and a taut silence filled the air. Acutely aware of the fact that she'd never lain this close to a man in her life, Maddie stared up at the sky. It was Kilpatrick who finally broke the quiet.

"Do you thrash and turn a lot in your sleep, Rutledge?"

"I'm a light sleeper," she admitted, still watching the stars above. "I'm always listening for the sound of a key in a lock. How about you?"

"I can't remember the last time I slept hard or without a gun. It's another occupational necessity." He paused a moment before adding, "I hear that there's some Quaker women up in Indiana who want separate prisons to be built for women."

Maddie smiled ruefully, but didn't look at him. "As long as the jailers are men, it won't make any difference."

"How long have you been locked up all together?"

"Two months before the trial. Four months awaiting transfer to Larned. Eighteen months since then. Which leaves only eighteen years to go on my sentence." She hadn't intended for the last to sound bitter, but the truth of it had crept into the words.

"There's always a cursory report that goes with any prisoner transfer assignment," Kilpatrick supplied. "The report on you said you'd been convicted of first-degree murder."

Maddie focused her attention on tracing the outline of Cassiopeia. "Well, I suppose that's pretty much the gist of what happened in the end."

Rivlin turned his head to study her in the darkness. She was staring up at the sky. "I've seen more than my fair share of cold-blooded killers, Rutledge, and you don't strike me as the type. Was it accidental or self-defense?"

"The latter to my way of thinking." She gave a little shrug as she added wryly, "But not to the judge or the jury and they were the ones that counted."

"Didn't your family hire you a decent lawyer?"

"I don't have any family, Marshal."

"I was wondering why the scads of brothers and cousins and uncles let you live in an orphanage."

A small smile tipped up the corners of her mouth. There wasn't even a trace of merriment in it. "Orphans are very good at conjuring up families, usually rich ones who don't know we're missing from the fold, but who'll come after us the minute they realize we exist." Her smile faded. "It's a farce, of course, and deep down inside we know it. But sometimes the pretending can get you through a rough patch." He couldn't tell whether she sighed or took a deep breath before she asked, "Do you have any family, Marshal?"

"My father's deceased," he supplied. "Almost five years ago now. My mother's still living. I have an older brother and five older sisters, all of them married. They live in Cincinnati, happily existing in each others' pockets."

"Five older sisters and you still know how to sew on buttons and cook?"

"It was the U.S. Army that impressed upon me the wisdom of learning how to take care of myself. If the matter had been left up to my mother and sisters, my keeping would have been passed into the hands of a wife a long time ago."

"There are worse fates."

He snorted. "I can't think of what they'd be."

"Then you're not trying, Marshal," she countered brightly. "Worse would be wanting to marry and have a family and being considered unsuitable by anyone worth having."

"I've never looked at it from that angle," he admitted, wondering if she were speaking in a general sense or about her own, specific regrets.

"Well, just be grateful that looking is all the closer you have to get to it."

Yes, Maddie tried to hide it under a blithe manner, but she saw her future in bleak terms. The honesty was there if you were listening for it. "You won't be locked up forever," he offered. "Like as not, the prosecutors will shave some of your time in exchange for testifying. Have you given any thought to what you're going to do when you get out of prison?"

"I thought maybe I'd head for California or Oregon and see if anyone needs a schoolteacher."

Her off-handed manner was telling; she didn't see it as likely to happen. It bothered him to think that she wasn't willing to dream. Everyone had to have dreams or there wasn't any point in living. "There's plenty of men out on the coast looking for wives and wanting families."

She drawled, "Yeah, I hear that middle-aged female ex-convicts go for a premium price out there."

Rivlin chucked. "You sure do have a way about you, Maddie Rutledge."

"I've been told that," she countered. "Of course, most people haven't found it as humorous as you apparently do. You have a nice laugh, by the way. You should do it more often."

"I can't say that I've found all that much to laugh about recently."

"How long a stretch are we talking about here?" she asked. "A week? A month?"

Since the night Seth Hoskins had died; a lifetime. "Years." He settled deeper into ground. "So tell me," he said, "who was it that commented on your ways?"

"Mrs. Parker, the head of the orphanage foundation, once said that my being there was proof that one of the other ladies had committed an unpardonable sin. She felt it wasn't fair that they all had to pay for it, though." She paused before adding, "She once told me that my parents had probably given me to the orphanage because I was so willful and disobedient. I believed her for a long time."

Rivlin knew to his bones that she'd spent her childhood trying hard to be good enough that her parents would magically reappear and take her back. It had been a cruel and unforgivable thing to say to a child. He couldn't even begin to imagine what it must feel like to have no family. Even out here, he knew he had people back East and that if he needed them, all he would have to do was send a telegram—not that he'd be at all likely to do that. But when all was said and done, and despite how they liked to meddle in his life, having them was a kind of comfort. Maddie had never known that kind of security.

"You're a long way from hearth and home, Kilpatrick," she observed, her gaze still fixed on the sky. "What brought you out this way?"

"Originally, I came west under General Grant's western command during the late war. The United States Cavalry stationed me here after the war and then I requested to be sent here when I joined the U.S. Marshal Service."

She didn't say anything for a long while, her gaze wandering among the stars. When she finally spoke again it was to quietly ask, "How many days is it going to take us to get to Leavenworth?"

"I figure it's close to three hundred miles so maybe ten to twelve days if we push hard. Why?"

"Just wondering, that's all."

The way she gazed into the night heaven prodded a memory to the fore. Emily, the youngest of his sisters, had always been fascinated by the constellations. She'd lain in the grass in the early evenings before their mother called them in for the night, naming them all and telling him the stories behind them. He'd been too busy chasing fireflies to pay her any more attention than it took to tease her from time to time. God, it had been years since he'd thought of those times. Rivlin smiled. "You can sleep without worrying about those stars, Rutledge. They're not going to fall on you."

"I haven't seen them like this in so long . . . a big, huge black blanket sprinkled with diamonds. And in twelve nights I won't be able to see them like this again. There's no harm in trying to memorize what they look like, is there?"

He couldn't tell whether it was the wistfulness of her voice or his realizing that particular price of being caged, but Rivlin felt his chest tighten nonetheless. He didn't like the sensation. He liked what it implied about his relationship with his prisoner even less. "No, there isn't any harm in it," he answered firmly. "Look all you want. 'Night, Rutledge."

"Good night, Marshal."

Rivlin closed his eyes and let himself drift toward the edges of sleep; his last deliberate thought was to remind himself of the dangers in remembering.

Chapter Four

RIVLIN CAME AWAKE with a start. The sound of a slowly sliding bolt sent blood through his veins like liquid lightning. Movement came in the same fraction of a second as recognition. He grabbed the front of his prisoner's shirt, her instant gasp drowning the soft slide of his gun coming free of the holster. She swore and tried to pull away, but he hauled them both over the top of the fallen cottonwood.

Her fight began in earnest as they landed in a tangled, unceremonious heap on the protected side of the dead tree. Trying to focus his attention on the shadows at the spring's edge, he was too keenly aware of her clawing at the hand fisted in her shirt front, of the snarling curses that punctuated her efforts to twist her body away from his. Desperate, he yanked her toward him and rolled her fully under him, pinning their bound hands under her and deliberately using his weight to crush the air from her lungs.

He clamped his gun hand over her mouth and looked down into eyes wide with fear. "Shut up and be still," he whispered harshly. "We've got company."

She glared up at him, her body taut and rigid, her breathing every bit as labored and raspy as his own. Cottonwood leaves rustled softly overhead. Beyond those sounds came another slow, cold metallic click. Rivlin swore and instinctively shifted his weight, using his entire body to leverage his prisoner between himself and the dense wood of their only cover.

The shot viciously tore the night, whining over them, the lead plowing into the earth not three feet from their heads. Realizations tumbled over him before the sound had died away; the weapon was indeed a rifle, the assailant had moved away from the spring, and Maddie had gone from rigid to pliable, molding herself against him. He gratefully accepted her surrender.

"Stay put," he whispered against her ear. "Don't make a sound."

The second shot came as he eased away from her. As it drove into the dirt a foot closer than the last, Rivlin rolled onto his side and fired blindly in the direction from which it had come. Sitting up just high enough to see over the tree he listened and watched. The rifle bolt slammed another cartridge into place and a flash of fire and another deafening boom answered his volley. It was all he needed. With instincts honed on surviving, he fired two shots in rapid succession.

From the darkness, Rivlin heard them strike flesh and bone. Wood and metal clattered against the ground and then came the gurgling rattle of death. His gut heaved, but he pushed it from his awareness, deliberately focusing on other sensations.

Maddie lay pressed tightly against the length of him, her hand fisted in his shirt. His left arm encircled her waist and held her to him with a force that should have cracked her ribs or at least broken her pinned arm. Rivlin eased his hold, asking, "Are you all right, Rutledge?"

She took a ragged breath and nodded. "And you, Marshal?" she asked, her voice quavering as she worked her shoulder and elbow.

"Not so much as a nick," he replied, removing himself from her and suddenly aware of the chill night air. He found his hat in the dirt beside him, settled it back on his head, then fished in his pocket for the key to the manacles. "Got any idea who your friend is?" he asked, removing the cuffs from their wrists.

He felt her stiffen. "I don't have family and I don't have any friends, Marshal." As he gained his feet, she scooted back in the dirt and added crisply, "I think the better question would be which of your enemies he is."

"*Was* is the proper verb tense," he corrected, climbing over the log.

"Oh, dear God," she whispered, scrambling to her feet. "Is he dead?"

Rivlin, adjusting his grip on the revolver, crossed to the body lying at the edge of their campsite. There were two dark holes in the center of the man's uniformed chest. He nudged the silent, still form with the toe of his boot just to be sure. "It's your beloved Sgt. Murphy and, yes, he's dead, dammit."

"He wasn't my beloved anything," she protested hotly.

He started at the realization that she had come to stand just behind him. He hadn't heard her move and that didn't speak well of his wits. If she'd been wearing her manacles and had been so inclined, he'd be lying face down on top of Murphy right now—not a position any fellow would want to find himself in.

"I only saw the man twice at my stay at Larned," she went on. "Once when I checked my belongings in and this afternoon when we checked them out."

Rivlin looked over his shoulder at her. "Well, then explain to me how it is that he's here in the middle of the goddamned night trying to kill us."

"If you hadn't killed him, you could have asked him that question!" she countered, her hands on her hips. "Couldn't you have just winged him?"

"I was planning to ask him to dance, but he didn't give me a chance."

"There's no need to be sarcastic, Marshal. It just seems to me that it wasn't all that necessary to go to the extremes you did."

"Well, there's the goddamn pot calling the kettle black," he retorted. "I don't see that you have any room to criticize me for doing what I did. In fact, in light of the fact that I just saved your ass, you might consider muttering something along the lines of *thank you, Marshal.*"

She clamped her mouth shut and glared up at him. The spark of fire in her eyes intrigued him; it hinted at a dangerous edge. "Now what I want to know, Rutledge, is why Murphy would want to kill you."

"Me?" she declared, stepping up beside him. "It was obvious back at Fort Larned that there was animosity between the two of you. I think it was you he wanted dead and I had to be eliminated as a witness.

Either that or he intended to let me live so he could accuse me of the killing."

Rivlin considered the possibilities from her angle and decided that, while they were sound in a logical way, they didn't make sense in the larger scheme of things. Unfortunately, Murphy was past the point of being able to explain the true particulars. There was only one recourse left. Rivlin holstered his gun, knelt on one knee, and thrust his hand into Murphy's trouser pocket, pulling it inside out. Three coins fell into the dirt.

Maddie Rutledge gasped. "Don't tell me that you intend to search the body."

"It's the only way we have of finding answers at this point," he countered gruffly, disliking the necessity of it, but accepting it. "Unless, of course, you know how to get a dead man to talk. Want to ask him about the weather?" He pulled the second pocket out. A folded wad of currency plopped into the dust. Rivlin picked it up to count. "Five hundred dollars," he announced, his mind racing.

"Which could easily be explained as the proceeds of his thievery."

As Rivlin shoved the money into his own pocket, it occurred to him that, for a murderer, Maddie Rutledge was oddly determined to see the better side of ugly situations and less-than-noble people. Pulling Murphy's boots from his feet, Rivlin explained, "Murphy never stole anything big enough to get him a stake of this size. And before you even suggest it, no, he didn't squirrel away his ill-gotten gains for a rainy day. If Murphy had money, he drank it as soon as he could."

"So the question is how he got five hundred dollars in his pocket."

"He got it from someone who felt it was worth

five hundred dollars to have you dead, Rutledge," he said easily, tossing aside the empty boots. He patted Murphy's sides, feeling and listening for the sound of anything tucked between cloth and flesh. "The question isn't how, it's *who*."

"And why," she added crisply. "Without a why, you have nothing but empty speculation."

Sweet Jesus. He knew enough about Maddie Rutledge to know for a fact that she wasn't brick stupid. She should have been able to see things just as clearly as he did. Rivlin stood and faced her squarely. "The why's easy," he snapped. "Someone doesn't want you to testify in Leavenworth."

The spark of anger lit her eyes again. "Then they know far more about it than I do," she retorted, her irritation every bit as evident as his own. "I wasn't lying to you back at Fort Larned, Marshal. I don't have the foggiest notion what it is I'm supposed to know and testify about in court."

He watched her carefully as he supplied, "The trial's about corruption among the Oklahoma Indian agents."

She rocked back on her heels, her hands fisted at her sides. She hadn't known; he could see the truth of it in the way she pursed her lips. "All right, Rutledge," he pressed. "Can you imagine what the prosecutors expect you to contribute to the grand and noble cause?"

She pulled a long hard breath before meeting his gaze. Anger was in her eyes along with a good dose of what struck him as resentment. "Do you have seven and a half years to listen?" she asked acerbically.

"We'll saddle our horses while you talk," he instructed, motioning her to follow him. "Start with how it is that you're in any position to know about these matters in the first place."

She nodded and followed him to where they had

picketed their animals. She'd tossed the blanket over her mount's back before she said, "I was raised in a Baptist orphanage in Iowa. When I was eighteen, they sent me to the mission at Tahlequah as a teacher. My responsibilities went beyond teaching white and Indian children, though. I was there as a representative of the church and was expected to see that right was done."

Rivlin snorted. *Churchy do-gooders.* "Meaning that you were supposed to see that the Indians weren't treated too badly."

"I was there to see that they were treated fairly," she shot back. "They're human beings, Marshal. They deserve food that's fit to eat, clothing that has more cloth than holes, farming implements that are actually sound enough to be used, and planting seed that hasn't rotted in the barrels and sacks."

It had been a fool's mission from the very beginning. "And what were you supposed to do when you ran across this unfairness?" he asked. For some unfathomable reason he liked her angry and so he added, "Quote them Scripture?"

"I was expected to report my observations to the proper authorities. And then be persistent in prodding them into seeing that justice was done."

Rivlin half-smiled and pulled Cabo's girth strap tight. The realities of reservation life were the same everywhere. Tahlequah wouldn't have been an exception to the rule. "Wore a rut in the road between the mission and the courthouse, didn't you?"

"I wore two sets of ruts, one between the mission and the Indian agents' office and one between their office and the courthouse."

"Let me guess. You didn't accomplish a damn thing except to wear out your shoes and irritate a whole bunch of folks."

She yanked tight her own mount's girth strap. "That's pretty much the gist of it."

"And these same irritated men were the ones who happened to have served on your jury. Right?"

"Yes," she answered, bringing the stirrups down and adding, "and it was the judge's nephew—Caleb Foley—that I killed. Caleb's father is an Indian agent, Tom Foley. One of the worst of them as a matter of fact. Tom's brother, George, is the judge."

Rivlin laid his arm across his saddle and turned to face her. "Christ almighty, Rutledge. You sure know how to pick your fights, don't you?"

With a shrug, she answered, "There wasn't a lawyer in the territory who'd take my side. The mission didn't want to be tarnished by association and I had to represent myself. I figure that losing had little to do with my legal skills. There wasn't a single second when I had a chance of actually winning."

Damn fine people, those do-gooders. They'd sent her out to do their work and when she'd needed them they'd left her dangling alone. Rivlin unclenched his teeth and motioned to their bedrolls. As she accompanied him and set to the task, he explained the larger picture as he saw it. "By killing the man you did, you played right into their hands, Rutledge. The agents railroaded you slick as a whistle, thinking they'd have you locked away for the next twenty years where you couldn't be a burr under their blanket anymore. Then along come a few ambitious fellows—the lawyers in this upcoming corruption trial—looking to make political reputations for themselves. They figure that they can get their names plastered all over the front pages of newspapers by charging a few of your

Tahlequah folks with fraud and God only knows what other ways of bilking the government. Scandal is always good news.

"So to that wonderfully noble end, the prosecutors start sifting through complaints looking for information and witnesses to support their case and, lo and behold, find your name. And for the Indian agents and their cronies, having you in federal custody isn't the grand solution it once was."

With the rolled blanket tucked beneath her arm, she rose to her feet. "Who's been charged in the case? Do you know?"

"Nope," he admitted, rising as well and snagging his saddlebags from the log. "But I aim to find out."

They were crossing back to their horses when she said, "I don't see that it makes any difference. Even assuming that you're right and Murphy came here tonight intending to kill me, he's dead. Their attempt to keep me from reaching Leavenworth has failed."

God, how could Maddie Rutledge persist in seeing the good side of things? Either she was a dyed-in-the-wool optimist or she stubbornly turned a blind eye to experience. Probably both, he decided. Mustering all the patience he could, he began by saying, "Let's assume Murphy accomplished the task he'd been paid to do. Do you think whoever paid him would want confirmation of your death? Or maybe even proof?"

"Probably," she admitted slowly.

"And what do you think will happen when Murphy doesn't turn up, and there's no proof of your death?"

She sighed. "They'll try again?"

"If I were in their boots, that's what I would do," he admitted. "I'd figure I'd have at least a dozen days to get the killing done and no shortage of men willing to take my money and pull the trigger." He paused to give her time to fully absorb the danger of their situation, then added, "Now, I, for one, don't intend to trot my pony across wide open spaces and make myself an easy target for whoever is throwing fistfuls of money around to see you dead."

"I'm sorry," she said softly, her gaze dropping to the ground between her feet.

"What for?" he demanded, ire shooting through him.

She didn't look up. "For getting you into this kind of trouble."

He resisted the impulse to physically shove her shoulders back. "Let's get something straight, Rutledge," he ground out. "*I'm* not in any trouble I can't handle. *You,* on the other hand, have been in trouble over your head for quite some time and, truth be told, seem to have a real ability for getting yourself into it."

As he'd hoped, her head came up and her eyes flashed with anger. Satisfied, he added more gently, "I'm a U.S. marshal, Maddie, and I knew going in what the dangers would be. My duty is to get you to a trial in Leavenworth. Safely. I'll get it done, even if it requires some adjustments."

"What kind of adjustments?" she asked, instantly wary.

Rivlin smiled. "I reckon they'll be looking for us between here and Leavenworth, don't you?"

Maddie answered with a nod, thinking that Rivlin Kilpatrick seemed to find a kind of pleasure in deliberately ruffling and then partially smoothing her feathers. It made him hard to read, hard to anticipate. She'd never met a man who seemed to prefer bristling over quiet compliance and demure apologies.

"We're going south," he announced. "To Wichita. We need to find answers to some questions and a place to hide while we look. Wichita's big enough and busy enough for us to dig ourselves a safe little burrow."

"Myra's from Wichita," Maddie supplied. "Well, not actually Wichita. She said Delano, on the west bank of the river, was considered a separate town. She's really from Delano."

He drew back slightly and studied her with knitted brows. "Myra?"

"Myra Florence," Maddie supplied. "She's the prostitute with whom I've been sharing the ladies' cell at Fort Larned for the last four months. Myra gets out next month. She was sentenced to five months for shooting a cowboy who owed her money and skipped out the upstairs window. One month for every bullet. She didn't kill him, in case you're wondering. She just nicked him repeatedly."

He grinned. "Myra isn't your garden-variety prostitute, Rutledge. Myra is a madam, a very successful madam."

It was her turn to study him in puzzlement. "You know Myra?"

He didn't answer for a long moment. "I've encountered her a time or two on a purely professional basis," he finally replied.

"Hers or yours?" Maddie asked before she could think better of it. She winced.

Kilpatrick laughed outright. "Mine. Sooner or later Myra meets most every man who's crossed the Missouri River. Asking Myra the right questions can save you a great deal of time and effort. Dollar for dollar, she's the best pointer I know."

Myra and Kilpatrick had an acquaintanceship. Then why had Myra not admitted to it? Surely Myra had recognized him. Rivlin Kilpatrick wasn't the sort of man one would describe as average in any way. In a crowd of men, he'd stand out. Standing alone, there would be no doubt as to who he was. Why had Myra pretended not to know him?

"Ready to ride, Rutledge?"

Maddie looked around their campsite. Her gaze trailed over Murphy's body. "We should give him a Christian burial."

"I was wondering when you'd get around to the suggestion," he drawled, unbuckling one side of his saddlebags. "I don't suppose you'd be content with muttering a few words over him as he is and considering it good enough, would you?"

"Is that how you'd like to be cared for in the end?" she asked righteously.

"I'd be dead and it wouldn't matter to me one lick," he replied, blindly rummaging around inside the hard leather pouch.

"Well, I can't just ride away and leave him for vulture and coyote food."

Drawing his hand out of the saddlebag, he turned to her and asked, "Have you ever dug a grave out of prairie dirt, Rutledge?"

She lifted her chin a notch to reply, "No. Have you?"

"More than I care to remember," he answered quietly. Handing her the trowel, he said brusquely, "It's an entrenching bayonet. Pick a spot and start hacking. I'll take care of his mount and belongings."

Maddie studied the miniature shovel in her

hand. If she had anything less than a week to get the job done, it was going to be a very shallow grave. She could only hope that if she ended up dead, Marshal Rivlin Kilpatrick would pause long enough to scrape out a shallow one for her.

Chapter Five

Rivlin watched, motionless, as his prisoner folded her hands and bowed her head. After a second, she lifted her face just enough to arch a brow in silent reminder. Rivlin scowled and reluctantly removed his hat from his head. It was all the decorum he was willing to observe for the likes of Murphy.

He heard Maddie sigh softly just before she said, "Dear Lord, we're sorry Sgt. Murphy is dead."

"Only in certain respects," Rivlin grumbled. "It would have been handy to have a few answers before he cashed out."

She cast him a dark look before resuming her dutiful litany. "We ask that you not judge him too harshly for his earthly misdeeds."

"If Murphy even made it as far as Saint Peter, he's doing better than I expected," Rivlin countered, irritated as much by Maddie Rutledge's piety as he was by the thought of actually begging on Murphy's behalf.

"I'm trying to offer a decent prayer for the departed, Marshal," she countered. "I'd appreciate it if you'd stop interrupting me with your disparaging remarks."

There was something about the spark in her eyes that prodded him to blunt honesty. "The Lord hates hypocrites and I don't aim to be one. I didn't like Murphy and he came to the end he deserved. The only regret I have is that I've got to stand here and listen to you pray over him."

"Well, the Lord knows what's in your heart, Rivlin Kilpatrick, so just keep your comments there and he'll still know exactly how you feel about Murphy. Keep in mind, however, that some day you'll have to account for your lack of Christian charity."

He'd seen enough in his lifetime to know that Christian charity was as rare a thing as a purple pig. If Maddie wanted to believe such a thing actually existed—even after all she'd been through—then he could only pity her. He sure as hell wasn't going to waste his time trying to convince her of the truth. "Lack of charity is going to be the least of the sins I'll have to atone for, Rutledge," he said. "I figure I'm in so deep, heaven's already given the devil leave to punch my ticket. And I don't much care."

"What a horrible attitude. Haven't you ever heard of redemption?"

"Yes, I've heard of it. The concept was frequently stressed in the wayward years of my youth."

"Obviously it didn't make a great impression on you."

"Let's just say that the war and the Indian campaigns made greater ones." Rivlin slammed his hat on his head and gave her a taut smile as he smoothed the brim. "Mumble whatever holy words you want, Rutledge. I'll wait for you over by the horses." As he walked away, he added over his shoulder, "Try not to spend too long at it, though. It's another one of your wasted efforts."

Rivlin leaned against Cabo's flank and watched her resume her prayerful stance. If she ever offered to pray for the redemption of his soul, he'd feel compelled to point out that her religious tendencies looked a mite contrived to him and thus earn himself a lightning bolt for sure. But the plain truth of it was that Maddie struck him as someone just doing what she thought she was expected to do for no more reason than that. From what he'd seen of her so far, she was a bundle of contradictions wrapped inside a blanket woven of forty-six different colors and an easy half-dozen patterns.

If he stripped away all her performances, what would he find? Certainly not a churchy do-gooder. His verbal pokes riled her every time and so far she hadn't made the slightest effort to turn the other cheek. She'd come back at him with fire in her eyes every time. He remembered the look in her eyes for the first few seconds after she'd vaulted into the guardroom. Yes, Maddie Rutledge certainly had fire in her. What would she be like if she abandoned all her pretenses? And why the hell was he wondering about it?

Rivlin expelled a hard breath. The truth was that his prisoner was a fine-looking woman and he wasn't close enough to dead not to notice. He'd told her he wouldn't force her onto her back and he'd keep that promise even if it killed him. But he acutely remembered the aftermath of Murphy's attempt to kill her—the feel of her curves pressed against his side, the warmth of her body. If she ever so much as hinted that she'd like to get that close again, he'd be sorely tempted to see just what kind of fire Maddie Rutledge possessed. There could well be some hefty price to pay for the pleasure, but he'd think about crossing that bridge if and when he came to it.

Rivlin snarled at himself in disgust. Maddie Rutledge was his prisoner and if he made so much as a single move to seduce her, he wasn't any better a man than William Hodges. He'd stake himself to an anthill before he fell that far. Hell, he'd ask Hodges to do it for him.

Maddie whispered a customary amen and turned away from the grave site. Rivlin Kilpatrick stood beside the horses just as he'd promised. She crossed to him, her step faltering as she drew close enough to see his face in the gathering dawn. He was angry about something; she could see it in the darkness of his eyes and the tension of his jaw and shoulders. Maybe she'd taken too long to do the right thing.

"Weather's coming in," she observed, trying to distract him and striding purposefully forward. "The wind's trying to shift around to come at us from the east. Like as not, it's going to rain before too much longer." Maddie reached the side of her horse, quickly put her foot in the stirrup, and swung up.

The marshal settled in his own saddle. "It's likely to set in. Usually does this time of year."

Maddie viewed the days stretching ahead. They were going to be cold and wet and very uncomfortable. "It might be best to find a dry place to hole up while it moves through," she suggested. "It would make our lives a whole lot less miserable."

"But it would also give whoever wants you dead time enough to figure out we're not on our way to

Leavenworth," he countered. "And since there aren't all that many other possible destinations, they'd have a fair chance of getting someone between us and Wichita."

Maddie silently cursed the telegraph lines. "I guess if the choice is between miserable and dead, I'll go for miserable."

"You don't have a choice, Rutledge," he reminded her, reaching behind him and into one of his saddlebags.

"I'm pretending that I do. It makes the prospects more palatable." Maddie went absolutely still as he turned toward her with the manacles in his hand. "They aren't necessary, Marshal."

"So you tell me. I'm pretending that they are. It makes the prospects more palatable. Put your hands out." When she didn't comply, he added, "You don't have a choice in this either, Rutledge. We can do it the easy way or the hard way, but in the end you're going to ride cuffed."

Maddie considered the choices he'd given her. She could either accept his decision gracefully or make him wrestle her to the ground. She'd been on the ground, pressed against Rivlin Kilpatrick, in just the last hour or so. Brief though the encounter had been, she could still feel where their bodies had touched. Maddie put her hands out knowing it was the safer road to travel.

Clamping the metal rings around her wrists, he said, "I'm not going to tether your horse. I'll trust you to ride beside me. But if you try to ride off, I'll catch you and knock you out of the saddle. Understood?"

"Why do you periodically feel this need to threaten me?"

He shrugged and took up his reins. "I just figure

that you should know the consequences before you take the action. It seems only fair."

"Well, thank you kindly, Marshal," she retorted. "It's nice to know that you think I'm that foolish."

"I didn't say I thought anything of the kind."

"It was implied. Just where do you think I'd run?" She didn't give him a chance to answer. "I've lived in three places in all of my twenty-seven years, Kilpatrick. The orphanage, the mission, and the cell at Fort Larned. The good ladies of the orphanage would turn me in to the constables the instant I showed up on their doorstep. The Indian agents would kill me if I went back to the Oklahoma Territory. And quite frankly, I can't think of anyplace I'd rather avoid than Fort Larned."

"It's a big country," he calmly replied. "It would be easy for a woman to get lost in it if she were of a mind to do that."

Maddie smiled tightly. "That's assuming, of course, that you wouldn't come after me."

"And if I came after you, I'd find you."

The marshal certainly had self-confidence. She suspected it was well deserved. When he nudged his horse in the flanks and started forward, Maddie did the same. As she drew abreast of him, she asked, "Just out of curiosity, Kilpatrick . . . How did you end up drawing the assignment of escorting me?"

"Hell if I know," he answered with a disgusted snort. "I was supposed to be heading into southern Missouri to investigate a death threat made against a federal judge, but the orders were changed at the last moment. For some reason, someone thought I'd be the best man to get you to Leavenworth. One way or the other, I'll get it done."

Maddie had the feeling that when he found the man responsible, Kilpatrick would make him pay for the decision. "Well, someone must really hate you," she observed. "Or maybe it's that someone wants you just as dead as they want me."

The marshal was silent for a minute and then he shrugged. "Well, I don't doubt that there's a few men who'd smile to see me planted, but they're not likely to be the same ones who want you dead and they're certainly not in any position to see that I drew this assignment."

Very probably true. It was interesting that Rivlin Kilpatrick had apparently given the idea some thought. As possibilities went, it was on the far side of ludicrous and yet he'd paused to consider it. Maddie wasn't sure what that said about him. Either he was a very thorough man or his definition of foolish was much narrower than hers.

She had no doubts that there were some who would want to see him dead. He struck her as the sort of man you didn't want to get crosswise with. He was gentleman enough to keep his back turned while a lady bathed and he was kind enough to replace missing buttons, but she knew that Rivlin Kilpatrick could be hard, cold steel when he chose to be. He'd killed Murphy without even blinking.

Maddie slid a glance at him. Damn, he cut a nice figure on horseback. How had Myra described him? A man's man? Maddie had thought it an odd expression at the time, but she could now see what Myra had meant. Rivlin Kilpatrick was the kind of man other men hoped to be.

What would he do if she provoked him? It was a sure bet he wouldn't let her get away with it. He could glare at her. He could curse at her. He could threaten her. If she was trying to escape, none of those would actually stop her. His only real recourse would be to wrestle her to the ground and hold her there as best he could without hurting her. Maddie's breathing caught as the memory filled her mind. Pinned between the earth and the power and steel of an angry, determined Rivlin Kilpatrick. . . . Maddie's heart raced and she forced herself to swallow and banish the vision.

She focused on the land rolling in long, endless swells before them. It had been a hot, dry summer and the short grasses had long ago faded into shades of pink and amber and dusty gold. The sky above was a thick, flat blanket of gray, the sun rising somewhere in a world just beyond this place and time. The air she breathed was cooling by the moment, the moisture in it thickening and swirling on the fitful gusts of wind that swung from the south to the east and back again. The storm was gathering in the northwest, preparing to roll down and over the land. Maddie counted the rolls of clouds at the front edge of the storm. Even in the faint light of dawn they were thick and black and heavy enough to stand out. Six. The wind would be vicious. She drew the collar of her jacket closer and settled deeper into the saddle.

"Hold up a minute," her keeper ordered quietly as he reined in his mount. Maddie did as instructed and watched him remove the oilskin slicker from her bedroll. He laid it across his lap as he fished in his pocket for the key to the manacles. Maddie waited until he motioned and then she extended her hands so that he could open the lock on one side.

She was pulling on the long coat when the marshal extracted his own coat and said, "Tell me about the Indian agents, Rutledge. Who are they? What do you know about them that they don't want you telling the world?"

Without prompting, Maddie closed the ring about her free wrist. "There's three that I had personal dealings with," she began. "Tom Foley, who's the head agent, and his assistants, Sam Lane and Bill Collins."

Kilpatrick nudged his horse forward. Maddie followed obediently, continuing on with her story. "As for what I know about them . . . Tom Foley's from New York originally. He wears gold and silver embroidered vests, a black beaver top hat, and spit shined shoes. He likes twenty-year-old brandy, fine cigars, and young women . . . preferably younger than his brandy.

"Sam and Bill are pretty much cut from the same bolt of cloth, but it's not nearly as fashionable as Tom's. Sam's got a temper and a lot of missing teeth to show for it. He likes to gamble and if he's not snoring in the corner of the agency office, you can find him at the nearest poker game. Bill you can find snoring just about anywhere, any time of the day. He's a drunk, pure and simple. On the rare occasion when he's upright, he's mean. Sam's from Ohio, Bill from Indiana.

"As for what they've done. . . ." Maddie stared out over the land. The grass was getting wet now and the colors were darkening. It was breathtaking; the amber and the gold contrasted against the dark pewter sky.

"What have they done?" the marshal prompted.

Maddie shrugged and told him what he probably already knew. "The circuit court judge said that what was happening in Tahlequah wasn't any different than what happened anywhere there were Indians. No one cared. Indians are Indians and they don't deserve any better than rancid meat, rat- and moth-eaten blankets, wormy flour, rotten seed, and broken implements. The judge would accept my complaints because the law required him to and then immediately dismiss them as being groundless. Of course, as I said before, the judge was George Foley, Tom's older brother, so I never did expect too much in terms of justice."

Rivlin turned his head and looked at her in amazement. She'd been making complaints about the agent to the agent's brother? Sweet God in heaven, Maddie Rutledge had to like throwing herself against brick walls. There was no other reasonable explanation for making such grandly futile gestures. Rather than point out the obvious reasons for her failure, he asked, "How'd Foley, Lane, and Collins get their jobs as Indian agents?"

"I don't know exactly. When I first got to Tahlequah, Reverend Winters told me they had all served in the Quartermaster Corps during the war. He said that that's how they'd gained experience in stealing." She smiled ruefully. "Rather like Murphy did, I suppose."

"This Reverend Winters," Rivlin prodded, his senses suddenly prickling. "Tell me about him."

Maddie's smile turned bittersweet. "He was a dear old man. I rather think that I was sent down to the mission as much to be his housekeeper and cook and companion as I was to be the teacher."

"*Was?*" Rivlin repeated.

"He passed away while I was awaiting trial for the murder."

"How'd he die?"

"He went to sleep one night and didn't wake up the next morning. He was almost eighty and it took every ounce of strength he had just to stand behind the pulpit on Sunday mornings and deliver a short sermon."

"Did the good reverend ever lodge official complaints against the agents?"

"He did before I got there, but it was one of the first responsibilities he handed over to me. The trip to the courthouse was very draining for him physically. And just 'tween you, me, and the next fence post, Marshal, I think he was tired of fighting a losing battle."

At least Reverend Winters had had enough good sense to know when to call it quits. Maddie on the other hand . . . If she hadn't been imprisoned, she'd still be making tracks to the courthouse and filing complaints against the judge's brother. "Is there anyone but you who could be called as a witness against Foley, Lane, and Collins?"

She considered his question for a moment and then shifted in the saddle. "I suppose they could call some of the teamsters who brought in the wagons of goods. There was an easterner who came through from time to time to drink and smoke with Foley, but he didn't stay long and didn't bring supplies or anything. Aside from those two possibilities, there's only the Indians themselves."

"Only citizens can testify in court and Indians aren't citizens," Rivlin reminded her. "And best of luck in trying to track down a teamster. They're not the most reliable bunch of men in the world. Their own mothers don't even know where they are. Do you have any idea of the name of the easterner?"

"He looked rich like Foley. I figured he was a friend of his from back home."

Rivlin turned the information over in his mind. "Being an Indian agent doesn't pay all that well," he observed. "Where does Foley's money for fancy waistcoats and expensive brandy come from?"

"I don't know. I heard Bill say one time that

Foley had invested for them all; that he had 'important business connections' and that someday they'd all take baths in champagne and ride in golden carriages." She laughed softly and the smile she gave Rivlin was delightfully bright and impish. "The general feeling was that no one cared what Bill bathed in as long as it happened fairly soon. And they didn't care what he rode in as along as he rode away."

Rivlin chuckled, but doggedly held to his inquisition. "Might that easterner you saw be Foley's business associate?"

"I suppose he could have been."

"Did you ever hear them discuss business?"

She laughed again. "I know you'll find it difficult to believe, but whenever I came into a room, they tended to fall into a deathly silence."

She'd succeeded in amusing him. "They actually let you into a room with them?"

"Not if they could help it." Her eyes twinkled and her grin broadened. "But then I can be persistent when I want to be."

She might indeed be persistent, but at that moment all he could think of was the fact that Maddie Rutledge could also be damn beautiful. Rivlin cleared his throat and forced his mind back to the larger situation. "What made you think this easterner was a friend of Foley's rather than a business associate?"

"Why would someone travel all that way to conduct business? Wouldn't they just send telegrams back and forth?" She shook her head. "And the easterner always brought him packages of his favorite things, which is, of course, what friends do when they come to visit."

"Makes sense," he admitted, wishing that it didn't.

"So tell me, Kilpatrick . . . What is it that I know that makes me worth killing?"

He didn't have so much as a pale glimmer of an answer for her. Rather than confess the truth, he forged ahead with another question. "How did the man you killed figure into all this?"

"I already told you. His name was Caleb," she said flatly.

The sudden change in her voice prompted Rivlin to look over at her. He found her gaze riveted on the land lying ahead of them, her chin up and her shoulders squared, and in that instant he had an inkling of just how she'd faced the judge and jury.

"He was Tom Foley's eldest son," she said, her voice still flat and distant. "Caleb didn't have a paying position or official responsibilities. He was there simply because he enjoyed preying on the weak."

Rivlin didn't want to ask, but he needed to find a reason someone wanted Maddie Rutledge dead and in his experience vengeful relatives were the best first bet. "Why did you kill him?"

"Eight Cherokee girls were raped and beaten to death in a six-month stretch. The youngest was eleven, the oldest thirteen. All were students of mine." She pulled the collar of the oilskin coat closer around her neck and stared out over the sodden land, her lips compressed.

"And you knew Caleb was responsible?" Rivlin prodded gently.

"I had my suspicions—as did some of the tribal elders—but there was no evidence that would have allowed me or anyone else to make so much as an informal accusation." Her chin came up another notch. "Then one day Lucy Three Trees didn't come to school. I rode out to their cabin and found Caleb beating her with a fireplace poker. He came at me with it and I shot him dead. I'd have killed him even if he hadn't come at me."

Matter of fact. No anger, no remorse. It had happened and she had done what had to be done. She'd had no other choice. Rivlin had walked in her shoes more than once. "Did Lucy recover?"

"She lived for two days. She was . . ." Her voice broke. "She was almost ten years old."

His gut wrenched. "I'm sorry, Maddie."

"Me, too," she said gruffly. She reached up and tugged the brim of her hat lower so that it shadowed her eyes. "Rain's coming in."

The words had no sooner been spoken than a cold, hard blast of air swept in from the northwest. There was the span of a single breath between it and the first drops of rain. They came fat and splattering at the beginning, wide streaks of gray from the blanket above. And then they multiplied a thousand-fold, narrowed, and turned knifelike, cold and stinging as the storm rolled down upon them.

Chapter Six

MADDIE COULDN'T REMEMBER a day she'd ever been so cold. It was hard to tell what time of the day it was; the sky had been the same dull gray for what seemed like an eternity. The minutes crawled past, marked only by a steady deepening of her discomfort. The prickling in her hands and feet had been almost unbearable for a long time and then, mercifully, she'd lost all feeling whatsoever. Now if only her nose would quit running. It was exceedingly difficult to look as though you were stoically enduring when you had to sniffle every two seconds. Of course Rivlin Kilpatrick rode on as if the sky were clear, the breeze were balmy, and the birds were singing brightly. Maddie scowled. She thought about wishing him to hell, but decided that such a fate would border too close to a kindness. Hell was dry and warm.

"I came through here a couple years back," he

said, breaking the long silence that had stretched between them. "I seem to recall that there was an abandoned homestead out this way. It wasn't much then and there's a good chance there's nothing left standing, but I figure we'll take a look-see."

"Might as well," Maddie countered, forcing a blitheness she didn't feel into her voice. "It's too windy to stack shot and too wet to dance."

He didn't look at her. "We'll dry."

Something in the way he said that made Maddie wonder if he had dancing of one sort or another in mind for later in the day. It was a troubling thought. "Fairness compels me to mention that I was raised by God-fearing Baptists. I've never danced in my life. It's considered a sin."

"I guess they're entitled to their opinion. What's yours on the matter, Maddie Rutledge?"

"I can't say that I've ever given it serious thought. I've never been in position of having a chance to decide if I wanted to dance or not."

"Never?"

"The good ladies at the orphanage watched us like hawks. Reverend Winters certainly wasn't about to risk damnation. And somehow or another the subject never came up while I was at Fort Larned."

"You might think about broadening your horizons just a bit."

"I don't much see the point in it. It's not as though there are going to be all that many opportunities for dancing in my future."

"Then maybe you ought to enjoy the chances while you have them."

"Maybe I ought to consider card playing and whiskey drinking as well," she countered flippantly.

"Well, I doubt that it would kill you."

"The ladies always said that dancing led to

drinking which led to gambling which led to . . ." She bit off the last word, realizing that she'd run headlong into a topic no decent woman ever discussed with a man.

"Other vices," the marshal supplied, struggling to contain his grin. "I reckon it could happen."

And she reckoned that with a man like Rivlin Kilpatrick it probably would and usually did. There was something about him that made her feel slightly edgy and definitely off her stride. Being around him reminded her of playing the orphanage version of hide-and-seek. You played with both dread and eager anticipation, knowing that your quarry could pop out of hiding at any moment and scare you half to death. You played tense, holding your breath, but you took chances because there was nothing that made your heart race like being caught.

Of course, Maddie firmly reminded herself, with the marshal, getting caught would amount to a great deal more than laughing and taking her turn at being "it." Rivlin Kilpatrick was much more dangerous than any little boy who had ever caught her behind the barn and tried to steal a kiss. If she let him think for one minute that she might like to play, that she might not mind being caught . . . She knew what the good ladies of the orphanage would say about letting herself get caught by the marshal. She also knew what Myra would say about the possibility. And somewhere between the two points, she stood, considering which way to go on the matter. She had to admit that, at least as she remembered them all, Myra certainly seemed the happiest with life.

ONE END OF THE ROOF had collapsed and the door hung by a single, rusted hinge. The rags that had once covered the windows had been either blown away by the prairie wind or carted off by practical, determined rodents. As hotels went, it wasn't worth noting, much less paying for. But as a reasonably dry shelter in the middle of nowhere, it served quite nicely. Rivlin had hung their sodden blankets from the low rafter, effectively closing off the roofed end of the cabin and drying the blankets while holding the heat of their fire around them.

He looked across the small fire at his prisoner. She sat cross-legged on the dirt floor, huddled in her wet coat, wearing her wet moccasins, staring at the two cooking pots sitting in the flames, and trying with all her might not to shiver from the cold. He hadn't noticed how chilled she was until he'd taken the manacles from her wrists. Her skin hadn't been a single degree warmer than the iron and he'd felt a stab of conscience for having failed to think of how the metal would have sapped her warmth. She'd hadn't said anything, of course. And she'd refused to follow his advice and peel off her wet clothing.

Stubborn woman, he thought, leaning forward to stir their evening stew. That task accomplished and the timing gauged, he set about making tea for them. He threw loose tea leaves and several strips of dried lemon rind into the pot of boiling water.

As he used his shirt cuff to pull the pot to the edge of the fire she spoke for the first time since they'd climbed down off their horses. "That smells good."

"And it'll warm you from the inside out when it's done," he replied, pulling a bottle from the saddlebag and adding a very liberal dose of whiskey to the tea. "Good for what ails you," he commented, then tossed in a chunk of sugar. He swirled the concoction to mix it all, let it steep for a few minutes, and then poured them both a cup.

Maddie took hers with a deep breath. "This is for medicinal purposes only."

"Absolutely," he assured her, staring into his own cup and wondering how much whiskey it would take for her to feel it. Remembering his first encounter with firewater took some doing, but he seemed to recall that novices tended to fall hard and fast. He didn't want her unconscious, just relaxed enough to consider shedding her wet clothes. He didn't much like the idea of delivering a prisoner suffering from frostbite. It would look bad in his file.

"Is there any more?"

Rivlin blinked and looked up. She held the empty cup out, looking sweetly hopeful. He lifted the makeshift teapot and obliged her, saying as he did, "You might want to take this cup a mite slower. Give it time to catch up to you."

She nodded and drank and he could tell she didn't understand the warning. "Whiskey tends to creep up on you. It keeps coming on for a while even after you've put the glass down."

Again she nodded and again she drank. Rivlin exhaled a long, silent breath and stirred the stew. He could only hope that his prisoner would be sober enough to eat some of it by the time it was ready. The fire crackled and popped. Rivlin carefully fed it small bits of the fallen roof timber.

"I've heard people extol the virtues of a good hot toddy," she said after a while. "I can see why they hold such high opinions. This is very effective."

Rivlin looked up to see her smiling into her cup. "Are you warmer?" he asked, knowing the answer already.

"Oh, yes. Much." She pulled her hat from her head and tossed it down beside her, adding, "In fact, I think I'm just a bit too warm."

She ran her finger along the collar of her oilskin coat, opened the uppermost button, and then stopped. Her gaze came up to meet his. "Marshal? I don't see any other course but to be bluntly honest."

Rivlin cocked a brow. "About what?"

She took a deep breath and moistened her lips with the tip of her tongue. "The rain soaked my moccasins and my pant legs. It also ran beneath the collar of my coat and soaked my shirt. The only way I can effectively dry my clothing is to remove my coat and footwear."

Rivlin scrubbed his lower face with his hand while he brought his smile under control. When he'd accomplished the task, he nodded slowly and replied, "I recall having already suggested that you do that."

"Yes, but there's a problem in doing so," she countered. "I wouldn't want you to construe the removal of some of my clothing as a tacit invitation to . . . well . . ."

Dance. "I'll stay on my side of the fire."

She tilted her head to the side and considered him with slightly narrowed eyes. "I have your word on it?"

"I believe that I've proven that I can be a gentleman when I want."

She went on considering him and then the corners of her mouth tipped up. Her eyes sparkled with mischief and whiskey. "And when you don't want to be a gentleman? What happens?"

He smiled and replied, "All hell tends to break loose."

She laughed softly. "I can see that quite easily. Your mother considered you a handful to raise, didn't she?"

"Yeah, she said something along those lines. Are you going to trust me to behave myself?" he asked, briskly stirring the stew. "Or are you going to sit in that wet coat all night?"

"I'll trust you for a ways." She laughed again and leaned forward to put her empty cup into his line of sight. "If you'd pour me just one more cup of your wonderful tea, I'd be most appreciative."

It occurred to him as he took her cup that if he were of a more predatory mind he could take advantage of her inexperience and trust. "Why don't we save it for after dinner?" he suggested, setting the cup aside.

Her smile was warm and bright. She stripped away the coat, the movement pulling her shirt tightly across her unbound breasts. Appreciation tightened his abdomen. "Speaking of dinner," he said, reaching for the tin dishes. "How hungry are you?"

"Now that I'm not likely to freeze to death, I'm starving."

"If it's not one thing, it's another," he quipped, ladling stew into the pans while acutely aware that she was stripping away the sodden leather encasing her lower legs. When she stretched her bare feet to the fire, wiggled her toes, and sighed, Rivlin had to suck a deep breath and remind himself of his oath of office. "Tell me about your moccasins," he said, handing her one of the plates. "Did you make them yourself?"

Maddie accepted the plate and leaned back against the wall of the cabin. "They were a gift from one of my older students," she said. "It was cold and she thought I needed something on my feet other than rags."

"The Reverend Winters didn't see that you had proper shoes?"

Maddie chewed and swallowed her first bite of stew. She quietly sighed in satisfaction before answering his question. "Oh, the reverend tried to get me some, but they were delayed for several shipments. I had the pair I wore from Iowa, but I tore the heel off the right one and it never was comfortable to walk in after that."

"I imagine." He ate a bite and then, without looking up from his plate, asked, "How'd you manage to tear the heel off? Tromping to the courthouse?"

"I kicked in a door."

His gaze snapped up to hers. "You what?"

She smiled at him and he knew that his surprise pleased her. "I told you I could be persistent when I wanted to be."

He gave up trying to contain his own smile. "Tell me the story."

"A wagon of goods came into the agency," she began. "You could smell the rotten meat an hour before it got there. I went to the agency to lodge a protest and found old Foley hiding behind a locked door. He refused to open it, and I got tired of pounding my knuckles against it and shouting through it, so I kicked it open. I lost my heel in the process, but no one seemed to notice my slightly awkward gait as I thumpity-thumped across the office. I just ignored Foley's fancy visitor and had my say. I even pounded on his desktop and flung a few papers for good measure."

Rivlin laughed quietly. "I bet you were impressive all riled up like that."

"They looked properly mortified." Maddie

grinned. "I was quite pleased with myself. Not that I accomplished anything beyond expressing my outrage."

"Did you pick up your heel and take it with you when you left?"

Chagrin edged his prisoner's smile. "Actually, Bill handed it to me on my way out. I took it graciously and then turned around and threw it with all my might at Tom Foley. He ducked and let it hit his friend. It caught him right above the eye."

"I'd have paid money to see that show of yours, Maddie Rutledge."

"The final act was a bit awkward," she admitted. "It's hard to retreat with any sort of dignity at all when you're missing the heel of your shoe. Afterward, I tried nailing a bit of wood on in its place, but it didn't work very well. Reverend Winters ordered me some new shoes, but by the time they finally arrived, I'd adopted the moccasins and I wasn't about to cram my feet back into those little leather prisons. Have you ever seen women's toes after years of wearing fancy shoes?"

He wondered if she realized that she'd crossed the line of propriety. Ladies didn't mention specific body parts in any conversation and they were never, ever to inquire after a gentleman's experience with them in even the most general way. "I can only imagine," he replied diplomatically.

"Most women have ugly toes," she observed. "All crossed over each other and scrunched up. Their feet are actually deformed."

He cocked a brow and let his gaze drop to her feet. "You seem to have escaped their fate."

She wiggled her toes. "No thanks to the good ladies, I assure you," she retorted, full of defiance. "They tried their best to see me crippled."

"But you resisted at every opportunity, didn't you?"

She quickly ate a bite of stew. "That's why they sent me to the Oklahoma Territory, you know."

"I don't quite track along the line you're drawing."

"I was considered ungrateful and exceedingly defiant of social convention," she explained. "They were convinced that I'd come to a bad end because of my poor attitude and unwillingness to be sincerely obedient and compliant. They didn't want me anywhere near enough that someone could point a finger at them. So they sent me into the territory, figuring that when I fell, they wouldn't be splashed with the mud."

They both ate for a moment and then he said slowly, "I don't think I'd much care for these good ladies."

"But they were the pillars of the community. Their reputations were above reproach. In the name of God they came down from their pedestals to improve the lot of us wretched bastards. I should have aspired to be just as good as they were."

"But you didn't," he said, studying her intently. "Why?"

She shrugged and pushed a bit of carrot around in her plate. "I wasn't tall enough to look down my nose at anyone except small children. It seemed cruel. And despite what the good ladies maintained, I don't believe children are responsible for the circumstances of their lives."

He nodded, ate a bite, and then looked up to grin at her. "And with your usual judgment in picking your fights, you told the good ladies just what you thought of them, didn't you?"

Maddie nodded.

"And they made you pay for your honesty by sending you off to the godforsaken end of civilization."

"Going to Oklahoma wasn't as horrible as they thought it would be," she said, her voice becoming more animated with every word. "Reverend Winters always insisted that I eat three times a day. I never ate that often before I got there. And I had my first real Christmas with the reverend, too. He gave me a half a bolt of brand-new black cotton fabric. I knew how to sew from taking in the seams of my hand-me-down dresses, but that fabric made the first new dress I'd ever had. It was so pretty.

"I had my first real birthday there, too. We just picked a date since we didn't know my real one, but it worked fine. I made a cake with raisins and Reverend Winters gave me a black bonnet to go with the dress I'd made. In many ways, sending me to the end of the earth was the best thing the good ladies ever did for me. I was happier there than I ever was in the orphanage." Then, as though she felt guilty for having once been happy, she sobered and quietly added, "And when I fell, they didn't get splashed with the mud."

Rivlin told himself that he was hearing the story of her life from only her side of it, that the good ladies of the orphanage could probably tell him tales of Maddie Rutledge that would curl his hair. And yet, despite being aware of the one-sidedness, he couldn't help but wish that she had a better life to look back on. "It seems to me," he said, choosing his words carefully, "that you didn't so much fall as you got pulled into circumstances that you couldn't get out of without using hot lead."

Maddie stared at the blanket curtain, her eyes darkening. After a moment she shrugged and focused on filling her spoon. "They said that I should have run away and told the law, that I shouldn't have acted as judge and juror and executioner on my own."

"Who are 'they'?"

"The church people." She ate, but her early enthusiasm for the food was clearly gone.

Damn do-gooders. "They weren't standing in your shoes that day," he countered firmly. "They were in no position to judge you or the decision you made. I wouldn't have done any differently than you did."

She almost dropped her plate. Her breathing quickened and she looked at him with such wonderment and relief that it struck him like a physical blow. In that instant he realized that he was the first person who had even tried to understand why she'd killed Caleb Foley.

"You would have killed him?" she asked softly. "You really would have?"

Her hunger for compassion struck him another blow. He thought of his sisters, imagined them in Maddie Rutledge's circumstances and faced with the choices she'd had to make. "I wouldn't have made his death as quick and easy as you did. He'd have paid dearly before he died."

Her smile was sad. "I sure wish you had been on my jury, Marshal."

Rivlin clenched his teeth against the pang of regret that twisted in his chest. He quickly reminded himself that it wasn't his place to be Maddie Rutledge's champion; there were lawyers and judges who were responsible for justice in these kinds of cases. His conscience suggested that he was obliged to nudge her in that direction. "Have you filed an appeal of your conviction? Have you asked for a new trial?"

"What good would it do me? I have no witnesses I can call."

She'd surrendered herself to her fate. He knew the dull tones of a funeral bell when he heard it. It saddened him in a way he couldn't explain. As a lawman, he should have been pleased to know that the fight had gone out of a prisoner. It made the job of controlling them so much easier.

"May I ask you a personal question, Marshal?" she asked softly, using her spoon to scoot a bit of potato around in her plate. She didn't wait for him to reply. "Had you ever killed a man before Murphy?"

Rivlin suspected the reason she asked. Part of him wanted to lie, but he didn't. "I lost count a long time ago."

"Do you have nightmares about them?"

"Just one." *Seth Hoskins.* "But it's been a long while since he came to haunt me." Rivlin stared down at the dirt floor, trying to close the doors of his memory, trying not to see the look in Seth's eyes, trying not to feel the horrible weight of guilt press down on his chest and squeeze the blood from his heart.

"How did you make him stop?"

Rivlin seized a deep breath and focused all of his attention on the woman sitting across the fire from him. She leaned back against the wall, her long legs stretched out toward the fire, her feet bare, the rough-cut edges of her pant legs lying softly on her slim ankles. "I made him a bargain," he said flatly, his gaze moving slowly upward. "As long as I stick to my end of it, he'll leave me be."

She moistened her lips and Rivlin knew what she was preparing to ask. He shook his head. "No. I'm not going to tell you what I offered in exchange for peace. You don't have any bargain to make, Maddie Rutledge. You don't have any wrongs that need to be righted. Next time that sonofabitch comes to visit, tell him to leave you the hell alone, then roll over and go back to sleep."

She smiled ruefully, closed her eyes, and leaned her head back against the rough plank wall. "I wish it were that easy."

"Give it time."

"Does drinking keep you from dreaming?"

Drinking. Reminded, he exhaled long and slowly, picked up the pot of now tepid tea, and divided what remained between their cups. "For a while," Rivlin said, gently rubbing the bottom of her cup over her perfectly shaped toes. She opened her eyes and with a lazy smile sat up to take it from him.

"I wouldn't make a habit of it, though," he added, as she settled cross-legged beside the embers, cradling the cup in both hands. "Whiskey has a way of taking over your life if you let it. Whatever it is that you're running from is still there every time you sober up enough to look past the bottle."

She sipped and looked at him over the metal rim of the cup. "That sounds rather like bitter experience talking."

Rivlin chuckled darkly, and then tossed the contents of his cup down his throat. "I won't deny that I tried it."

"It's a pleasant feeling, like being wrapped in the softest, warmest blanket," she said quietly. "I can see why the good ladies were so opposed to imbibing strong spirits. But then again, they were opposed to anything that felt good, that made you smile. They didn't like us to laugh at all. They said we should have been spending our waking hours praying earnestly, asking for God's forgiveness." She laughed quietly and looked up to smile at him. "Earning forgiveness is a very serious business, you know, Marshal."

"Yeah, I know."

Maddie heard the resignation in his voice, saw the shadows in his eyes. She'd been the cause of it, she and the questions she'd had no business asking. He'd tried to make her feel better and she'd repaid him by reminding him of a past that obviously troubled him. Maddie caught her lower lip between her teeth, wanting to ease the sorrow she'd inadvertently brought him. How?

"I'll bring the horses in and get some more wood for the fire," he said, rising smoothly to his feet. "While I'm about all that, you might want to pick the spot where you want us to pass the night."

Maddie nodded and watched him step past the blanket curtain. She still felt badly about triggering his memories, but a new problem had been presented and it demanded her immediate attention. There couldn't have been any more than twenty-five square feet of dry dirt in their ramshackle haven. The fire had been built smack in the middle of that. And Maddie didn't believe for one second that Rivlin Kilpatrick was going to allow her to sleep without being cuffed to him. That fact, when combined with the smallness of the space, meant that she and the marshal were going to be sleeping in very close quarters.

Maddie eyed the blankets that trapped the heat in the little space. Were they dry enough to sleep in? Would the marshal take them down even if they were? Removing them would allow the heat to follow the smoke right out the open roof. If they remained draped over the rafter, then she and the marshal would be using their slickers as blankets. As barriers to physical contact, they'd be less than ideal.

Recognizing the problem seemed to be all she was capable of doing, however. Finding a solution other than accepting matters as they were was simply beyond her grasp. The warm, soft blanket of alcohol was numbingly comfortable. All she wanted to do was sleep. Maybe if she took a couple of minutes to rest, she'd be able to think of something when Rivlin Kilpatrick came back. Maddie leaned her head back against the wall and let her eyes drift shut.

She felt the iron slide around her right wrist. The other end would be clamped around his left, she knew. His gun hand would remain free. Maddie opened her eyes to find him sitting beside her, his back against the wall. She could feel the heat gently washing over her as the fire popped, consuming the fresh wood. The marshal leaned forward to flick her coat over her legs.

Maddie let her eyes drift shut. She was warm and comfortable and safe. As life went, it was all she ever hoped for.

Chapter Seven

MADDIE SNUGGLED HER BACK deeper into the warmth, vaguely thinking that the mattress was horribly hard. She came fully awake when the bed snuggled back. She half-turned and looked into Rivlin Kilpatrick's eyes. Her heart lurched. She turned and stared at the embers of their fire, realizing that her head was pillowed on his outstretched arm and that her body was curled into the curve of his. His arm lay over her waist so that their cuffed hands nestled together against the slight swell of her abdomen. Heat suffused her cheeks. How did one go about extracting oneself from such situations with some degree of aplomb? she wondered.

"Good morning, Marshal," she finally ventured. "Did you sleep well?"

"Apparently. And you?"

Maddie felt the low vibration of his voice and

the pleasant ripple it sent through her. She took a steadying breath. "Apparently I slept quite soundly."

"I gather this is the first time you've ever awakened in this particular situation?"

The amusement in his voice added to her discomfort. "Of course it is," she countered. "Any suggestions you might be willing to offer for how to extract myself with some dignity would be deeply appreciated."

"You're assuming that I have some experience at this?"

"You don't?"

His laughter was silent, but she felt it in the way his body moved against hers. She was considering abandoning any pretext of poise when he said, "I've noticed that you have a tendency to be the schoolmarm—use fancy words and string them together formally—when you're a mite uncomfortable with something."

Maddie knew it for the gentle dare it was. She'd always had a problem with resisting the temptation of meeting a challenge. She half-rolled back to look up at him. "And how is that observation of any value to me?"

"It probably isn't," he admitted, his smile soft and knowing. "I'm just saying that it tends to give you away."

"You're implying that I'm attempting to hide something."

He cocked a brow and his smile widened. "So tell me, Maddie Rutledge . . . Are you in pain?"

"I beg your pardon? What does that have to do with anything at all?"

"Well," he drawled, "you're blustering about how to get out of the situation and yet you don't seem to be in any great hurry to get away. It couldn't be hurting too bad."

His frankness pushed her past any concern for panache. "I really thought you were a better man, Marshal," she declared, scrambling out of his loose embrace. Her flight was abruptly curtailed when he drew his cuffed arm back to his side. Whirled around by his action, Maddie caught herself, and on hands and knees, met his gaze squarely.

"The fact that I'm a man pretty much limits how good I can be," he said quietly. "Don't expect the impossible and that way you won't be disappointed."

It was a warning if she'd ever heard one. Part of her was thrilled, intrigued by the possibilities. Another part of her cringed. Good judgment said she needed a safe distance between them. "Uncuff me."

"I'm the marshal and you're the prisoner, remember?"

Two years of imprisonment had done nothing but make her resent her lack of power. She bristled at his reminder. "You're being loathsome."

"And you're being childish," he countered, sitting up easily. "What's wrong with waking up and discovering that you're warm and comfortable?"

I liked it. Startled by the silent admission, Maddie quickly tried to turn the discussion away from herself. "You didn't look all that pleased at your first glance," she pointed out.

He considered her for a second and then grinned. "The truth is I was trying to remember whether or not we'd danced and was feeling a mite put out that if we had, I didn't remember it."

"I assure you that we didn't!" she declared, hoping that he couldn't hear the sudden hammering of her heart.

"I figured as much," he drawled. "If we had, your feathers wouldn't be all ruffled."

Completely unable to think of a pithy rejoinder, she was left with glaring at him and hoping that he could supply the epithets on his own.

"Has anyone ever told you how pretty you are when you blush?"

To Maddie's horror, the heat in her cheeks intensified. "No!"

"Well, you are," he said softly. "Very pretty."

No one had ever spoken to her as he did. Never had mere words so thoroughly stirred her blood. Alarmed, Maddie lifted her chin, resolving to make their conversation less personal. "Are you planning to stay here today and wage an assault on my dignity," she asked with what she hoped passed for nonchalance, "or are we going to ride on?"

He was silent and still. Maddie waited, holding her breath and hearing for the first time the sound of rain falling on the sod and wood roof overhead, the low, mournful wail of the wind outside.

"Why is being told you're pretty an assault on your dignity?"

The gentleness, the sincerity of his question affected her deeply and something inside her threatened to crumble. Maddie lifted her chin a notch. "Vanity is one of the mortal sins, Marshal."

Another long silence stretched between them, broken only by the sound of the wind and the rain. "All things considered," he finally replied, "I'd think that being accused of vanity wouldn't be your chief concern."

It wasn't, but she couldn't very well admit it. Maddie forced herself to swallow. "I happen to believe that it's unwise to burn your moral bridges."

"That's assuming that you want to go back to

the place where you started," he countered, his voice suddenly flinty. "Most of us don't. And some of us flat-out can't."

Murderers like you, for instance, Maddie silently finished for him. She didn't care if he knew she was angry. "Are you implying that there is no point in my maintaining a sense of moral decency?"

For a fraction of a second surprise and confusion clouded his eyes and then they were gone, replaced by a cold, steely hardness. "I'm not implying a damn thing," he countered. "I'm saying—"

The roof squealed, the sound high-pitched and long and desperate. Maddie instantly looked up, sensed Rivlin Kilpatrick do the same. A half-dozen muddy rivulets cascaded down, carrying bits of dried grass away from the widening slivers of light above. The squealing deepened into a shivering groan and then a bone-numbing rumble. The horses whinnied in panic. The planks parted. The rivulets gushed, thick and black. Above the noise of the collapsing roof, Maddie heard Rivlin swear. He moved with breathtaking speed, half-pulling her into his arms, half-meeting her, and tumbling both of them into the near corner.

She clung to him, keenly aware of the mass of sinew and heat wrapped around her, shielding her from the mountain of falling debris. Protected, she only half-heard the crashing come to its end. It was beyond Rivlin Kilpatrick, beyond her realm of concern. He had pinned her upright into the shelter of the corner, holding her there, pressed hard against her, his breath quick and warm against her temple, his heart hammering hard against her breast.

He eased his shoulders back and brushed wet tendrils of hair from the side of her face. "Maddie?"

She looked up into dark, searching eyes. Her

throat tightened. She couldn't breathe, but it didn't matter.

"Are you all right, Maddie?"

No. I want you to kiss me. "I'm fine. You? Are you all right?"

He nodded. For a long moment he studied her and she sensed that he knew the secret of her wish. Her pulse skittered at the thought that he might oblige her temptation. Instead, he looked away, drew a long, slow breath, and then eased the rest of his weight off her, saying, "Guess that pretty much decides the matter of whether we stay or ride on."

He reached into his pocket, produced the key to the manacles that bound them together, and without a word, unlocked them.

Slumping weakly into the wall, Maddie absently rubbed her wrist and watched him turn away. His back, from his shoulders to the hems of his pant legs, was splattered with mud. She forced herself to breathe and found her balance. Gathering her wits, she asked, "You don't happen to know of another abandoned farmstead along the way, do you, Marshal?"

"Nope." He pushed open a path for them with his foot, saying, "I'll see to the tack and the horses if you'll start rounding up what you can of our blankets and other things."

She nodded and set about the task. It wasn't easy; everything was buried beneath the jumble of broken, rotted boards and mounds of heavy black mud. Maddie worked resolutely, using one of the longer boards to lever away the rest and reclaim their sodden and muddy belongings. Despite her best efforts, her mind refused to dwell solely on the salvage effort. With maddening detail, she remembered the look in Rivlin Kilpatrick's eyes as he'd studied her in the aftermath. Now, just as then, her heart pounded and her throat tightened. Maddie sternly warned herself of the danger inherent in courting even so much as a single kiss. It didn't help. Her intellect seemed to have completely separated itself from her emotions.

That realization was not only deeply troubling, but very sobering, and the implications of it consumed the better part of her awareness as she worked. She and Rivlin Kilpatrick were tethered, when and if they would reach Leavenworth largely unknown. It was pointless to deny that she considered him an attractive man; any woman would. And if she were being honest with herself, she'd also have to admit that for the first time in her life she wasn't repulsed by the idea of an intimate relationship with a man. It was equally clear that the marshal wasn't disinterested in her as a woman. He had, in fact, warned her that being male made him susceptible to temptation and cautioned her not to expect too much from him.

As far as she could tell, only two considerations stood between her and what some would see as perdition: her resolve to keep her life from getting any more complicated than it already was and the marshal's sense of professional duty. In the moments after the roof's collapse, she'd faltered. Rivlin Kilpatrick had held himself in check. In that frozen moment was the essence of the road ahead. As long as one of them could exercise common sense, they'd be able to maintain a safe distance between them. If they both stumbled at the same time, though . . .

Maddie sighed. There had been a time in her life when she would have seen the possibilities before her as black and white, as clearly defined good and evil. She would have prayed for deliverance from temptation and held rigidly to religious and social strictures. But all the shoulds and oughts that had ordered her existence had been turned inside out in the moment she'd faced Caleb Foley and pulled the trigger. In the days that had followed, she had come to understand that all she had been taught as truth wasn't, that life was really various shades of gray, that good and evil were relative definitions and that in a blink of time one could easily become the other. How you made your way through the days and years couldn't be decided on the basis of ironclad rules and precepts. Oak trees stood unyielding before the wind. They often shattered and died. Cottonwood trees yielded when they needed to, and in doing so, survived storm after storm.

And that, Maddie decided as she assembled the blankets, their coats, and her moccasins, was the only way she had of approaching the days ahead. What came of her journey with Rivlin Kilpatrick would be what came of it, and she wouldn't batter herself for whatever course it ultimately took. Carrying the salvaged items outside into the drizzling rain, Maddie joined him beside the well and silently set to the task of washing away the mud as best she could.

SOMETHING ABOUT HER was different. Rivlin couldn't say exactly what it was, but he sensed it nonetheless. He slid a glance over at her. She sat her horse as she had before, her shoulders squared and her moccasined feet set well into the stirrups. The rain had stopped hours before and she'd unbuttoned her coat in the warming temperatures and pushed her hat brim back on her forehead so that the occasional ray of sun shone on her face.

He suspected, however, that it wasn't a physical change he sensed. It seemed to have more to do with the way she wore the world. His first inkling had come when she'd brought their belongings out of the ruined house. Those had been the first moments they'd been together since the collapse of the roof. More accurately, he admitted, those had been the first moments since he'd looked down at her in the corner and struggled with the temptation to kiss her.

Did she know what had gone through his head? he wondered. Did she know how close he'd come to forgetting his sworn duty? She'd have had to have been deaf and blind not to have noticed his strain. Oddly enough, though, she didn't seem distressed or angry by it all. In fact, she seemed a bit more . . . settled? Yes, *settled* was the right word. She'd been skittish and temperamental until the last few hours, but now she gave every sign of having decided to accept the bit. His pulse jolted at the implications in that possibility.

Damnation. If ever there were a woman he shouldn't become involved with, it was Maddie Rutledge. She was his prisoner. Professionalism mandated that he avoid any personal relationship with her. No matter how one looked at it, kissing her was definitely unacceptable conduct. But the plain truth was that he wanted to do just that. Hell, if given the chance, he'd be tempted to do even more with Maddie Rutledge. He'd had a fair idea of what was hidden under her baggy clothing, but waking up with those lush curves curled into him had been just about the most wonderful bit of enlightenment he'd ever had.

Rivlin considered the immediate future. If he were an intelligent man, he'd wire for a replacement the minute they reached Wichita. He'd hand her into the custody of the local marshal and ride away as fast as he could. He wouldn't spend one more second with her than absolutely necessary. But Maddie had been buffeted hard by her past experiences with the law and its representatives and he didn't want to be responsible for more of the same. With her kind of luck, Hodges would be sent to take her into Leavenworth. No, whether or not it was smart, staying with her and seeing her through to the end was the right thing to do. He'd simply have to keep his head square on his shoulders, his hands to himself, and hope that Maddie didn't take up sides in the battle waging between his conscience and his desire.

"Just out of curiosity and to keep myself from being swept away in the heady revelry," she said, breaking the long silence, "what kind of name is Rivlin?"

"Irish. It's my mother's maiden name."

"It's an interesting name, Rivlin Kilpatrick. I've always thought that Maddie Rutledge sounds drab and plain, rather like a mud hen."

Rivlin thought about telling her that he thought it was a pretty name, but decided that she wouldn't take that any better than she had his comments about her blushing. But since a response of some sort seemed in order, he asked politely, "Who named you? The ladies at the orphanage?"

She nodded, her laughter dry. "I suppose I had a name before I got there, but since I was only four, I don't remember what it might have been. They picked Madeline because it sounded polished and refined. Rutledge was given to me in honor of a prominent citizen from somewhere in Iowa. During the war, they began to give us all names of military men. Sherman and Grant are two of their favorites."

He tilted his head to grin at her. "No Lincolns?"

She whipped her hat off her head and held it over her heart. "That's a sacred name, Marshal."

The sparkle in her eyes told him she didn't consider it in that light. "I don't suppose there were any Jacksons or Lees."

"Heresy!" She lifted her face to the sky. "Forgive him!"

"Truth be told," Rivlin countered, "they were the better tacticians and officers."

She plopped her hat back on her head. "I've heard it said more than once that if the Confederacy had had stronger supply lines, they would have won the war."

"There are no winners in a war, just survivors." He hadn't intended for the words to sound embittered, but there was no calling them back, no hope of making them anything but the truth they were. Rivlin frowned at the land stretching before them, remembering despite knowing better.

Several moments passed and then she asked softly, "How old were you?"

"I was all of seventeen when I ran away to enlist." So young. Too young to know any better.

"I gather that your parents opposed it?"

There was a kind of blessed distraction to be had in answering her question. "My father was a munitions manufacturer with sizable government contracts and even more impressive government connections. I could have worked for him and been exempt from military field service. My parents thought that was what I should do."

"So why didn't you?"

"I was convinced I'd never get my fair share of glory if I stayed at home and pushed paper across a desk every day."

"Did you find your glory?"

"I found that there's no such thing in a war, Maddie. There's only blood and death."

Rivlin felt her gaze slide over to him and knew that she'd heard every measure of his regret and disillusionment. Odd how he didn't mind her knowing. It made her the only person on earth who did. He sensed that the secret was safe with her.

"Does your family still make munitions?" she asked, artfully shifting the conversation away from his wounds.

Rivlin chuckled dryly. "It seems there's always a need to blow something up or shoot someone down."

"So why didn't you go into the family business after the war? Why did you stay out here and marshal?"

"I did go home, twice," he answered with a shrug. "The first time right after the war and then again when my father died and the business passed to my brother and me." Giving her a quirked smile, he added, "I discovered that I didn't like it any more than I had when I'd been seventeen. The first time I reenlisted and the second time I wired the U.S. Marshal Service—throwing pride to the wind—and begged them to help me escape my misery. They were kind enough to oblige before I lost my mind."

Her brows knitted as she considered him with narrowed eyes. After a moment she shook her head. "I can't imagine you in an office and wearing a fancy suit."

"Would you be willing to write that in a letter to my mother and sisters?"

She laughed, the sound light and musical and somehow both soothing and exhilarating. "Maybe

I'll just send them a telegram. How far it is to Wichita?"

"From Larned, a bit shy of a hundred miles as the crow flies." He quickly added, "And in answer to your next question, at the rate we're traveling, we'll drag in about midnight tomorrow."

Midnight tomorrow. And then her world would be reduced to four walls again. For how long? She had to be in Leavenworth in ten days. If the answers weren't ready and waiting for Kilpatrick when they reached Wichita, it might take a while to find them and then he'd be forced to transport her by train to reach the trial in time.

Maddie lifted her chin and gazed around her, reveling in the relative freedom she had for the moment. The air was cool and damp, the sun masked by a thick blanket of pale gray clouds. The earth was soft from the rain the night before and the sound of horse hooves was muffled and low. The land that had been flat and sparsely grassed outside of Larned had changed as they'd moved southeasterly. There were long, easy rolls to it now. In the shallow valleys, where there was some protection from the ravages of the south wind, cottonwoods grew. For miles in every direction the vista was the same: dun and amber grass swells dotted with stands of paling green. The wind came softly from the north, its touch a whisper against her ear.

As they rode into the relative shelter between two hillocks, Maddie remembered what this part of the world had looked like when Hodges had brought her through. It had been in the late spring. The grass had been the purest green, dancing in waves under the wind. The trees were seeding, their leaves shimmering greenish silver as the wind passed through. And the sky over it all had been a clear azure, filled not with clouds, but with the drifting bits of white cottonwood fluff. She'd thought it beautiful in an open, quietly wild, and forever sort of way. Even now, as the land settled in for the coming winter, it possessed a simple beauty that was soothing. It was a world so different from the bluffs and manicured farmland of her childhood in Iowa, from the densely wooded hills of eastern Oklahoma, from the often parched, flat land that lay around Fort Larned. If someone said that she had to spend the rest of her life here, she wouldn't have seen the edict as a bad thing at all.

She pitched forward in the saddle, her horse snorting and dancing beneath her, returning her awareness to the immediate moment with heart-wrenching suddenness. Time crawled, each bit of realization coming full formed and slowly. Rivlin Kilpatrick had moved his horse to block the path of hers. His mount pawed the ground, nervously shifting against the hard control of the reins. Beyond Rivlin, on the other side of a little creek of runoff water, sat two horsemen, one with a gray grizzle of a beard, one young and clean-shaven. A rifle lay across the lap of the older man. As she watched, the corners of his mouth lifted with a smile.

Satisfaction. Maddie swallowed to force the lump out of her throat. In front of her, Kilpatrick shifted in the saddle, effectively making himself a wider shield. His left hand held the reins, his right lay on his thigh, inches from the butt of his gun. Too many inches, she judged, glancing toward the muzzle of the older man's rifle. Rivlin would never be able to draw and beat the bullet.

"Afternoon, gentlemen," Rivlin said with all the

ease of a man rocking on a front porch. "Might I ask what brings you out here?"

Maddie looked at Rivlin's back and wondered how he could be so calm and collected. She shook so badly that she wasn't at all sure she wouldn't rattle herself right out of the saddle. For a long moment there was only the sound of the other riders' horses stamping nervously.

"Would you happen to be Marshal Kilpatrick?" asked the older man.

Damn.

"Might be. Might not be," Rivlin answered conversationally. "Why do you ask?"

A gun; she needed a gun of her own. If something happened to Rivlin Kilpatrick. . . . She looked at the ground in front of her horse and saw too clearly the image of Rivlin sprawled in the grass, his life pouring out of him. Would she have time to get down, pull the revolver from his hand, and defend them both? Probably not.

"Been sent to find you and your prisoner."

Maddie caught the almost imperceptible movement of Rivlin's right arm and knew that he was preparing to reach for the revolver. *Don't,* she silently pleaded. *He'll kill you before it clears the holster.*

"Oh, yeah?" Rivlin drawled as though only barely interested. "By whom? And why?"

The impulse came and she acted on it in the same instant. Clutching the saddle horn with one hand, she pulled her left foot from the stirrup and swung her leg back, dragging her foot across the horse's flank. As it had in the yard at Fort Larned, the animal instantly snorted, jumped sideways and spun. She hung on with blind desperation as she bounced around the animal's back.

Twin explosions shook the air. Her horse scrambled sideways with a snort, requiring every bit of her strength to haul back on the reins and bring her under control. Over the sound of her gasping struggle came a whinny, the squeal of saddle leather, and a hard thump. Thick acrid smoke drifted slowly over her. Through it she saw Rivlin Kilpatrick sitting squarely and pointing his gun with a steady hand. She set her left foot back into the stirrup, sparing only a glance at the body of the older man sprawled in the mud at his horse's feet.

"*You* have a choice, mister," she heard Rivlin say to the remaining rider. "I recommend you drop that gun and put your hands up where I can see them." There came an instant soft thud and then he added, "Now, how about you tell me who it was that paid you to come out here and find us."

"He didn't tell us his name."

"What did he look like?"

"Short, little sawed-off fellow," the young man answered, his voice earnest with fear. "From back East somewhere. Can't tell you exactly where, but it wasn't the South. Wore a bowler hat. Big mutton-chop sideburns. Fancy suit."

"Tell me the particulars, every single one of them."

The man expelled a hard breath. "Not much to tell. The guy came into the saloon in Florence and—"

"When?"

"About three weeks ago," he quickly answered. "We was to see that you and your witness there didn't make it to Leavenworth if the first plan didn't work. A hundred to wait and another four hundred if we was the ones to bring you down. If we didn't get some sort of word by yesterday morning, we was supposed to come looking for you. Jim there thought you might have figured it all out and be making a line for Wichita. Which is how we happened to come this way instead of looking for you up north."

"Did he say why he wanted us dead?" Rivlin pressed.

"No. And we didn't ask."

Maddie mentally sorted through the information the stranger had provided, quickly recognizing the implications. Her hands trembled and she tightened her grip on the reins to still them.

"What proof were you supposed to provide that you'd killed us?" Rivlin demanded.

"Your hat and badge. Her left foot from above the ankle. Seems she's got a scar."

They'd been planning to cut her foot off her body? In her mind's eye she saw the dull glint of an ax in midarc. Her blood went cold and she couldn't suppress the deep shudder than ran up the length of her spine.

"And how were you supposed to provide the proof and collect your money?"

"We was to send a telegram to Kansas City—to William B. Jones—general delivery and then meet him in Emporia so's he could see and pay us if'n we had the right things."

She heard Rivlin swear under his breath. "Maddie," he commanded, "climb down and go get the rifle and the gun. Make sure you get the one that's still in the holster. Bring that extra horse back with you, too."

She scrambled to obey, being careful not to look at the dead man's face. Having manacled hands made tucking the guns into the waistband of her trousers awkward but she managed it. Then, with the rifle in one hand, she snagged the reins of the riderless horse with the other and led it back to her own.

"You can't leave me out here without a weapon," the young man declared as she handed Rivlin the rifle.

"Yes I can," Rivlin countered with cool indifference. "I can leave you without a horse, too. Climb down, keeping your hands high, and back up about fifteen paces."

Settling into the saddle, Maddie watched the man hesitate and then warily do as he'd been told. He finally stopped and stood, glaring at Rivlin. "If I die out here," the stranger said, "it'll be on your head."

Keeping the muzzle aimed at the man and using his knees to command his mount, Rivlin eased the animal forward to take the abandoned reins in his free hand. "Well, if you feel that strongly about it," Rivlin drawled, "I guess I could leave you with both a gun and a horse. Only problem, as I see it, is that you're gonna have to be dead enough not to use either one to come after Maddie and me. Seems to be a case of six of one and a half-dozen of another. How badly do you want 'em?"

"You son of a bitch."

Rivlin slowly dropped his chin. "You remember that. And know that if you decide to come after me again, I'll kill you for sure and for certain. Think twice about it, young man."

Rivlin holstered his revolver and wheeled his horse about, bringing the extra mount with him. Maddie, too, turned her animals. She rode beside him, her mind filled with thoughts of what they'd just learned. They'd covered a mile or two when Rivlin finally drew to a halt, dismounted, stripped the saddles from the extra horses, and then turned them loose.

He was back in the saddle when he extended his hand toward her and said, "The guns, if you please."

She gave him one, saying, "Considering the circumstances, maybe I ought to keep the other one to protect your backside."

"Or maybe you'd use it to put a bullet in me." He held out his hand. "Give it over."

"I would think," she said, "that I might have earned just a small amount of your trust in the last few days."

"Your horse isn't tethered, is it? I've gone all the farther along the road of trust that I'm going to. Give me the other gun, Maddie."

"I created the diversion for you, you know. If I hadn't set my horse to dancing, you'd be dead."

"Probably. And I'm appropriately grateful. Now give me the gun."

She surrendered it, commenting, "Just so you know, Marshal . . . If something happens to you, I intend to pick up your gun and use it."

One corner of his mouth quirked up. "To defend yourself or finish me off?"

"Both," she retorted just to prick his amusement.

He sobered and met her gaze squarely. "Well, for God's sakes don't make a mess of it." Putting his index finger on the bridge of his nose, he added, "Lay the muzzle right here and pull the trigger clean."

Her stomach clenched. She could never do such a thing, of course. It was the cool, matter-of-fact way that Rivlin Kilpatrick approached the subject that so deeply disturbed her. It was almost as if the thought of dying didn't bother him in the least. Why? She shivered and resolutely changed the course of their conversation. "That man back there said the offer on us was made three weeks ago. Did you know then that you'd draw the assignment to escort me?"

"Nope," Rivlin replied, nimbly dismantling the first gun. "But somebody apparently did."

"Do you have any idea who? Could it be someone at the Marshal Service?" She watched his hands, sensing that he was accomplishing the task by second nature and without conscious thought.

"Could. Or it could be someone with the kind of influence it would take to get things done like they wanted." He threw away all the pieces of the revolver except the cylinder. That he put into the pocket of his coat as he asked, "Do you think the man spreading the money around could be that friend of Tom Foley's?" He began dismantling the second gun.

"Sawed-off and muttonchop sideburns would fit him," Maddie admitted, squinting to remember him. "He also wore a bowler. I suppose it could be him."

"Or his cousin or his uncle or his brother," Rivlin observed on a derisive snort as he discarded more pieces, again keeping the cylinder. "That's the problem with men from back East, they all look alike."

He disassembled the rifle with breathtaking speed, flinging the parts away, keeping only the trigger. Then, with a glance back over his shoulder, he set his horse into motion.

Maddie fell in beside him. "I can't help but wonder . . . Why do they want you dead, too? It can't be a case of needing to kill you just so they can kill me or they wouldn't bother with wanting proof that you're dead." He didn't answer, but she didn't let the silence discourage her. "What if you know about something else and they're trying to kill two birds with one stone? It sure seems as though someone went to a great deal of effort to make sure we were together out here."

He looked over at her, his eyes dark and hard. "Sure does, doesn't it?"

Chapter Eight

IT WAS AGAIN MIDNIGHT *on that horrible moonless night. Seth was curled up under a bush, his knees drawn tight against his chest. Jesus Christ, Seth, what's happened? A whimper and tightening of his arms around his legs. Look at me, Seth. Who beat the hell out of you? But Seth wouldn't answer. He cried out softly and jerked away when Rivlin reached to touch him. Look at me, Seth. Please. Tell me what happened. I can't help you if you won't talk to me. Seth cried, deep, silent sobs that wracked his body.*

Rivlin awakened with a heart-jolting start, his chest heavy and his throat tight. It had been years since that memory of Seth had come to him in his dreams with such clarity. He reached into his saddlebags for his cigarette makings, knowing that he couldn't keep from remembering the rest of it any more than he could undo the past. Just one week after that night, Seth had lain dying in his arms, the killing bullet fired from the barrel of Rivlin's own rifle. Seth had finally looked up at him then, his eyes brimming with tears of shame and regret. And then Seth had slipped away forever and without a word.

Rivlin licked the edge of the cigarette paper, stuck it into place, and twisted the ends closed. He struck a waxed match on the heel of his boot, drew the fire into the end of his hastily fashioned cigarette and a draft of hot, acrid smoke into his lungs. Blowing out the match, he tossed the charred remnant into the glowing embers of his and Maddie's evening fire. While Seth had never told him what had happened to him that moonless night, he'd made a reasoned guess. As he had all those years ago, Rivlin deliberately closed his mind to the details of imagining what Seth had endured. It was too ugly, too unnatural.

Rivlin took a pull on the cigarette and watched the end glow bright orange in the dark of the prairie night. It was the question of who that had opened the doors of his memories, of course. Who wanted Maddie Rutledge dead? Who wanted him dead? And as his mind had searched for answers in his sleep, it had brought an older, still troubling and unanswered question to the fore: Who had brutalized Seth?

Rivlin felt a gentle tug on his left wrist and looked down. "Go back to sleep, Maddie," he said quietly. "Dawn'll be here soon enough. Tomorrow will be a long, hard ride. Best go into it rested."

Maddie sat up slowly, asking quietly, "Are you all right?"

He scrubbed his hand over his stubbled chin. "Yeah."

It was a lie. She could feel it. "Do you want to

talk about him? The ghost that haunts you? Maybe it would help."

"What makes you think there's a ghost?" he asked.

"Almost every man I've ever met of a certain age served in the war. And not a one of them came out of it unscarred. With some, it's physical and obvious. But others are scarred in spirit. You strike me as one of the latter."

Maddie felt the sag in his shoulders. The sound he made was akin to laughter, but there was no humor or merriment in it, only the brittleness of recognizing a sad joke. Resisting the urge to touch him, Maddie stayed where she was and watched him struggle with his memories.

"Seth Hoskins and I grew up together," he said softly, the sudden end to his silence startling her. "We were like brothers, inseparable. And when the call came for volunteer enlistments, we went together to join the army. We served in the same unit, shared the same tent."

Maddie waited as he pulled on his cigarette and blew out the smoke in a long, hard stream.

"I had the midnight watch and it was around about the middle of it. There was movement in the scrub about twenty feet out ahead of me. When I called for the man to stand and identify, he whirled back. All I could see in the moonlight was the glint of the bayonet on the Enfield as it came around to point at my chest. I didn't know it was Seth until I went out and . . ."

His voice broke. He cleared his throat, but said nothing more.

"It was an accident, Rivlin."

"No, it wasn't," he said with absolute conviction. "Something horrible had happened to Seth a week before that night. He refused to say anything of it, but I've always had my suspicions and . . ."

His voice trailed away as he once again stared into the distance. "What happened?" she gently prompted.

"War brings all manner of men together and then brings out the worst in their personal natures. Four-legged animals are compassionate predators. The human kind . . ." He shook his head. "Gentlemen don't discuss such matters with ladies, Maddie," he said firmly, flicking what remained of his cigarette into the embers of their fire. "Hell, they don't discuss it among themselves, either. Just let it suffice to say that while the bruises on Seth's body healed, those of his mind and soul didn't. I think he walked out past the picket line that night fully intending to draw a bullet."

What had happened to Seth? she wondered. What was so horrible that men didn't talk about it? "You can't hold yourself accountable for another man's decision to die," she offered softly. "You aren't God, Rivlin Kilpatrick."

He looked up at the stars. "I failed him, Maddie. I didn't see the danger before it caught him and I didn't protect him from himself in the aftermath. Instead, I pulled the trigger and Seth died. He never got the chance to learn to live with what had happened to him. He never got to go home to his family. He never had a chance to find a woman he loved. He never got to marry or have children."

Understanding came with heart-wrenching clarity. "So you promised him you wouldn't have those comforts, either," Maddie said quietly. "That was the bargain you made with Seth, isn't it? That you would atone for your sins by having no forevers of your own."

"Something like that," he answered with a shrug so dismissive that she knew that she'd guessed the truth.

"Does Seth's family blame you for what happened?"

"How can they not?"

"They can live by forgiveness and understanding."

He turned and faced her, his face deep in the shadow of his hat brim. "Can you forgive the jury that sent you to prison for defending Lucy Three Trees's life? For defending your own life?" he asked. "Can you forgive the Foleys and Collins and Lane for all that they did to you and the Indians of Tahlequah?"

"I can try."

He shook his head slowly. "Try all you want, Maddie. Pretend 'til the cows come home. But if you were being honest, you'd have to admit that underneath it all, you can't forgive a hurt like that. I didn't tell Seth's parents everything; just how he died. They've hugged me, told me they understand. But I know how deep the pain goes and that the wound I've caused them will never heal."

Because your own never has.

An expression of bittersweet sorrow slowly softened his features and the smile he gave her slipped gently around her heart and held it. In a voice that would have soothed the most fretful infant or the most frightened animal, he said, "Don't look so sad, Maddie. It's my burden and I've learned how to bear it. It can't be fixed, no matter how much you might like for that to happen. Don't you lose any sleep over it."

And with that, he eased back down into the blankets, drawing her with him. Maddie settled into the prairie that was their bed, thinking that Rivlin was the most intriguing man she'd ever met. On the surface, he didn't appear to be very complicated—a lawman with a clear sense of duty, an equally clear sense of right and wrong, and a streak of honesty that made him unable to abide pretenses of any sort. Underneath, though, he was a tangle of contradictions. He had grown up wanting for nothing. He'd had a huge, apparently loving family, money, and quite likely the social position and power that almost always came with wealth. Despite his rather folksy manner of speech, every now and then she caught a glimpse of an educated man. No doubt, given his family's resources and their business hopes for him, his education had been far more extensive than hers.

And yet he'd turned his back on all of it and walked away. He'd chosen to live a solitary, dangerous, and essentially nomadic life on the edges of civilization out of a sense of having to atone for his failures as a young man. In a way, he had no more of a future than she did. He was simply existing from day to day, accepting what life brought with an almost casual indifference as to whether he lived or died. She remembered when she'd suggested burying Murphy and his calm instruction in how he wanted her to kill him and knew that, in his way, Rivlin Kilpatrick was courting his own death just as surely as Seth Hoskins had that long ago night. And there was nothing she could do about it. Maddie swallowed back the lump forming in her throat and reached over to tuck the blankets more closely around him.

Rivlin studied the stars overhead and smiled ruefully. If Maddie Rutledge had ever put half as much effort into taking care of herself as she did others, her life wouldn't be nearly the mess it was. Instead, she'd taken risks to feed hungry children between meals at the orphanage. She'd gone to the Oklahoma Territory because justice had needed a servant. And she'd dutifully battled in the name of fairness, despite never once winning even the smallest victory. And now she was trying to soothe his regrets and banish his guilt. In a way, Maddie Rutledge had spent all of her years trying to be good enough to earn her parents back. The futility of it all saddened him.

MADDIE STRETCHED HER BACK and shifted her position in the saddle. The afternoon sun beat down on them relentlessly and she marveled at the number of flies that had seemingly come from nowhere to buzz about their ambling horses.

"Almost makes you have fond memories of the rain, doesn't it?" Rivlin Kilpatrick asked from beside her.

She nodded.

"Wagon ahead."

Oh, dear God, please. Not another attempt to kill us. Maddie focused on the sweep of prairie before them. In the shallow valley below a single wagon sat in the sea of grass. The canvas cover, patched and loosely tied down, fluttered fitfully in the soft breeze. The pair of oxen stood in their yokes, hitched to the wagon, nibbling idly on the grass at their feet. A man sat with his back braced against the front wheel. As Maddie studied the scene, he slowly climbed to his feet. He wore baggy clothing, a ratty hat and a holster worn high on his hip. She guessed him to be at least forty years old or so.

"We'll ride in," Rivlin said very quietly, his eyes narrowed. "But I want you to stay behind me and to my left so that my gun hand's always between you and him. Understood?"

Maddie nodded, wondering if he ever encountered a person without initial suspicion. If not, it was a cold and lonely way to live. Out of the corner of her eye, she saw him ease his hand down his thigh, carefully take the tether from his revolver, and then rest his hand casually over the butt of the weapon. She dropped back as he'd instructed.

"Afternoon," Rivlin called, drawing his mount to a stop a fair distance from the stranger. "Is there a problem?"

"Naw," the man answered, looking between her and Rivlin. He jerked a thumb toward the wagon behind him. "I'm just waitin' 'til my wife is done birthin'."

It was as though she'd met this man a thousand times before. The West seemed to be full of his kind, oblivious to all but his own narrow needs and desires. Some were simply mean-spirited. Others were simply simpleminded and didn't truly realize there was a world beyond themselves. She couldn't yet tell which kind this man was. She deliberately unclenched her teeth and touched the tip of her tongue to her lips, resolved to find out. Rivlin Kilpatrick asked the question before she could.

"I assume you're waiting out here because she has someone else assisting her?"

The man shrugged and smiled. "I figure she'll do fine on her own, it being a natural female event and all."

She knew that she shouldn't have been surprised or disappointed by the man's pronouncement, but she was nonetheless. The fact that he appeared to be a simpleton didn't matter. Maddie tried to swallow back an angry growl, the effort apparently a failure because Rivlin glanced over his shoulder at her. "Have you ever delivered a baby?"

Both relief and dread swept over her at the same time. "I've assisted the midwives twice," she replied, swinging down off her horse. "I wouldn't say that I'm any storehouse of knowledge on the particulars. Both births went without a hitch. If there are difficulties with this one, I'll be in well over my head."

Rivlin, too, dismounted, saying as he did, "You've got two times more experience than me and Mr. . . ."

"Reynolds," the other man supplied. "Edgar Reynolds. And I'd imagine Sally would be grateful for the company. It's been a while since she had another female to talk with."

Talk? The man actually thought his wife would be in a state of mind to appreciate conversation? Once she took care of Sally, she was going to find a heavy object and beat the man soundly about the head and shoulders. Turning to Rivlin, she held out her hands, saying, "I can't do this cuffed, Marshal."

Rivlin had no more reached into his pocket for the key than Edgar Reynolds took a step forward. Maddie staggered as Rivlin turned and shoved her behind him.

"Wait a minute!" the other man sputtered. "Why is she in irons?"

"She's a federal prisoner," Rivlin replied, handing the key to Maddie without looking back at her.

Maddie quickly opened the locks as Reynolds said, "Sally is a good, God-fearing woman."

Dropping the manacles into the grass at her feet, Maddie pushed the key into her pants pocket and stepped up to Rivlin's left side. "Not to worry,

Mr. Reynolds," she offered with all the calm she could muster. "The tarnish doesn't rub off."

"I don't know." He repeatedly looked between her and the back of the wagon, clearly making no progress in deciding what to do about the situation.

Beside her, Rivlin asked incredulously, "You'd rather risk having your wife and child die than let Maddie help?"

Only the drone of the flies broke the taut silence for a long while. Rivlin finally bent, scooped up the irons, and half-turned to face Maddie. "Climb back up. We're riding on."

Her heart slammed into her throat and her blood raced so hard it hurt. She desperately grabbed a handful of his shirtsleeve. "I can't ride on, Rivlin. Please, please don't do this. Don't ask me to do this. What he thinks of me doesn't matter. It's his wife's decision to make."

He blinked down at her and she saw misgiving flicker in the depths of his eyes. Drawing a deep breath and then sighing heavily, he shook his head and said quietly, "All right, Maddie. I'll take the point for you. Hang on one second."

Turning and stepping toward the other man, he said with flinty coolness, "Reynolds, here's how we're going to play this out. You and I are going to stand right where we are and you're not going to utter so much as a tiny squeak of protest as Maddie climbs into the back of that wagon and checks on your wife."

"I don't know," Reynolds said again. "What if she hurts Sally?"

The blur of Rivlin's gun coming out of the holster stole Maddie's breath. "We're wasting time," Rivlin drawled, his hand rock steady as he aimed the weapon at the center of the other man's chest and drew back the hammer. As Edgar Reynolds's hands inched into the air, Rivlin added, "All right, Maddie, go check on Mrs. Reynolds. Stay well out and cross behind him."

Maddie ran and didn't look back. The tailgate of the wagon was up and bolted closed. She didn't take the time to lower it, but simply scrambled up and over the top. One glimpse inside and she nearly lost her grip on the rough wooden planks. It was bad. Very bad. There was always blood with childbirth, but there was too much with Sally Reynolds. Way too much. The pool was so wide and deep that it trickled through the floorboards and onto the grass below. The tiny woman lay in the middle of it, motionless, her baby lying in the blood between her thighs, just as still.

For an instant Maddie was frozen, overwhelmed by the stench and the utter hopelessness of the situation, not knowing what to do. But something had to be done. Maddie swallowed down her stomach, blinked back her tears, and forced herself into the shade of the wagon bed and the cloud of droning flies.

Sally Reynolds was no more than fourteen, Maddie judged as she found the materials the girl had prepared for her own delivery. Too young, too small to be having babies. Maddie splashed whiskey over her hands, remembering all she'd seen the midwives do. The baby's needs came first. Quickly tying off and cutting the cord, Maddie used her finger to sweep clear the infant girl's mouth and then held her up by the heels to slap the tiny rump. The cry was quiet and weak and didn't last long, but the blue that had tinged the little mouth instantly began to fade and Maddie's heartbeat slowed a bit in relief.

A large rag and a clean blue cotton shawl were

among the items Sally had assembled and Maddie used the former to clean the child a bit before she carefully wrapped it in the latter. Then she moved up to carefully place the small bundle on the mother's chest. Pressing her fingertips against the young woman's neck, she felt the faintest of pulses. Tears filled Maddie's eyes again and she resolutely blinked them back. With her fingertips, she gently brushed wet tendrils of blond hair off the girl's forehead.

Sally's chest rose with a shudder and her eyes slowly opened. *Old, old eyes,* Maddie thought. And in their depths she saw that Sally knew she was dying.

Maddie beat back another wave of tears and smiled down at her. "Hello, Sally. My name's Maddie. I'm here to help you as best I can."

She didn't move, didn't look anywhere but at Maddie's face. Her voice was the thinnest of whispers. "Is my baby alive?"

"Yes," Maddie answered, gently taking the girl's rail-thin hand and placing it on her child's back. "You have a daughter."

"A girl?" Tears clouded Sally's eyes. "God forgive me. I prayed so hard. . . ."

Maddie's heart twisted. "Have you chosen a name for her, Sally?"

"Will she live?"

Maddie didn't know, thought it wasn't likely, but she wasn't willing to add to Sally's grief. "I'll do all that I can to see that she does."

Sally's gaze slid to the fluttering canvas overhead. "Grace. I want to call her Grace."

"It suits her well."

Sally plucked weakly at the shawl and Maddie quickly drew it down so that the mother could touch her baby's skin. After a long moment, the young woman's gaze sought hers again.

"Don't leave her with him," Sally pleaded, her breath rattling in her lungs. "Promise me you'll take her."

"Ma'am," Maddie began, not knowing what to do, what to say, and desperately trying to decide what was right.

"Promise me. Please."

The raw regret and fear in Sally's eyes as the meager light in them began to fade . . . "I promise. I'll raise her as my own."

"Thank you." The hand that stroked the baby went still and with one last shuddering breath, the light in Sally Reynolds's eyes went out.

Whispering, "Godspeed and peace, Sally," Maddie gently closed the lifeless eyes and then gathered Grace into her own arms. She rocked back and forth, patting Grace's back. She wouldn't cry. She couldn't. There were too many things that had to be done, too many decisions that needed to be made. She had to keep a clear head. She needed the cool steadiness of Rivlin Kilpatrick. Wiping her cheeks with the corner of Grace's shawl blanket, Maddie sniffled once and then made her way to the tailgate.

Rivlin's gut clenched the instant he saw Maddie's leg swing over the back of the wagon. It was blood red from the knee down. Reynolds must have noticed his attention shift because the man began to lower his arms and turn.

"Don't move," Rivlin commanded, freezing the man. "Maddie, come back over here the same way you went."

She didn't say anything, but then she didn't have to. He could see the grief in her face as she carefully brought the small blue bundle out of the wagon with her. Rivlin silently swore and hoped that Reynolds would be sufficiently overcome by his loss that he wouldn't pose a threat to Maddie.

She stopped halfway between the two of them and looked at Rivlin with the saddest eyes he'd ever seen. Her face was pale, the tear stains evident. She looked weak, as though her legs would give out at any moment. Tears rimmed her lashes, but she blinked them away and lifted her chin before turning to face the father of the child cradled in her arms. Unwilling to risk gunfire near the infant, Rivlin holstered his revolver as he stepped to Maddie's side, prepared to place himself between her and Reynolds if it became necessary.

"I'm sorry, Mr. Reynolds," she said softly, "but there was nothing I could do for your wife. She's been taken into the arms of her maker. She left you a beautiful daughter." She held the infant out toward the man, adding, "Sally asked that she be named Grace."

Reynolds didn't even look at the baby. The dull look that clouded his eyes vanished, replaced by a sharp light that struck Rivlin as bordering on madness. "You killed my wife!" the man screeched.

Color flooded Maddie's cheeks. She pulled the baby back against her chest and calmly replied, "Sally was far too young and far too small to bear children, Mr. Reynolds. She was all but gone by the time I got there. She hung on only to see that her daughter was in safe hands."

"Don't you make excuses for what you've done!" He shifted his weight and leaned forward. "You're nothin' but trash, a federal prisoner riding in irons an' no doubt spreadin'—"

Rivlin stepped between Maddie and Reynolds and ended the tirade with his fist. The man toppled backward like a tree, his lower face smashed and bloody. Maddie's eyes were wide as she looked up at him. Rivlin rubbed his knuckles and said, "There was no point in letting him finish it."

"Thank you."

He smiled. "My pleasure. Are you all right?" She nodded, but he sensed that she was offering the assurance only for the sake of being polite. "You've got the look of a problem in your eyes, Maddie."

She studied the back of the wagon for a long moment and then turned to face him, her shoulders squared. "Sally Reynolds made me promise to take the baby with me, not to leave her with him. I told her I would just so that her passing would be easier."

"But you want it done that way," Rivlin guessed. "Christ almighty, Maddie," he groused, yanking his hat off his head and slapping it against his leg in frustration. "As if this assignment isn't awful enough already. My prisoner—who happens to have a bounty on her head—wants to haul a sick newborn baby along? It's downright stupid. And more than goddamn dangerous. We don't have any business even so much as thinking about taking that baby with us."

She drew back the blanket so he could see the tiny head. It was rather pointed and covered with a dark fuzz. The face beneath it was thin and red and wrinkled and he wondered if all babies were as ugly as this one.

"As you can see, Grace is very small," Maddie said with such earnestness that he felt a deep twinge of guilt for thinking so uncharitably about the child.

"She's not a strong baby," Maddie went on, stroking the little cheek with the back of her finger. Little lips weakly puckered. "She needs to be under a doctor's care as quickly as possible. She needs a wet nurse. Maybe Reynolds will be of a mind to see that she gets to Wichita, that she gets the care she needs to survive, but . . ."

The look in Maddie's eyes as she looked at him would have crumbled even the hardest of hearts. Rivlin hung his head and silently admitted defeat. "I'll dig a grave," he said, resigned to his fate and putting his hat back on, "if you'll get Sally Reynolds ready. We'll see what Mr. Reynolds is of a mind to do after that."

"What if he wants to keep Grace?"

"She's his child, Maddie," he answered honestly, placing the tether over the hammer of his gun. "He has a right to her." The tilt of her chin prompted him to add as he walked toward the fallen man, "Don't look so grim. I can be very persuasive when I need to be." He bent, grabbed the back of Reynolds's collar, and started to drag the unconscious form toward the wagon.

"What are you doing with him?" Maddie asked, following along, Grace once again wrapped tight and cradled to her.

"We're going to be busy for a bit," he explained, "and I don't feel like having to take the time to knock ol' Edgar here on his ass again. When he comes to, he's going to find himself cuffed to the wagon wheel."

"I don't suppose we can ride off and leave him like that, can we?"

He laughed quietly. "Sorry, Maddie. But I will admit that it's a tempting thought."

She left him to his task and carried the baby to the back of the wagon to begin hers.

EDGAR REYNOLDS HAD COME TO with his head on his shoulders a bit more squarely than when he'd been taken down, his anger replaced by a kind of fuzzy awareness that allowed him to stand upright but kept him from moving with any deliberate speed or purpose. Still, Rivlin didn't trust him enough to close his eyes during the prayer Maddie was offering for the soul of poor Sally. It was a shallow grave the three of them stood around; he'd hit flint within a foot of the surface and it had taken a pick to hack another foot beyond that. To go any deeper would have required dynamite.

"Amen."

"Amen," Rivlin muttered in chorus with the dead woman's husband. They both put their hats back on their heads and turned to face each other. Maddie stood silently, holding the baby and watching intently.

Rivlin seized the initiative. "We're heading into Wichita, Mr. Reynolds, and will be glad to ride along with you and the baby."

The man puckered his lips, nodded, and scratched his stomach as he said, "I figure to be headin' on west toward Santa Fe like I planned."

Rivlin held his ground. "The baby needs a doctor and a wet nurse. The nearest ones are in Wichita."

"Well, I've been givin' it some thought," Reynolds replied, hitching up his pants, "an' I reckon the baby an' me will be partin' company. It seems to be the Lord's will."

Maddie's shoulders slumped with relief, but she kept her silence. Rivlin asked, "Will you be staying in Santa Fe?" At the man's confused look, he added, "So we can send you word on Grace."

"Oh." He shrugged. "I don't know exactly what my plans are after I get there. Might stay, might just as likely move on to California. You can send a letter general delivery, I guess. I'll get it eventually."

"I'll do that," Rivlin countered, knowing that the effort would be a waste of time, paper, and ink. By sundown tonight Edgar Reynolds would have only the vaguest recollection that he'd ever known a woman named Sally, much less that she'd died in giving him a daughter.

"Well," Reynolds said, looking toward his wagon, "I reckon you'll be wantin' to get on to Wichita an' findin' that doctor right quick here. Don't see any reason for me to be lingerin', either." He looked back at Rivlin to add, "Much obliged for you diggin' the hole, mister."

"It was the least I could do," Rivlin managed to say.

Without so much as acknowledging Maddie or the baby, Reynolds walked off. He climbed into the wagon box, took up the reins, and flicking them against the backs of the oxen, set out toward the southwest. Rivlin watched him until he crested a hill and dropped from sight.

"He never once looked back," Maddie said, coming to stand at Rivlin's side.

"My guess is that once he got back in the box, he forgot why he'd stopped." He turned to smile at her. "I'd say the chances of him turning around and coming after Grace are pretty slim. Sally can rest in peace."

Maddie nodded. "We need to be going, too."

"Yep." He reached down and took the flour sack she clutched in her hand, asking, "What's in here, Maddie?"

"Two cans of tinned milk, all the clean rags I could find, and a necklace," she supplied as they started toward their mounts.

"A necklace?"

"It was Sally's. I took it so that Grace would

have something that had been her mother's. Someday it will mean all the world to her."

Leave it to Maddie to think of such a thing. She had the biggest, softest, kindest heart of any woman he'd ever met. He looked down at the silent bundle of blue in her arms. Maddie had draped her medicine pouch around it. "Was this your mother's?" he asked, carefully touching the leather cord.

"Lucy's aunt made it for me after I was arrested. She said the spirits had told her that I needed their protection."

And Maddie had given it up so that Grace could be protected. Grace was one lucky baby to have ended up in the care of Maddie Rutledge. He, of course, was a damn fool for allowing it. He sighed and reminded himself that there was no rule that said life had to give you sensible choices. You did the best you could with what came your way just so you could look yourself in the eyes when you shaved.

Rivlin picked the cuffs up out of the grass as he passed, considered them for a moment, and then tucked them into a saddlebag.

Chapter Nine

It was several hours after midnight when they reached the confluence of the Big and Little Arkansas Rivers and turned south. They'd had to skirt a good distance to the north to avoid a huge herd of grazing cattle and it had cost them at least an hour. The rise on which they paused was a very small one, but it and the moonlight afforded Maddie a clear view of what could have been called a city in only the most charitable sense of the word. On the eastern side of the wide, shallow river was a wide, muddy road flanked on either side by a jumble of brightly lit wooden buildings. A brass band sat on the balcony of one of the buildings, its musical efforts seeming to be largely ignored by the men moving up and down the wooden walkways. Lights glimmered here and there beyond the main road, suggesting that the burg sprawled for some distance outward across the plain.

On the western side of the river, connected to the other side by a wide wooden bridge, was another jumble of buildings. It was a much smaller collection of wooden structures, but the light and noise streaming from them far outdid that coming from the eastern side of the river. There were men moving up and down the wooden walks here, too, but they seemed to be staggering more than walking.

Maddie smiled, remembering that Myra had called all of this the Peerless Princess of the Plains. Daylight might make a difference, but Maddie suspected that it wouldn't be a significant one. It appeared that, as usual, Myra had been poetically generous. If there was a God, Myra had spoken accurately about the welcome Maddie could expect at her house.

Maddie looked down at the silent bundle in her arms. Grace had cried only once in the hours since her birth. Once her diapers had been changed, she'd settled back into a sleep so deep that Maddie had taken to placing her fingertips on the infant's chest just to be sure that she was still breathing. Maddie checked again and felt the now familiar wave of relief wash over her.

"Is she all right?"

Maddie nodded, wondering if Rivlin Kilpatrick knew that she could hear the tension in his voice every time he asked her that question. He'd periodically groused about the insanity of bringing Grace with them, but Maddie knew that he couldn't have abandoned the innocent any more than she could have.

"So what do you think of Wichita and Delano?" Rivlin asked quietly, his arm resting across his saddle horn as he surveyed the scene before them.

"Well, to be honest, from all of Myra's glowing

praise, I did expect Delano to have more than one street."

"One street, yes. But that street's a whole two blocks long."

"That's not a cross street," she pointed out, shifting her hold on Grace. "It's nothing more than an alley. How on earth do you think we're going to become lost in that?"

"Don't let the size fool you," he countered, straightening in his saddle. "There's a lot that goes on in Delano and anyone who wants you dead would have to think very seriously about whether it would be worth coming in to look for you."

"Why?"

"What did Myra tell you about Delano and Wichita?"

"She said Delano rarely sleeps, was a good place to do business, and that the cowboys were generally a much more gentlemanly bunch than people gave them credit for. As for Wichita . . ." Maddie looked across the river. "Myra always sniffs when she talks about the east bank. She says that's where the hypocrites live."

"I can understand how Myra would see them that way. Let me tell you what *I* know about Wichita and Delano. Wichita has a gun law, Maddie. Everyone has to turn their weapons in to the marshal upon arrival. You pick them up as you're leaving town.

"Delano, on the other hand, is free-wheeling and everyone's armed to the teeth. If you pull a weapon in Delano, you'd best expect to have one pulled on you in the same blink of an eye. Liquored-up cowboys and professional gamblers stay alive by keeping to one simple rule: Shoot first and ask questions later—which doesn't leave much leeway for making your intentions clear with regard to exactly who it is you intend to kill. That's the long way around, Maddie, of saying that anyone who came after you would have to be courting a death wish."

"There are other ways to kill someone besides using a revolver," she rebutted softly. "Sam Lane always carried a knife. He called it his tummy tickler."

"Knives require close quarters," Rivlin said solemnly. "No one's going to get that near you except me and Grace. Only a fool would even think of trying to come at you with a knife."

It occurred to her that anyone who was willing to so much as contemplate going through Rivlin Kilpatrick to get to her was a fool to begin with, but she kept the observation to herself. "Well, I suppose Delano's small size is a blessing in a way. We certainly won't have any difficulty finding Myra's place."

"What makes you think we're going to Myra's?" His horse shifted its stance impatiently and Rivlin gave him the reins.

Maddie's horse followed his down the rise and toward town. "Why wouldn't we go to Myra's?" she asked as she drew abreast of the marshal. "Myra's my friend. She told me if I ever found myself here, I was to come see her. I helped her write letters to her girls and she mentioned me in them, so I won't be a complete stranger showing up on their doorstep. And besides, she has a washerwoman named Katherine O'Malley and Katherine is nursing a child."

"Ah, I see your logic," he drawled, his gaze touching the baby cradled in the crook of her arm before he looked up at Maddie. With a cocked brow and a half-smile, he asked, "Have you ever been in a . . . house of ill-repute?"

"No," she admitted, finding his effort at discretion endearing.

"You might want to think twice about holing up there."

"Thank you for being worried about my reputation. It isn't necessary, but I appreciate it nonetheless."

"I wasn't thinking as much about your reputation as I was your sensibilities, Maddie. They don't exactly skirt politely or delicately around certain matters and I wouldn't want you to be offended."

Maddie felt her cheeks flush and was grateful for the relative darkness. "Ah, yes, those certain matters," she replied. "I had my eyes opened and my jaw dropped more than once during the time Myra and I shared a cell. Among other things, Myra tends to be both earthy and frank. I'm relieved to know, though, that you can't tell that I've been so dubiously enlightened."

The man riding beside her was silent for a moment. "I always knew what my father did for a living," he finally said. "But I discovered that there was a big difference between knowing and actually smelling the gunpowder, hearing the clank of machinery, and feeling the grit in the air. And there's a whole world of difference between knowing and actually seeing what that gunpowder can do to men and beasts."

She recognized the tone of his voice, heard once again his regret and the hardness of his memories. He'd led her to believe that he'd left his family and come west because of their determination to see him married and because he wasn't temperamentally suited to fancy clothes and paperwork. Those explanations might well be part of the reason for his decision, but they weren't all of it. Rivlin Kilpatrick had been to war, had seen the horrible carnage, and realized that his family had become wealthy by supplying men with the means of killing one another by the hundreds of thousands.

What he had seen on the battlefields of the war and in the Indian campaigns had given him a perspective that no one else in his family had. He *knew* what put food on the Kilpatrick table and fancy clothes on their backs. And he wanted no part of what blood bought. He'd walked away from hearth and home rather than profit from the business of death. She knew it to the center of her bones.

"There are a few things we have to have an understanding on before we get into town, Maddie."

She smiled. "The first being that if I try to escape, you'll have to stop me. By brute force if necessary."

"The first being that you don't go anywhere without me and I don't go anywhere without you," he clarified. "You pretend we're still cuffed together or we will be in cold metal truth."

"And the second?" she asked.

"I can't see that there'll be any problem with who and what we are at Myra's. They know who you are and I've been there often enough that I'm known, too. And the nature of their business isn't to ask questions anyway. Wichita's a different kind of critter all together, though. When we cross the bridge, don't tell anyone anything more about yourself than you have to. The less folks know, and the fewer that know anything at all, the better. I'm willing to bet Murphy's money that whoever wants us dead will come looking for us here sooner or later."

He was right, of course. He always was. Jim—the second man who'd died in the attempt to kill them—had made the assumption that they'd be seeking refuge here. Others would, too. Lord, she wished she knew what it was that made it so important that she die before getting to Leavenworth.

"It's been my experience that people are as curious as the proverbial cat," Maddie countered, carefully shifting Grace into the curve of her other arm. "There are bound to be questions asked about us. How do you intend to explain our being together?"

He grinned at her and replied, "I'm going to tell whoever asks that it's none of their damn business. I'd suggest that you do the same."

"That will go a long way toward satisfying curiosity," she retorted, rolling her eyes. "Not to mention that whoever asks is going to be standing there fumbling for a graceful way to get away from us as fast as they can."

"They deserve to feel uncomfortable for being so rude in the first place."

Maddie smiled. She might have guessed that Rivlin Kilpatrick's finely honed sense of justice extended to social situations, too. His mother probably cringed at the thought of him making his way through a drawing room affair.

They came into Delano from the back side, rode through the space between two buildings, and halted at the back door of Myra's place. The hand-painted sign overhead announced that Myra's never closed and that all services were to be paid for in cash. Rivlin swung down from Cabo and then ducked under the animal's neck to come to Maddie's side. As they had done every time they'd stopped since Grace had come into their care, she handed the baby to him and waited until he stepped back before she, too, dismounted.

"Maddie? One more thing," he said softly,

giving Grace back to her. "Don't call me 'Marshal' while we're here. Myra's girls know, but if there's anyone else around, it might well lead to questions that we don't need asked. Call me Rivlin. All right?"

"I think I can manage that easily enough," she said, wondering if he'd noticed that she'd been doing just that since she'd clutched his shirtsleeves and pleaded with him to let her help Sally Reynolds.

He winked and then gestured for her to precede him to the door. She went, pausing when she got there to take a deep breath to fortify herself. He reached over her shoulder and knocked sharply on the wooden panel, then drew back to wait. Maddie felt the warmth of him and, for a second, she was tempted to lean back against him in the hope that he'd put his arms around her and hold her. She closed her eyes and broadened her stance. A long moment passed and Rivlin knocked again, harder.

The tapping of hard-soled shoes against wooden flooring heralded the arrival of someone on the other side. The handle turned and the door swung open just wide enough to throw a line of lamplight across Maddie.

A tall, thin, dark-haired woman looked her up and down. "Yeah?" the woman asked, her expression hardening as she studied the bundle in Maddie's arms. "What do you want?"

With her free hand, Maddie pushed the brim of her hat back so the lamplight shone full on her face. "My name's Maddie Rutledge, ma'am. I'm a friend of Myra's and—"

"Myra isn't here."

"Yes, ma'am, I know. At the moment she's incarcerated at Fort Larned."

"And how do you know Myra?"

Maddie quickly moistened her lips. Rivlin stood

behind her in the shadows, silent and still, no doubt waiting to see how matters progressed. "I'm from Fort Larned, too," Maddie ventured carefully.

A hand suddenly gripped the outer edge of the door and pushed it wide. Into the suddenly broader opening stepped a rather plump young woman with bright red hair and a huge smile. The first woman was nearly knocked off her feet as the second reached for Maddie's shoulder and exclaimed, "You're *that* Maddie Rutledge! Well, why didn't you say so?" She drew Maddie forward saying, "Come in, come in."

"You must be Helen," Maddie guessed, blinking as her eyes adjusted to the brightness of the kitchen light.

"How did you know?"

Maddie smiled. "Conversation is one of the few ways to pass the time. Myra described everyone in Delano to me—especially those she calls 'her girls.' She said you were the friendly one, that you never met a stranger, and that you have a beautiful smile. Myra wasn't exaggerating."

She heard Rivlin's boots scrape the floor as he crossed the threshold. The dark-haired woman shifted her stance and all the harshness in her manner suddenly turned silken and warm. "Why look what the cat dragged in. Marshal Rivlin Kilpatrick."

From the corner of her eye, Maddie saw him touch his hat brim and lower his chin slightly. His eyes were narrowed slightly as he drawled, "Miss Meredith."

"Can I get you a drink? Whiskey, isn't it?"

"Thank you, but no, ma'am."

"That's Meredith Grun," Helen whispered.

"I gathered," Maddie whispered back. Myra

hadn't been at all complimentary about Meredith. In one of the kinder observations, Myra had described Meredith as a vulture who fancied herself a regal peacock. Myra put up with the woman's pretensions only because Meredith both had a head for bookkeeping and appealed to a very specific group of clientele. Clearly Meredith had decided that Rivlin was one of them.

"What's this, Maddie?" Helen asked, plucking ever so gently at the blue shawl.

"Her name is Grace," Maddie answered, drawing the cover down so that the baby's face was visible. As Helen stroked the little cheek with a plump finger, Maddie softly explained, "She was born this afternoon out on the prairie north and west of here. Her mama died and her father didn't want her. I remember Myra said that Katherine O'Malley was nursing a child of her own and we came here hoping to prevail upon her kindness."

Helen nodded crisply and stepped back with a smile. "Well, everyone knows that Katie's kindness is every bit as big as her—"

"Where could we find her?" Rivlin cut in.

"Her room's here off the back hall," Helen answered, turning and motioning for Maddie to follow with the baby. "I'll take you, introduce you, and explain. Katie won't mind at all, I'm sure. Andrew's never taken all she has."

Maddie followed, saying, "You'll never know how much I appreciate this, Helen," and feeling both relief and sadness at having found a haven for the infant. Grace would be put to the breast, and if she suckled, her chances of survival would be dramatically improved. If she didn't, she would probably die. Either way, Maddie knew that once she reached Katie's room, Grace would have to be surrendered. It was the way it should be, the way it needed to be for the sake of Grace's life.

"It's no bother at all," Helen declared, stopping before a closed door and quickly knocking. "Even if you weren't Myra's friend, we couldn't turn you away. Why, it would be like the innkeepers who turned Joseph and Mary into the night. Can't have that."

A voice called out for them to enter and Helen instantly obeyed. Maddie held Grace tightly and followed, breathing deep the scent of new baby and knowing the hours she'd gotten to hold Grace would have to be enough to last a lifetime. The pretending that had been so soft and sweet withered as Helen explained it all to Katie and turned to a bittersweet ache as Maddie handed Grace into Katie's arms.

RIVLIN WATCHED MADDIE until she disappeared into the room behind the good-hearted Helen. "Who's in charge here while Myra's gone?" he asked Meredith. "You?"

"I am indeed, Marshal." She inclined her head in a regal way. Her gaze dipped to his gun belt and then came up to meet his before adding, "How may I be of service to you?"

Robert E. Lee would be president before he took Meredith Grun to bed. He'd lost count of the number of times he'd tried, politely and kindly, to convey that certainty to the woman. He had no interest in the kind of games Meredith liked to play and couldn't understand how any man could find pleasure in being bullied. The very idea of surrendering to her made his skin crawl.

But he understood that conquering resistance

was part and parcel of the whole thing and that Meredith enjoyed bending others to her will—both in the bedroom and out. Every conversation he'd ever had with her had been a battle for dominance of will. This one wasn't going to be any different and there was no point in dancing around trying to avoid the inevitable contest. "Maddie and I need a room for a couple, three days. It doesn't have to be much."

Her gaze flicked to the hall where Maddie had gone. "You know that this isn't a boardinghouse," she declared, turning back to smile thinly at him. "There are, however, some across the river that won't mind catering to you and your . . ." Her smile took on a derisive edge. "Woman friend."

He ignored the insult. "Myra's out of prison soon and she's not going to be all that pleased when she learns you wouldn't put Maddie up."

Meredith crossed her arms over her corset-cinched midriff and gave him a smug smile. "You're of course assuming that she would ever find out."

"I'll make sure that she does." She searched his gaze and her smile faded. "And in case you haven't noticed on your own, Miss Meredith, while Myra's got a generous heart, she's also got a hard sense of justice to go with it. I wouldn't want to poke her with a sharp stick. It wouldn't be smart."

She clenched and unclenched her teeth, then managed to grit out, "If there's anything we can do to make your stay more pleasant, I hope you won't hesitate to prevail on our hospitality."

Meredith Grun had a way of saying much without really saying it. If she were a basically nice person, he might have thought they'd reached an amiable accord. Rivlin knew better, though. "Much obliged, Miss Meredith," he offered, touching the brim of his hat. "Do you have a boy around who can see to our horses?"

"Henry Stutzman's probably out in the alley somewhere. He usually is at this time of the night."

"Which doc in town does the best with babies?"

As he'd fully expected, she drew her shoulders back. Her eyes darkened to ebony as she replied, "No doctor will be coming here, Marshal. That would imply a problem in the house and wouldn't be at all good for business."

"I'm thinking, Miss Meredith," Rivlin drawled, "that for the sake of a baby's life, those concerns might be set aside. I'll have the kid, Henry, fetch the doc with instructions that he come to the back door. That way you won't have to fret over your nickels and dimes too much."

"You don't own this house, Kilpatrick," she declared. "Neither are you in any position to declare what will and what won't happen within it."

"You don't own it either," he reminded her. "I'll take my chances with Myra when she gets back."

She seethed in silence for a long moment and then, apparently realizing that he wasn't going to back down, said with flinty coolness, "We have one empty room. Edith ran off with a cowboy last week and I haven't had a chance to replace her. You may rent it at the same price she was charged to use it, five dollars a day. It's number twelve, on the far end of the upstairs hall."

"Fair enough. I'll have the key now. That way I won't have to bother you for it later."

She reached into her pocket, produced an iron key, and then held it up well out of his immediate reach. "That will be fifteen dollars, please."

Rivlin pulled Murphy's money from his pocket

and peeled a twenty-dollar bill from the wad. He tossed it on the kitchen table.

"I don't have change," she said, her tone still flinty as she considered the money.

"Didn't expect you to," he replied, stepping forward to take the key from her while her attention was riveted on the table. He left then, feeling the intensity of Meredith Grun's gaze even after he closed the door behind himself. The hair on his nape prickled and he scowled, sensing that in finding a place to hide Maddie while he looked for answers, he'd blindly managed to buy them another avenue of threat. As marshaling went, he sure as hell wasn't going to be nominated for any awards for brilliant service.

Chapter Ten

Henry had pronounced Dr. Fabrique the best "baby doc" in town, and from what little Rivlin knew of the subject, it appeared that the boy was correct. The gray-bearded physician had arrived at the back door of Myra's with a quiet knock and a professionally determined manner. Rivlin had escorted him to Katie's room and then stepped aside to let the man do his work.

Fabrique was a thorough man, carefully examining every square inch of Grace while asking Maddie questions about the delivery and the baby's behaviors since. Maddie answered, the information so detailed and precise that Rivlin wondered if anything but Grace had been on her mind since they found her. Surely, even Sally Reynolds wouldn't have known more about her baby's every living moment. Katie, a generously sized woman wearing a white cotton nightgown, sat propped by pillows in her narrow bed and, when questioned by the doctor, supplied observations that she'd made while nursing the infant.

"You've done a fine job, young lady," Dr. Fabrique announced, smiling at Maddie as he closed his medical bag. "Had you not arrived at the wagon when you did, there's no doubt the child would have died. I think," Dr. Fabrique added, stroking the cheek of the sleeping baby, "that it would be best to leave the child in Katie's care for the immediate future. Grace will need to be fed on demand to bring her strength up and matters will be much simplified by such an arrangement." He turned to Maddie again, asking, "What are your plans for the baby's future? Are you thinking to keep her as your own or give her for adoption?"

Rivlin's stomach dropped at the look of yearning that passed over Maddie's face. A sad smile touching the corners of her mouth, she answered, "As much as I'd like to keep her, Dr. Fabrique, the circumstances of my life at the moment make that impossible." She paused to take a deep breath before adding, "If you know of a family who would welcome and love her, I think that would be for the best."

Rivlin heard the strain in her voice and his gut twisted. Doctor Fabrique softly cleared his throat. "I'll make inquiries." With that comment and a glance at Rivlin, the doctor picked up his black leather bag and headed for the door.

Rivlin quietly followed him out. "I need to pay you, Doc."

The elderly physician turned to face him in the shadowy hall. "I don't want your money, young man," he said quietly. "Grace isn't your child and you more than saw to your humanitarian duty in bringing her here. You've done enough where the baby is concerned."

"I'm much obliged for your coming over," Rivlin offered.

The good doctor tugged at his beard. "I have no idea of what the nature of your relationship with Miss Rutledge is," he said slowly, "and I'm fully aware that it's none of my business. But if I may ask one thing of you, Mr. Kilpatrick, it's that you be mindful of her care. She's physically exhausted and needs to sleep long and well. And surrendering that baby tore her heart. I saw it in her eyes and I suspect you did, too. It's my professional opinion that it would be in her best interests to move on as quickly as possible so that she doesn't form any deeper attachments to the child than she already has. Let her rest and then be on your way."

Rivlin knew the old man was right on every count. "We've business in Wichita, Doc, but I'll do the best I can."

Dr. Fabrique nodded and, turning away, said, "If you need me for anything, you can stop by my office or send a message. I'll let Katie know when I find a family for Grace and I'll be responsible for seeing that she gets there."

Rivlin nodded and silently watched the doctor depart. He heard the door open behind him and turned. Maddie closed it softly and then stopped, her hand still on the brass knob as though she were tempted to go back in.

"Maddie?"

She stepped away from the door to face him. "He seemed like a good doctor," she said with a brave smile. "Katie is thrilled to hold a little one again. Andrew's almost a year old. Did you see him sleeping in the bottom drawer of the chest? He's such a handsome boy."

"I saw him," Rivlin lied. How could he tell her that she'd been pretty much all he'd been aware of? "And, yeah, Doc Fabrique seemed competent." He motioned toward the back stairway, adding softly, "Let's get some sleep, Maddie."

She smiled as she came toward him. "The peacock vulture let us have a room?"

"Not happily," he admitted, falling in behind her.

"But you were persuasive."

"I told you I can be when I need to be."

Her moccasined feet didn't make a sound as they made their way upstairs. The heels of his boots rang in the narrow corridor. Neither of them said a word until they stood before the door and Rivlin fished in his pocket for the key.

"Aren't we going to see to the horses?"

He'd have had to have been deaf not to hear the quaver in her voice and been as stupid as a mud brick not to know she didn't want to go into that room with him. "I've already taken care of our animals," he answered, opening the door and gesturing for her to proceed him across the threshold. As she stepped into the dimly lit room, he added, "I hauled our saddlebags upstairs while I was waiting for Dr. Fabrique to get here."

She went halfway to the double bed, stopped, and slowly surveyed the small room as she said, "You've thought of everything."

"I tried." He locked the door behind them, put the key back in his pocket, and then gave her an apologetic smile. "I'm afraid that I couldn't get you a bath or clean clothes, Maddie. They'll have to wait 'til morning."

"I'll take the bath with profuse thanks. As for the clothes . . ." She shrugged and went back to studying the room. "A good scrubbing of what I've got will be enough, but I appreciate the thought just the same. It's very kind of you to offer."

He considered her in the soft light of the oil lamp and knew that he'd never in his life met a woman like Maddie Rutledge. She was capable of being fierce when she wanted or needed to be; he'd seen her use her irons to smash the guard's face, seen her lash Edgar Reynolds with angry words. She'd stoically endured the god-awful conditions of their travel, not once complaining of being cold and wet and miserable. She'd begged for the right to help Sally and had shouldered the responsibility for Grace with resolute purpose. There was a grit to her that many a man would envy.

And yet she was vulnerable in ways he hadn't anticipated when they'd first met. Life had battered her hard from the very beginning and it almost seemed as though she'd accepted her lot as an inescapable destiny. She would beg for others, fight for others with all her might, but when it came to her own needs and wants, Maddie all but withered away. In a way she reminded him of soldiers who had seen too much, had too much asked of them, and had surrendered hope for anything beyond what existed in the moment. When backed into a corner, they'd fight to stay alive, but in the aftermath always question why they bothered. He'd traveled along that road himself and it had taken a conscious decision to turn back. Could Maddie? There wasn't much for her to hope for.

A soft, sad voice ended his contemplation. "I suppose you're going to cuff me to the bedstead."

"Do I need to?" he asked quietly, knowing the answer.

She turned to face him with a bittersweet smile. "Would you believe me if I told you that you didn't?"

"Yes."

She blinked, clearly surprised by his admission. And then the steel went out of her back. Her shoulders slowly slumped. She didn't make a sound as tears filled her eyes and spilled over her lashes.

"Don't cry, Maddie," Rivlin cajoled, fighting the impulse to reach for her. "If you want to be cuffed, I'll oblige you."

She tried to smile, tried without success to brush the tears away. "I don't want to be cuffed."

"Then why are you crying?"

"I don't know." A sob broke the end of her words and she covered her face with her hands.

Rivlin surrendered to instinct. "Ah, Jesus, Maddie. Come here," he said softly, drawing her against him. He wrapped one arm around her shoulders and with the other stripped the hat from her head and blindly tossed it away. Stroking her hair, he whispered over her muffled sobs, "Cry all you want, darlin'. You've been through enough to deserve a good, long wail."

Her arms around his waist, she gathered handfuls of his shirt into her fists and sobbed, "Why are you being so nice to me?"

Because he was a damn fool who thought too much and felt a larger sense of responsibility than he properly should. He kept the truth to himself, saying instead, "You're only human, Maddie, and every man and woman alive has a breaking point. You've reached yours."

His words calmed her. Her shoulders ceased

their shaking and he felt her take a deep breath. Still, she didn't try to step away from him. She turned her head and cradled her cheek against his chest. Softly she said, "But you're the federal marshal and I'm your prisoner. There are rules. I don't think you're supposed to be letting me cry all over your shirt."

In that instant something deep inside him shifted, easing a pressure he hadn't known was there. He couldn't fully explain the whys of it, but he knew it had something to do with the warmth of Maddie's body against his. He considered the road ahead and the one back. The decision was surprisingly easy to make.

"Well," he drawled, using his thumb to gently tilt her tear-stained face up so he could look her in the eyes. "I can't say that I haven't had that conversation with myself the last couple of days, Maddie, but the truth is we seem to have crossed a line somewhere along the way to Delano. I could tell you that I'm just trying to keep my prisoner in one piece so she can testify, but it'd be a lie. I like you, Maddie, and I like holding you. Those are the plain, simple facts and I don't feel the least bit inclined to apologize for them."

Maddie looked up into somber dark eyes. Tears tickled her throat, but she knew she wasn't going to cry again. Her heart was lighter than it had ever been. She knew what Rivlin Kilpatrick was saying, knew what he wasn't saying outright, and she found herself wanting to embrace the possibilities. They would eventually go their separate ways, there was no avoiding that reality. And while whatever they might have together would be temporary, there were possible consequences that could follow them both for the rest of their lives. She felt honor-bound to remind him of that fact, to give him a graceful way out of the situation. "You take up with me, you're asking to have your reputation ruined."

"My reputation isn't all that shiny, darlin'," he answered, tracing the curve of her jaw with the pad of his thumb. "The road I've traveled has been long and hard and with more than its fair share of low spots. Letting you cry on my shoulder qualifies as one of the higher points in my life."

"You're one of the kindest men I've ever met, Rivlin Kilpatrick."

One corner of his mouth quirked up and he shook his head slowly. He tilted her chin higher, saying, "It probably wouldn't be wise or charitable to let you go on thinking that."

Never in her life had she been kissed as Rivlin kissed her then, gently and tenderly, but with an intensity that stole her breath, her strength, and all thoughts of consequence. His possession deepened by slow, delicious degrees, and when he parted her lips, she melted against him, reveling in the wondrous spiraling of her senses. Such warmth, such pleasure . . . They were heady, rare gifts and stirred her to return them in kind.

Rivlin groaned at the touch of her tongue to his and his knees buckled, threatening to take them both to the floor. For a moment his arms tightened around her and then he slowly released his claim to her lips. Still held within the circle of his arms, Maddie looked up at him, her own breathing as uneven as his.

He exhaled long and hard and struggled to smile. "You're supposed to call me a cad, Maddie, and then slap my face for taking such liberties."

"But I don't want to," she answered softly, honestly. He was everything she wasn't: power and certainty and strength. She'd never wanted anything as much as she wanted to burrow into him, to be a part of him, to be safe for as long as he'd hold her.

"You'd better scrape together some of the good ladies' words on proper deportment, Maddie, darlin'," he said, his embrace easing. Taking her by the shoulders, he held her steady as he took a step back, saying, "I'm not nearly as good as you think I am, and right this moment I'm having a real hard time finding the last line."

But he'd found it nonetheless. Part of her knew she should be grateful for his determination to be a good man. A selfish part of her, however, was sorely disappointed, lonely, and nursing a throbbing kind of hunger she'd never known existed. Disquieted by the discovery, she chose to set it aside and act on good sense. Saying, "Perhaps it would be best if we got some sleep and came at this again when we're not so tired," she stepped out from under his hands.

"A fine suggestion," he seconded, turning to grab the straight-backed chair that sat beside the bureau. He placed it firmly in front of the bedroom door.

"What are you doing?"

"I'm putting this chair in front of the door."

"I can see that. Why?"

"The primary reason is that if anyone tries to come in while we're sleeping, the door will hit it and the noise will wake me up." He dropped into the seat without ceremony. "The second reason is that I'm sleeping in it."

She watched him stretch his long legs out and cross his booted ankles. Her hands went to her hips. "I appreciate your gallantry, Rivlin, but it's ridiculous. You're every bit as tired as I am and that chair is going to give you a miserable night's sleep. We can share the bed. It's plenty big enough for the both of us."

"Temptation is a restless bedmate, darlin'," he drawled, pulling his hat forward so that the brim shadowed his face. "You're safer with me sleeping in the chair."

Safe, yes. But she also remembered the pleasant sensations of awakening to find herself curled into the hard warmth of his body, of the feel and taste of his kiss. Was it so horrible to want more of such wondrous things? How many times had he proven that he could be trusted not to take advantage of her? "I'm not afraid of you, Rivlin."

"If you had any sense, you would be."

"If I had any sense, I wouldn't be in prison for murder, now would I?" she countered. "Stop being foolish, Rivlin. Leave the chair there to serve as your alarm and come take your half of the bed."

He crossed his arms over his chest. "Save your breath, Maddie. I'm planted right here and I'm not moving."

"Stubborn man," she groused under her breath.

"Yep."

For the first time since retrieving her moccasins, Maddie wished she had her heavy prison shoes on her feet. Stomping across the plank floor to blow out the lamp didn't have nearly the enraged sound she wanted. She worked at it anyway and then flung herself onto the bed so that the boards beneath squeaked in protest. The iron headboard smacked the wall, producing a hollow sound. She scooted to the far side of the mattress, pulled one of the feather pillows from beneath the coverlet and punched it with her fist before stuffing it under her head. She knew that Rivlin couldn't help but hear the production she made of retiring, but he offered no comment from his chair and made no move to concede to her way of thinking.

Damn his hide. He was doubtlessly thinking she'd lie there and remember all the words the good ladies had given her on the evil inherent in carnal knowledge. Truth was, she did. The litany had been given too often for her to have forgotten it. She could recite it from memory just as ably as she could the Lord's Prayer. But if Rivlin Kilpatrick thought that remembering the dour attitudes and condemnation of the good ladies was going to change the way she perceived the possibility of a carnal relationship with him, then he was badly mistaken. It felt good to be held in his arms. Kissing him felt right, more right than anything ever had in her life. What had the good ladies ever done for her that made her feel as safe and wanted as she did when she was with Rivlin? Nothing, that's what. *Nothing.*

Myra had said that the good ladies were full of prunes and had hearts just as shriveled up and dried. Myra had said that there was nothing wrong with desire between a man and a woman, that making love was a natural instinct and that as long as both the he and the she were willing, there was more harm in denying the urge than in giving in to it. Myra was startlingly frank about the pleasures she'd found in taking men to her bed.

Maddie smiled into the darkness, remembering how she'd often blushed from the roots of her hair to the tips of her toes and just as often discounted Myra's florid descriptions as being overly dramatic. Kissing Rivlin had changed her way of thinking entirely. It now seemed quite likely that Myra hadn't been exaggerating in the least.

"Maddie?"

She liked hearing the low rumble of his voice in the dark, even if it was coming from the other side of the room. "What?"

He hesitated a long moment and then said, "Good night."

"Good night, Rivlin," she whispered.

"Sweet dreams, darlin'."

Darlin'. She liked the sound of that; it made her feel special, almost cherished. It also twisted her heart, but she decided that it was best to pretend that it didn't.

Chapter Eleven

RIVLIN STRETCHED HIS BACK and legs, admitting to himself that Maddie had been right. He'd had a miserable night's sleep. It was only partly a consequence of having slept in the chair, though. Every time she'd rolled over in her sleep, he'd awakened and had to fight the temptation of going over to that bed and sharing it with her. Somewhere around dawn he'd faced up to the fact that he was going to have to come to some sort of resolution on the subject before the next nightfall or risk being permanently crippled and perpetually ill-humored.

What was he going to do about Maddie? he wondered, watching her sleep. He was a marshal and making love with his female prisoner wasn't either right or a very good idea. On the other hand, there was no denying that simply looking at her stirred a fire in him that couldn't be tamped out by reason or rules. Kissing her had fanned the flames into a red-hot urge that had taken everything in him to ignore. Just remembering the taste of her and how she felt pressed against him tightened his belly and sent the heat spiraling into his core.

Looking at her even now, her clothes pulled askew in sleep, her dark hair fanned across the pillow . . . It was so tempting to lie down with her, take her in his arms, and kiss her from slumber into passion. She would sigh as only she could and she'd return his caresses and there'd be no dredging up honor to save them this time. All he had to do was take three steps and accept that having her was more important to him than his badge.

Rivlin adjusted the lay of his gun belt, sucked in a deep breath, and turned away. He closed the door behind him soundlessly and slowly turned the key in the lock. Sternly reminding himself of the things that needed to be done, he made his way down the hall to the back stairs. He reached the bottom to find Katie heating water on the huge cast-iron stove and Meredith seated at the kitchen table wearing a black silk wrapper and nibbling on toast.

"Good morning, Marshal," Katie said brightly, handing him a steaming cup of coffee. "Baby Grace is sleeping snug as a bug in a rug. Full and content, she is."

"That's good to hear," he answered before taking a sip of the precious elixir.

"You look as though you had a restless night," Meredith ventured.

Rivlin felt her gaze pass over him just before she turned on her seat to let the wrapper fall open to display a long, shapely leg.

He took another sip of the coffee before he

replied, "I've slept sounder. But then I've had worse nights, too, so I'm not going to complain."

"I always say that a hard night is best eased by a friendly morning."

A friendly morning? He thought of Maddie as he'd left her, so sweetly disheveled and innocently inviting. A friendly morning with Maddie could well turn into a friendly afternoon, evening, and night. Hell, with Maddie friendly could become a nice way of passing a good week or two.

"I'm glad to see the notion appeals to you."

Rivlin winced and put the images of Maddie from his mind. With his vision focused on the here and now, he noticed that Meredith had reclined into the back of the chair to allow the wrapper to fall open to her upper thigh. He silently swore and then forced himself to smile amiably as he said, "I'm much obliged for the kindness of your offer, Miss Meredith, but I'll have to pass."

"It seems to me that a woman who can't give a man ease doesn't deserve exclusive claim to him, Marshal. I assure you that I know how to please in ways Miss Rutledge has yet to so much as imagine."

"Well, I reckon you're entitled to think whatever you'd like in that regard, ma'am. But the fact remains that I'm not inclined to accept your invitation." He turned to Katie who stood silently by the stove, stirring her pot and trying hard to go unnoticed. "I was wondering, Katie, if it would be possible to find something for Maddie to wear besides what she's got on. And to arrange for her to have the luxury of a hot bath. The trail's been hard on her and I'm sure she'd appreciate it greatly."

Katie turned with a smile, but before she could answer, Meredith said, "She can have something out of the ragbag, Katie. As for the bath, let her go over to the public bathhouse if she wants one."

"No self-respecting woman goes to the bathhouse!" Katie protested, her hands going to her ample hips. "I'll heat the water for her, Marshal."

"No, you won't," Meredith countered calmly, rising to her feet, the wrapper sliding down her shoulder. "I make the rules and I set the terms of exchange in this house. If Marshal Kilpatrick wants favors for Miss Rutledge, then he has to be accommodating in return."

It occurred to him that walking away would be the easiest course. It wouldn't, however, resolve anything. "You seem to have your mind set against Maddie," he observed. "Care to tell me why?"

Meredith smiled in what she no doubt considered a seductive manner. "She has something I've always wanted for myself: you."

She had brass, he had to give that to her. Hoping to get out of the situation without having to be blunt, Rivlin replied, "Well, begging your pardon, Miss Meredith, but in case you haven't noticed, I'm not the only man in town."

"That's not the point. I've always been drawn more to quality than ease of acquisition."

"That goes both ways, ma'am," he countered as gently as he could. His efforts to cushion her feelings didn't garner the least bit of appreciation. Meredith snorted indignantly, jerked her wrapper back onto her shoulder, shot a murderous look at Katie who was quietly choking on the steam from her water pot, and then glared at him in icy fury.

Before she could spit venom through her teeth, he tossed the last of his coffee down his throat and said, "Much obliged for your willingness to help,

Katie. I'll just head over to the bathhouse and make the necessary arrangements."

Heading out the back door, he knew that the sparring with Meredith had gone as well as it could have, given her determination to force the issue. Myra had handled her rejection with considerably more grace than Meredith had ever mustered. Maddie on the other hand . . . Rivlin smiled and shook his head as he made his way down the alley. Maddie was just going to wait him out. She'd spent her entire lifetime cultivating patience. He hadn't—and she knew it.

RIVLIN HAD SPARED no expense. The bathhouse had been hired for their exclusive use and he'd insisted that the proprietor put fresh water in the tubs for them. Maddie sunk to her chin and reveled in the luxury of hot water and the lavender soap he'd bought her. Life simply didn't get any better than this. She felt almost human again. Now if only she could figure out how to get around Rivlin and to Grace, she'd be completely content.

Grace had been the only sticking spot of the morning. Rivlin had awakened her with a tray containing a large cup of freshly brewed coffee, a plate of hotcakes drenched in syrup, and a pile of bacon a good three inches high. She'd dined in bed for the first time in her life and Rivlin had gone out of his way to see that she enjoyed it. And when she'd all but licked the plate clean, he'd lured her from the bed with a dress and a bundle of undergarments Katie had found for her use. Her suggestion that she go check on Grace had momentarily narrowed Rivlin's eyes and led him to brusquely mention that she'd slept most of the day away. It was clear that he didn't want her going anywhere near the baby and that he was determined to keep her busy enough to prevent it. She understood his reasoning. It was a shame he didn't understand how good she was at pretending and then putting it away.

"I don't hear any sounds over there," he called through the canvas curtain separating their bathing areas.

"I'm trying to drown myself," she answered. "It requires great concentration."

He laughed and she heard the water splash over the rim of his tub. "If you're not decent by the time I am, you're going to be embarrassed."

Maddie quickly climbed from the watery heaven, eying the clothing Katie had provided. There was a fancy, lace-trimmed whalebone corset among the items and Maddie frowned at it. She hadn't been allowed one in prison, of course. The stays could be removed and fashioned into knives and the lacings could be made into an effective noose. Going without had been one of the few positive aspects of being a prisoner and she was reluctant to consider climbing back into the torturous device.

Social convention mandated that she wear it, though. Such trappings of femininity were the silent testaments to being a civilized person and in this part of the world people tended to cling to such things with fierce determination. To forego the contraption marked a woman as being beneath even minimal respect. She had no real choice but to wear the damn thing. Resigning herself to her fate was the easier part of the decision, however. The corset laced up the back. There was no way she could contort her arms to accomplish the task on her own. That left asking Rivlin Kilpatrick for his help.

Deciding that she had best be as covered as she

could be before she asked for assistance, Maddie pulled on stockings, garters, pantalets, and a chemise. Using a piece of polished tin as a mirror, she did what she could to pin her hair atop her head. She eased the corset up over her hips and settled it into place.

"Decent, Maddie?" Rivlin called from the other side of the canvas.

"As much as I can be without your help," she replied, dejectedly. "I'm afraid that you're going to have to come in here."

He lifted the flap while saying, "You don't have to sound so repelled by the—" He froze for a moment, his gaze traveling over her scantily clad body. "Idea," he finished, swallowing hard and letting the flap fall closed behind him. He tipped his hat back on his head, suddenly fighting a smile. "I gather you need to be laced."

Maddie nodded and, her pulse racing, presented her back to him. "I hope you know how to do this."

"I can't say that I've ever tightened a corset before," he answered, coming to stand behind her.

She felt the heat of his body even before his fingers brushed against her back. "You've loosened your fair share though, haven't you?" she asked, wondering what he'd do if she leaned back against the hard expanse of his chest.

"Probably loosened *more* than my fair share."

Would he put his arms around her and hold her close like he had last night? Would he kiss her again? Would he make her feel safe and wanted?

"Let me know when it feels right," he said, tugging his way methodically down her back.

Afraid that she'd act on an impulse, Maddie deliberately put away her fantasies and answered, "The only time a corset feels right is when it comes off."

He leaned forward, his breath brushing her shoulder as he quietly said, "I'll be happy to oblige with that part, too. All you have to do is ask."

Maddie locked her knees and closed her eyes, gathered fistfuls of chemise into her hands. "You're a true gentleman."

"I'm trying. It's painful, though."

Painful? He wasn't in pain. She could hear the smile in his voice. He was enjoying himself immensely. And there was something exhilarating about knowing she was the cause of his happiness. "I'm sorry to have to put you through this," she offered teasingly. "Unfortunately, your agony is going to be prolonged. The dress buttons down the back and you'll have to manage that for me, too."

"Oh, well, we'll muddle through somehow," he replied, the smile still in his voice as he tied the strings at the base of her spine. His hands slipped around her waist for a moment and then he abruptly stepped back, softly clearing his throat.

Maddie exhaled and darted forward to take the faded teal-colored dress from the wooden bench. "I'm hardly knowledgeable about fashion," she admitted, turning back and holding it up before her, "but judging by the neckline, I'd say this is an evening gown. Wearing it at this time of the day is going to create comments."

"Not in Delano." He took it from her, his fingers brushing lightly over hers. He immediately lowered it so that he could see her. His smile was wide, his eyes sparkling with amusement. "Do you want to step in or would you prefer to have me drop it over you like a large sack?"

Maddie considered her alternatives and then raised her hands over her head. Rivlin sucked in his cheeks and resolutely stepped forward.

"It may be acceptable in Delano," Maddie said through the yards of draped brocade, "but we're on our way over to Wichita." As Rivlin settled the gown's bodice into place around her shoulders, she added gloomily, "Where the good and virtuous people live."

He tilted her chin up with the pad of his thumb until she met his gaze. The amusement in his eyes was gone. "Don't give them a second thought, Maddie," he said softly, earnestly. "They're not worth it. They're not one bit better than you are. Remember that. You hold this chin of yours high."

Her heart filled, making it impossible to speak.

He studied her for a long moment and then he winked and smiled. "Turn around, darlin', and let me at those buttons of yours."

His fingers worked the buttons into place blindly, his attention focused on the satin skin displayed by the low-cut bodice. What would she do, he wondered, if he were to lean down and kiss her shoulder? If he pressed a trail of kisses upward along her nape? What would she do if he reached around her and cupped her breasts in his hands? Stroked the creamy swells with the pads of his thumbs?

If she sighed and leaned back into his caress, he'd be fighting a temptation stronger than touching would satisfy. And Maddie sure as hell deserved better than to be taken for the first time on the floor of a public washhouse. He sucked a slow, deep breath and focused his attention to the work of his fingers, willing the hardness in his loins to ease.

THE SKY WAS A CLEAR, deep blue, dotted here and there with puffy white clouds. The sun shone bright and warm and the breeze blew gently in from the southwest, softening the notes of the city's brass band. It was a beautiful autumn afternoon, a perfect day to stroll the sidewalk of Wichita with a beautiful woman on his arm. If Maddie saw the censorious glances cast her way, she didn't falter before them. And whenever she felt his gaze on her, she would look up at him and give him a smile as dazzling as the day. It was as right as his world ever came and he felt a pang of regret when they reached the Wichita city jail.

He opened the door and, holding her elbow, guided Maddie across the threshold just ahead of him. The room was considerably dimmer and cooler than the world outside, but not so dim that they couldn't clearly see the boy seated behind the desk vault to his feet and whip the hat from his head.

"Afternoon, ma'am. What can I do for you?"

Maddie gave him a smile that made the hat suddenly hard to hang on to. As he bobbled the misshapen bit of black felt, Maddie said, "We're looking for Marshal Mike Meagher. Could you tell us where we might find him?"

The hat slipped from the boy's grasp, and as he bent to scoop it from the dusty wooden floor, he answered, "Marshal'll be back directly, ma'am. Him and Wyatt went out to find them fellers that stole that wagon and mules out of Fort Sill. Word was they was in Delano just an hour ago and took off toward the north."

"Do you mind if the lady and I wait?" Rivlin asked, gently guiding Maddie toward the chair placed before the large mahogany desk.

"No, sir." The boy clamped his hat back on his head and hitched his pants up a notch before heading toward the door and saying, "Make yourselves at home. I need to sweep the walk. I'll let you know when I see Mike comin' this way."

They watched him take a broom from the peg by the door and step out into the sunlight. He didn't bother to close the door behind himself and a wide shaft of bright light spilled across the small room. Dust motes danced lazily in it and Maddie watched them for a long moment, a sad kind of smile touching the corners of her mouth.

"Are you all right, Maddie?"

She blinked and the brilliance of her smile returned when she looked up at him to nod. It crossed his mind to bend down and kiss her; nothing that would get past his control, just a light caress so that she'd know how beautiful she was sitting there. Even as he considered the merits of the idea she turned her attention to Mike Meagher's desktop.

"Rivlin, look," she declared, pulling a newspaper from the clutter. "It's a week old, but there's a front-page article about the trial."

The discovery had made her breathing quicken and the cut of the dress bodice afforded him a view of her breasts that was as inspirational as it was distracting. At the moment, he didn't care one iota about the trial or a newspaper account of it. Still, he had enough of his wits about him to know that he should and so he managed to ask, "What does it say?"

She angled the paper to put it into the light from the open door. "The prosecutors are Wilfred T. Parker, James S. Williams, and Homer F. Fogelman. All esquires, of course. Do you recognize any of those names?"

"Nope. Keep reading." One of her shoulders was in light, the other in shadow. The temptation of the bathhouse returned, more intense for having been denied, and he was sorely tempted to trail his fingers over the smooth, pale curves of both.

"The presiding judge is Henry C. Abbott."

"Iron Pants Abbott," Rivlin contributed with a grin, walking around the desk and dropping into the other chair. "He's renowned for his physical endurance. Jurors and attorneys have to plead desperation before he'll consider calling even a brief recess. People have been injured in the race for the privy." Rivlin sobered. "He's a stickler for being thorough, though. A conviction in his court is a fair one. Who's been charged?"

"Oh my. Both Tom and George Foley. Sam Lane and Bill Collins, too. Let's see . . . Yes, here it is. Tom's been charged with one count of conspiracy to defraud. George Foley, the judge, is charged with eleven counts of misuse of public office. Tom, Sam, and Bill each face an additional five counts of grand theft and two counts of embezzlement of public funds."

Putting a desk between them had seemed like a good way of curtailing the urge to touch her. It hadn't worked, though. It took great effort to keep his attention on business.

"It says in a related story that Senator Harker—Republican of Illinois—is expected to be there in support of the prosecution. There's speculation he's going to use ending corruption as a major campaign issue in his bid for the presidency in the next election."

Rivlin snorted in disgust. "That's the joke of the century. It'd be funny if the man weren't such a bastard."

Maddie looked at him over the edge of the paper. "How do you know the senator?"

"He wasn't always a senator. I had an opportunity

to observe his command in the late war. If I'd had my way, the son of a bitch would have been court-martialed and locked in the stockade for the rest of his natural, black-hearted life. I sure as hell tried to put him there. So did my friend Seth."

"What did Harker do that was so bad?"

The question jolted him. Rivlin shook his head, refusing to consider his darkest suspicions about the man. They were only suspicions and there were plenty of documented sins. "He signed the payroll as dead men, taking for himself the money that should have gone to widows," Rivlin answered. "If supplies weren't nailed down, he sold them and pocketed the profit. The units he led did without blankets and food and went into battle with as little as two cartridges a man. The high casualty rates eventually got him stripped of his field command and transferred to the Quartermaster Corps. He made Murphy look like a goddamned saint."

"And he's going to run for the presidency on promises of ending corruption?"

"Like I said, it'd be funny if it weren't so damn twisted." He didn't want to deal with any more of the memories and so he deliberately changed the subject, asking, "Does the article say who the witnesses are expected to be?"

Maddie nodded and went back to reading the paper. "The prosecution says it will produce documents to support the charges of wrongdoing. They also have several teamsters who have agreed to testify. And then it says that the prosecution is planning to produce an eyewitness—a federal prisoner—who will describe the long pattern of the defendants' malfeasance and provide specific details in support of the conspiracy to defraud charge."

"That would be you."

Maddie shrugged her delectable shoulders. "The article reports that the defense attorneys don't believe that such a witness truly exists. They accuse the prosecution of pandering to the public's fascination with sensationalism."

"Does it say who the defense team members are?"

She took a deep breath and squared her shoulders, forcing Rivlin to adjust the lay of his gun belt and be thankful there was the desk to hide behind.

"No," she said, shaking her head, "It says that the original attorneys were recently dismissed and new ones have just arrived. It doesn't mention them by name. It just says they're from the firm of Wordsworth, Long and Kirkman."

"New York," he said, suddenly focused on what she was reading.

She looked up from the paper, her brows knit. "I beg your pardon?"

"It's a Wall Street firm, Maddie," he supplied, his mind racing over unsettling tracks. "Very prestigious and very expensive."

"Well, the Foleys are from New York. I suppose they could have family connections."

Rivlin shook his head and came to his feet. "I doubt it," he said, beginning to pace. "Somebody with those kinds of friends doesn't end up as an Indian agent in the Oklahoma Territory."

"How do you know about this law firm?"

"They've handled the legal matters relating to financing for some of the family's munitions operations. They don't normally deal with criminal matters and it's my guess they had to dig deep to find someone in the firm with any trial experience at all."

"It must be a very big favor they owe the Foley family."

"That or someone in the firm stands to lose a great deal if the prosecutors win their case."

"Perhaps it's all the money that Tom's stolen and invested over the years."

"Wordsworth, Long and Kirkman don't broker, Maddie. They take care of the legalities for those who do."

"Then perhaps something wasn't legal."

"I'd take that as a good bet."

"The question is what, though."

"The larger question is how you fit into all of this," Rivlin said, pausing to study her. "What is it that you know that the teamsters don't? Why is someone willing to pay to have you murdered before you can testify?"

She sighed and laid the paper back on the desk. "You've already asked those questions, the day you shot Murphy. And, if you'll recall, we added the question of who wants *you* dead the day the two riders came after us."

"And we're not one bit closer to answers than we were then."

She smiled. "We know for certain that it's one of the men on trial."

"Maybe," Rivlin offered. He gave her an apologetic smile before he added, "Then again, maybe not."

"Who else would care if I did or didn't testify?"

"Good question, Maddie."

"Well," she countered, exasperation evident. "I think we should just head for Leavenworth and be done with it. We're bound to find the answers once we get there."

Rivlin crossed his arms over his chest and shook

his head. "That's assuming we get there at all, Maddie. Nope. I want a clear idea of who to watch for before we go one step further."

She opened her mouth to reply, but at that moment the boy darted into the doorway to exclaim, "Marshal Meagher's coming, mister. Him and Wyatt got those polecats. You might want to move the lady out here so she's out of harm's way if'n they go to resist being locked up."

The boy dashed away after delivering the pronouncement and Rivlin snorted. "As if I needed to be told." He stepped toward Maddie, bending his arm for her to take, saying as he did, "I don't have sawdust for brains."

She laughed and rose to stand beside him, her gloved hand on his forearm. "No, you have a very fine brain, Marshal Kilpatrick. I like watching it work. It's quite stimulating."

He cocked a brow, and escorting her toward the door, asked, "My mind appeals to you?"

She didn't hesitate before replying, "You have a great many attributes which I find appealing."

He knew he was heading out on a limb, knew he was flirting with a course he couldn't easily reverse. It didn't give him so much as a pause. "Attributes such as?"

"Would you prefer the character list or the physical?" she asked, smiling up at him.

His blood turned to fire. "You have lists?"

"Very extensive ones."

It was hard to breathe as he led her over the threshold and back out onto the sidewalk. The light was bright and he squinted into it, saying quietly, "We're going to talk later, Maddie."

"If that's what you'd like to do."

He'd like to do much more than that, but his

Chapter Twelve

"Isn't that there something to see?" the boy asked in awe. "Bet there'll be a dime novel about it all—with three-color pictures and everything."

Maddie watched the scene coming down the middle of the street. Two Negro men and what, from his clothing, appeared to be a Mexican, were being marched, hands raised, toward the jail by a man on foot who pointed a six-shooter at their backs. Behind him, bringing up the rear of the small procession, a large, blond man drove a wagon with three mules and two horses tied to the tailgate. Everyone in town had stopped where they stood to watch. Men called out, apparently cheering the lawman on foot. He responded to each comment with a smile and a tip of his hat.

Rivlin, standing at her side, snorted in obvious disgust, and then, his right hand on the butt of his revolver, moved her well back from the door to the jail as the lawman herded the captives in that direction. Beneath her hand, she felt the muscles of Rivlin's left forearm tense as they passed, felt the muscles vibrate as the lawman acknowledged her presence with a smile and touch of his hat brim.

As the wagon pulled up at the edge of the wooden walk, Rivlin's stance shifted and he drawled, "They don't exactly look like vicious desperados."

"Hey, Riv!" the wagon driver called, tying off the reins and grinning broadly, his blue eyes bright.

"Good to see you still in one piece, Mike."

"What brings you to this haven for misfits?" the other asked, jumping down from the box and striding forward to vigorously shake Rivlin's outstretched hand.

Mike glanced toward her and Rivlin laid his hand over hers. "May I present Miss Madeline Rutledge," he said genteelly. "Maddie, this is Mike Meagher, Wichita's marshal."

"It's a pleasure ma'am," the other replied, removing his hat to reveal blond curls plastered to the crown of his head. He smiled broadly, his grin accentuating the squareness of his face. "But we should be clear that, unlike Rivlin Kilpatrick, my title of marshal is purely honorary."

"I'm pleased to make your acquaintance, Marshal Meagher," Maddie answered politely. Mike was a good, decent, hard-working man; you could tell it just by looking at him.

Plopping his hat back on his head, he turned his attention back to Rivlin. "You didn't answer the question, Riv. Why are you and Miss Rutledge here?"

"I'm assigned to get Maddie to Leavenworth. There've been two attempts to kill her since she came into my custody and I'm here looking for answers to a good number of questions."

"And hoping I've got some for you, huh?"

"It'd sure be nice if you did."

Mike looked casually up and down the street and then jerked his thumb over his shoulder, saying, "Let's step into my office."

Rivlin shook his head. "Let's stay out here."

Mike's pale brows inched upward. He looked over his shoulder into the jail office and then back to Rivlin. "Is it Wyatt?"

"I don't trust a man who makes a public spectacle of himself."

Mike grinned and nodded. His voice low, he said, "Well, I'll admit that Policeman Earp does like to impress. But he's a good officer for the most part. A bit of a temper and downright pushy when it comes to his brothers, though. Wish he'd shut up about hiring them. And then there's the blind eye he gives his mother and sister over in Delano. But, all in all, he's one of the better officers I've ever had."

Rivlin chuckled. "That's not saying much, Mike."

"Would you like a job?" Mike asked, clamping his meaty hand on Rivlin's shoulder. "The pay's lousy, but you can sleep in your own bed every night."

Rivlin laughed outright. "I'll pass, but it's right kind of you to offer."

Mike leaned close to offer in a conspiratorial whisper, "And it goes without saying that there'd be regular helpings of Mother Meagher's apple pie for you."

"Your mother does make a good pie," Rivlin admitted, grinning. "Maybe we can talk when my appointment comes up for renewal." He glanced toward the office and then added, "Get rid of ol' Flash in there so we can talk privately."

Mike nodded, released his hold on Rivlin's shoulder, and walked over to the door. Sticking his head just inside, he called, "Hey, Wyatt! Do me a favor and meet the *Eagle* reporter halfway this time, would you? The last time we like to never got rid of him."

Mike barely had time to get out of the way before Policeman Earp came through the doorway, his step springy and his manner deliberate. "Be happy to, Mike," he declared as he brushed past. "Ma'am," he added, tipping his hat yet again as he passed Maddie and headed down the dusty street.

"Never met a reporter he didn't like," Mike observed, watching his deputy go. With a sigh and a shake of his head, Mike led the way into his office, asking as he went, "So what kind of questions are you asking, Riv?"

"Any seedy-looking strangers come into town in just the last couple of days?"

Mike waited until Maddie had taken the seat in front of the desk before he dropped into the one behind it. He rubbed his hand across the back of his neck. "You're going to have to be more specific than that, Riv. The train rolls in three times a day and spits out at least a half-dozen drifters every time. I've got farmers coming in for the first of their winter supplies." He looked between them, his eyes sparkling. "Talk about your *seed*-y types." He exploded in laughter, slapping his thigh.

His amusement was contagious and Maddie laughed despite the rather poor quality of the pun. Rivlin grinned, rolled his eyes, and muttered, "Forget the farmers and the bad jokes, Mike."

Wichita's marshal slowly sobered and came back

to the business at hand with a good-natured sigh. "Let's see. . . . There have been three herds come into the stockyards this week alone and there's a fourth coming off pasture and forming up out west of Delano. It'll be in before nightfall. Which, when it's all said and done, means I've got more strangers in town than I can shake a stick at and not a one of them's fit to sit in my mother's parlor."

Rivlin leaned on the corner of the desk, his arms crossed over his chest. "Has anyone come into town either too eager or too reluctant to give up his gun?"

"Oh, hell, Riv." Mike winced and met Maddie's gaze. "Pardon my language, ma'am," he offered hastily and with utter sincerity.

"That's quite all right," she assured him. "Please speak freely, Marshal Meagher. I won't take offense."

"But my mother would if she caught wind of my manners. She taught me better." With a smile he leaned his forearms on the desktop and gave his attention to Rivlin again. "Riv, I can't say that anyone's real happy about the gun law except the locals who, by the way, happen to be better armed than me and Earp combined."

"Has anyone come into town asking questions about Maddie or me?"

"Not that I've heard of. I'll keep an ear to the ground, though. Where are you staying?"

"Myra's." Mike's brows went up in silent question, prompting Rivlin to add, "It's a long story."

Maddie could see the questions churning in the depths of Mike's eyes. But his mother had apparently done a good job of raising him because he didn't pry. Instead, he said, "Well, be careful. Ol' Red Beard and Rowdy Joe Lowe are going at each other like wet cats over there. Make sure you keep out of their way. Those two are going to end up slinging bullets before too much longer. Wouldn't want Miss Rutledge to get caught in the crossfire. We had to bury a man just last month 'cause he didn't duck fast enough."

"I'll keep that in mind, Mike."

"How long will you be staying?"

"No longer than we have to. Maddie's got an appointment she has to keep."

Maddie watched another set of questions play across Mike Meagher's mind. This time he decided to ask one of them. "You said you were heading toward Leavenworth. Miss Rutledge's appointment wouldn't be in any way related to the big government trial going on up there, would it?"

Rivlin snorted softly. "Mike, you're lousy at subtlety, you know that? Yes, Maddie's to testify for the prosecution."

Mike looked at her long and hard and she knew that while Rivlin might have refrained from telling him she was a federal prisoner and he her escort, Mike had just put all the facts together on his own. Mike glanced back and forth between them appraisingly, then pushed his hat back on his head. "You might want to reconsider making the trip, Riv. Word is the agents are going to be acquitted."

Rivlin tensed but managed to keep his posture relaxed. "Oh, yeah? Who's saying that?"

"A couple of the local lawyers I was playing cards with the other night. According to them, the case is built entirely on circumstantial evidence. Now personally, I happen to believe that if it sounds like a duck and looks like a duck, you've got a duck, but these lawyer fellows say it's not enough to deprive a man of his liberty."

"The prosecutors seem to think that Maddie's an eyewitness to something."

Mike nodded, the information clearly not news to him at this point. "That goes a long way toward explaining how things have gone for you. You arrive in Leavenworth with Miss Rutledge and those men stand a good chance of going to prison. You don't arrive there and they walk free. I can see the temptation."

"Unfortunately," Maddie contributed, "I don't know what it is that I'm supposed to have witnessed."

Mike studied her again. "I'd make a point of trying to remember, ma'am," he finally said. "It may be the only thing that keeps you and Rivlin alive."

Rivlin gained his feet and came to stand at her side. As he extended his arm for her, he asked, "Who's the most discreet man at the depot, Mike?"

"Charlie Roberts. He's an old-timer with a snow-white beard clear to his belt buckle. You can't miss him."

"And how likely is Marsh Murdock to know anything outside of what he's read in the *Kansas City Star*?"

Mike snorted. "Marsh knows a lot, Riv. It's getting him to admit and print it that's the problem. Marsh is determined to make Wichita into the New York City of the plains and anything that might discourage folks from coming this way tends to be overlooked when the type is being set for the next edition of the paper. According to Marsh, we've never had a shooting or a theft in our little corner of Paradise."

"Think he might have heard anything new related to the trial?"

"Hard to tell. Guess you could ask him. He's probably over at the paper. The next edition's due out tomorrow and he had parts for the press come in on the noon train. Like as not, he's going to be in a foul mood when you find him. I'd stay well back and be ready to run."

"You know I don't run," Rivlin countered with a wide smile, guiding Maddie toward the door.

"Oh, that's right," Mike countered, chuckling. "You only make strategic retreats."

"It was a pleasure to meet you, Marshal Meagher," Maddie said over her shoulder.

"I hope to see you again, Miss Rutledge. And under better circumstances. In the meantime, you take good care of my friend there."

"I'm doing the best I can."

Mike nodded, offering her a curious smile that somehow managed to be both happy and sad at the same time.

MARSH MURDOCK DIDN'T HAVE the time of day for them. He was up to his elbows in grease and printer's ink and curtly told them to go read the paper for themselves. Rivlin tipped his hat, thanked the man politely, and then guided Maddie out of the *Eagle* offices. As they made their way down the wooden boardwalk toward the train depot, the cattle herd came through town as Mike Meagher had predicted. It was a wide, bawling, dusty parade of longhorned cattle, prodded forward by a ragtag group of men who looked every bit as wild as the animals they drove. While Rivlin went to find Mr. Roberts, Maddie watched the sea of hooves and hide slowly pound its way east on Douglas

Street. As each cowboy passed, he acknowledged her presence with a touch of his hat brim. Not a one of them seemed interested in her beyond the fact that she was a female and a welcome sight for weary eyes.

"See anyone you know?"

Maddie smiled and turned to find Rivlin leaning against the side of the depot. "How long have you been standing there?"

"A while," he admitted, straightening and then coming to her side. Putting her hand back on his arm, he started them down the sidewalk as he added, "I stood there long enough to know that I'm not the only man in town who knows a beautiful woman when he sees one."

Heat fanned across her cheeks. "In answer to your question, no, I didn't see anyone I knew. And no one seemed to be looking for me in particular, either. Did Mr. Roberts have anything to tell you?"

"No. But he promised to watch and send word over to Myra's if anyone caught his attention." He eased their pace, and saying, "Let's step in here," slipped his hand to her elbow.

Maddie quickly surveyed the shop window. Hats and gloves and beaded reticules—all displayed on purple satin-draped boxes. A milliner's store. "But I said—"

"Yes, I know," he countered, pulling open the door. "But I'm pretending that you're a typical female and all giddy at the thought of a new dress."

"I'm not a typical female," she protested even as she was propelled over the threshold, her arrival heralded by a jangling bell overhead.

"I noticed that, Maddie," he said, his voice silken. "In the first two seconds I met you."

"How may I help you?" offered a matronly woman coming around the end of the glass-topped counter.

Rivlin didn't give Maddie a chance to respond. "Good afternoon, ma'am. The lady needs a traveling costume and we're hoping you might have something ready-made that might fit the bill."

Maddie endured the woman's narrow-eyed appraisal, prepared for the sniff of censure that never came.

"I have only one that I think might do," the proprietress said, heading back behind her counter. From the shelf she pulled a huge gray cardboard box. It no more than touched the countertop before the lid was removed and the dress presented with a flourish. "It, of course, comes with a matching half-fitting *paletot*. I also have a reticule, gloves, a hat, and a shawl which would complement it nicely."

Maddie clenched her teeth to keep her jaw from dropping. It was simply the most beautiful outfit she'd ever seen. The fabric was a fine foulard, the color a deep reddish-bronze. Four deep rows of kilt pleats comprised the lower skirt, topped by a band of intricately folded black grosgrain ribbon. The upper skirt was gathered tightly at the waist, unadorned in the front, covered on the sides and behind with a draping overskirt of black foulard, trimmed in long ruffles of the same fabric. The bodice was tailored and decorated with a row of jet buttons that marched up the front to end somewhere beneath a black grosgrain bow and a flounce of black lace. The sleeves were set in and fitted, ending at the cuff with a narrow band of knife pleats. It was a lady's dress and it was undoubtedly worth a small fortune.

"The overskirt is lined, of course," the shopkeeper

said quietly, turning the piece to reveal a dark tan-colored Duchesse satin. She lifted one of the skirt flounces, revealing the same lining there. "And the overskirt can be draped six different ways so that it's quite versatile." She smiled. "A lady should always look attractive and novel—whether she's arriving or departing."

Maddie couldn't resist. She brushed her hand over the foulard and gently stroked the cool softness of the satin. "It's very lovely," she said, drawing back.

"Would you like to try it on, Maddie?" Rivlin asked. "I think it would look good on you. The colors suit you well."

She couldn't. It was too expensive, too fine. "No, but thank you," she said, smiling at him and hoping her regret didn't sound in her words.

He beamed at her and then said to the other woman, "We'll take it. And the reticule, and the gloves, hat, and shawl. Wrap it all up so we can take it with us. All except the shawl, that is. We'll have that to use now. The sun's setting and I wouldn't want the lady to catch a chill."

"Very good, sir," the woman answered, neatly folding the dress and returning it to its box. "Shall I send the bill to your hotel?"

"But Rivlin," Maddie began.

"I'll pay for it now," he said, ignoring her protest.

Maddie stopped breathing as she watched him pull Murphy's money from his pocket. He winked at her, then turned so that she couldn't see him peel off the bills. The woman behind the counter could see him quite clearly, however, and she watched, nodding when the appropriate amount had been separated out. Rivlin passed the thick stack into her hand and she quickly tucked it into her pocket before going back to her packaging.

Not knowing precisely how much he'd just spent on her, but certain that it was an appalling amount and far more than she should properly allow, Maddie touched Rivlin's elbow and drew him around to face her.

His smile was wide, the corners of his eyes crinkled. "If you should ever get the chance to meet my sisters, Maddie, please promise me that you'll show them the proper way to shop for clothes. You have no idea how many days it takes for them to choose a single costume. The fitting room sessions are endless. I spent most of my childhood bored mindless in dress shops."

Protesting wasn't the right thing to do, she realized. Rivlin was bound and determined to buy the dress and the cost meant absolutely nothing to him. Expensive dresses were a normal part of his world. The least she could do was to be gracious in accepting it so that she didn't spoil his happiness. She suspected that it had been a very long time since Rivlin had enjoyed a moment as much as he did this one.

And so she watched the matron wrap a fringed reticule in tissue paper and pack it into a little box. She smiled and agreed that the small black velvet hat decorated with loops of grosgrain and fluffy ecru feathers was the prettiest she'd ever seen. The gloves were a fine quality kid leather and made with obvious craftsmanship. The shawl was a deep tan cashmere, soft as butter and as light as a cloud. But, as luxurious as it was, its warmth came from Rivlin's tender care as he took it from her and draped it around her shoulders.

"Thank you," she whispered.

"My pleasure, Maddie," he whispered back. "Shall we go home now?"

Home. Home was wherever she happened to be when the sun set. Tonight it would be Myra's again. Tomorrow it could be anywhere. What would it be like to have someplace that you belonged, that belonged to you? she wondered.

"Maddie?"

She started and quickly put away her sad musing. "I'm ready to go whenever you and the packages are," she answered brightly.

"And your purchases are indeed ready," the matron said, placing the box containing the reticule atop the others on the counter. It was an impressive pile.

Rivlin stepped up and took the entire stack in his arms, saying, "If you'll get the door, Maddie, we'll be on our way."

She did as he asked, but with misgiving. He had to peer around the side of the boxes to see his way to the door and out onto the sidewalk. Maddie fell in beside him and held her breath as they made their way west on Douglas. The city band played from the upper balcony of a downtown building and lights were being lit within the drinking gardens and gaming halls. Tinkling piano music drifted out into the street along with the sounds of feminine laughter. Maddie noticed that she was the only woman out and about, that the passersby were all male and purposefully moving toward their havens of choice. A few of them didn't seem to be pleased with having to move out of the way to let her and Rivlin and the mountain of boxes pass.

She bit her tongue for as long as she could stand it and then said, "Please let me carry something, Rivlin."

"A gentleman never permits a lady to carry packages."

"Be that as it may, you can't see over the top of the stack and you're going to run into something and get hurt."

"I'm tougher than I look."

"So am I," she countered, quickly reaching up to snag the strings of the reticule and hat boxes.

Rivlin looked at the top of the stack that now reached only to his shoulder and then over at her. "Do you always do as you please, Maddie?"

"If I always did as I pleased," she answered as they started across the bridge to the west bank, "I'd have pitched a proper fit and all of these packages would still be back at the store."

"Why didn't you protest any harder than you did?"

She smiled and gave him the truth. "Because I saw that it made you happy to buy it." Maddie paused as a realization struck her. "Now that I think about it," she added, chagrined, "I did do as I wanted. And I was selfish twice over. I have a new dress *and* I had the pleasure of seeing you enjoy yourself."

He chuckled. "So we've come back to my original question. Do you always do as you please?"

"I'll have to think on that," she answered, deliberately avoiding the discussion. "I'm not sure."

But she did know the answer to his question. Rivlin had said they were going to talk. This probably wasn't the subject he had in mind, but it was one that needed to be addressed. How to go about opening it wasn't quite as clear to her as the need to do so, however. They had reached the back of Myra's when she asked, "Do you want an honest answer to your question, Rivlin?"

"Is there one?"

She sighed and nodded. Rivlin put his packages down on the steps, added hers to the pile, and then leaned back against the railing, his arms crossed over his chest.

"I suppose," she began, searching for her way as she went, "that I could tell you that, as a federal prisoner, I don't have the choice to do anything beyond what I'm told. But the truth is that, even locked in a cell, I do have choices. I can be a difficult or a cooperative prisoner. What I choose to do to pass the time is my decision to make.

"It's taken a good many years, Rivlin, but I've learned that living to please others is generally a wasted effort. What pleases them one minute, doesn't the next, and it's exhausting trying to figure it out and change myself. From time to time I'll make an attempt to be what someone might want me to be, but only if it seems like the way of least resistance. For the most part, though, I do what I think will keep me safe and make me happy."

"I had the impression early on that you were trying to please me."

"I did. I thought that it would keep me safe while I was with you. But I discovered that being someone besides myself wasn't necessary and so I stopped."

"Thank you," he said quietly. "I much prefer the Maddie Rutledge who speaks her mind and does what she wants."

"Why? I'd think that you'd prefer me docile and compliant. It would certainly make your job easier to do."

Rivlin considered the toe of his right boot, knowing that they'd worked their way around to the grit of their relationship. Part of him wanted to ignore the thorny issues and hope it all ended well by pure luck. His conscience wouldn't let him take the small man's way out.

"We've passed the point where you're just part of the job, Maddie," he said, meeting her gaze. "We may still be the lawman and the prisoner on the surface, but there's more to us now. The stake's become personal. I didn't want it to happen and Lord knows I should have had my wits about me close enough to head it off, but the horse is out of the barn and there's no use in saying that it isn't."

"And that makes the situation difficult for you, doesn't it?"

"It depends on what part of the situation we're talking about."

"Getting me to Leavenworth alive and in time to testify?"

"Actually," he admitted, "that part's still pretty clear cut. I like your company, Maddie. There aren't any rules against that. And I'll admit that I'm not looking forward to the end of the trip and that I'm going to drag my feet for as long as I can about getting you there. No one cares how long it takes me—as long as I have you there on time. As for keeping you alive . . . It's my sworn duty to see that you keep breathing. I've always been willing to do what it takes to see that you do. Nothing's changed about that."

She nodded slowly. "Then what part *has* been complicated?"

His pulse skittered like a damn schoolboy's. Rivlin clenched his teeth, reminding himself that he was a grown man and Maddie sure as hell wasn't the first woman he'd ever come to terms with. "I told you that first day that I wouldn't lay you down on your back unless you wanted me to, Maddie. I meant it. I still mean it and I'll live by those words if you want to hold me to them."

"Do you want to lay me down?" she asked softly.

His chest tightened and hunger shot through his veins. He resisted the impulse to reach for her. "It's not the least bit smart, but, yes, I do."

"I wouldn't be opposed."

"But are you trying to be a cooperative prisoner, Maddie?" he wondered aloud, studying her in the twilight. "Or are you honestly wanting? There's a big difference between those two. In the first, I'm the lawman and you're the prisoner who'd be giving in to the power I have over your life. That's not right and I won't have it that way. I have to know that you're looking at this the same way I am. There's nothing permanent here for us, Maddie. Sharing a bed wouldn't change how things end. I'm going to take you to Leavenworth and I'm going to turn you over to the prosecutors. Do you understand that?"

"God, Rivlin," she whispered. "Do you honestly think I live on hope?" She laughed softly, sadly, and shook her head. "I did when I was young, when I actually thought that if I was good enough my parents would come back for me. But I gave up believing, for better or for worse, a long time ago. What my life is at any moment is all there is, Rivlin. Whether it's good or bad or somewhere in the stream of things between, that's all there is. The good doesn't last forever. Neither does the bad. All things pass. I don't know what tomorrow's going to be like, what it will bring my way. Yesterday's done and over and I can't change it. Today is all there is.

"You say you're going to get me to Leavenworth. I think there's a fairly good chance of that happening. You're intelligent and resourceful and determined. After that . . ." She shrugged. "I don't hold the reins on my life. What will happen, will happen. All I can do is ride along and get through it the best I can.

"I'm your prisoner, Rivlin, and you have your duty. There's no putting that truth aside. What happens between us until you hand me over to the prosecutors . . ." A bittersweet smile lifted the corners of her mouth. "If a scrap of happiness comes my way, I'll certainly accept it and appreciate it. But I'm not going to try to hang on to it, Rivlin. I'm not going to hope that it's my future. I know better."

He'd suspected that was how she looked at life, but hearing her say it hurt in a peculiar way. It knotted his gut and made him want to hold her and promise her that she could dream of good tomorrows.

She took the hat and reticule boxes off the stack and headed up the stairs. Her hand on the doorknob, she looked back over her shoulder and asked, "Are you coming in or are you going to stand out here all night?"

Good judgment said he needed time to sort through the jumble of his thoughts. "I think maybe I'll have a smoke out here first," he answered, standing squarely on his feet. He fished in his pocket and produced the key to their room. Stepping forward, he handed it to her, saying, "I'll be up in a few minutes."

She looked at the key and then back at him, her brow arched. "Aren't you afraid that I'll walk out the front door while you're not watching me?"

"Are you?"

She laughed softly. "No."

"Then I'll trust you."

"You've come a long way since the water hole, Rivlin," she observed, letting herself into the kitchen.

"How far have you come, Maddie?" he asked quietly.

Either she didn't hear him or she did and didn't want to answer. The door closed behind her and he was left standing in the alley, the boxes containing her dress and *paletot* at his feet. He'd squarely faced the difficult issue that lay between them and Maddie had just as squarely told him what he needed to hear. She'd been completely honest; he should feel gratified and comfortable. He should be seeing the way ahead as clear and certain. But he wasn't. Something was gnawing at his insides, burning deep in his chest. It was a hunger of some sort, but not the kind that eating or taking a woman to bed would ease.

Rivlin reached into his vest pocket and drew out his makings bag. He had no illusions, knew that he wasn't going to find any answers in the smoke. But he rolled a cigarette anyway, hoping that the motions would somehow soothe his uneasiness.

Chapter Thirteen

MADDIE DROPPED THE KEY and the boxes on the kitchen worktable, then turned and looked at the door. Should she go back out and tell Rivlin the whole truth? Admit to him that she honestly didn't hope for anything after he left her in Leavenworth, but that in the time between now and then . . . No, she decided, removing her shawl and laying it over the boxes. She knew better than to hope for anything at all. Telling him about it would only compound the foolishness of the mistake. Rivlin would do what Rivlin decided his conscience could allow. And while she waited for him to choose a path, she might as well indulge in the comfort of holding Grace. Babies didn't set conditions, they accepted everyone just as they were.

"Maddie, honey!"

She whirled toward the parlor door, knowing the voice. "Myra!" Open arms invited her and

Maddie laughingly flung herself into them. Hugging and being hugged, she managed to gasp out, "It's so good to see you, Myra! I thought I never would again!"

Myra set Maddie from her and while visually surveying her from head to toe, said, "I could hardly believe it when Helen said you were here. Tell me your version of the story, honey."

"Rivlin's supposed to take me to testify at the trial going on in Leavenworth," Maddie said, determined to make quick work of the tale. "But Murphy from the fort came after us and tried to kill us. Then there were two others who tried the same thing the very next day. Someone's paying to have us killed, Myra; me so that I can't testify. We don't know why they want Rivlin dead. We came here to hide and see if we could find some answers."

Myra nodded, looking gravely concerned for all of a half second. Then, as usual, her great optimism took hold. "And the story of baby Grace! Katie told me that one!" Myra exclaimed, beaming. As always, Myra's hands did as much talking as her mouth. They fluttered and Maddie stepped back out of harm's way. "There's a dimer in that one, Maddie. Can't you just see it? *The Marshal, His Pretty Prisoner and the Abandoned Baby.*"

Myra and her poetic tendencies. Maddie laughed and shook her head. "Tell me your story, Myra. I thought you had another month to go before you were released."

Myra launched into her tale with gusto. "I was released by order of the governor himself. His imbecile secretary *finally* gave him my letter and he saw that justice was done as quickly as he could. He was most apologetic for the delay. And the pea-brained secretary is now filing papers over in the land office."

"You really do know the governor?"

"Honey, I know all kinds of people. And most of them owe me big favors."

"Speaking of knowing people," Maddie countered, her hands going to her waist. "Why didn't you tell me you know Rivlin Kilpatrick?"

"Maddie, you do real well at accepting what I do for a living, but if I'd told you I knew Rivlin, you'd've assumed the worst no matter what I said to the contrary and you'd've ridden off with him with your heels set and your hackles raised. The poor man wouldn't have stood a chance with you all bristled up."

"Stood a chance with me for what?"

Myra rolled her eyes and threw her hands up in exasperation. "Of charming your drawers off you. What else?"

"And you think this is something that should happen?"

"Well, hell, Maddie," Myra retorted, her own hands going to her hips. "Lord knows I've tried to get him interested in mine and haven't had so much as a wink from him. I figure that if I can't have the pleasure myself, then maybe I can have the thrill by you telling me about it."

"And what makes you think that I'd get a wink from him?"

Myra laughed softly, her blue eyes sparkling. "Maddie, honey, you're every man's fantasy; a curvy little package of fire and innocence. If Rivlin Kilpatrick doesn't reach for you, there's something wrong with the man."

There wasn't anything wrong with Rivlin. Having a conscience was commendable. "There are rules governing his conduct," Maddie countered.

"Oh? Meredith tells me that you two are sharing Edith's old room."

"You can just wipe that smile off your face, Myra Florence. Nothing has happened between us."

The smile left Myra's face. "Then, honey, you're not trying hard enough," she said firmly. "Rivlin Kilpatrick may be a lawman, but he's a man, and there isn't a man alive whose thoughts don't turn to lovemaking at the mere *sight* of a bed."

"Myra . . ."

"Honey, life is short. Live it while you have the chance. You've got a long stretch of lonely in front of you and a smart girl like you should know enough to grab some pleasure when it comes your way."

"Myra," Maddie said, arching her brow, "you told me this when I left our cell however many days ago it was. I heard you."

"Oh?" Myra breathed, her eyes widening. She grinned. "Well, that puts a different light on the matter. What seems to be holding Rivlin back?"

"Decency."

That gave Myra a pause for all of a second and a half. With a nod, she *tsked* and said, "I'll just have to have a talk with the man and set him straight."

Maddie could well imagine how that would go. Her pulse skittered. "Please don't."

Myra looked around the kitchen. "Where is that handsome man of yours?"

"He's not mine, Myra. He's the marshal assigned to see me to the trial."

"We'll quibble over that later. Where is he?"

Maddie knew there was no dissuading Myra once her mind was made up. "Out in the alley," she supplied quietly. "Smoking a cigarette. He'll be in directly."

"He'll be delayed," Myra declared as she marched toward the back door. "Have something to eat while you wait."

"Myra!"

"Trust me, honey. I'll see that Rivlin does right by you."

Maddie covered her face with her hands and groaned. The door closed with a sharp bang.

RIVLIN WATCHED THE DOOR OPEN as he lit his second cigarette. But it wasn't Maddie who came through the opening and down the steps at him. He flicked away the match and braced himself.

"Rivlin Kilpatrick, I want a word with you."

"Hey there, Myra," he drawled. "The governor finally heard of your plight, huh?"

"He's a good, kind man."

"I'll have to take your word on that. Have you seen Maddie?"

She stopped in front of him, put her hands on her hips, and nodded crisply. "Yep, left her in the kitchen with her face buried in her hands."

What had . . . ? "Jesus, Myra," he growled, starting past her. Myra's hand shot out and stayed him.

"She's all right, Riv. I wouldn't hurt that girl for anything. She's like a daughter to me. And this mama wants to know what you think is wrong with my girl."

"Wrong?" he repeated. "There's nothing wrong with Maddie."

She released her grip on his arm. "Then why haven't you seduced her?"

Oh Lord. Rivlin took a pull on his smoke. "Most mamas don't want their daughters bedded, Myra. Leastwise not before there's a ring on their finger."

"I'm open-minded," she shot back. "Why haven't you wiggled Maddie down yet?"

He decided to try the high road first. "Myra, please don't take offense, but that's none of your business."

Her arms still akimbo, she leaned forward to say with cool precision, "Well, if you think I'm above extortion, you can think twice, Rivlin Kilpatrick. You ever hope to get me to point for you again, you'd better square up to this and square up to this fast."

So much for the high road. The middle one was the next logical choice. "Maddie's had a rough life." Rivlin took another pull on the cigarette. In the wake of a hard stream of smoke, he added, "She doesn't need it any more complicated than it already is."

"And what's complicated about you two sharing a bed for a while?"

Everything. He dropped the cigarette and crushed it out with the heel of his boot. "She's a good person, Myra. I don't want to be another in the long line of people who haven't given a damn about what happens to her."

Myra didn't respond and the hairs on the back of his neck prickled. He looked up to find her studying him, her head tilted to the side. "What?" he asked warily.

"Do you love her, Riv?"

His mouth went dry. "Nope," he declared, clearing his throat. "I'm just trying to be a gentleman and do what's right."

Myra arched a carefully painted brow. "Are you by any chance having a hard time with it?"

Myra was both smart and experienced enough to know desire when she saw it and so there wasn't any point in him denying it. "Can't say that there hasn't been a time or two when I've been tempted to ignore common sense."

"Good. Next time it occurs to you to be a gentleman, Rivlin . . . Ignore the impulse. Maddie doesn't have much to hope for and a bit of loving isn't going to hurt her in the least. Maddie's a smart girl. More importantly, she's practical. You're not going to be bedding a girl dreaming of a white lace dress and showers of rice."

"I'll think on it," he replied, wondering if Myra had had her ear pressed to the door while he and Maddie had talked.

"Well, while you're thinking on that, Riv," she said with quiet earnestness, "think on this, too: Maddie's as chaste as she came into this world, not an easy accomplishment given all she's been through. The odds of her finishing out her sentence in the same condition are pretty damn slim. And if you don't accept the honor of being her first . . ." Myra shook her head. "For God's sakes, Rivlin, her first lover should be one she wants. You can give her some good memories to see her through what's ahead."

If Myra had intended to knock the air out of him, she'd succeeded. "So seducing Maddie would be an act of charity, huh?" he managed to say. "I'll *really* have to think on that one, Myra."

"That's your problem, Rivlin Kilpatrick. You think too much. Takes all the fun out of feeling."

He wished he hadn't stomped out the half-smoked cigarette. "Feeling's a double-edged sword, Myra."

"Then be careful with it. Tell me about these attempts to kill you and my Maddie."

She'd finally asked for something simple and straightforward. He breathed a sigh of relief and told her about everything that had happened, about all the shadows he saw looming over them.

"Talk about your double-edged swords," Myra said sadly. "Poor Maddie gets a taste of freedom and a chance to be a woman, but it all comes with the possibility of dying for it."

"She's not going to die if I can help it."

"Who are you thinking might be behind it all?"

"There's money there, Myra. Lots of it. Wordsworth, Long and Kirkman don't come cheap. I don't know about the Foleys, if they've got that kind of money or the kind of connections they'd need to pull off something this big."

She smiled ruefully. "It could be that they're just as good at extortion as I am."

"That thought's occurred to me. But whose arm would they be twisting?"

Myra shrugged. "Could be anyone's from the Oklahoma Territory to the east coast."

"That's a great help, Myra."

"What are you planning to do? Hole up here forever? You're welcome to, of course."

Rivlin shook his head. "I figure they'll make another attempt to kill us before too long. I aim to be waiting for the next man who comes after Maddie. With any luck, I'll get some decent answers out of him."

Myra considered it all for a moment, sighed, and then nodded in acceptance. "How long do you think it will take for them to send someone?"

"I think we're already living on borrowed time," he admitted. "If I were on the other side of this, I'd have had another man waiting on the trail just in case Murphy and the other two failed. When I didn't get the news that my quarry'd been taken care of, I'd have sent someone to Wichita to finish the business."

"And the train makes the trip a quick one. Have you talked to Mike Meagher?"

"Yep. He's watching. As best he can, anyway. Also spoke with Charlie Roberts this afternoon."

"We'll just have to keep Maddie tucked in the nest until this plays out. I gather you paraded her around town today so whoever's looking for her will know she's here and where to find her?"

"That was one of my purposes," he answered, stepping around Myra to retrieve the boxes he'd left on the step.

"And the others? Would they be professional or personal?"

He lifted the boxes slightly, saying, "I bought her a traveling suit so she doesn't arrive in Leavenworth looking like trail trash."

"Why, Rivlin Kilpatrick," she drawled, "that's very thoughtful of you."

Oh jeez. He knew that tone: the mama whose daughter had been asked to dance. "Don't read more into it than there is, Myra," he cautioned.

"I wouldn't dream of it."

She would, too. "I need to find Maddie," he said, heading up the stairs. "I don't like letting her out of my sight." He winced and quickly added, "And don't read any more into *that* than there is, either, Myra. She's my prisoner."

"Of course. Your prisoner. That's all."

Rivlin froze, one hand balancing the boxes, the other on the doorknob, his teeth clenched. She'd been nice as pie in all but out and out calling him a liar. He couldn't be mad at her, though. She was right.

He didn't know exactly what his relationship with Maddie was all about, but being with her wasn't entirely a matter of duty. It had become a pleasure he looked forward to and sorely missed when deprived of it. All in all, that didn't bode well for the day he was going to have to ride out of Leavenworth alone.

"Thinking again, Riv? I warned you about that."

Her words stung. "Done thinking," he declared, twisting the doorknob.

Noise blasted through the crack at him. The door wasn't open far enough for him to see anything, but Grace was crying to beat the band and over the gulping wails he very clearly heard Meredith screech, "That *thing* is disturbing our customers!"

Rivlin froze, not at all sure if he wanted to walk in on a contest between Katie and the peacock vulture. Wisdom said he should duck back and try to come in again later.

"Babies tend to cry from time to time, Meredith," Maddie replied calmly. "She's not doing it to deliberately hurt business or to irritate you."

Rivlin silently swore. Maddie hadn't gone up to their room. Odds were she was holding Grace. Damn, *damn.*

"Well, either make it shut up or take it outside."

"It's too cold to take a baby outside."

"And then if you were to do that," Meredith countered snidely, "you might miss the chance to show Rivlin Kilpatrick what a good and virtuous woman you are, how you'd be a wonderful, caring mama for his brats."

Rivlin snarled and started forward. Myra grabbed him by the belt and hauled him back, whispering harshly, "Let Maddie fight her own battle. You stay out of it." He started to protest, but Grace suddenly quit her wailing and the cool tones of Maddie's voice rang loud and clear.

"I don't know that I need to demonstrate anything of the kind for Rivlin."

"Well, it certainly isn't good business sense you're showing him. An intelligent woman never gives her services away for free."

"Not that our relationship is any of your concern, Meredith," Maddie countered, her tone icy, "but Rivlin is escorting me to my destination and nothing more. I am neither giving nor selling my services to him."

"That's not what he said."

Rivlin growled. Myra tugged his belt again. "Let her fight."

"Rivlin is a gentleman," Maddie said, each word sounding as though chipped from a block of ice. "Whatever your understanding is of our relationship, I'm sure it's not from anything Rivlin has said on the matter, but rather is the result of your desire to believe as you want to."

There was a taut silence and then Meredith said, "That's my dress you're wearing."

Katie answered indignantly, "You said this morning that Maddie could have something out of the ragbag and that's where I got that dress for her."

"What was it doing in there?" Meredith demanded. "I certainly didn't throw it away."

Katie huffed. "I remember exactly what you said when you put that dress in the pile, Meredith Grun. You said you didn't want it anymore, that it was too faded and worn to be presentable."

Grace started wailing again. Meredith and Katie went on, shouting over her.

"What we remember are obviously two very different things," Meredith said. "I want my dress back."

"You're just being mean and petty. You don't want the dress, you just don't want Maddie to have it."

"It's my dress and I want it back now."

"You never liked that dress in the first place. You always said the color made you look giddy and brainless."

"I did not. It's one of my favorites and I want it back."

Rivlin gnashed his teeth. Myra whispered, "Patience."

Maddie's voice came quietly, like a lull in the storm. "I'll see that it's returned to you, Meredith. It wasn't my intention to impose."

"After you've let that baby puke all over the front of it? No. I want it now before you ruin it."

Maddie's voice was cold, hard steel as she said, "Here, Katie. Hold Grace for a moment, please."

Myra yanked Rivlin's belt so hard she nearly threw him off the top step. "Now," she declared, pushing past him and throwing the door wide. He caught his balance just in time and went after her. It took half a second for him to wish he hadn't. Meredith was a slit-eyed cat who looked like she'd spit green any minute. Katie was as puffed up and red as an overstoked stove. If she exploded, they'd all be killed.

And Maddie . . . His chest went tight and his breathing came hard. Maddie was angrier than he'd ever seen her. She met Meredith's gaze square on, her jaw set, her chin up and her hands fisted at her sides.

"Myra," she said through her teeth, "would you

be kind enough to undo my buttons so Meredith can have her dress back?"

Myra stepped to the task with a blithe "Be glad to."

Rivlin saw the course of things and put the boxes on the table, saying, "Maddie, why don't you go upstairs and—"

"No," she said, without looking away from Meredith. "Miss Grun wants her dress back *right* this moment and she'll get it *right* this moment. I wouldn't want her to fear for either its safety or its return."

"Well, maybe Meredith shouldn't always get what she wants," he offered, watching Myra's fingers fly down Maddie's back.

"She's going to this time."

"Darlin' . . ."

"There. Done," Myra pronounced, pushing the shoulders down Maddie's arms.

"Thank you, Myra." And then Maddie proceeded to yank the sleeves off her arms and shove the whole thing down her body faster than Rivlin had ever seen a woman get shed of her clothes. She stepped out of the pool of damask, bent down, snatched it up with both hands, and then flung it at Meredith, saying, "Here's your goddamned dress. Are you happy now?"

Meredith found the shoulders and shook it out. "It's wrinkled."

"Then press it," Maddie shot back.

Meredith huffed. "I'm not the one who wrinkled it."

Maddie's hands went to her hips. Her breasts rose and fell, threatening to come over the top of the corset. "Go to hell."

Myra chose that moment to step from behind

Maddie and head for the parlor door. As she went, she said serenely, "Meredith, I'll have a word with you. In my room. Now."

Meredith glared at Maddie, silently threatening murder, then turned on her heel and marched out, the dress in her hand.

Rivlin expelled a hard breath, relieved to see the monster go. Maddie didn't move, didn't say anything. She stood there, her arms akimbo, staring at the door.

"I need to change Grace and then put her down. It's past her bedtime," Katie said, her voice shaky in the aftermath. "Are you all right, Maddie?"

"I'm fine. Thank you, Katie."

Katie nodded and without another word retreated to her room with the baby.

Maddie stayed right where she was—as though she'd been rooted to the spot. Her breathing was ragged and fast and her jaw was still rigid with fury. Color had flooded her cheeks and washed down over her shoulders and breasts. Her arms were at her sides, her hands fisted, as she stared straight ahead.

She was close enough that he could easily touch her. Something told him not to. Rivlin swallowed the lump down his throat. "You got so riled up that you pulled some of your hairpins loose."

"I don't care." She reached up and pulled the loose pin from her hair. She looked at it for a moment and then turned to toss it on the table beside the boxes and her shawl. A second hairpin followed it. Long, shiny, dark tendrils tumbled down. Rivlin struggled to breathe.

"Do you care that you're standing in the kitchen only half-dressed?"

"No, frankly I don't," she answered, her anger still there, barely banked.

"You probably should."

Her gaze came up to meet his with an almost audible snap. Her eyes were a dazzling blue and brimming with defiance. Hunger coiled hard and deep inside him.

"I'm in the kitchen of a bordello, Rivlin. I doubt that I'd get so much as a second look if anyone walked in here."

"Shows you how little you know, darlin'. If someone walks in, I'll have to kill them before they clear the doorway."

She looked away and pulled another pin from her hair and threw it down on the table.

"Fair warning, Maddie," he said slowly, evenly. "You stand there and pull out one more hairpin, I'm going to do more than look."

She lifted her chin, met his gaze, and then very deliberately reached up and pulled a pin from her hair. She held it up for him to see and then opened her hand to let it fall to the floor.

"You're going to be sorry you did that, Maddie."

"No, I'm not."

Instinct wanted her against him hard and fast, but he forced himself to reach out and slowly trail his fingertips over her breast just above the corset's lace edge. "I wanted to do this in the bathhouse," he said quietly. "And in Mike Meagher's office."

Her eyes drifted closed as she arched forward into his caress. Through the lace of her corset, he saw her nipples bud and the invitation was too much to resist. Brushing his thumbs over the peaks, he watched her face. A smile touched the corners of her mouth just before her lips parted to emit a soft sound of pleasure.

Rivlin bent down and brushed his lips over hers. "And I wanted to do this outside the depot," he whispered, slipping his arms around her and drawing her against the length of him. He kissed her again, this time as he'd ached to do all day—with a slow, fiercely gentle deliberation that he intended to serve as a warning. If Maddie was going to surrender, it was only fair that she know how deeply and thoroughly he was going to possess her.

Sensation washed over her in delicious, intoxicating layers; the boldness of Rivlin's touch, the deepening hunger of his kisses, the warmth and strength of his body pressed against hers. Her skin tingled where he touched her, making her feel alive as she never had before. And deep inside there was wanting, hard and undeniable. Threading her fingers through the silken strands at his nape, she drew Rivlin closer, rose to meet him.

Her virginity flitted across his mind and Rivlin tried to keep the thought, to hold it between what he wanted from her and what he needed to give her. But she was heaven in his arms, warm and hungry and so responsive. She rose on her toes, pressing herself closer, holding him, asking for more with an openness and honesty that stole his breath . . . and his resolve.

Breathing wasn't important; getting her out of the corset was all that mattered. He devoured her mouth as his fingers plucked the laces loose. His shirttail had come free of his belt, the sensation stirring and then startling. Common sense took advantage of the moment. It hurt to put her from him, but he did it anyway, taking her by the shoulders and gasping, "Not here. Upstairs."

Chapter Fourteen

Maddie nuzzled into the curve of his neck, breathing deep the scent of sun and wind and male. She kissed him there, reveling in the taste of his skin, in the way she could make his breathing catch and his arms tighten around her. Somewhere along the stairs she lost a slipper; she vaguely heard it clatter on the steps. She deliberately kicked the other one off.

"You've got to the end of the hall to change your mind," he said, reaching the top of the stairs and turning toward their room.

"I don't want to change my mind," she answered lazily, kissing his neck again. "Do you?"

"No. Probably should, though."

He set her on her feet in front of their door and she obediently turned to insert the key into the lock. His lips caressed her nape, sending a wave of pure pleasure rippling through her. The lock clicked in the same moment his arms slipped around her and he whispered against her skin, "I can give as good as I get."

Rivlin smiled as she sighed and melted back against him. With one arm around her corseted waist, he pulled the key from the lock, opened the door, and somehow managed to get them both into the room. Getting the door locked behind them, however, required a moment of focusing his attention on something other than kissing a trail down Maddie's delectable, lavender-scented neck. She took advantage of his distraction and turned out of the circle of his arm.

Stepping beyond his reach, Maddie turned to face him and watched him toss the key onto the table beside the door. He took off his hat, dropped it on the table, too, and then roughly tousled his hair with his fingers. He looked boyishly innocent, yet dangerously roguish, too, and her knees went weak.

A tiny, knowing smile touched the corners of his mouth. Watching her, he reached down and pulled the string tethering the holster to his leg and then very deliberately undid the buckle of his gun belt. He pulled it all from around his hips and, with it in hand, started forward. He paused in passing her to press a feathery kiss to her ear and whisper, "Breathe, darlin'."

Maddie grinned. Breathe? Who cared about breathing? She turned and watched him put the gun belt on the bedside table, watched him sit on the mattress and casually pull the boots from his feet.

Did she dare torment him as he did her? Even as she wondered, a rush of boldness coursed through her, drowning reserve. Her heart hammered as she slowly tugged the string of her pantalets. The movement, slight though it was, instantly caught his attention. Rivlin sat on edge of the bed, watching, his chest rising and falling in quick cadence.

A tiny voice in the back of her mind gasped at her wantonness. Acknowledging it and admitting that she didn't care, Maddie let the pantalets fall and then stepped from the pool of white cotton. The hem of the chemise brushed lightly over her upper thighs as she crossed the room to stand before him. He looked up at her and smiled, his eyes blazing amber and black, beckoning her to continue the game.

Her heart raced as she reached out and opened the first button on his shirt. "I'd like to see what's beneath this," she whispered. "If you don't mind, of course."

"Not at all." He stood, his hands at his sides.

The buttons opened and she finished the task she'd begun in the kitchen, pulling the rest of his shirttail from his trousers. Somewhere in her mind, Maddie knew that he was appraising her. It didn't matter. Nothing mattered but touching him. She wanted to know the feel of his skin, the ripples of his muscles beneath her hands, the warmth of him, the power of his body. She wanted to bury her hands in the crisp curls that covered his chest, to trace the thin line of darkness that led down across his muscled belly and disappeared into his trousers.

She splayed her fingers upward across his chest. His heartbeat pounded against the hardened planes, pulsed in the hollow at the base of his throat. The words escaped before she knew they were there. "You feel so good."

It took every bit of his control to keep himself

from throwing her down on the bed and finding his release in her. Never had he wanted a woman like he did Maddie Rutledge. Something strangely akin to both joy and terror swept through him when her hands slid down across his chest. He caught her wrists and held her still as he struggled to sort through the torrent of his thoughts for the one that alarmed him.

Through the walls of their room came the raucous sounds of Delano—the tinkling of piano music, the tinny notes of the brass band, the thudding of hooves, the laughter and shouts of women, the bellowing of men. Through an interior wall came the sound of rhythmic thumping. It was all from beyond the silence that hung between him and Maddie and yet is was a part of them, too.

His conscience stabbed and he closed his eyes, silently groaning beneath the weight of certainty. "No, Maddie," he whispered. "This isn't right."

For a second she froze and then she tried to pull her hands free and step away.

"Listen to me, Maddie," he pleaded, refusing to let her go. "It isn't that I don't want you. Christ, I want you so bad I ache." He saw pain and humiliation in her eyes and it hurt to know he'd been the cause. "We're in a whorehouse, Maddie. You deserve better than this."

Her smile was tight and her chin came up, neither of which hid the shimmer of tears in her eyes. "Deserving and getting aren't tied together, Rivlin. Sometimes it's best to settle for what you can have."

"If I did that right now," he admitted, "I wouldn't be able to look at the fellow shaving in the mirror tomorrow morning."

She blinked to hold the tears at bay and pulled

against his grip, saying with sad bitterness, "Because you're the marshal and I'm the prisoner and there are rules."

He let her go. "Because I know I'm going to have to turn you over to the prosecutors and ride away," he explained as she picked her pantalets up from the floor. "You being willing doesn't make that end any less callous. No matter how you look at it, Maddie, making love to you is using you."

"No more than I'd be using you."

He watched her sit on the edge of the chair and pull on the pantalets, turning her words over in his mind. Using him? For what? Maddie didn't know how to use people. A possibility niggled into his awareness. His stomach clenched.

"Maddie," he asked as she rose to her feet and tied the waist ribbon, "are you thinking? . . ." Words failed him and he drove his fingers through his hair in an effort to find a way to handle the matter with some degree of compassion and finesse. She met his gaze, her brow arched in silent question, and he saw no course to lay the truth out for her. "Darlin'," he said gently, "they'd take a baby away from you. You'd have to give it up just like you had to give up Grace."

And it would hurt a hundred times more, Maddie silently added. *Because it would be your child.* Her anger and frustration at being physically denied ebbed away in the face of Rivlin's obvious distress. He was such a good man, trying so very hard to do what he thought was right.

"I wasn't thinking that, Rivlin," she assured him quietly. "I know the rules of being a prisoner. There are ways to keep from having babies; Myra told me about them. I know enough to avoid a heartache if I can. When I said I would be using you, I meant for my own selfish pleasure."

He gave her a quirked smile that didn't reach his eyes. He raked his fingers through his hair again as he said softly, "God, you don't know how badly I wish I could see a simple way out of this."

"Only simple men see simple ways, Rivlin," she replied, reaching behind her back to finish loosening the laces. "That you can't speaks well of you. Are you planning to sleep in the chair again tonight or are you going to be sensible and take your half of the bed?"

He sighed hard. "I'll sleep on the floor."

"I suppose that's a reasonable compromise," she admitted, pushing the corset down over her hips and stepping out of it. She picked it up and tossed it onto the chair.

"I'm sorry, Maddie. I shouldn't have started something I wasn't willing to finish. It wasn't fair to you."

"It's all right," she assured him with an easy smile. "I understand. It's just a little surprising to find a man with a conscience. Give me a while to think about it and I'll probably come around to actually appreciating that such goodness exists."

He snorted and took a blanket from the chest at the end of the bed. "If I were truly good, keeping my hands to myself wouldn't feel like such a goddamned sacrifice."

"You're a good man, Rivlin, not a saint."

"Darlin'," he drawled, fashioning himself a pallet beside the bed, "even a saint would be tempted by the sight of you standing there dressed like that. For God's sakes have some mercy on me and either get under the covers or blow out the light."

She did both, tossing him his hat, a pillow, and a wish for a good night.

COTTONWOOD LEAVES RUSTLED *overhead. Maddie stood silent in the clearing, her chemise and pantalets gossamer wisps in the pale light of the moon, her hair cascading in dark waves over her shoulders. The hand that pointed to the woods beyond her was his. "I can't want you. It's not right."*

Tears filled her eyes as she squared her shoulders and lifted her chin. He tried to call the words back, tried to find others to change what he'd done, but they tangled in his mind and he couldn't stop her from turning and walking away. He hurt. God, he hurt for what he'd done to her. She needed him and he'd sent her away.

The moonlight faded to nothing. Weeds and brush pushed their way up through the ground and the trees were cottonwoods no more. Ash and oak and elm, the leaves of the carpet on which he knelt. He couldn't look down. He didn't want to see the bloody proof of what he'd done.

"You know what he did to me."

The sobs were his own. "Yes, Seth. I know."

"You know who did it, too."

He screamed inside, tried to climb to his feet and run away. He couldn't move, couldn't escape. "No. You never said." Believe me, Seth. Please believe me.

"But you can guess, Riv. You'd be right. Why didn't you go after him? Why did you let him get away with it?"

Rivlin tore his way from the nightmare, rolling onto his hands and knees, gasping for air, his body wracked with uncontrollable shivers. The instincts of his dream clawed at him and he scrambled to his feet, desperate to run as far and as fast as he could. Where the hell was he?

Maddie awakened suddenly, searching the darkness of the room for what had started her from sleep. Rivlin stood beside the bed, staring at the far wall, his breathing labored, his shoulders rigid with tension. He looked the same as the night he'd wakened out on the prairie and told her the story of Seth Hoskins's death.

"Rivlin?"

He whirled about, his hands fisted in front of him. The music drifted up from the street outside, sounding oddly muffled and distant as Maddie watched regret and pain wash across his features.

"What can I do, Rivlin?" she asked quietly. "Do you want to talk about it?"

He exhaled hard—once, twice—and then ran his fingers through his hair before giving her a smile that spoke of profound sadness. He sat on the edge of the bed and reached for his boots.

"Where are you going, Rivlin?"

He crossed to the table by the door and settling his hat on his head, answered, "I'm going to wander over to Rowdy Joe's and see what I can do to numb my brain."

And drown your memories. "You'll be careful?"

"I learned the need for that the hard way."

"I'll be here when you get back," she assured him.

He hesitated for just a second, then pulled the key from the lock and laid it on the table, saying, "Lock the door behind me and don't go anywhere while I'm gone. You leave this room and you make yourself a target."

"I'll lock it," she promised. "And I'll wait for you right here."

He studied her for a long moment and then stepped to the chair where he'd tossed their saddlebags. He opened one, rummaged for a minute, and came to the bed with his hand extended. Maddie looked down to see a tiny, pearl-handled gun lying in his palm.

"It's loaded," he said. "Someone comes through that door, I want you to shoot 'em."

Maddie took it from him, asking, "Do you give all your prisoners loaded derringers?"

He smiled so softly and sadly that her chest tightened at the sight of it. "Only you, Maddie. You're the first." Then he turned and headed resolutely toward the door, adding as he went, "You have to cock it before the trigger spring will pull. Remember that."

Maddie let the door close before she climbed from the bed and went to lock it. She hesitated, torn between doing what Rivlin trusted her to do and going after him. But what more could she say that hadn't been said already? What could she do to ease his pain and guilt? Heartaches healed in their own time. She knew that. She also knew that someone telling you to simply walk away from them didn't work. You had to wait out the pain and find your peace in your own way. Maddie locked the door, saying a little prayer that Rivlin would find his before it was too late, and then considered the bed. She didn't feel like sleeping. With a sigh, she decided that the room could use some straightening.

BY THE TIME HE SAW MYRA in the kitchen, it was too late to turn back up the stairs without looking like a yellow-bellied coward.

"Good evening, Rivlin."

"Myra." He touched his hat brim and headed for the back door.

"You just hold it right there, mister. Where's my Maddie?"

He stopped, resolved to get through the ordeal and gone. "Upstairs. I gave her a derringer to protect herself. You hear a shot from that direction, you send one of the ladies over to Joe's for me at a dead run."

"Why are you going over there? I have whatever you want to drink right here. It's up in the parlor. And it's not watered and I'm not going to charge you for it. Besides, Joe and Red are going at it tooth and nail tonight and you don't want to get caught in that fight."

He half-smiled. "I can handle a fight, Myra."

She laughed. "Riv, honey, you're so wrapped up in your frustration you'd have a hard time beating your way out of a flour sack. From the looks of you, I'd say you and Maddie haven't come to a happy meeting of the minds yet. You'll feel a helluva lot better when you give in."

He silently swore and said, "Night, Myra," as he turned on his heel and yanked open the door.

"You stay out of Joe's and away from Red's, too."

Rivlin closed the door and stood on the step, breathing deep. Angry shouts came from the direction of Rowdy Joe Lowe's and Red Beard's neighboring saloons. Breaking glass—lots of it—inferred that someone or something had been pitched through a front window. And then smashing wood; that would either be chairs or tables or maybe both. Myra was right. He didn't have much starch in him at the moment. If he'd thought there was a reasonable chance of sleeping without Seth haunting his dreams again, he'd head back up to Maddie and settle in with her. It's what he wanted to do, for sure and for certain. And that was the root of the problem. Rivlin patted the side of his vest to make sure his makings bag was still tucked in the pocket, then went down the steps and headed toward the river.

He thought about the promise he'd made Seth and understood it in a way he never had. It had seemed a sacrifice equal to his sin at the time, but the truth was that it hadn't taken any effort to hold to it in the years since. He'd come home from the war to find that his family had pretty much gone on without him. His father and John were a perfect team for managing the munitions factory and didn't need his help to so much as get the floor swept. Emily and Anne had married while he'd been gone and, like his three older sisters, were immersed in filling the nursery and managing households of their own. His parents had insisted that he live at home, but it hadn't taken long for him to realize that they'd become accustomed to being alone together. He'd learned to clear his throat well before rounding a corner and entering a room.

It wasn't that his family didn't want him; it was that there wasn't an easy place for him there. He'd changed in the years he'd been gone. Walking away and living apart from them had been far simpler to do than figuring out how he was supposed to fit among them again. He'd been the dutiful son and gone home again after his father had died, but he hadn't found any greater sense of belonging than he had the first time he'd tried. And all of it made keeping that part of the promise to Seth easy.

Life in the army and the Marshal Service had made keeping the other parts of the promise just as easy. He moved from place to place at the drop of a hat, pulling up stakes and moving on without so much as a look back. Women to be found around army posts were either faithfully married or not the kind to inspire thoughts of anything beyond a quick and meaningless dalliance. The Marshal Service was an all-male society in which the only women you met were wives and mothers. The life was even more nomadic than that of the army.

And then he'd drawn the assignment of escorting Madeline Marie Rutledge to a trial. She'd intrigued him from the minute he'd laid eyes on her. An admitted murderess with a heart of gold when it came to caring for others weaker than she was, Maddie had affected him like no other woman in his life. His duty was to keep her alive and deliver her to the prosecutors, but, despite knowing better and digging in his heels every inch of the way, protecting her had become a personal mission that he couldn't surrender. Beneath the soft curves and gentle smiles, Maddie had a backbone of steel and a wisdom far beyond her twenty-seven years. He didn't love her, of course, but he sure as hell respected her strength and goodness.

His life had been nicely simple before Maddie had come into it, his decisions clear and easy to make, his promise to Seth one he could live with and keep without a second thought. But Maddie made him feel and look at things in a whole new way. She made him have second thoughts about the solitude of his existence. And that was why Seth had appeared in his dreams again.

Rivlin looked up at the sky. A cold, heavy truth wrapped around him, body and soul, refusing to be denied for one more day. He'd made the promise he had because he'd known deep in his heart that it would be easy to keep. He'd been pretending for ten long years that he was paying penance when in reality all he'd been doing was running away from an ugliness he didn't want to face. The promise to Seth was only half of what he should have made his friend that night. He couldn't run anymore. He had to confront what had happened and see that justice was done in Seth's name.

Who? The Seth of his dream had said he could guess and be right. Rivlin snorted. Seth had always considered him to be wiser than he actually was. Still, there was a niggling sense that he did know.

A high-caliber blast slammed out of Delano and boomed over the water. Rivlin whirled back as a woman screamed, high pitched and panicked. *Maddie!* He ran, his heart hammering, his mind a tumult of thought and gruesome images. He'd left Maddie alone and he shouldn't have. If she was dead . . . In his mind's eye he saw her sprawled across the bed, her chest blown open, life pouring out of her.

Red Beard, a shotgun in his hand, staggered into his path. Rivlin sidestepped him and kept going. He hit one step at the back of Myra's and only a couple on his way upstairs. The door was closed and intact and he allowed himself to gulp some air as he slammed his fist against it. "Maddie, let me in!"

The lock clicked instantly and the door flung open. Maddie stood there wearing her prison blues, her eyes wide, her body whole and blessedly unharmed.

"Are you all right?" she cried, grabbing him by his shirt front and half-hauling him into the room. "I heard shots and screaming and I was afraid that—"

He wrapped her in his arms and kissed her, hard

and deep and thankfully. And she met him with a hunger just as consuming as his own. What tendrils of fear remained were evaporated in the heat of quickly soaring desire. His heart thundering and his pulse burning, he ran his hands over her, touching, feeding and fueling the desperate need for more of her. A solution flitted through his mind, only half-formed, but it was enough for him to grasp.

Devouring her mouth, he swept her into his arms and carried her to the bed. Kneeling to place her in the center of it, then balancing his weight on one side, he laid a fiery trail of kisses down her throat. The buttons of her shirt opened easily and he brushed the fabric away to bare her breasts. She arched up with a moan and he accepted the invitation, slowing his assault to savor the taste and feel of her, reveling in the feast of her passionate response.

Her fingers threaded through the hair at his nape, then upward to push away his hat. He vaguely felt it tumble off as Maddie arched still higher and held him to her breast. He suckled her, teasing the hardened tip, feeling the tremors that passed through her, hearing her throaty murmurs of delight. Rivlin trailed his fingers downward over heated satin skin, eliciting a gasping cry from her when he reached the waistband of her pants.

Her hands slipped down to his shoulders and then around to work the buttons on his shirt front. With a slow, hard pull he lifted his head and released his claim to her breast. "No," he declared softly, catching her hands in his and pinning them to the pillow over her head. She looked up at him, her eyes bright with desire and sparking with frustration. "It's my way, Maddie, or not at all. Just accept it."

"But I want to touch you."

If she did, he wouldn't be able to hold back and

they'd both pay the price for his weakness. "It's not my turn to be touched," he countered quietly, watching her eyes as he slowly opened the buttons on her trousers with his free hand. "Trust me, Maddie. I promise you won't be sorry."

Her breath caught and her eyes widened as his hand slipped beneath the fabric. He leaned down and brushed a kiss over her lips, then drew back to watch her face, to find his pleasure in devoting himself to her.

Maddie's senses reeled, at once overwhelmed and craving more. His touch, his kisses were deliberate, knowing, and sure, sending wave after wave of deliciously intoxicating sensation spiraling into her core. Her body throbbed, aching with the strain of reaching, of riding the building swells of heated yearning. She arched to meet them, embracing their power and letting them bear her upward and inward in ever-tightening spirals. The speed and intensity of the ascent was magnificent and she gasped, breathless with the potency of desire, mindless to all but the dizzying rush toward the beckoning pinnacle. The waves came faster, deeper, jolting through her, casting her higher and higher.

The universe bloomed bright for a timeless heartbeat and then shattered into a million glittering pieces, each flickering golden rose as they drifted slowly down from the heights of heaven. She floated with them, at once as fragmented as the world and more whole than she had ever been. Then, one by one, the lights dimmed and disappeared, leaving her to drift in sated darkness.

Rivlin's breathing came in great, greedy gulps. His heartbeat raced, pounding hard through every inch of him. The emotional satisfaction went deep, taking the sharpest edge from his physical wanting and allowing him to tenderly take Maddie in his arms, to kiss her gently back to earth.

Her arms slipped loosely around him and she snuggled against him, her breathing as ragged as his own as she returned the soft caress of his lips. He drew back and tilted her chin up so that he could see her face. God, she was beautiful, her skin still flushed from the heat of desire, her eyes full of dreamy wonder, her smile soft, satisfied.

"I liked that," she whispered.

He grinned. "I could tell."

"Thank you."

"My pleasure, Maddie." He kissed the tip of her nose. "Any time."

A bit of the dreaminess left her eyes, replaced by a wispy kind of sadness. "I don't see how you could have gotten the same satisfaction out of it that I did."

He managed a lopsided smile. "Well, considering the alternatives, it'll have to do."

"That doesn't seem fair to you. Will you allow me to return the favor?"

The mental image was immediate and so searingly detailed it crushed the air from his lungs and slammed his heart against the wall of his chest. He clenched his teeth as he hardened to an unbearable degree.

"I know how," she assured him with the quiet certainty of absolute innocence. "Not that I've ever done it, mind you. When you share a cell with Myra you don't have much choice but to listen."

He knew better than to think he'd be content with only a shadow of satisfaction. Maddie was a novice and didn't know how much more there was to be had. He did and he wasn't at all sure it was a wise idea to flirt any closer around the edges of it. It would be too easy for temptation to trample good sense. Even now it was getting one helluva beating.

"Go to sleep, Maddie," he said, gently drawing her closer. "We'll see what tomorrow brings."

She sighed and nodded and soon drifted into a deep slumber. Rivlin held her, staring into the darkness, breathing deep the scent of lavender in her hair, feeling the warmth of her soft breaths caressing his skin. The sounds of Delano filtered through the walls and he closed his eyes, wishing for another time and place, hoping for a chance he wasn't likely to get.

Chapter Fifteen

SHE STARTED AWAKE when Rivlin reached for his gun. The knock on the door came in the same second that the weapon cleared the holster. "Rivlin?" Myra called from the hallway. "Maddie? Oatmeal's on and not getting any warmer. Get yourselves presentable and come on down."

She walked away before either of them had the presence of mind to tell her they'd heard the summons. Rivlin shook his head, slipped the revolver back into the holster, and then smiled at her. "Mornin', darlin'."

"Good morning."

"We'd better not make her wait," he said, his gaze sliding over her, the amber sparks in his eyes bright. "Patience isn't one of Myra's virtues." He half-rolled across her, putting an arm on either side of her head. He nibbled at her lower lip. "You're just as beautiful in the morning as you are at night. Do you know that?"

He could set her afire so easily. All it took was a look, a simple touch. She threaded her fingers through his hair, reveling in the silken feel of it. He trailed kisses across her cheek, then burrowed into her hair to tease her earlobe. Maddie took a ragged breath. "I thought you were worried about Myra's patience."

He laughed, nipped her ear, then pushed himself up and rolled off the bed in one smooth motion. Drawing her out after him, he said, "Let's go eat."

She loved to hear Rivlin laugh, loved the way the corners of his eyes crinkled when he smiled broadly. He didn't laugh often enough to her way of thinking. And she wasn't going to tarnish his happiness by telling him that she sensed a good-natured inquisition waiting for them over breakfast. She just smiled, pulled on her moccasins, and let him lead her down the back stairs.

As Maddie had expected, Myra was indeed waiting for them in the kitchen. She laid aside her newspaper and looked between them as they came in. She smiled and opened her mouth to speak, but Rivlin cut her off, holding up his hand and saying, "Not one word, Myra. No observations, no comments, no advice. No nothing. It's between Maddie and me and it's private."

"My, my," she ventured, fluttering her lashes innocently. "You're a bit edgy this morning, aren't you, Riv?"

Maddie fought a smile as Rivlin glowered at the older woman and headed toward the pot steaming on the stove. "What's in the paper?" he asked, artfully changing the subject as he got himself a bowl from the warming area at the back. "Anything worth the time and effort to read about?"

Myra smiled and winked at Maddie, then picked up the paper. "Oh, there's a big article on Senator Harker coming out West. Everyone's all excited at the thought that he even knows we're here," she supplied, folding it so the front page lay face up. She tapped the daguerreotype picture gracing the center. "Frankly, I wouldn't trust that man any further than I could toss him."

"Why is that?" Maddie asked on her way to get her own bowl of hot cereal. "Do you know him, too?"

"Never met him, honey. And I'm not ever likely to, either. He's of the different persuasion." She cleared her throat and then added slyly, "If you know what I mean."

Maddie felt the tension shoot through Rivlin. He turned from the stove, the serving spoon laden with oatmeal and suspended over his bowl. "How do you know that, Myra?"

"Well, I don't *know* it," Myra admitted. "But it's something I sense. You don't go long in this business without developing an ability to read customers, Riv. For one thing, the lives of you and your girls depend on being able to read a man right. For another, rubbing up against the wrong tree not only doesn't get your itch scratched, it's also a waste of time and the loss of money. Trust me on this, Ol' John Harker has the look of a man who likes other men."

Maddie watched Rivlin plop the oatmeal into his bowl and make his way to the table, noting the tightness of his shoulders and the set of his jaw. She recalled all that he'd told her about Harker's conduct in the military. Nothing he'd shared seemed to warrant Rivlin's reaction to Myra's observations about the man.

"Can't you see it, Maddie?" Myra asked, rising from the table and bringing the newspaper to the stove. She thrust it forward, adding, "Look around the eyes."

Maddie obediently studied the picture of Senator John Harker. "All I see is cold and calculating," she finally ventured.

"Yeah, I'd say he's got a mean streak, too," Myra said, looking at the picture again as Maddie served herself. Together they joined Rivlin as Myra went on with her commentary. "I wouldn't let him in the door of my place. No, siree. He's trouble all the way around. I'll betcha he fits right in in Washington, though. Guess that means he has the skills to be a typical president." She tossed the folded paper into the center of the table just as a bell jangled from the front of the house. "Someone's here," Myra announced, heading toward the kitchen door. "I'll be right back."

Rivlin stared at the picture of John Harker, remembering bits and pieces of the past that had meant nothing to him at the time—things men had said in what had then seemed to be cruel jest, the looks that had sometimes come to Harker's face as he'd walked the camps, the casual—and declined—invitation to join Harker in his tent for a drink. Rivlin remembered the myriad details of the night he'd found Seth curled in the brush, of the eternity between that night and the one Seth had courted a bullet and death. It all meant something now, the balance making for a gut-clenching certainty. There but for the grace of God and youthful ignorance . . . If he'd only understood then what he did now.

Maddie sat blindly, her awareness wholly

consumed by Rivlin. He sat frozen, staring at the grainy picture. His lips were thinned, his skin was pallid, and his breathing was alarmingly shallow. She'd never seen him like this; it was almost as though he'd seen a—*ghost. Seth.* With a suddenness that lurched her heart, Maddie understood it all—what had happened to Seth, who had hurt him, and why Seth had felt such deep shame that he'd wanted to die. And she knew that Rivlin was staring into that past and being consumed by the guilt of his failure to save his friend. "Rivlin?" she said softly, laying her hand on his.

"Leave it alone, Maddie," he said, pulling away from her touch. He shifted his gaze to the window and the sunlit world beyond it. "Please," he added softly, shaking his head. "I can't talk about the past with the same kind of distance that you can."

His regret and pain tore her heart. "Then we won't talk," she whispered, rising from her chair and stepping into his line of sight. She took his face gently between her hands and trailed the pad of her thumb over his lower lip.

He took a deep breath, but it couldn't hide the strain in his voice as he said, "I know why you're doing this, Maddie."

I don't care. "Does it matter?"

"Only if I pause long enough to think," he admitted, his breathing quickening.

"Well, don't do that." Maddie bent down to press a lingering kiss to his lips. A soft cry strangled deep in his throat as he slipped his arms around her waist and drew her closer. Maddie went, straddling his lap and sliding her arms around his neck, her lips parting beneath his tender assault.

The hunger he'd satisfied for her in the night returned, made more ragged and demanding by the speed at which he pursued the distraction she offered him. There was a certain tenderness in the way his hands moved over her, but also an intensity of purpose that wouldn't be delayed or denied. He pulled her shirttail free and the feel of his hands, warm and rough on her skin, sent shivers of delight coursing through her. His kiss deepened, stealing her breath even before his hands came around to cup her breasts. She melted into him, desire throbbing through her, making her oblivious to all but the heady taste and feel of Rivlin Kilpatrick. He shifted beneath her and moaned softly as she settled closer against him.

"Riv—"

They both started at the sound of Myra's voice. Rivlin wrapped his arms around Maddie's waist and held her close, his forehead pressed to hers, as they both tried to catch their breath and Myra said from the doorway, "Damn. Sorry to intrude, but Mike Meagher's here and looking grim. He wants to see you and Maddie. I've stuck him in the front parlor. Take a minute to cool off there, but please don't make poor Mike suffer any longer than he has to."

The door closed with a click and Rivlin eased back to meet her gaze. "Jesus, Maddie," he whispered raggedly. "You're hell on a man's honorable intentions."

"Good," she replied, brushing her lips lightly over his.

"Yeah, you are, darlin'." His hands slipped back under her shirt, up her sides, and around to tease her hardened nipples. "You're very good."

"How about tempting?" she asked, twining her fingers through the hair at his nape.

His eyes were dark and searching and she could feel the driving rhythm of his heartbeat everywhere their bodies touched. She slowly, deliberately shifted on his lap and he groaned in surrender as his hands slipped to her hips and he hungrily sought her mouth with his.

"Although," Myra said from the doorway and startling them just as she had before, "come to think of it, he deserves to suffer for his lousy timing. You two just let things progress naturally and I'll keep Mike entertained."

Maddie sagged forward, cradling her head on Rivlin's shoulder and struggling to accept her frustration. "I'm going to kill her and you can't stop me."

Rivlin laughed silently, then hugged her tightly before swatting her playfully on the rear and saying, "Let's go see what burr Mike's got under his blanket this morning."

"It's not likely to be at all good," she reminded him, sliding off his lap. Her legs were shaky and she leaned against the table to steady herself. "Myra said he looked grim."

Rivlin slowly gained his feet. "Darlin', like as not, his grimness has little to do with what he's come to tell us. Mike's a good Catholic boy. Stepping through the door of Myra's has him terrified of God and Mother Meagher and the penance he's going to have to do for being here."

He adjusted the lay of his gun belt with a wince and a tight smile, then threaded his fingers through hers and led her from the kitchen. He was still holding her hand when they walked into the parlor. Myra, sitting in a chair opposite Mike, grinned and emitted a contented sigh that vaulted Mike to his feet and twisted his hat in his hands.

"Good morning, Mike," Rivlin said brightly.

"I've yet to see the good part of it."

Rivlin guided Maddie to a third chair and, squeezing her hand before letting go of it, deposited her into the seat. He stepped behind her and placed his hands on her shoulders, saying, "I gather that you've got problems?"

Mike took a deep breath. "A fisherman pulled a body out of the Ar-Kansas River up around the island this morning. Turned out to be Meredith Grun."

Maddie went cold. Myra gasped and pressed her hand over her mouth. "How horrible."

"Yes, ma'am," Mike said, nodding. "Horrible's the right word for it." He looked back to Rivlin. "Doc Fabrique says it looks to him like she was strangled to death." His gaze shifted to Maddie. "It's my duty as marshal to examine the bodies of the unfortunate, and when I did in this case, I happened to notice that Miss Grun was wearing a dress just like the one you were wearing in my office yesterday, Miss Rutledge."

Ugly certainty filled her, making her stomach roil and her heart pound. Rivlin's hands tightened on her shoulders and she took a deep breath. "It was Meredith's dress. I gave it back to her last night after returning from Wichita."

Mike met her gaze squarely. "It occurs to me that in the dark, you and Miss Grun might be mistaken for one another. You're both tall and slender. Both have dark hair. If a man had seen you in the dress earlier and then Miss Grun wearing the same dress later . . ."

Rivlin finished the thought for him. "It was Maddie they wanted to kill, not Meredith."

"That's what I'm thinking. Can you tell me why whoever killed her also lopped off her foot?"

Her stomach leapt, but she fought it down. "I

have a scar around my left ankle," she managed to say. "If someone wanted proof that I had been the one killed, they could have requested . . ." The rest of it was lost in the battle to keep herself from gagging.

"How did you get this scar?"

The cool precision of Mike's voice settled her. She swallowed and lifted her chin. "There are actually two scars, one over the other. Both are from manacles."

"And who would know about these scars?"

Her pulse was beginning to slow. "The ladies of the orphanage where I grew up in Iowa, most of the people of Tahlequah, and maybe a soldier or two at Fort Larned—depending on how observant they were."

Mike turned to Myra. "Do you know if Miss Grun had a similar scar, Mrs. Florence?"

"Not that I ever noticed, Marshal Meagher."

"When was the last time you saw her?"

"She and I met to discuss some affairs of the house and she left my room just after seven, saying she was going to look for a job at another establishment. I didn't see her again and assumed she'd gone off to do that."

"Can you think of anyone who might have had a reason to kill Miss Grun?"

Myra sighed. "There's probably a lot of folks who might have thought about it a time or two, but I can't say that any of them would have actually done it. Meredith wasn't an easy person to like, Marshal."

Mike smiled ruefully. "It would appear to have been a bad night for those kind of folks." Once again he looked back to Rivlin. "Red Beard was killed, shot in the chest just this side of the bridge.

Rowdy Joe thinks he may have done it, but he's not sure. Seems he was drinking quite a bit and remembers only bits and pieces of last night. I've been asking questions, looking for witnesses. People remember seeing a man out that way last night who, from the descriptions I'm hearing, sounds a lot like you, Riv. Would you know anything about that?"

Maddie felt him shrug. "I steered clear of both Red's and Joe's last night. Tempers and whiskey don't make for a good mix and so I wandered down to the river for a smoke. When I heard the shots, I headed back to here to make sure Maddie was all right. I passed Red on the way. He was headed toward the bridge with his shotgun. I figured he was on his way over to swear out a complaint against Joe Lowe. I didn't see Joe anywhere."

Mike considered it all for a moment and then said quietly, "And Red Beard dies where you were smoking just a few minutes earlier. Did you hear the shot that killed him?"

"Nope. It was a bit noisy around here last night."

Myra nodded hard enough to make her blond curls bounce. "That bunch that brought the herd in yesterday afternoon hit Delano about ten last night, Marshal. You must've heard them over on your side of the river. They damn near deafened us on this side."

"Yes, ma'am, we heard them," Mike said without looking at Myra. His gaze was locked with Rivlin's and Maddie saw both determination and sadness in his blue eyes.

"Let me save you the breath, Mike," Rivlin said quietly. "You'd appreciate it if Maddie and I left town before the undertaker runs out of boxes."

There wasn't the slightest flicker of relief in

Mike Meagher's expression and Maddie's pulse skittered.

"They say bad news comes in threes, Riv. I got a telegram just before I headed over here. It was from the Marshal Service. Charlie says copies went out to every peace officer between Kansas City and Santa Fe. They've issued a warrant for the arrest of you and Miss Rutledge. She's wanted as an escaped prisoner, you for aiding and abetting her."

Rivlin literally held her in the chair. "Who sent it?" he calmly asked.

"Wallace out of St. Louis."

"Well, that's a wrinkle I didn't expect."

Mike stood, saying, "I'm going to pretend I left the office before that telegram got there, Riv. I'm going to make a point of being out and about most of the day. But, when I do go back there this afternoon, I'm going to have no choice but to read it and then come looking for you and Miss Rutledge. I don't want to find either one of you."

He took a deep breath and slowly shook his head. "I don't care where you go, Riv. I don't *want* to know where you go. But I'm thinking that now would be a fine time to make one of those strategic retreats."

Rivlin stepped to the side of the chair and extended his hand without looking at her. Maddie took it and rose to her feet as Rivlin said, "I've got two horses at the livery, Mike. Will you see to them until I can get back here for them?"

"It's not a problem."

"Appreciate it."

Mike turned his hat over, reached into the crown, then stepped forward with a wad of folded currency, saying, "It's a loan to help get you and Miss Rutledge someplace safe. It's not much, but it was all I could lay my hands on without stirring up curiosity over at the bank."

Rivlin hesitated and then accepted it with a crisp nod. "Thanks. I'll pay you back the next time I see you."

Mike Meagher clamped his hat on his head, touched the brim to both Myra and Maddie, and then headed toward the door. "Wire me when you've got this mess sorted out."

"Thank you for trusting us, Marshal," Maddie said as he went past them.

"Just watch Riv's back," he said, not looking back. "Friends don't grow on trees."

The front door had barely closed behind him when Rivlin squeezed her hand in reassurance and turned to Myra. "Myra, have you got a good-sized traveling bag we can borrow?"

"Of course," she answered, coming up out of the chair. "What else can I do to help?"

"What I'd like you to do, Myra, is head over to the depot and tell Charlie that I need that car hooked to the northbound train the minute it comes into the station."

Myra grinned and winked. "I've always liked your style, Rivlin Kilpatrick," she said, sweeping past them with a rustle of skirts. "I had Helen take Maddie's boxes upstairs, so get on with getting my girl ready to travel. I'll have that bag for you in the shake of a lamb's tail."

"Car?" Maddie repeated as Rivlin led her up the stairs.

"Do you think I'm moving a valuable prisoner cross country packed in a car with some fifty other passengers? Any one of whom could be someone hired to kill you? Nope. Private car is the safest way to travel. It's got two doors and a long stretch between. It gives me control over who comes near you and room to move in case they do."

"But it's so expensive," she protested as they entered their room.

"You're worth every penny ten times over and then some."

Maddie dropped down onto the chair, and stripping her moccasin away, said, "I didn't know you felt that strongly about ending corruption."

"Corruption's as old as dirt, Maddie, just as common and just as perpetual. But that's not why you're—"

There was a knock at the door. Maddie rose from the chair and went to answer it.

Katie said from the doorway, "Myra asked me to bring the bag up while she heads over to the depot. I brought Grace along so you could say your goodbyes."

The baby. Rivlin's gut knotted. The teeter-totter of his emotions that had begun with Myra's comments in the kitchen crashed downward again.

"Hello, sweetheart," Maddie crooned, taking the infant from the washerwoman. "Aren't you a pretty girl? Can you take my finger and show me how strong you're getting?"

Rivlin watched Maddie wiggle the baby's hand, watched her tickle the little cheek and smile. Katie looked on approvingly, the bag still in her hand. His breathing came hard. "Any word from Dr. Fabrique on a home for her?" he asked brusquely, striding forward to relieve Katie of the bag.

"Not yet. It'll take him a bit of time," Katie said as he strode to the bed and tossed down the leather satchel. "I wouldn't worry about her, though. Myra said we'll keep her here until things work out."

"Would you write and let us know how she's

doing?" Maddie asked. Something in the tone of her voice made Rivlin look back toward the door. Grace was back in Katie's arms.

"I can't write," Katie replied, tucking the blanket under the baby's chin. "But Myra said you'd been teaching her so we'll get it done one way or the other. Where should we send the letter?"

Maddie clasped her hands behind her back. "Leavenworth, I suppose," she said. "General delivery. If it comes after I've been sent on, they'll forward it. Thank you for everything, Katie."

The other woman stepped back into the hall. "You take care, Maddie. You write us, too."

Maddie nodded and closed the door. She slowly turned back into the room. The smile on her face was tight and didn't ease the sadness in her eyes.

"Doc Fabrique will find her a home. It's for the best, Maddie."

The smile faded as she considered him. "I know she's not mine, Rivlin," she said, going back to the chair and her undressing. "I know that I won't ever see her, won't ever hold her again. I also know when it's all right to pretend and when it's time to stop pretending. And if there's any lesson I've learned over the years, it's to keep my heart out of the whole thing." She rose and on bare feet went to where Helen had stacked the boxes in the corner of the room.

He angrily dumped the contents of their saddlebags into the satchel without ceremony or care. If she thought he believed her, she fancied herself a better liar than she was. His conscience prickled. If Maddie hadn't kept her heart safe from Grace, had she managed to do any better where he was concerned?

"Rivlin? Why did they put warrants out on us? I haven't escaped. We're not overdue for the trial."

He put away his personal musings, grateful for the reprieve. "I've been wondering that myself," he answered, picking her moccasins up off the floor and tossing them into the bag. "Wallace knows me. He knows how I work. Someone had to have pushed him into acting against his better judgment and experience."

"The same someone who wants me dead."

"Sounds like a reasonable guess to me."

"Or is it the someone who wants you dead?" she posed. "Are we talking about the same person? Or is it two people? Are they working together or separately?"

Questions, questions. And not one goddamned answer. He swore and snapped the strap across the top of the satchel, then pitched the whole thing toward the door. He was glowering at it when she came to him, presenting him with the laces on her corset, and adding, "I suppose the question of who isn't really all that crucial at the moment. But if that telegram went out to every marshal between Kansas City and Santa Fe, it means one of two things, doesn't it? Either they don't know where we are and they're using the marshals to find us, or they do know where we are and they're trying to flush us out in the hope that we'll be arrested."

"You've got to admit that it's pretty clever to think of using the U.S. Marshals to track down someone you want to kill. Downright efficient, too." He worked quickly, tugged the last of the laces snug and tied them off.

"Your reputation is ruined," she observed, walking away.

His emotions edged upward and he laughed dryly. "Darlin', every lawman who knows me is scratching his head and thinking that Wallace has lost his mind. Mike Meagher isn't the only one who's going to give me the benefit of the doubt. Don't worry about it. I'll get it sorted out."

"Good. I wouldn't want you to suffer any negative consequences because of me."

No negative consequences? There was a warrant out for his arrest and hers, too. Meredith Grun was dead. So was Red Beard. Finding their murderer was Mike Meagher's job. His was to figure out who was paying to have Maddie and him killed and why. He was running blind and hoping luck would keep them one step ahead of a bullet. He'd deliberately cast caution, common sense, and professional duty to the wind and all but made love to his prisoner.

No negative consequences? Once he delivered Maddie into the hands of the prosecutors, they'd be responsible for her protection. Could they handle it? The odds weren't good. Christ. He stood a good chance of riding out of Leavenworth tomorrow or the next day with his badge still pinned to the inside of his vest, but he'd never ride that way again without remembering Maddie and how he'd failed her. That was going to hurt like a son of a bitch. First Seth and now Maddie.

Chapter Sixteen

Myra was waiting for them inside the car. Rivlin set the satchel on the dining table, pretending that he didn't notice that the bed had been dropped from the wall and the sheets turned down. Maddie, every inch the lady in her new traveling costume, walked past him and into Myra's outstretched arms.

"Maddie, honey, don't you worry about anything," the older woman crooned, rocking Maddie gently back and forth and patting her on the back. "Rivlin will keep you safe. You just do what he tells you, all right?"

"Myra, I think maybe this goodbye really is the last one."

Rivlin wished that Myra hadn't stayed to say farewell. Maddie was crying and he hated to see that. He'd rather be dragged behind a mustang five miles through cactus than hear Maddie cry.

"Oh, honey, don't you cry now," Myra continued to croon. "Everything will be fine. You'll see." She held Maddie at arm's length and then said firmly, "Tell you what you're going to do, honey. When you get to Leavenworth, you're going to square right up to those fancy lawyers and tell 'em that unless they're offering to get you out of prison with time already served, you'll be going into court a deaf mute. You make 'em give you what you want for what they want from you, Maddie. Do you hear me?"

Rivlin silently swore. He'd have to make sure Maddie didn't believe that was possible—because it wasn't.

"And when you're free and clear, Maddie, you come back here. You make Rivlin bring you back here."

Maddie nodded and Rivlin scowled at Myra.

"Now give me a smile," Myra said, smiling herself as she tilted Maddie's chin up with her fingers. "Show me the Maddie who knows how to fight for herself."

"Goodbye, Myra."

Myra kissed Maddie on the cheek and then patted it on as though to make sure it stuck for a good long while. "I'll see you in a couple of weeks, honey," she said, stepping around Maddie and heading toward the rear of the car. Myra didn't look at him as she swept past. "You. Outside."

"Be right back, Maddie," he said, turning to grudgingly obey the summons. "Why don't you draw the curtains while I'm gone."

He'd barely lit on the platform when Myra started in, her hands on her hips. "Where are you taking her?"

"Into Kansas City and then straight on to Leavenworth."

She looked at him incredulously. "You're going to turn her over, aren't you?"

He looked down the tracks. When he thought he could control his anger, he looked back at her and replied, "I don't have any other choice, Myra. Do you have any idea of how many marshals there are out there looking for us? How many of them I *don't* know and who'd just as soon kill us as arrest us? Handing her over is the best way I know of keeping her alive."

"And what if it's one of the prosecutors who wants her dead?" she countered derisively. "You hand her to them and you might as well put the gun to her head and pull the trigger yourself."

He saw Seth's face. He saw Maddie's head being blown into fragments. It took everything in him not to scream, to keep from spilling his guts on his feet. "Jesus, Myra," he ground out, using anger to keep his stomach at bay. "You'll never know what a low goddamned blow that was."

"If it was a low blow, I'm sorry," she said softly, studying his face. "I don't take cheap shots, Rivlin, and you know it. All I want is my Maddie safe and I was just trying to say something to get through that hard head of yours."

He yanked his hat off and ran his fingers through his hair. "Hell if I know which way to go. I don't like not having answers, Myra."

"What's your gut telling you, Riv? Deep down inside what do you wish you could do?"

He slapped his hat against his leg and stared back through Wichita toward the river and Delano and the prairie beyond. "Take the horses out of the livery and ride west. Take Maddie to the end of the earth so they'd never find her."

"Then why don't you do it?" she snapped. "Mike said he didn't care where you went. No one does as long as it's away."

The conductor sang, "All aboard!" The whistle blew a long, mournful wail.

"Because," Rivlin snarled, slamming his hat back on his head and settling it low on his brow, "I'd have to spend the rest of my life looking over my shoulder and worrying that every man I met was the one who wanted her dead."

"Beats getting yourselves killed in Leavenworth."

"I'll figure something out," he said, grasping the handrail of the car and vaulting onto the step. "I'll keep my eyes open and my wits about me. I won't turn her over until I'm sure she'll be safe. I promise, Myra."

"And you'll bring her back here when they let her go?"

He turned back to face her squarely. "It isn't going to happen that way, Myra. You may have high-placed friends who will flex their muscles for you, but Maddie doesn't. She can threaten the prosecutors six ways to Sunday and it's not going to get her anything but brutal treatment when they drag her into the witness stand. And if she does what you've told her, she'll be serving a sentence for contempt of court on top of the eighteen years she already faces."

The whistle blew twice. The train lurched and slowly rolled forward. Myra stomped along, keeping pace, her eyes blazing. "You're going to let them put her back in prison, aren't you?"

"I'll see that she gets a good attorney, that an appeal gets filed for a new trial."

"Are you planning to stand by her until that happens? Or are you thinking to kiss her and ride off with a tip of your hat and a thank you kindly, ma'am?"

Dammit, he didn't have the time or the inclination for this conversation. "Myra . . ." he began.

"You son of a bitch!" she yelled, shaking her finger at him, her curls bouncing furiously as she all but ran to keep up with him. "You leave her in Leavenworth, don't you dare set foot on my doorstep ever again. You do and I'll shoot you myself and consider it a kindness."

She ran out of platform and stopped, but she was still stomping her feet and shaking her fist at him, calling him vile names as he turned his back on her and let himself into the car. Maddie stood in the center of the long, rolling room, her hands clasped in front of her, her lower lip caught between her teeth. He went to the bar and poured himself a glass of whiskey.

"Do I want to know what you and Myra were arguing about?" she asked softly.

"No."

Maddie watched him throw a healthy dose of liquid fire down his throat and wondered how long it would take him to explode and whether the whiskey would hasten the inevitable or prolong the agony of waiting for it to happen.

"Maddie," he said, whirling around on her, "it doesn't matter how I feel about surrendering your custody. I'm going to have to do it. I don't have any other choice. You know that, don't you?"

Her pulse skittered as she realized what had set him off. She took a deep breath and gave him a reassuring smile. "Myra's a romantic, Rivlin," she said calmly. "She believes in true love and hopes for all the things that go with it. She's like a prospector, sifting through men, looking for the golden nugget she knows she'll eventually find. And her belief in that is so strong that she can't even begin to imagine how others don't believe in happily ever afters."

His expression didn't change. His only movement was to throw more whiskey down his throat. "I didn't ask about Myra's views on love. I asked whether you understood what I have to do."

Maddie nodded. "And you asked because Myra tried to make you promise to bring me back here." She crossed to the liquor cabinet and stood before him. "Rivlin," she said with gentle firmness, "we've covered this ground already. You have your duty and I have no illusions about you casting it aside. You'll deliver me to the prosecutors and we'll be done. I've always known that would be the way we end. There isn't any other way *for* it to end. I know better than to love you, Rivlin. And you know better than to love me. In the time we've been together, we've found a bit of pleasure in each other's company. But that's all there is between us."

"Are you being honest, Maddie?" He turned from her to refill his glass and ask, "Or are you trying to please me by saying what you think I want to hear?"

"Why would I try to please you?" she asked, hoping to appeal to his logic. "Is there anything I could say or do that would keep you from turning me over to the court?" She didn't give him a chance to answer. "No, Rivlin, there isn't. And so there's no point in pretending there is."

He drank, two hard tosses, one right after the other. "Goddammit!" He slammed the empty glass down on the bar. His hat went flying across the room a half second later.

"What's wrong, Rivlin?" she asked quietly. "What's gnawing at you?"

He gripped the edge of the cabinet with both hands and hung his head. "I don't know."

"I think I do." She brushed the hair off his collar, saying, "You're not in control of your circumstances and you don't like it the least little bit. You have questions and no answers. You're having to accept a course that you don't like and isn't of your choosing. And you're angry that there's nothing you can do to change any of it."

He turned his head to look at her. "How do you know that?"

"You've been tied to me and you're having to live with the circumstances of my life. It won't last forever, though. Your world will come right the instant you turn me over to the prosecutors."

"Your life isn't going to change," he said flatly.

"No, it isn't. But then I know how to survive it, how to endure and get through it. You don't." She brushed her fingertips across his cheek. "Please don't look so distressed. It's not your responsibility to try to change my circumstances. It's not possible. Just accept it, Rivlin. Just accept what we have for the moment for what it is and don't hope to keep it for any longer than we have."

He studied her, his turmoil and regret so obvious in his eyes that her heart ached. "How the hell can you live without hope, Maddie?" he asked, his voice a rough whisper. "What makes waking up every morning worth the bother?"

She smiled at him, knowing that she was going to miss him for the rest of her life and that she wouldn't have traded their time together for her freedom and all the money in the world. "Sometimes, out of the blue, truly wonderful things come my way. Like you did."

He straightened and slowly took her face between his hands. He didn't say anything; he simply stood there, his gaze sliding gently over her every feature as though he was trying to memorize the way the she looked. Her heart pounded, the ache terrible and yet sweet. And when he lowered his head and kissed her with gentle reverence, she knew it for the end it was. Her heart swelled, twisted, and tore in two.

RIVLIN STOOD AT THE REAR DOOR of the car and watched the sun set, a brilliant ball of blood-red fire. Maddie sat on the divan, silently staring at the same sunset. What the hell was he going to do? The train was going to roll into Kansas City within the hour and all the pacing and thinking hadn't helped in the least. He didn't have any idea beyond finding a train northbound on the trunk line and grimly boarding it with Maddie at his side.

Good evening, Mr. Esquire. I'm Marshal Rivlin Kilpatrick and this lovely woman is Miss Madeline Rutledge, the prisoner you wanted out of Fort Larned. Thought you'd like to know that we haven't tried to evade the court and that we're here in town. If you need us, we'll be over at the hotel. And don't worry about having to arrange for Maddie to go back to prison when it's all over. I'm hiring a lawyer and seeing that she gets a new trial. Nope, I don't love her. It's a simple case of injustice that needs to be righted and I'm honor bound to see that that happens. I'll just keep her with me until all that dust gets settled.

Rivlin closed his eyes. He wouldn't get the chance to so much as say howdy before they clamped him and Maddie into irons. They'd both be hauled off in separate directions and he'd be lucky if he only got his brains bashed in in the process. And Maddie . . . Once again Maddie would be at the mercy of a world that didn't care about her.

After he screamed and hollered and pitched things around, someone from the Marshal Service would spring him and he'd be able to pick up his life. Maddie, on the other hand, would sit in her cell and quietly endure. And when he finally managed to get to her, she'd thank him for his determination to see that she got a fair trial and the chance to be free and never for a minute hope that it would actually happen.

It would happen. He'd see to that. But if the verdict came back the second time the same as it had the first . . . Eighteen years was a helluva long time. Could Maddie survive that long? Or would she decide one morning that there really wasn't any reason to wake up?

"Penny for your thoughts, Rivlin."

He wasn't about to tell her the truth. "I'm wondering if I ought to wire ahead and let the prosecutors know I'm bringing you in."

She looked over her shoulder at him. Her smile was soft and gentle and real. "It would be the polite thing to do. And it would give them time to get the band down to the station to meet us properly. I rather got the impression from the newspaper article that the esquires have an appreciation for pomp and circumstance. It would probably be in our best interests to give them a chance to make proper public spectacles of themselves. Frankly, I'd like to see the show. I'll bet it's impressive."

God, how could she do that? he wondered. How could she actually face it all with grace and humor?

He let her chatter as the train rolled on, tossing comments back at her when she paused long enough to let him. And by the time the train pulled into the station she'd managed to make him smile a time or two. When the car came to a stop, they were ready to go. Maddie's chin was up as she accepted his assistance down the stairs and when they walked up the platform, she tucked her arm around his and smiled at everyone who passed them. And, somehow, he felt fortunate for the moment.

Maddie slid a glance at Rivlin as they came into the central portion of the station. He was doing better, actually smiling like he meant it. He'd been absorbed in his own thoughts for the greater part of the journey and toward the end of it he'd looked as though he were facing the prospect of an inept firing squad. It had taken forever for him to join in pretending, but he'd finally seen the advantage of it and accepted it for the best. He'd given her so many wonderful memories in the time they'd had together, it seemed the very least she could do in return was to make sure that he didn't feel guilty and responsible when they parted.

She looked about for something to comment on. There were certainly people enough in the station to make a full evening of fashion commentary and frivolous speculation as to everyone's destinations. Unfortunately, she didn't know much about fashion and any mention of destinations had the potential for making Rivlin think of their own.

Her gaze passed from knot to knot of travelers changing trains, looking for something amusing that she could point out and make Rivlin smile. There was a man over by the baggage desk with a ridiculously tiny bowler hat on his head. He reminded her of a monkey she had seen when a troupe had passed through town when she'd been a child. The monkey had danced and then run among the audience, collecting coins in his cap. Everyone had laughed and—

Maddie considered the man again, her eyes narrowed. Her heart tripped. "Rivlin!" she said, looking up at him while tightening her hand on his arm and drawing him to halt. "Over by the baggage desk, standing next to the tall, older man in the top hat and fancy suit . . . See the man in the plaid coat and tiny bowler? The one showing the tall man the book and talking a mile a minute?"

He glanced that way briefly and then politely away. "Yes."

"That's Tom Foley's friend from back East," she explained. "The one I hit on the forehead with the heel of my shoe that day."

His gaze snapped back to the group. His jaw went rigid and she saw his pulse hammering in the side of his neck. "Jesus," he snarled. "Jesus H. Christ."

Maddie looked between him and the group of men. The tall, older man was looking back at them, his expression full of recognition and every bit as granite as Rivlin's. "What is it?" she asked, focusing on Rivlin again. "Do you and that man know each other?"

He took her hand from his arm and held it tight in his own. Saying, "Move your feet and don't look back," he whirled them about and headed back the way they'd come at all but a flat-out run.

Moving quickly in a corset didn't leave her

breath to spare for questions. It wasn't until he'd found a storage closet and yanked her inside that she managed to gasp out, "Rivlin? What is it?"

By a sliver of light from the barely open door, Rivlin pulled open the valise and grabbed a slicker. "I've figured it out, Maddie. It's Harker who wants you dead. And me, too. The son of a bitch."

"Senator John Harker?" she asked, incredulous. "Why? How do you know that?"

Rivlin tugged the buckle open on his gun belt with one hand, untied the holster with the other, and crisply explained, "The man with Tom Foley's friend back there is John Harker, the same John Harker whose path crossed mine and Seth's in the army. Foley's friend is what's called an aide. He handles all the details of Harker's life so the bastard can look competent. As a side benefit of the weasel being in his employ, Harker gets to hide behind someone while doing his thieving."

Her blood went to ice. Her mind raced, putting the facts together. "I can testify that Harker's aide is at the agency on a regular basis," she said aloud over the hammering of her heart. "That's what I know that makes me worth killing. If I testify to that it would be the end of Senator Harker running for the presidency on the platform of fighting corruption."

Rivlin nodded as his revolver came out of the holster in one smooth motion just before he tossed the belt into the bag. The gun went into the waistband of his trousers, his hat into the bag with the other things.

"But I didn't know that, Rivlin. Not until just now," she reasoned, trying to understand the whole of the frightening picture.

"But his aide knows that you've seen him at the

reservation," Rivlin countered. "What if one of the Foleys or Collins or Lane starts singing to the prosecutors to save their own hides, Maddie? If they can give the prosecutors Harker . . . Harker can't take the chance that you'll corroborate their testimony or offer it on your own. You have to die before you get to Leavenworth."

Understanding filled her with a dread like none she'd ever known. "But why does Harker want you dead, Rivlin?" she asked, trying to keep her knees from buckling. "It doesn't have anything to do with Tahlequah, does it? It's about something that happened while you were in the army. You can't be the only one who knows about his stealing supplies and payroll."

"It's not about thieving, Maddie. It's about what happened to Seth. Harker can't be sure if Seth took the secret to the grave with him. But whether Seth told me or I figured it out on my own, Harker knows he can't afford me as a loose end." He rammed his fingers into his hair and ruffled it, pulling it forward around his face. He looked at her then, the first time since they'd raced from the central portion of the terminal.

Maddie fought down panic as she took in his suddenly changed appearance. "Why are you—"

"You stay right here," he commanded, yanking the coat on. "And don't you so much as stick your head out until I get back, do you understand me?"

"Yes." Her heart was pounding high in her throat. "Where are you going?"

He reached back into the bag and, after a swearing and rustling around in it, produced the derringer. He handed it to her, his eyes hard. "Fix your bustle so it looks as different from the way you have it as you can. Change the way you're wearing your hair, too. And get rid of those goddamned feathers in your hat. I want to have to look twice to know it's you when I get back here."

"You're scaring me, Rivlin."

"You've got every right to be scared, Maddie." He inched the door of the closet open just enough to peer out. "There's a good chance we're both going to die right here in this station unless I can find us a fast way out. Now stay put."

And then he was gone, leaving her standing there, her knees trembling, his name a whisper echoing in the dark.

RIVLIN STRODE BACK the way he'd brought Maddie only minutes before, his mind racing. They were in trouble so deep and thick it would be a miracle if they ever saw the sun rise again. He should have kissed her before leaving her. If things went badly in the next few minutes, he'd at least die with the sweet taste of Maddie on his lips. It was too late to go back now, though. Every second counted.

Ahead of him in the hall, a middle-aged businessman stood beside a marble pillar, his suitcase at his feet, a newspaper tucked beneath his arm as he checked his pocket watch. Putting it away, he picked up his satchel, turned, and stepped into the shadows, heading toward the door that led out to a platform. Rivlin quickly judged the man's height and the width of his shoulders and then smiled grimly as his mind tracked through the maze he needed to run. He wasn't beaten yet. The bastard wasn't going to win without a fight. Rivlin fell in behind the unsuspecting, God-sent stranger.

And when he got Maddie the hell out of here and someplace safe, all bets were off. The Marshal

Service be damned. Good judgment and tomorrow be damned, too. If he had only a few days left to live, then, by God, he was going to spend them making love with Maddie Rutledge.

Rivlin followed the man through the doors and onto the deserted platform. Pulling his gun from his waistband, Rivlin quickly closed the distance between them and brought the butt of the revolver down at the base of the man's skull.

Chapter Seventeen

SHE WAS SHAKING SO BADLY the derringer fell out of her hand. The sound of it clattering on the floor startled her, silencing her chattering thoughts long enough for reason to catch hold of her mind. She didn't know how long Rivlin would be gone. It might be only minutes. He'd given her specific instructions and she needed to have completed her tasks by the time he came back through the door. Maddie bent down, scooped up the tiny gun, and then carefully placed it on the floor beside the open valise.

She quickly took off her *paletot,* folded it, and put it into the leather satchel. The bustle, which she'd fixed to display as much of the Duchesse satin as she could, was rearranged so that not a scrap of the lighter fabric showed. And as Rivlin wanted, the feathers came out of her hat. She dropped them into the bag with all their other worldly possessions. Her hair . . . Maddie sighed. Without a mirror there wasn't much she could do with it that would look even halfway presentable. The best she could do was to change her single plait into two, wind and pin them, and hope the hat would hide the worst of it.

When she was done, she picked up the derringer and stood facing the door, her breathing ragged and her heart beating wildly. And, in the absence of distraction, her fears blossomed. Surely Rivlin should have returned by now. It had taken her forever to make the changes in her appearance. Where had he gone? What was he doing? Was he all right? What if he was in trouble and needed help? She wasn't any good to him hiding in the closet. But he'd said to stay here. He'd been adamant about it. And she'd promised him.

The closet was too small to let her pace, too dark for her to judge in any way the passage of time. She heard train whistles and snatches of conversation as people occasionally passed to and fro. She listened for gunshots, for excited exclamations and sounds of fighting, and took what comfort there was in not hearing them. God, where was Rivlin? It was Senator Harker who wanted them dead; her because she knew he was tied to the corruption at Tahlequah, Rivlin because he knew that Harker had brutalized Seth. If either of them lived to tell what they knew, Harker's political aspirations would be completely and forever destroyed.

The door opened suddenly and a well-dressed man wearing a bowler and carrying a leather suitcase slipped inside. Stunned, Maddie gasped and fumbled with the derringer. He stripped it from her hand, chuckling.

The familiar sound instantly soothed her nerves

and calmed her spirit. She threw herself into Rivlin's arms. "Thank God, you're all right."

He hugged her close, then held her away just far enough to give her a hard, quick kiss. "How're you doing?"

She sensed a shift in the way he faced their circumstances. The need for quick, decisive action was still there; so was the resolve. But the feeling of desperate urgency had been tamped down and Maddie knew that he'd found a solution. "Fine, now that you're back," she admitted. She fingered the fine fabric of the jacket he wore. "Where did you get these clothes?"

He grinned and even in the darkness she could see the sparkle in his eyes. "Some poor son of a bitch is going to wake up with a helluva headache. And then, to add insult to his injury, he's going to discover he's wearing only his union suit and missing his suitcase."

"You attacked a man and stole his clothes?"

"I attacked him from behind, too. No honor in it at all." He sobered. "Desperate situations require desperate actions, Maddie. Are you ready to go?"

She nodded and picked up the satchel Myra had loaned them. Rivlin took it from her, saying, "Ladies never carry their own bags."

"But your gun hand won't be free if you're carrying both bags."

"It's a calculated risk, Maddie," he said with calm assurance. "I'm trying to look like anything except a lawman. We're just going to have to grit this out and hope for the best."

"Where are we going?" she asked, watching him ease the door open another inch so he could see the world beyond their haven.

"To our next car," he answered, pushing the door open and motioning for her to follow. Maddie fell in beside him as he added, "And we're going across the station like a couple out for a leisurely evening stroll."

"We're heading to a different track than the one we came in on," she observed as they moved away from the central portion of the station.

"That's because we're going out on a different line than we came in on."

It didn't really matter to her where they were going, but she wanted to know just the same. "Will this one take us to Leavenworth?"

"Darlin', we're making yet another strategic retreat."

Her heart went insanely light and she exhaled in trembling relief. "You mean we're running away."

"Like rabbits," he admitted, chuckling darkly. "As fast and as far as we can."

They turned a corner and passed through gilt-lettered glass doors that opened to a covered platform. A long train sat on the tracks, the steam from the engine wisping back, rolling around and through the trusses overhead. People moved up and down the wooden walkway and porters loaded huge stacks of baggage into a car at the center of the train. A man in white livery stood at the rear of the last car, watching them approach.

"Good evening, Mr. Tillotson," the man said as they neared. "Mrs. Tillotson. Welcome aboard."

"Thank you," Rivlin said smoothly, all but stopping Maddie's heart. "If you'd be kind enough to see that we're not disturbed before leaving the station, we'd be most appreciative."

"Very good, sir."

Rivlin smiled at her and offered her an abbreviated bow. "After you, my dear."

"Allow me, madam," the other man said, quickly stepping forward to offer his hand in assisting her in climbing the stairs of the car.

She managed the task without tripping over her hem, thanked the porter for his help, and entered the car. The curtains were drawn and the oil lamps had been lit. Even in the soft light, she could see that the car was appointed beyond her imagination. A luxurious feather bed had been turned down, the brass headboard all but hidden by a fluffy bank of lace-trimmed linen pillows. Rivlin came behind her, dropping the bags just inside the door and locking it behind them. He whipped the bowler from his head, grimaced, and flicked it into a corner. Maddie looked at him with an arched brow and said, "Tillotson?"

"I've borrowed the name of one of my brothers-in-law," he explained, coming to her and slipping his arms around her waist. "You're my wife, in case you didn't figure that out. Anne Tillotson."

Maddie twined her arms around his neck. "Your sister."

"Anne is, but you're not." He grinned. "Not by a long shot."

"You could have warned me about the charade," she admonished. "You're lucky I didn't make fools of us both."

"I'm sorry, Maddie." He kissed her tenderly and she forgave him even before he eased away to add, "You handled it beautifully, though." He winked and released her. "I say we've earned a drink. Brandy, darlin'?"

As Rivlin stepped to the beverage table and

poured, Maddie removed her hat and tossed it on the dining table, then stripped off her gloves and tossed them aside as well. Dropping onto the divan, she kicked her slippers off and wiggled her toes. Rivlin handed her a brandy and then went to the bags by the door. She sipped the aromatic liqueur as she watched him take his gun belt from the bag and strap it around his hips. As he came back toward her, she smiled, liking the contradiction of the elegant suit and the easy confidence with which he wore his gun.

He settled into the other corner of the divan, his right foot on the floor, the left on the upholstery so that he used his knee as a rest for his brandy glass. He took a sip, savored it, and then studied her for a long moment before grinning. "For a woman who likes to see the good in people, you did very well back there when we were unraveling the conspiracy."

"It's terribly complicated, isn't it? But at the same time, very simple, too."

"Yep," he drawled. "And above all else, it's high stakes deadly."

From the platform, the conductor called all aboard. The train's whistle blew. The lurch forward came a second later, accompanied by the grinding of metal and the clank of couplings, and followed by two short whistle blasts. With a slowly accelerating clickity-clack, the train rolled forward and out of the station.

Maddie felt the tension ease from her shoulders. She took another sip of the brandy and said, "I remember from my own trial that there are rules about calling witnesses. The prosecutors at Leavenworth had to tell the defense attorneys what they expected me to say. Do you think they know about Harker's connection to the corruption?"

"I can't help but think that they do, Maddie. If you were in the shoes of the Foleys, or Collins or Lane, would you be willing to go to prison while your partner used your trial to get himself elected president?"

"I'd make sure he went with me," Maddie admitted. Rivlin saluted her with his glass and a smile.

"But if the prosecutors know of Harker's involvement in the corruption at Tahlequah," she continued, "why haven't they charged him along with all the others?"

"All I can give you is my best guess, Maddie," he answered. "What would happen if they charged Harker and for some reason or another the jury doesn't buy your testimony linking him and Tom Foley?"

"At the very least Harker would see that they never practiced law again."

Rivlin studied the light through his brandy, saying, "And their personal ambitions would be dashed on the rocks of overconfidence." He took another sip. "No, they're thinking to bring the information to light, let the newspapers run at it and do the digging for dirt. The esquires will bask in the glory of having opened the door to a major scandal and, with any luck at all, be asked to prosecute Harker when the time comes. They'll dance out the other end of it all as candidates for the Supreme Court."

The way his mind worked awed her. He saw threads and the patterns they made that she never would have known to look for. "How do you know all this?"

He gave her a quirked smile. "I didn't just walk away from a suit and a munitions factory, Maddie. I walked away from a world where a man has to think like this every waking hour of his life. There are a helluva lot of Harkers out there and they don't let morality stand in the way of what they want."

His calm acceptance was somehow reassuring. "If the senator is willing to have me killed to keep me from testifying, Tom's life isn't worth a bent penny."

Rivlin finished his brandy. "Tom Foley's a dead man no matter how the trial goes," he said matter-of-factly. "Harker isn't going to leave that loose end dangling. Sam and Bill are dead men, too."

"I saw Harker's face in the station, Rivlin," she ventured solemnly. "He knows we've figured it out."

"He's got to catch us before he can kill us, darlin'," Rivlin declared, rising from the divan and carrying his snifter back to the bar.

"Which is why we're running like rabbits," she observed.

He set his glass down, then turned to lean against the cabinet, his arms crossed over his chest. "We're falling back, Maddie," he said, smiling at her. "We're going to make a stand, but we're going to get to high ground before we do."

Suddenly, she realized that Rivlin wasn't smiling to make her feel better. He wasn't pretending everything would be all right in an effort to get her through a rough patch. He was actually happy. "Rivlin, please correct me if I'm wrong," she said, "but aren't we in a great deal of danger? Surely Senator Harker will move heaven and earth to find us just as fast as he can."

He considered that a moment and then replied, "I'd say you have a very firm grasp of the situation."

"Then why are you smiling?" she asked outright. "Given the gravity of our circumstances, I can't see what it is that you've got to smile about."

"You don't?" His eyes sparkled with amusement.

"No, I don't."

"We have answers to our questions, Maddie," he explained, his voice buoyant. "We're not moving blind anymore. We don't have to helplessly endure circumstances. We can plan and we can act to protect ourselves. We have a better chance of coming out of this alive than we've ever had."

"All right," she said, accepting that he was right about the change and that it was indeed something that fell into the category of generally good. But the clouds of ignorance hadn't been the only ones hanging over them. "We're also earning the warrants for our arrests," she reminded him.

"I suppose we are." He shrugged. Coming back toward the divan, he added, "We'll get it straightened around in the end. We've got good reason for flight." He didn't sit, but leaned down and braced his weight with a hand on either side of her.

"Best of all," he said softly, "I don't have to surrender your custody. And that makes me happy."

Her heart swelled, but she couldn't allow herself to hope. It was false and she knew it. "You'll have to eventually, Rivlin," she gently reminded him, trailing her fingertips along his jaw.

"We'll cross that bridge when we come to it," he countered, leaning closer. "Let's not go looking for it any sooner than we have to, all right?"

His lips brushed hers and Maddie twined her arms about his neck, accepting her uncommon good fortune. The future would come as it willed, but the present was hers to enjoy while she could.

She tasted sweet and one kiss wasn't enough. The second was so warm and delicious that he decided he had to have a third. And the third made him realize that kissing Maddie wasn't enough. Not anymore. Rivlin shifted the balance of his weight, freeing a hand. Laying gentle assault on her earlobe, he drew her skirt upward until he found the hem. Her breathing came in soft, slow catches as he trailed his fingers up her thigh. She sighed in sanction when he unhooked her garter and drew it down.

A knock came at the front door of the car—only a half-second before she gasped and Rivlin vaulted away from her, his hand on the butt of his gun as he put himself between her and the door. He relaxed almost instantly. Casting her a sheepish smile, he started toward the door, saying, "It's the porter."

Her heart racing, Maddie straightened on the divan and smoothed her skirts. The door opened with a rush of wind and noise.

"Good evening again, Mr. Tillotson," she heard the porter say over the clacking of the wheels. "Compliments of the Missouri Pacific Railway."

"Thank you," Rivlin replied. "Over on that table, if you'd please."

The same man who had helped her aboard came into the car, bearing a cloth-covered tray in one hand and a lidded silver bucket in the other. "Madam," he said, acknowledging her with a dip of his chin as he passed. He put the items on the table as instructed and then turned to bow in her direction. "If there's anything we can do to make your journey with us more pleasurable," he said, "please let me know. I'm at the rear of the next car forward. You need only pull the silver cord to summon me."

"Thank you," Maddie answered with what she hoped looked like a serene and gracious smile. As he turned and moved toward the forward end of the car, Maddie rose and went to the table, reminding herself to ask Rivlin how one was supposed to properly respond to servants. She'd never been waited on in her life and she didn't want to make a mistake that would give them away.

As the porter and Rivlin exchanged parting pleasantries, she lifted the cloth on the tray. Apples and pears and plums had been arranged in the center, surrounded by little crustless sandwiches and wedges of cheese. A silver-handled knife had been tucked carefully along the edge. Maddie lifted the lid on the silver bucket and found a green bottle nestled in chipped ice. She turned it just enough to read the label. *Champagne.* She'd heard of champagne. It was supposed to have bubbles in it that tickled your nose.

"Looks good, doesn't it?" Rivlin said, coming toward her.

"Compliments of the Missouri Pacific Railway?" she asked.

"I'll tell you about that later," he promised, stepping behind her and wrapping her in his arms. He pressed kisses to her nape, saying, "At the moment, I'm tired of talking. Now, where were we when we were interrupted?"

"We were on the divan," she whispered, her body thrilling at his touch.

He kissed his way to the hollow behind her ear as he began opening the line of buttons up the front of her dress. "What were we doing?"

She could hardly breathe. "You were kissing me in a most delightful and suggestive manner."

"Suggestive? I thought I was being very direct about it. I was also working on your garter."

"Yes, I know." Leaning back into him, she closed her eyes and sighed. "It's creeping down my leg."

"Must be terribly uncomfortable," he said,

drawing down the bodice of her dress. "Would you like to get rid of it?"

As though you could think about garters when a man was sliding your bodice off your shoulders and down your arms. She laughed softly and said, "It would be very kind of you." Her gown pooled around her feet and his hands trailed back up her arms to her shoulders, the caress making her shiver with delight.

"And wouldn't you like to get rid of your hairpins, too?" he asked, kissing her bare shoulder even as he set to the task.

"Yes, please," she heard herself whisper. "That would be lovely."

Rivlin smiled. Lovely didn't even begin to describe how he felt about the seduction of Maddie Rutledge. It was as if he'd waited his whole life for this chance. He dropped the hairpins on the carpet and uncoiled her braids, then unbound them to run his fingers through the dark cascade of shimmering waves. They were warm and scented of lavender.

"It's your turn to be touched," she said quietly, drawing away from him.

"Then touch," he offered, guiding her out of the circle of her discarded dress.

She looked up at him, her eyes bright with happy anticipation. "Truly? You'll let me?"

All he could do was nod. She smiled as she undid his stolen tie and dropped it among the hairpins, then began unbuttoning his shirt. He watched her, intoxicated by the joy with which she accomplished the task. Blindly, he untied his holster and unbuckled his gun belt. He tossed it in the direction of the bed, but couldn't say whether it hit the mark or not. Maddie's hands were skimming over his chest, her lips parted and her breasts rising and falling in quick cadence. His shirt was pushed from his shoulders with artful ease and as he extracted his arms from the sleeves she leaned forward to kiss the place where his heart hammered against the wall of his chest.

Her hands came down his sides, over his hips, and then slipped around to glide with gentle pressure upward over the muscles of his thighs. He closed his eyes, the expectation pounding through his veins. His breath caught as she deliberately traced the hard length of him. She did it again and he strangled on a moan of pleasure.

"You don't like that?" she asked quietly, touching him.

"I like it very much," he managed to say. "How do you know—"

"Myra talked. I listened."

"God, you listened well, didn't you?"

"I hope so," she whispered, slowly tracing the length of him again. She unbuckled his belt and worked open his buttons. Her hands, warm and sure, followed the angle of his hips downward, sliding his pants before them. Her fingers trailed up his thighs.

"Maddie," he groaned.

"Mmm?"

He exhaled long and hard to steady himself. He opened his eyes and met her gaze. She smiled, moving slowly and without the slightest hint of subterfuge. He knew what she was about to do and that he wouldn't have stopped her even if he could have. When she took him in her hands, his universe collapsed until it contained only her touch and his only need became drowning his desire in the full promise of this incredible woman. He endured the exquisite torture for as long as he could and then reached for her, slipping his hands around her narrow waist and bending down to capture her mouth with his.

He kissed her with fierce tenderness, a wordless confession of the hot spur of desire and a warning of what was to come. Her lips parted and she leaned into him, her hands skimming over his back and lower. He felt the firmness of her breasts against his chest, the smoothness of her thighs warm against his own. He wanted to go slowly, wanted to savor the delights of her, but the hunger was too demanding. He worked the laces of the corset, wanting it gone and knowing that he didn't have the patience for stockings and garters. He'd apologize later. He'd love her, apologize, and then love her again—the way she deserved and needed to be loved.

He reached the top of the lacings and Maddie sighed, low and hard, as the tension eased. She arched, further loosening the laces. He brought his hands around to cup the fullness of her breasts, to tease the hardened crests with the pads of his thumbs.

Maddie spiraled into a universe of shimmering, ruby heat and throbbing desire, a world she didn't know, a place where Rivlin had taken her. Rivlin. . . . Had she called his name? It didn't matter. He was there. He touched her. He kissed her with a feverish hunger equal to her own. She was whirling downward, falling, but she went without struggle, safe in Rivlin's arms.

For a heartbeat another reality intruded, the feel of the cool cotton sheets and the soft feather mattress against her side. And then it was gone, obliterated by the warmth of Rivlin's body hard along the length of hers, easing her back and pressing her down, his hips circling against her own. She moved beneath him, instinctively answering his body with her own. Low sounds rumbled in his chest as he settled between her thighs.

Rivlin moaned at the willingness of her surrender, at her readiness. She moved beneath him, arching up to accept him, and he gasped at the shuddering, gripping welcome of her body. Her hands were on his chest, her long legs wrapped around his, holding him as she arched up in a primal plea.

He answered it and found her maidenhead. She cried out, instinctively let go of him and tried to scramble back. Rivlin went still within her, caught her hips with his hands, and held her as he whispered, "Easy, Maddie. Easy."

She looked up at him. Her hair fanned across the pillows, framing eyes wide with apprehension. Her lips were wet and swollen from his kisses, her skin flushed with desire, her breasts taut and hard budded.

He dredged up every scrap of gallantry he could find. "I'll stop if you want."

She searched his eyes and then slowly shook her head. Her hands slipped up his chest to rest on his shoulders. "What I want is you."

The words echoed softly, touching a place he had long ago closed away. He braced his lower body, angled her hips, and claimed her. The cry strangled in her throat as she closed her eyes. He went still as her fingers dug into his shoulders, returning to him in part the pain he'd given her. If he could have, he'd have taken all of it for her.

"I'll never hurt you again, Maddie," he whispered. "Never again."

Maddie knew that he meant it, knew to the center of her soul that she was safe with him. In the warmth of that certainty, the pain ebbed. She felt his hands ease on her hips, felt him shift his weight and begin to draw away. The friction of his movement within her triggered a wave of exquisite pleasure that obliterated all memory of pain. "Don't go," she gasped, reaching for him, desperate to keep him where he was, wanting more. "Please."

Rivlin groaned, both in delight and frustration. He couldn't deny her command, couldn't deny the heady wonder of possessing her, of being possessed by her. He'd thought to begin again, to seduce her gently, to gradually make her forget the hurt he'd caused. He'd made her his and he'd thought he had all the time in the world to see that she didn't regret her surrender. But she arched up, drawing him deeper, and forever ceased to matter. There was only Maddie and now and the overwhelming need to loose himself in loving her. God, he was going to spend forever apologizing to her.

He came back to her, filling her with an achingly delicious warmth that washed through and consumed her. She was at once satisfied and starving, reveling in the attainment and yet craving a deeper taste of its sweetness. Obedient to ageless instinct, her hands slipped down the length of his torso, stopping only when they found the lean hardness of his narrow hips. She held him to her, delighting in the corded strength of the muscles beneath her hands, rising to meet him, riding ever upward on the driving, pulsing rhythm of their dance.

Rivlin rode the waves of her glorious, shuddering climb, letting her draw him higher. The swiftness of their ascent was breathtaking, magnificently beyond his power to control, the intensity of their hunger impossible to resist. Reckless abandonment was his only choice, an explosive, soaring release his reward.

The downward spiral was lusciously slow, thrumming his sated senses. God, if he died right now, it'd be all right. He'd never in his life felt so good, so absolutely, mindlessly completed. Maddie. It was Maddie who made him feel this glorious.

He tilted her chin up and brushed her lips with his. The corners of her mouth lifted in a sated smile. Her eyes fluttered open. Her breathing was as winded as his own, her eyes dark, soft, and full of wonder. "Oh, Rivlin," she whispered.

He was light-headed. "I ought to tell you I'm sorry for taking you so fast. I didn't mean to."

She snuggled closer to him, kissed his shoulder. "But are you sorry?"

"Oh, God, Maddie, I should be," he admitted, his senses slowly grounding. "But it was too wonderful to regret. You're wonderful."

She laughed, softly, luxuriously. "You *do* give as good as you get."

Rivlin grinned. "Yeah, well, you're no small inspiration, darlin'." He nuzzled his face in her hair and decided that while he had his wits about him, it was time to get rid of her corset. And her garters and stockings, too. "What do you say to spending the next week right here in this bed?" he asked, pulling the laces from the eyelets. When the lace came out of the last hole, he threw it blindly away, then trailed his hands up her back.

She arched against him, murmuring, "That feels delicious."

He smiled and gently rolled her onto her back. The corset went the same way the lace had. "I haven't even started toward delicious yet, Maddie," he said softly, leaning down to kiss the swell of her breast. "But we'll get there."

SHE LAY IN RIVLIN'S ARMS, her back to his chest, his warmth and power curled around as he slept. Maddie smiled. They'd found delicious. And then divine and then exquisite. She'd had no idea how infinite were the ways to make love, how many sensations there were to be had. And there was something to be said for slow and easy, for savoring each little tingle, each small ripple of pleasure. She'd accused him of torture and he'd laughed and in the end the completion had been more than she could have ever expected. Myra had been right. Rivlin Kilpatrick could indeed make the stars burn brighter and the world spin crazily. He'd made her laugh and moan and gasp and feel so wondrously alive, so special and wanted. Maddie sighed and snuggled back against him. His arms tightened around her and she knew that if she were ever granted just one wish, it would be to spend the rest of her life making love with Rivlin Kilpatrick.

Chapter Eighteen

It was dark outside when Rivlin stirred and she awoke. He kissed her cheek and asked, "Can I get you some champagne?"

"Oh, yes, please," she answered as he climbed from the bed. "And while you're up, tell me how we've come to have such luxury compliments of the Missouri Pacific Railway."

Rivlin grinned and pulled the bottle from the ice. "Albert's a major stockholder in the company." He ripped the foil off the top of the bottle. "If you're going to command a private car on word alone, it's best to use an owner's name."

Maddie inched upward until her back was propped up by the pillows. He'd attacked a man, stolen his clothes, and then commanded a private car pretending to be his brother-in-law, who happened to own part of the railroad. She'd always considered Rivlin to be the epitome of right and law-abiding conduct. But he was apparently very good at being bad. For some unfathomable reason that realization thrilled her. "Well," she managed to say, "you did tell me that your sisters married well. I wasn't thinking in terms of this well, though."

"For wealthy women, they're remarkably down-to-earth." He turned the bottle away and worked the cork up with his thumbs. "I'm not saying it's going to happen right from the git go, but eventually you'll like my sisters. You'll like my mother, too."

The cork blew across the car with a loud, accompanying pop. Maddie's pulse shot through her with much the same sort of suddenness.

"You look like a rattler just slid under the sheets," Rivlin observed offhandedly, carrying the bottle to the bar.

She knew the answer, but asked anyway. "Are we going to Cincinnati?"

He poured a tall glass full of bubbles. "I didn't mention that?"

"No. No, you didn't."

He poured a second glass of the champagne, saying, "I was working my way there when the porter interrupted. And then I got distracted by other things.

"Maddie," he said, bringing her a glass, his expression somber as he slipped back into bed and wrapped an arm around her shoulders, "if we hope to come out of this alive, we're going to need help that's just as powerful as Harker. I've been cut off from the Marshal Service and the only place I have left to go is home. The only people we can trust are my family."

"And you think your family can beat Harker?"

He smiled and winked. "I know they can. All we have to do is get there in one piece."

"That might prove to be a bit difficult."

"Have faith, Maddie," he said quietly. "Trust me and have faith."

She did. She believed in Rivlin Kilpatrick to the center of her soul. He clinked his glass against hers and the confidence and warmth of his smile wrapped around her heart. Beneath her feet, the wheels rolled over the tracks and sang a simple, repetitive song. *Love*him*love*him*love*him.

She could hardly breathe. Love him? Oh, dear God. No, she couldn't love him. The heartache would destroy her.

"Did that rattlesnake bite you, darlin'?"

She blinked, startled from her panic and momentarily confused. Maddie grasped blindly at the straw he'd given her. "What rattlesnake?"

"The one that slid in here when I mentioned meeting my mother and sisters. You have that just-bit look on your face."

"Yes, it did," she lied, desperate for distraction. "I'd prefer to avoid meeting your family if at all possible."

"Why?"

Her heartbeat was mercifully slowing. She took a deep breath. "Rivlin, you're an intelligent man. Think."

"You're afraid you won't fit in my family," he said quickly and with certainty. He gave her a quirked smile as he added, "Darlin', *I* don't fit in my family."

"And that's supposed to make me feel better about the prospect?" she countered dryly.

"They'll be nice to you."

"Of course they will. They're undoubtedly very well mannered." She decided there was nothing to do but confess the most elemental truth. "Rivlin, I don't know how to be a lady. My stomach goes cold at having to deal with the porter. I don't know if I'm doing it anywhere close to right. And you want to plunk me down in front of a wall of privileged petticoats?" She closed her eyes and imagined her reception in the parlor. "God, I'd rather go back to prison."

He tilted her chin up and waited until she opened her eyes before saying, "You'll do fine, darlin'. Being a lady doesn't have a thing to do with money or social privilege. You did perfectly well with the porter. All you have to do is be yourself, Maddie, your naturally gracious self."

He had the most wonderful eyes, so soft and gentle. You could believe anything was possible when you looked into Rivlin's eyes. And when he smiled . . . When he kissed you . . . It would be easy to love him. Her pulse skittered again. "Do you intend to tell your family what I am?"

"They'll be able to see for themselves what you are, Maddie—an incredible, beautiful woman." He hesitated for a moment. "But I know what you're asking and, yes, I've got to tell them what's happened to you. I need their help and the only way they can do what needs to be done is if I tell them the whole story."

It was going to be awful. Better, she told herself, to know just how awful before heading into it. "When was the last time you wrote a letter home?"

"Can't say that I remember," he answered offhandedly. "I don't think I have since joining the Marshal Service, anyway."

Good God. It was getting worse by the second. "And after years of silence, you intend to walk back into your family's lives, present your murderess lover, tell them about the plot to kill us, and then expect them to happily help us?"

"That's what families do for each other, Maddie," he replied quietly, not the least bit daunted by the picture she'd painted.

Maddie took a long drink of her champagne. The Kilpatricks might be willing to help because he was one of theirs, but she had no illusions about how they were going to feel about her. There was no point in trying to get Rivlin to see the situation from her perspective, however. He couldn't. He wouldn't. It was going to be horribly, horribly unpleasant, but there was no way to avoid it as long as she was with Rivlin and his mind was set. She'd just have to get through it somehow.

"I sent Everett a telegram from Kansas City," Rivlin said, obviously trying to soothe her disquiet. "They know we're coming in, Maddie. It won't be a complete surprise to them. They also know trouble's coming on our tails and that we need help."

Wonderful, she silently groused. *They'll meet us at the station with stones in hand and I won't have to worry about Harker.* "Who's Everett?" she asked gloomily.

"Emily's husband. He's a newspaper publisher."

A faint ripple of relief crept through her. "And you're hoping he'll print our story in his paper."

"There's no hoping to it, darlin'." His smile was wide again. "The minute he reads that telegram his eyes are going to light up and he's going to start setting type. Count on it. The only thing he's going to grumble about is the fact that this didn't fall into his lap last fall when it could have made a difference in the presidential election."

"I gather he supported Mr. Greeley," Maddie

offered absently, wondering just how much Rivlin had managed to put in the telegram.

"He and Horace are good friends. They go way back."

Good friends. Of course. Maddie sighed in exasperation. If he was going to drag her among the lions, the least he could do was flat-out tell her how big and how mean they were so she could start looking for a big enough stick. "You have one brother-in-law who owns a sizable portion of the Missouri Pacific Railway. Another who's personal friends with Mr. Horace Greeley, who happens to have run for the presidency last year. That's two of the five. No more surprises, Rivlin. What do the other three do?"

"Charlotte's husband, Will, is a federal judge. Liz's husband, Lawrence, owns both a shipping company and a transport company. Mary's husband, Leander, is an Ohio state senator. He'll probably be governor someday soon."

He didn't talk about his family any differently than he did cowboys, railroad conductors, and saloon keepers. "That's very impressive."

He drank, shrugged, and countered, "Like I said, I don't fit in with my family."

"I suspect that's by choice." The movement was tiny, but she felt it nonetheless. She'd hit the truth so square on he'd flinched.

"Darlin'," he drawled, recovering quickly and raising his glass in salute, "the sad truth is that I lack serious ambition. It's a typical character flaw of boys who are raised wealthy. We grow up into men who don't like to work. I'm sorry to disillusion you."

Disillusion her? No. He was lying to her through his teeth. "Ambition isn't necessary. You could have easily ridden your brothers-in-law's coattails to a social position just as lofty as theirs, but you didn't. You walked away from all the money and the power. Why? If you're going to drag me into your family, I deserve to know the truth, Rivlin."

As he had the night he'd told her about Seth, he held his silence for a long while. Maddie waited, watching him struggle with the decision of how much of himself he was willing to share. He emptied his glass and climbed from the bed. He stepped to the table and stood there looking at the food, not seeing it, his eyes dark as he stared into the past. The rails sang.

"When I was young," he said softly, "I was going to own the world, be a captain of industry like all the men who came to my parents' parties. It was just a matter of picking which industry to conquer first." He laughed dryly and reached for the champagne bottle, adding, "And then I marched blithely off to the war and had my sights readjusted."

He filled his glass, put the bottle back in the ice, then picked up the tray of food and brought it to her.

"I remember the first night I was home when it was over," he began, his voice softly cynical, as he settled in beside her again. "My parents threw a huge welcome home Rivlin affair, inviting most of Cincinnati and all the lords of power. I was the hero, the prodigal son returned to their bosom with the rank of captain and a stack of sterling commendations signed by General Grant himself. I had my hand pumped and my back slapped until I hurt. And my father's business associates laid the world at my feet, promising me all that I'd dreamed of when I'd been a boy."

He sighed and gave her a bittersweet smile. "And I stood there, Maddie, watching it all swirl around me and thinking that everyone was putting a helluva lot of effort into getting things that didn't matter. I was alive. I had clothes on my back and my stomach wasn't empty. I had both my arms and both my legs and my mind hadn't been twisted by the horror. It was enough for me, Maddie. I stood there and realized that I didn't want anything beyond what I already had."

The rails sang loudly in the wake of his words and the song echoed in her soul.

"I should have left the next morning, but I didn't," he went on, his voice suddenly more animated. "I stayed, trying, I suppose, to catch the fever again. It didn't work. Then one Sunday afternoon we were all together for dinner. I don't remember what the conversation was about or even what contribution I made to it, but Emily turned to me and asked where her brother was; told me she didn't know the man I'd become. And I looked around the table and saw that they were all thinking the same thing and that only Emily had the guts to say it. I didn't fit anymore and I knew I never would again. They knew it, too." He drank. "I left the table and the house and the next morning I reenlisted."

"But you tried again when your father died," she said.

He nodded sadly. "Duty wasn't enough, Maddie. It didn't change what was there and how I felt about it. I fit even worse than I had the first time and everyone was as miserable as I was." With a shrug he added, "So I spared us all and left again."

"And now you're going home a third time."

"It won't go any better than it has before," he said on a hard sigh. "I know that. I wouldn't even *think* about going back if I had any other choice."

His gaze came to hers and held it, searching. The corners of his mouth lifted the tiniest bit. "Just stand by me, Maddie. I won't feel so alone if you do. You understand."

The song came again, not from the rails, but from the depths of her heart. It was a mistake, but it was made and couldn't be undone. She loved him. He needed her and if he had a thousand sisters, she'd face them, every single one of them, and defend him with all her might. Let them think whatever they wanted to of her. The only person in the world who mattered was Rivlin.

She would never tell him. It would be easier that way. It would keep things from getting more complicated than they already were, the goodbye from hurting any deeper than it was going to. But in the time they had left together, she'd let her heart whisper it to her soul. And in all the tomorrows there would be without him, she'd listen to the echoes of the refrain and remember how she had been so close to completely whole.

Maddie set her glass on the table, took his from him, and set it aside as well. He put the food tray out of harm's way. "I'll be right there," she whispered, settling astride his legs. "All you'll have to do is reach for me."

RIVLIN LIFTED THE CURTAIN just far enough to see the hazy sunrise on the horizon, then let the cloth fall back into place and watched Maddie sleep. They'd crossed another line together; he could feel it even if he couldn't name it or explain why he felt it so profoundly. They'd taken turns in their first trysts, one leading, the other following, shifting their roles without a word, each sensing what the other needed and wanted and willing to give it. It came as close to perfection as he'd ever imagined.

But the last time . . . Rivlin closed his eyes, remembering. There had been no leader, no follower. It was almost as if they'd been one person instead of two. They'd made love slowly, as though they'd had all eternity to reach the end. And the end . . . God almighty. He'd fallen asleep with his head pillowed on Maddie's breast, knowing a whole new definition of satisfied.

Something had changed between them as they'd come together that time. Like the morning Maddie had come from the ruins of the collapsed farmstead with their muddied belongings, he'd sensed a shift in the way she wore the world as she'd slipped her arms around him. If he'd thought of her as settled that day, he could only think of her as firmly grounded now.

He gently brushed a tendril of hair from her cheek. Madeline Marie Rutledge. A big name given to a little girl nobody wanted. Maddie. A simple name for the complex woman that little girl had become. If only the paths of their lives had crossed earlier.

She stirred and slowly opened her eyes. A soft smile touched her lips as she looked up at him. "Good morning, Rivlin."

"Morning, Maddie," he whispered, tracing the curve of her delicate cheekbone with his fingertip.

"How long before we get to St. Louis?"

She was so beautiful, so gentle and sweet and strong. "Judging by the haze on the horizon, another hour or so."

"Then," she drawled, stretching languidly, "we should be getting up and dressed."

The sheet slid lower on her breasts and caught

tauntingly on the peaks. Rivlin smiled. It was nice to know he could want again after last night. And they didn't need an hour or two to get dressed.

THE PORTER HAD VAULTED up the back steps of the car before it had come to a complete stop, pushed open the door, and nearly fainted as he'd looked down the barrel of Rivlin's revolver. Being held by his shirtfront had undoubtedly been part of the problem, but the man had eventually stammered his way through a cursory explanation. Rivlin had released him, allowed him to take their bags, and then they'd dashed through the St. Louis station for the train literally waiting for them to board.

Maddie suspected that it was a combination of self-preservation, indignation, and a tardy train that led the railroad man to unceremoniously fling their bags into the car behind them and stomp off to the center of the platform. Through the window, she watched him face the front of the train and wave his arms over his head. The whistle blasted once and the train lurched forward on the second.

"This is the last leg, Maddie," Rivlin said, taking off his suit coat as the train surged forward and gathered speed. He grinned. "Damn nice of Lawrence to send one of his cars for us, wasn't it?"

"Lawrence is the . . . ?" she asked, heading toward the silver-laden table in the center of the car.

"Shipping and transport companies," Rivlin quickly answered. "Nothing moves in the Ohio Valley that his people don't touch. Keeping track of it all requires him to travel a great deal."

"And in considerable style," she declared, lifting one of several domed covers. Eggs, bacon, and toast thrilled her senses. "We have breakfast!"

"Smells good. I'll be right there."

He went to the side of the car, his jacket draped over his arm as he stripped away his tie. Maddie covered the plate again and watched as he began working the window latches.

"Thank God I don't have to wear this damn suit anymore," he said, sticking his hand outside and letting the tie flutter away. The jacket quickly followed it. He closed the window and came back to the table, smiling and saying, "If I'd known Lawrence's car was going to be here and that I wasn't going to have to beg, borrow, or steal one for us, I could have pitched the whole god-awful getup out the window the minute we left Kansas City. I'll get shed of the rest of it after I eat. What have we got?"

She lifted the silver cover with a flourish and his smile broadened. "Have a seat, Miss Rutledge," he said, drawing out a chair for her. "And allow me to serve."

She smoothed her skirt and sat. "You'll tell me how I'm supposed to be served so I'll know when we get your mother's house?"

"If you think it's necessary and it'll make you feel better." He picked up the silver pot from the tray. "Would you care for coffee, madam?"

"Yes, please."

He made a move to pour and then stopped, his grin roguish and his eyes bright with mischief. "It's going to cost you a kiss."

She laughingly paid the price and while he held to his end of the bargain and filled her cup, she asked, "And what's the cost of eggs and bacon and toast?"

He set the coffeepot down and picked up the platter. He winked as he held it down for her to scoop a portion onto her own plate. "It's a damn good thing we've got a day and a half before we roll into Cinci."

"Outrageous," she countered, enjoying their game.

"I'm thinking there's a pretty good chance of that."

His eyes twinkled and she decided that she'd never seen him happier.

Chapter Nineteen

The last few days had been more than she'd ever had reason to expect, Maddie told herself as the train came into a tiny station, a few miles east of Cincinnati. She should be remembering the wonder of them and not dreading the hours ahead. But being even slightly cheerful was impossible. The respite was at an end.

Looming ahead of her was a wealthy family and the shadow of Senator John Harker. And beyond that—assuming she survived both of the ordeals—waited a return trip to Kansas City, the trial, and then eighteen years of prison. If Rivlin wouldn't have been so disappointed in her, she might have seriously considered throwing herself under the wheels of the train and being done with it. It wasn't as though she had anything particularly pleasant to look forward to once she stepped from the car. And simply enduring didn't promise the same kind of satisfaction it once had.

"You're not thinking about bolting on me, are you, Maddie?"

"Not exactly," she replied, giving him what she could muster of a smile. "But I am thinking that I'd really rather not get off this train."

He settled his hat low across his brow as the train stopped. "I wouldn't mind riding a while longer with you, Maddie," he said, opening the rear door.

"But it's time for us to pay the piper," she finished for him, accepting his hand and allowing him to assist her down the steps. "I've enjoyed the journey, Rivlin. Thank you."

"We'll have the one back to Kansas City, too."

She didn't mention that she thought it highly unlikely that the Marshal Service would let him escort her across a street much less across the country again. If he managed to keep his badge once the truth of their relationship was known to his superiors, he'd be lucky if they didn't chain him to a desk somewhere.

"Well, I'll be damned," Rivlin drawled, as they made their way down the platform and toward the depot. "Everett's thought of everything."

Maddie followed the line of his gaze past the building and saw the closed carriage parked in the street. A driver sat holding the reins. Another man stood at the carriage door. He was fiftyish, short, slender, and impeccably dressed.

As Rivlin guided her in his direction, the man smiled, turned on his heel, and smartly opened the carriage door. "Good evening, Master Rivlin. It's good to see you again."

"And it's good to see you, Stevens," Rivlin said,

drawing her to a halt before the man. "May I present Miss Madeline Rutledge." As Stevens bowed his head in acknowledgment, Rivlin added, "Maddie, this is Stevens. He's been a family retainer since I was in short pants. He knows enough to blackmail me forever."

"It's very nice to meet you, Stevens," Maddie said, sensing that blackmail would never cross Stevens's mind. "But how on earth did you know that we'd be getting off the train here rather than in Cincinnati?"

"Mr. Broadman anticipated Master Rivlin's caution," the man explained. "In the unlikely event that he hadn't appeared on the platform, I was to search him out and advise him that the constabulary is quite prepared for his arrival in Cincinnati."

Rivlin asked, "Do they have the house under surveillance?"

"A fact which is not sitting well with your mother, sir."

"I can imagine," Rivlin admitted with a wry smile. "So what's Everett's plan for getting us into town?"

"It was actually Mr. Caruthers's idea, sir. The family is assembling at Spring House for a late supper. Should anyone happen to inquire, the pretext is your sister and Senator Billington's return from Columbus. They should have arrived within the last hour."

"Everett certainly marshaled the clan, didn't he?"

Stevens fought to keep the corners of his mouth still. "Miss Emily was of the opinion that a two-page telegram warranted such an assembly. I do believe her exact words were: 'Rivlin hasn't strung this many words together in ten years.'" He indicated the carriage with a sweep of his gloved hand. "If you and Miss Rutledge would care to board, we'll be on our way."

"Hello, Jansen," Rivlin called up to the driver as Maddie climbed inside.

"Good to have you home again, sir."

"Thank you."

Rivlin came through the door and settled into the seat beside her as Stevens closed the door behind him. The carriage rocked slightly as the Kilpatrick retainer climbed up to the box and in the next second they rolled smoothly into the twilight.

"Spring House?"

Rivlin tossed his hat on the seat opposite them. "It's a place Father bought so Mother could escape the city. Over time it's become something of her tribute to Marie Antoinette's gardens at Versailles."

Her stomach pounded. "I've seen pictures of Versailles in books."

"It's not a replica of the palace, Maddie," he assured her. "Don't let it overwhelm you. Remember that it's just a house. It's nothing more than walls and furniture." He took her hands in his, adding earnestly, "And don't let the throng intimidate you, either. By my count, there should be six men besides myself, seven if John brings his eldest, Adam. There'll be seven women and you."

Fourteen strangers. "And will everyone be carrying name placards so I can keep them straight?"

"It'll be all right, Maddie. They don't bite."

She'd have preferred that they did. She could have consoled herself with the knowledge that if they so much as bared their teeth, she could pick something up and smack them on the nose with it.

Rivlin released one of her hands and slowly trailed his fingers over the curve of her breast. She gasped as the warmth of his touch rippled through her and he drawled, "You look like you need distracting."

And he could easily do so. But for once, trepidation and common sense were stronger than desire. "I don't need to add difficulties to my reception by arriving at your mother's looking . . . looking . . ."

"Tumbled," he supplied, grinning wickedly.

"Thank you," she countered, fighting a smile. "Tumbled."

He laughed and took her hand again. "Just so you know, darlin' . . . You wouldn't be the first woman to arrive at Spring House hitching up her garters. I've seen Em, Anne, and Liz come out of their husbands' carriages with very rosy cheeks and extremely wrinkled skirts."

Maddie mentally tallied those three sisters as having potential for being a bit understanding of their brother's relationship with her. "What about Charlotte and Mary?" she asked warily.

He winced. "Charlotte, as the eldest daughter, will inherit the position of family matriarch when Mother passes to the great beyond. Char's been practicing *staid* since she was fourteen years old. Mary is very conscious of what people think of her. She always has been. I'm sure it's what makes her a good political wife."

"She must be shy."

Rivlin snorted. "Mary's not shy. She just doesn't want anything said about her that might be considered even slightly scandalous. Of all my sisters, she's the one I have the least patience with."

No, he wouldn't have patience with anyone who compromised themselves for the sake of others' expectations. He hadn't lived by pretenses in his own life and he'd prodded her to honesty when she'd tried to be someone other than herself with him.

Still, it was one thing to be true to yourself and another to blatantly disregard social conventions. Walking the fine edge was a daunting challenge, especially after having been with Rivlin and so free to be herself of late. "I'll try not to step on anyone's toes or create any scenes while we're here," she promised. "Which of the husbands should I be careful not to offend?"

He considered her for a moment and then replied, "Don't worry about the men, darlin'. Come at them as square on as you'd like. They'll appreciate the directness. As for stepping on toes and creating scenes . . ." He tightened his grip on her hands. "Maddie," he said firmly, "don't you *dare* let anyone wipe their boots on you. If they ask to have their toes smashed, you oblige them. If they want a scene, give them one they'll remember for the rest of their lives. And if there's a problem bigger than you can handle, you come find me. Understood?"

"Yes." He would stand between her and his family. *I love you, Rivlin.* She kept the words to herself, but couldn't resist the urge to lean forward and kiss him soundly.

"Careful," he admonished, his eyes sparkling, his arms going around her waist and drawing her close. "I wouldn't want to look tumbled when I get out of the carriage."

THE CARRIAGE SLOWED, turned to the right, and began a slow ascent up what was—judging by the sound—a cobbled drive. Maddie reached for the window flap, but Rivlin caught her hand and brought it to his lips.

"Are you trying to keep me from seeing the house?" she asked.

"Take it a little piece at a time," he advised. "It's easier that way."

She wasn't properly grateful for his intervention until Stevens opened the carriage door. They sat in a portico before a set of granite steps at least fifteen feet wide. Six tiered slabs led up to a massive set of oaken doors. Huge oil lamps burned brightly on either side of the panels and smaller lamps flanked the stairs on each end.

Rivlin snatched his hat from the seat, slapped it on his head, and stepped out of the coach. As he turned back and extended his hand for her, she heard a booming voice fill the space behind him.

"It's high time you dragged in here!"

He grinned, extracted her from the carriage, and then turned, shaking the offered hand and saying, "Good to see you again, Everett."

Maddie barely had time to note the man's rather bearlike appearance when Rivlin drew her forward and said, "Maddie, this is Everett Broadman. Everett, Maddie Rutledge."

"It is indeed a pleasure, Miss Rutledge."

"I've heard a great deal about you, Mr. Broadman," she said, feeling instantly at ease. "Thank you for your assistance in getting us here safely."

His dark eyes twinkled and his smile was broad. "Well, I couldn't have done any less and hoped to continue living at home. We'll be sitting down together fairly soon so that I can get the details of the story from you. If it would be acceptable to you, I'd like to dispense with the formalities and use our given names."

"It would be a relief," she admitted, liking the man more with every second that passed.

"I'd encourage you to approach the others with

the same sense of freedom," he went on, heading up the steps. "All except Mother Kilpatrick, of course. She tends to be a bit traditional. One of the privileges of age, you know."

Maddie tucked her hand around Rivlin's arm and gathered her skirt in her free hand, saying, "I'll bear that in mind, Everett, and thank you for mentioning it."

They were halfway up the stairs when Everett paused with his hand on the brass door pull. He looked between them and his smile turned wide again. "You'd best clearly establish your claim on her, Riv. Adam's every bit the young man you were."

"Adam's welcome to try to take her from me if he's a mind to," Rivlin replied easily. "Every young man should be knocked into next week at least once. It's good for his character."

Everett's laughter boomed through the portico as he yanked open the door and preceded them inside. Maddie would have frozen on the threshold if Rivlin had given her half a chance. He didn't though, and she had no choice but to keep moving through what looked like a long stone cave. The walls were made of granite blocks and decorated with large oil paintings in ornately carved and gilded frames. The ceiling was vaulted and paneled in deeply recessed boxes of dark wood. The floor was marble and their footsteps rang around them as they made their way toward the far end of the cavern. Her hands and feet were cold and numb by the time Rivlin steered her toward an open set of double doors. Rivlin removed his hat and dropped it on a large chest sitting just outside.

As formidable as the entryway had been, going back was preferable to going any further forward. Rivlin's family all stood, en masse, at the far end of the richly appointed and softly lit room, a wall of suits and fancy dresses and keen appraisal. Maddie instantly felt poor and inconsequential and horribly overwhelmed. Rivlin placed his free hand over hers and squeezed it as he led her further into the lions' den.

The lone older woman stepped forward as they did, the lamplight glinting in her silver hair, her arms outstretched and her smile wide. "Rivlin, sweetheart. Welcome home, son. I've missed you so much."

Mrs. Kilpatrick met them halfway and Rivlin released his hold on Maddie to step into his mother's embrace and kiss her cheek. It occurred to Maddie that now would be the time to bolt if she were going to. Mrs. Kilpatrick had Rivlin by the shoulders and it didn't look like she was planning to let loose of her son anytime soon.

Rivlin must have read her mind because he chose that moment to step back and reach for her. Gently taking Maddie by the hand, he drew her forward to stand at his side in front of his mother.

"Mother, I'd like you to meet Miss Madeline Rutledge."

The gaze that met Maddie's was appraising. Her voice as cool as the polite smile she offered as she said, "Miss Rutledge. Welcome to Spring House."

"Thank you, Mrs. Kilpatrick." Then, because she felt she needed to say something more, Maddie added, "You have a lovely home."

"Thank you. How is that you've made Rivlin's acquaintance?"

The question was casually posed, but Maddie knew it had been meant to knock her off balance. It had worked. How was she supposed to answer?

Even as she scrambled for a solution, Rivlin tightened his grip on her hand and intervened.

"I consider it to have been by fortuitous circumstance," he said, his smile easy.

"I am under the impression, Rivlin," his mother countered, "that your circumstances at the moment could better be described as perilous."

"I'd say that's fairly accurate."

Maddie caught the inside of her lip between her teeth as Mother Kilpatrick's brow inched slightly upward.

"Would it also be accurate to conclude that Miss Rutledge is the cause?"

Again, while the tone of the question was conversational and polite, the underlying intent was anything but. Rivlin's shoulders shifted back and he lowered his chin. Maddie felt the tension vibrate through his body and she held her breath.

"Mother," he said slowly, "understand this very clearly. Maddie and I met because of circumstances beyond our control. And while those circumstances still bind us, they are *not* the foundation of our relationship. Yes, we're in trouble, both of us, and equally so. If you don't want it brought into your house, we'll understand completely. All you have to do is say so and we'll turn around and walk right back out that door."

There was no dainty inching to Mother Kilpatrick's brow this time. It shot up. She considered her son for a long moment and then she said with regal calm, "You should introduce Miss Rutledge to your family."

His family! She'd all but forgotten they were there. Maddie quickly glanced around the half-circle of people standing behind the Kilpatrick matriarch and saw a sea of faces intently watching Rivlin and his mother. They seemed to have forgotten Maddie existed and an intense wave of relief washed over her.

Rivlin gave his mother a quick nod and drew Maddie around her. As he did, a young man separated himself from the herd and stepped forward, grinning broadly. His shoulders weren't as wide as Rivlin's, but she knew that they would be someday. It looked like he'd been poured from the same mold as the man at her side. This is what Rivlin had looked like, been like when he'd gone off to the war, she realized.

Rivlin chuckled and tucked Maddie's hand around his arm, saying, "This eager person is my eldest nephew, Adam. Make a move to touch her, Adam, and I'll beat you to within an inch of your life."

The threat took just enough wind out of the young man to give him pause. Maddie filled it. "It's a pleasure to meet you, Adam. People tell you all the time how much you favor Rivlin, don't they?"

"Yes, ma'am," he replied, finding his poise and a charming smile. "They do."

"I hope you take it for the compliment it is."

"I do, ma'am. I do."

A shorter, narrower, gray-haired version of Rivlin stepped to Adam's side and clapped a hand on his shoulder. "A fatherly point of advice, Adam. A man should avoid using the phrase *I do* unnecessarily. If it becomes a habit, it can have lifelong consequences." He smiled at Maddie. "I'm John, Rivlin's favorite brother."

And it began. Rivlin didn't so much introduce his male relatives as they eased their way forward and smoothly inserted themselves into the polite conversations. Maddie made careful efforts to keep them straight. Everett, of course, was the bear with the booming voice and easy manner. Albert Tillotson was the pocket watch, carefully trimmed mustache, and rather large paunch covered by an expanse of gray-green brocade. Lawrence Caruthers was a quiet, much more compact version of Everett with piercing dark eyes and huge, gnarled hands. She would have guessed Will Sanderson to be a judge just by looking at him. He was tall and angular, wore wire-rimmed glasses, and his sandy hair was graying at the temples in a way that made him look very distinguished and wise. Senator Leander Billington was impeccably dressed, had a resonant voice and a way of being both open and formal at the same time.

And then there were the women. They were much more reserved than their spouses and the introductions were tight and stiff. John's wife, Martha, soundlessly floated forward to be presented and then just as silently retreated to the rear of the assembly. The moment was so quick that Maddie formed only the vaguest impression of her. It seemed to be exactly what Martha wanted. As Adam favored Rivlin, Charlotte favored their mother. Mary, tall and fair-haired, lacked her political husband's sense of ease, but possessed all of his formality and attention to detail. Elizabeth, or Liz as she ventured to propose, was quiet, but had a generous smile and understanding eyes. It occurred to Maddie that Anne, though a small woman in stature, was accustomed to having the world move at her whispered command. And then there was Emily. Emily had the same unrestrained smile as Rivlin, the same amber sparks in her eyes. Only Emily reached out to touch her in welcome. Only Emily offered her home for

Maddie and Rivlin's use. Gratitude tightened Maddie's throat.

"I see that dinner is served," Mother Kilpatrick said the moment the introductions had been completed. She extended her hand, clearly intending for Rivlin to escort her to the table. There was a tiny moment in which no one moved and then Adam vaulted forward to do the honor. As he led his grandmother past Maddie and Rivlin, she said regally, "Rivlin, please try to remember your manners and remove your weapon before joining us at the table."

Maddie looked up to see Rivlin watch his mother pass through the dining room doors. His smile was quirked, his brow cocked, and Maddie knew that he wasn't going to do as he'd been told. His family paired up by couples, then lined up by age to follow in Mrs. Kilpatrick's wake. As they fell in at the rear of the procession, he leaned down and pressed a kiss to her cheek. "You're doing fine, darlin'," he whispered.

"Are you sure defying her about the gun is a good idea?"

"She's testing to see how far she can push. I've backed up all I'm going to."

Emily looked back over her shoulder to whisper, "And don't you give another inch, either, Maddie. Mother respects strength if nothing else."

They passed into the dining room and while Mother Kilpatrick's scrutiny made a reply impossible, Maddie took the advice to heart and suddenly everything became not only bearable, but almost a game that she had permission to win if she wanted to. It made all the difference in the world. She had to fight a smile when Mother Kilpatrick frowned as Emily *tsk*ed and blithely set about rearranging the place cards on the table so that Maddie and Rivlin were seated side by side and opposite her and Everett. Charlotte sniffed and Mary looked acutely uncomfortable as her gaze darted to each of the others. They were ignored as everyone shifted to take up their newly assigned positions. Adam pulled his grandmother's chair from beneath the table and after a regal pause, she lowered herself into it, granting the others permission to do the same. As the last man seated himself, the servants appeared to wordlessly begin their serving tasks. Maddie carefully patterned her actions after Emily's as the dinner conversation began.

Everett started by asking, "Have you seen any newspapers in the last few days, Riv?"

"The only time we've dared to poke our heads out of a car was to make a run for the next one. Anything interesting to read about?"

"One of the defendants out in Leavenworth hanged himself in his cell."

Rivlin froze for a second, a slice of beef halfway between the serving tray and his plate. "Which one?"

"The alleged ringleader of the conspiracy, Tom Foley."

Rivlin went back to serving himself. "Tom isn't—or rather *wasn't*—the ringleader. And I'll bet you Spring House that he had help climbing into that noose. Any mention of Sam Lane and Bill Collins?"

Everett pondered a moment and then replied, "Not that I recall."

Will added his judge's perspective to the conversation. "With Foley dead, the conspiracy charge will, of course, be largely moot. It was likely to be dropped anyway. The papers also report that the prosecution's witness to the conspiracy escaped custody and can't be found. Without his testimony they have no credible evidence to support the charge."

Maddie saw Everett wince ever so slightly just before Rivlin said, "You didn't tell them the particulars, did you?"

"I thought it best to leave that to you."

Rivlin quietly growled and then met Will's gaze. "The prisoner hasn't escaped. And it's not *his* testimony, it's *hers*."

"The prisoner they want to testify is a *woman*?" Mother Kilpatrick asked. "How do you know that, Rivlin?"

"I'm the marshal assigned to get her to the trial."

Maddie had to give them all credit for the speed with which they put the facts together and arrived at the logical conclusion. The silence was deafening, their frozen motions and stunned expressions as they gaped at her, almost comical. A tiny part of her wanted to laugh. The greatest part of her, however, wanted the floor to open up and swallow her.

"How absolutely fascinating," Anne said with great enthusiasm.

Liz quickly followed her sister's lead. "Rivlin, you really *must* start at the beginning and tell us *everything*."

Maddie exhaled, thankful for Rivlin's sisters' gracious rescue.

"We had no idea that anyone wanted either of us dead until we were out on the trail and the first two attempts were made," Rivlin explained. "A third attempt was made in Wichita and we left there still not knowing who or why someone was trying so hard to see that we died. It wasn't until we reached Kansas City that we figured out Senator Harker was behind it all and why."

"Harker?" Leander repeated, clearly stunned. "John Harker out of Illinois? Are you sure?"

"Not one doubt."

"Oh, for heaven's sakes, Rivlin," Charlotte scoffed. "Senator Harker is a prominent and well-respected member of the Republican party. Why would he want to kill you and Maddie?"

"He wants Maddie dead before she gets to Leavenworth because her testimony is going to implicate his involvement in the conspiracy to defraud."

"Implicate?" Mary gasped. "Have you thought of the possible repercussions? The likelihood of scandal?"

"I know full damn good and well what the repercussions are going to be," Rivlin snapped. "I'm not stupid, Mary. Just because I live west of the Missouri River doesn't mean I don't know what goes on east of it. And—"

He bit off the rest of his words as Maddie gently laid her hand over his. She gave his sister a small smile. "It's the repercussions that motivate Senator Harker to try to kill me, Mary," she said evenly. "If I testify, there'll be an investigation and he stands a good chance of eventually going to prison. Rivlin drew the assignment to escort me to the trial because he and Harker crossed paths during the war and Rivlin knows something of a personal nature that the good senator doesn't want to become public knowledge. As long as Rivlin and I are alive, Senator Harker's chances of becoming president are jeopardized. If we die, then his ambitions can be realized."

Everett beamed. Albert and Lawrence eased back in their chairs as though to better study her.

Leander looked like he was mulling it all over. Will almost smiled and John did—in a most satisfied way. Adam looked awed. The women quickly looked back and forth between Maddie and Rivlin as though seeing them for the first time. All except Charlotte.

"What do you mean 'something of a personal nature'?" she demanded.

Rivlin drew a long, slow breath. "It's not a subject fit for either the dinner table or mixed company and I'm not going to discuss it. You can speculate all you like. I'd suggest that you'll get closer to the truth if you consider the darkest crime you can imagine one man committing against another."

Every man at the table blinked and then slowly eased back in their chairs, their expressions hard and filled with barely contained disgust. Rivlin met each of their gazes in turn, nodding in acknowledgment of their correct assumptions.

"If he's guilty of the crimes you've alleged," Charlotte countered, clearly not grasping the nature of Rivlin's accusations, "then I hardly think you'd be the only two people who pose a danger to him. He would have a very long list of people who would need to be killed."

"Not really," Rivlin drawled. "There's the four men from Tahlequah on trial who know about his involvement in corruption. The most threatening of them—Tom Foley—is dead already. The other three can be disposed of easily enough. No one's going to raise a hue and cry over their demise. What I know, I alone know."

"But what of his staff?" Albert posed. "Surely some of them have to at least suspect that the senator is involved in such nefarious activities."

Everett answered. "There was another interesting

bit of news to come in over the wires in the last few days. Out of Kansas City. It seems that while Senator Harker was en route to lend his moral support to the prosecutors in Leavenworth, his senior aide, Jacob Evans, slipped and fell beneath the wheels of a train arriving in Union Station. Senator Harker immediately canceled his plans to attend the trial and is taking the body back to Washington for burial. He's reported to be heartsick and determined to console the Evans family in person."

"Goddammit."

"Rivlin!" his mother said, slapping her hand on the tabletop.

He ignored her censure. "I should have seen that one coming. Evans was the link between Foley and Harker. Lane and Collins can testify to the connection, but—"

"Their testimony," Will said, "will be regarded as unreliable since they stand to benefit if they can place culpability elsewhere. Maddie, however, has nothing to gain. Her testimony would be extremely damaging. Yes, I can see Harker's motivations very clearly."

"Killing Evans," Emily chimed in, "eliminates a potentially dangerous witness and taking his body back east is the pretext for the senator to so abruptly change his plans about attending the trial. No one will think it at all odd. He'll probably even manage to gain public favor for such a selfless and compassionate response to the tragic—and oh-so-very-timely—death of his senior aide. You have to admit that it's a truly masterful move."

Rivlin nodded. "And Harker knows that this is the only place I had left to go. He's closed down all my other choices. On his way back to Washington, he'll conveniently pass through Cincinnati and tie up the last two loose ends." He looked around the table. "We've been damn lucky so far, but it's time to make a stand and put an end to this." His attention focused on the judicial expert in the family. "Will, what kind of evidence do we need to put Harker behind bars?"

"Given what you've told us," Will said, removing his glasses and cleaning them with his napkin, "I wouldn't focus on tying Harker to the conspiracy to defraud at this point. While it would certainly instigate an investigation, he'd be free while it dragged out. You need him locked away immediately so he no longer poses a threat to your safety." He put his glasses back on his face, adding thoughtfully, "If it were me, I'd want at least a dozen impartial witnesses to his overt attempt to commit murder in the first degree."

"Would one count be sufficient?" Rivlin pressed.

Will shook his head slowly. "Two would make for a stronger case against him. An informal rule of legal thumb, Riv: Always go for more than you think you're going to need or get. Of course, you have to balance that against the danger you're willing to put Maddie in."

"One count will have to do."

"We need to be sure," Maddie protested quietly. "We need to go for the two counts."

"Maddie," he said, turning his head to look at her. His eyes were dark and bright. "It's my sworn duty to keep you safe. You'll do as I say."

She was acutely aware of his family watching them. "Perhaps we should continue this discussion later and make what plans we can at the moment."

"I'm not going to be swayed, darlin'."

She pulled her hand back from his, saying,

"Then it will be one of our more memorable exchanges. I look forward to it."

Albert immediately took the cue and commanded Rivlin's attention. "What do you need us to do to help, Riv?"

"Well, in case I haven't said so, I appreciated the use of one of your cars out of Kansas City. Since Maddie and I will have to go to Leavenworth once Harker's taken care of, it'd be nice if you'd take care of the arrangements for that."

"Consider it done."

Rivlin looked across the table at Everett. "Is Robert Baker still the chief of police in Cinci?" At the other man's crisp nod, Rivlin turned to his political brother-in-law. "Lee, there are federal warrants out for Maddie and me. There's nothing we can do about the marshals who might attempt to execute them, but I'd like to have room to move without worrying about getting arrested by the local police. You and Robert go back, Lee. Can you talk to him for me?"

"I'll go see him first thing in the morning. I've a chip or two I can call in for you."

"Thank you." He met the gaze of the man seated to Leander's right. "Lawrence, I want to know the minute Harker pulls into the station. He can't take his time about coming after Maddie and me without raising questions. He'll come at us fast and I need to know every move he makes. Can you put some of your people on it?"

Lawrence grinned and his eyes shone brightly. "You'll know when he's going to sneeze before he does. How far behind you do you think he is?"

"He'll be in sometime tomorrow. More late than early, I think. It cost him time to deal with Evans and he didn't have the ease of waiting rail cars like we did."

Lawrence pulled a watch from his pocket checked the time, and then put it away, saying, "I'll have men in place by midnight tonight, just in case."

Rivlin smiled at the judge in their midst. "Will, I want you to pretend that you're not hearing any of this."

"Huh?" Will rejoined, cupping his ear and leaning forward. "You'll have to speak up."

Rivlin nodded his thanks and then looked around the table. "I want suggestions from all of you for how to go about forcing Harker to come out in the open to take his shot. I want someplace where he can't hide and where the risk to innocents can be kept to a minimum. The floor's open and I'm listening." He looked at his brother. "John, what are you thinking?"

Maddie ate, listening to the give and take of lightning-fast conversation. Emily and Anne made occasional contributions, but for the most part the female members of the family were spectators. Maddie kept to their ranks, watching them watch Rivlin and finding great pleasure in their wonder.

Chapter Twenty

His mother had decreed it time for the men and women to move to their separate postdinner rooms. Maddie hadn't wanted to go; he'd seen the plea in her eyes. Emily had forestalled his intervention, though, linking her arm through Maddie's and leading her away with a bright, reassuring smile. Maddie wasn't reassured, but she'd lifted her chin, squared her shoulders, and gone nonetheless.

"Damnation, Riv," Everett said, closing the study doors behind them. "That is a very interesting woman."

Interesting? Oh, yes. And so much more. "I like her," Rivlin admitted, accepting a brandy from Albert and a cigar from Lawrence.

Adam snorted from somewhere behind him. "I'd do a *lot* more than like her."

Everett was right, the boy was a great deal like he'd once been. "Watch your mouth, Adam," Rivlin cautioned without looking back at his nephew. "It's going to get you into trouble."

"C'mon, Uncle Riv," Adam persisted. "No man on earth could resist trying to get a taste of that little morsel."

Rivlin slowly turned and took a deliberate step toward his nephew. "*No* one talks about Maddie that way."

Adam's hands instantly came up in a gesture of surrender. "All right. I'm sorry. I won't mention it again."

"Don't even *think* it again," Rivlin declared. "Have I made myself clear?"

Adam nodded, crisply replying, "Yes, sir."

John chuckled quietly and laid his hand on Rivlin's shoulder. "Welcome back, Rivlin. Nice to see you being yourself. It's been a very long time."

He knew what his brother meant, could tell by the others' expressions that they were all thinking the same thing. The subtle lifting of their snifters in a congratulatory salute suggested that it was best to set the matter straight right from the beginning. "Nothing's changed about me, John," Rivlin said with quiet firmness. "I still look at things the same way I did the last time I was here. I'm not planning to stay any longer than I have to."

"What if Maddie wants to stay?" Everett posed, lighting his cigar. "Would you stay if she wanted to?"

The hopeful looks on their faces . . . Rivlin laughed, and biting off the end of his own cigar, replied, "Maddie will be ten steps ahead of me out the door. She doesn't belong here any more than I do and she damn well knows it. If I'd given her a choice in the matter, she'd be a thousand miles away from here already."

Albert considered the closed study doors. "Do you think it's wise to let them have her alone? You know they're going to put her through an inquisition, don't you?"

Yes, he did, and he had mixed feelings about it. The memory of Myra holding him back by his belt came to him and he knew along which path wisdom lay. "I've seen Maddie scrap with the best of them. She can handle anything they throw at her." He lifted his brandy snifter to Albert. "My mother and sisters have met their match."

Will cocked a brow and quietly observed, "Then she's more resilient than she looks."

"Jesus, Will," Rivlin countered, leaning his shoulder against the ornately carved mahogany mantel. "You have no idea what she's been through in her life. Resilient doesn't even begin to describe Maddie." He paused to consider and then added, "Having said that, though, I also have to tell you that she's got a loving heart and a soul as warm and good as I've ever met."

Leander entered the conversation observing, "She certainly seems to have come through your adventures with her grace and pride intact. I don't think I've ever seen anyone put Mary and Char in their places quite so effectively."

"And speaking of the table," John said, "I, for one, feel much more comfortable with certainty rather than assumption. You told us long ago about how he died, but tonight you alluded to . . ." He paused, clearing his throat in an obvious effort to hide the fact that he was fumbling for words. The others shifted about, their gazes darting to each other, their expressions drawn and tight.

"You want to know what happened to Seth

before he died," Rivlin supplied. There were slow nods and quick fortifications with brandy. Rivlin drained his glass and crossed to the sideboard saying, "You've surmised correctly, gentlemen. Seth was beaten and sodomized."

The sound of brandy gurgling from the decanter filled the room. The crystal stopper dropped into the neck with a dull, heavy clunk.

"And it was Harker?" John asked quietly. "Are you sure?"

Rivlin looked down at the dark amber liquid, remembering all the bits and pieces again. "I'm sure," he said, tossing some of the brandy down his throat.

"Why didn't you have him brought up on charges at the time?"

He turned to Albert and gave his brother-in-law the truth. "I was a coward. I thought that if I pretended I didn't know what had happened to Seth, in time I'd either forget or convince myself that it was something other than it was. I assuaged my conscience by thinking that dragging Seth's name through the mud wouldn't bring him back or erase his suffering. And I was wrong on all counts."

"You were only a boy, Rivlin," his brother offered. "You were all of what? Seventeen? Eighteen?"

"Eighteen. And it's no excuse." He emptied his glass again, set it aside, then turned and faced them. "I trust that I have everyone's word that nothing will ever be said of this to Seth's parents. They don't need to know."

Every man nodded somberly. Adam drew a cross over his heart, the gesture so childlike and earnest that Rivlin felt a stab of regret for having spoken so bluntly in the young man's presence. Innocence was such a fragile thing.

"But . . ." Lawrence said quietly. He shifted in

his chair. "The present situation with Harker may take the issue of Seth's parents out of our hands, Riv. If, as Harker fears, you were to make public accusations against him, the Hoskinses couldn't help but hear of it."

"I don't see that he has any other choice," Everett countered. "It's the only leverage Rivlin has."

"I disagree," Will chimed in. "If we can lure Senator Harker into making an attempt—safely and before witnesses, of course—on Rivlin's and Maddie's lives, then he can be incarcerated on those charges and he's politically ruined without Seth's name or the shameful incident ever being mentioned. I'm assuming," he added, turning to Rivlin, "that's how you'd prefer to handle the matter if at all possible."

Rivlin nodded absently. Would it be enough? Would the ruin of Harker's political career be sufficient justice? Could that be accomplished without telling the world what had happened to Seth? Powerful men walked away from criminal charges every day, but matters of morality tended to elicit public outrage that demanded retribution. Could he sacrifice Seth's name and the Hoskinses' illusions to the larger end? God, it would be so much cleaner to simply kill Harker and be done with it.

Rivlin turned the sudden notion over in his mind and saw both merits and drawbacks, the former far outweighing the latter. Given Harker's determination to see him and Maddie dead, killing Harker would be seen as a simple matter of self-defense. Seth would remain unknown to those outside the circle of his family and friends. There was true justice in Harker paying for Seth's life with his own.

And when it was all over, if his obligation to

Seth had been met . . . "Will," he said, bringing his vision into focus on the family's legal expert, "I need to talk to you about getting Maddie an appeal and about how to go about keeping her out of prison while we get ready for a new trial."

"Well, you don't pick small problems, do you?" the man countered, with a small sigh. "The first we can do if we can come up with sufficient grounds. The second . . . Rivlin, you're both fugitives. No competent judge is going to give her the benefit of the doubt and release her to prepare for trial."

"Maddie . . ." Rivlin began, trying to find the words to express his deepest fears. "She doesn't hold to hope, won't let herself do that. There's only a whisker's difference between living with no hope and dying, Will. I'm afraid that if she goes back to prison—even for just a while—she's going to choose the latter."

Everett spoke quietly for a change. "She doesn't strike me as the sort of woman who'd kill herself, Riv. You've said yourself that she's tough."

Rivlin shook his head. "I've seen strong men look at their lives stretching out ahead of them and then calmly ask death to take them. It usually does and without a second invitation. I can see Maddie giving up. I can see it too easily."

Leander, lighting his cigar, said through a blue cloud, "You didn't go into the particulars of her conviction earlier, Riv. What kind of battle are you fighting?"

"She walked into the cabin of one of her students to find a man beating the child to death. He turned and came at Maddie and she shot him. What should have been seen as a case of self-defense went to court as first-degree murder. The judge was the dead man's uncle. Maddie couldn't get a lawyer who'd represent her, and so she defended herself. The judge in the case is the surviving Foley on trial. Tom, his brother, was the Indian agent and the dead man's father."

Will removed his glasses to clean them on his coat sleeve, saying crisply, "She has grounds for appeal on two counts: inadequate representation and a prejudicial bench. Do you have any idea of what evidence she can present in her defense?"

"Only her word," Rivlin supplied. "The girl died."

Will all but deflated in his chair. He managed a semblance of a smile as he said, "I'll talk to Maddie sometime in the next couple of days. Perhaps there's circumstantial material that can be presented to strengthen her position. I'll start the appeal paperwork and find a good lawyer for her."

It was better to know than to just guess, no matter how accurate you thought you were. "You're not optimistic, are you, Will?"

"If I were standing in your shoes, Riv, and having the concerns about Maddie that you do . . ." He cleared his throat quietly. "Speaking not as a judge or even as a member of the bar, just as your brother-in-law . . . I'd be visiting with Lawrence as to where he could get me a quick, safe passage for two."

"I'd suggest South America," Lawrence instantly offered. "It's easy to get lost down there. Say the word, and I'll have you both a berth on the next steamer headed that way. Talk with Maddie tonight and let me know what you want to do in the morning. I'll be back here for a late breakfast."

Rivlin nodded, trying to imagine how Maddie would respond to the idea. If she was willing to consider it . . .

"Tomorrow's tomorrow," Albert declared from his seat by the window. "I think that the matter of Maddie's future rather depends on what we decide to do about Harker, don't you? I say it's high time we started nailing down some specific plans."

As the others agreed and put forth the ideas first sketched at the dinner table, Rivlin deliberately set aside his thoughts of Maddie. He lit his own cigar and, through the cloud of aromatic smoke, watched and listened and then artfully prodded the other men in the direction he needed them to go.

MADDIE KNEW THE INSTANT Mrs. Kilpatrick stopped in the middle of the drawing room and turned back that it didn't bode well for her. Emily squeezed her arm before releasing it and gliding away.

"If I may be so bold as to ask, Miss Rutledge," Mrs. Kilpatrick said as her daughters silently settled into velvet-upholstered chairs. "What is the precise nature of your relationship with my son?"

Maddie saw two ways to go; she could try to dodge for the sake of propriety or she could be bluntly honest. Maddie looked around the room, meeting each of their gazes individually. Emily smiled and winked. Anne and Liz, their eyes bright, were leaning slightly forward in their chairs as though awaiting the unveiling of a large, ornately decorated package. Mary quickly looked away and smoothed her skirt, her lips pursed. Charlotte sat ramrod straight, her hands folded primly on her lap, and looked at Maddie down her patrician nose. Martha blinked as though she were trying to hold back tears and quickly set about arranging the little china figurines on a skirted side table. Mother Kilpatrick waited, her white brow arched.

"I am indeed in Rivlin's custody as a federal prisoner," Maddie began, hoping for the best. "I'm officially under his protection and to be escorted to the trial in Leavenworth, Kansas."

Mother Kilpatrick waited. The silence had grown uncomfortable by the time she said, "I have somehow formed the impression, Miss Rutledge, that your relationship with Rivlin is more personal than it is official. Am I incorrect?"

One more try. "You're correct."

"And again, I ask . . . What is the precise nature of that relationship?"

Accepting that she wasn't going to be allowed a graceful evasion, Maddie saw no course but to go straight to the heart of the matter. "Rivlin and I are lovers."

"That was rather bluntly put," Charlotte said disdainfully.

Despite the ire flooding through her, Maddie calmly countered, "I was given no choice but to answer honestly and in a straightforward manner."

Mrs. Kilpatrick tilted her head. "You're a different young woman, Miss Rutledge," she observed, her tone implying that she was more intrigued than condemning.

Hoping that Emily was right and that her mother did indeed respect strength, Maddie took a deep breath and the bull by the horns. "Mrs. Kilpatrick," she said evenly, "I think you should know that when Rivlin told me he was bringing me here, I told him I'd rather go back to prison than have to face you all. I meant it. I'm not any happier about being here than you are to see me. But he asked me to stand by him and I will. I'm not going to cut and run. And I'm not going to slink around the edges of the room, either. For Rivlin's sake alone,

I hope we can find a way to gracefully endure each other until this is over."

The matriarch's brow inched up. "I don't believe I've ever heard a lady speak in such a *direct* manner."

"Mrs. Kilpatrick, I'm not a lady," Maddie rejoined calmly. "I'm an orphan out of Iowa, a teacher out of Tahlequah, and a federal prisoner out of Fort Larned."

"How predictably Rivlin," Charlotte muttered.

Emily instantly and hotly countered, "And what an incredibly nasty and rude comment, Char."

A porcelain shepherdess tottered and Martha fumbled to catch it before it fell off the table. Anne and Liz nodded in full support of their younger sister's censure. Mary was suddenly absorbed in smoothing nonexistent wrinkles from her lap. Mother Kilpatrick looked at her eldest daughter and in a granite-edged voice, said, "You will apologize to Miss Rutledge."

"I meant no disrespect to you," Charlotte said, her smile as false as the honey in her voice. "I was simply referring to the fact that Rivlin has long marched to the beat of his own drummer."

Maddie had to give Charlotte credit; the woman had certainly perfected the art of the backhanded insult. The thought of politely murmuring words of acceptance rankled Maddie's pride. She wasn't of a mind to surrender to Charlotte's bullying. Neither was she willing to spend the rest of her stay skirting around the underlying issue.

"In the interest of all of us getting through this ordeal with the least amount of unpleasantness possible," Maddie began, meeting Mother Kilpatrick's gaze squarely, "please let me assure you that I'm perfectly aware that I'm not what any of you have in mind for Rivlin. He knows it, too. Our relationship is temporary. I was convicted of murder. I've served two years of a twenty-year sentence. Once I testify, I'll be sent back to prison and I'll be gone from Rivlin's life. You needn't be concerned with trying to imagine how I can possibly fit into this family. It's an effort none of us are going to have to make."

A heavy silence descended in the aftermath of her words. Emily finally broke it, saying softly, "I'd be willing to try, Maddie. You've brought home a Rivlin I thought I'd never see again. I suspect you're responsible for the change in him and I'll be forever grateful to you for that."

"He *was* different tonight, wasn't he?" Anne contributed. "It was almost as though the war had never happened."

Liz nodded. "I noticed it as well."

Mrs. Kilpatrick raised her hand, silencing her daughters. "What are your feelings for my son, Miss Rutledge?" she asked softly.

I love him with all my heart. "Private," Maddie answered.

"If returning to prison were not in your future," Mrs. Kilpatrick pressed, regarding Maddie intently, "would you wish to continue your relationship with Rivlin?"

Her heart raced at the idea and she knew the danger it signaled. As much for herself as to answer the other woman, Maddie said firmly, "I don't allow myself to hope for things I know can't happen, Mrs. Kilpatrick."

Mother Kilpatrick didn't pause to so much as blink before coming at the matter a third time. "If Rivlin asked you to, would you be willing to face us every day for the rest of your life?"

That question Maddie *could* answer. "Yes, Mrs. Kilpatrick. If Rivlin asked, I'd stare you down twice a day, every day."

The matriarch smiled as she turned away. "You *are* a most interesting young woman, Maddie Rutledge," she said, seating herself in the middle of a velvet-upholstered settee. "Do you imbibe spirits?"

"Only since I've met Rivlin," Maddie answered as Emily beamed and glided toward the beverage cart.

Mother Kilpatrick laughed, the sound musical and light. "Yes, Rivlin could drive a parson to drink. And it wouldn't be sherry he drowned himself in, either."

A truce had been reached and Maddie knew that if anyone cared to tally points, she'd be declared the victor. The tension in the air evaporated just as obviously as Anne's and Liz's sighs of relief. Charlotte and Mary settled into the backs of their chairs. Martha let her hands fall into her lap and allowed her shoulders to relax.

"How long have you known Rivlin?" Emily asked, presenting Maddie with a tray of glasses filled with dark amber liqueur.

Maddie selected a glass and answered, "I've lost track of the time, actually. It feels like my whole life. Certainly the best part of it, anyway."

"That's a striking costume you're wearing," Anne offered with a smile.

Maddie remembered Rivlin's tortured groans at her own attempt to make parlor talk. She understood exactly how he felt. But since there was no escaping it, she dutifully and politely replied, "Thank you. Rivlin bought it for me in Wichita."

Anne's eyes widened. "He went *shopping* with you?"

Emily laughed. "Did you have to hold a gun on him?"

"Actually, it was his idea," Maddie replied, smiling and remembering how Rivlin had asked her to teach his sisters the proper way to shop for clothes.

Liz shook her head. "You must tell us how you accomplished this, Maddie. Rivlin is the world's worst about dress shops. The *worst*. He's been banned from most of those in Cincinnati."

Maddie sipped her sherry. "I'm afraid that I didn't do anything beyond surrendering and watching him enjoy the moment."

"Enjoy?" Anne repeated. "Rivlin?"

"Someone should notify the church," Emily said, placing the empty tray back on the beverage cart. "A miracle has happened."

"Don't blaspheme, Emily."

"I'm sorry, Mother." Emily's sparkling eyes said she wasn't the least bit contrite.

"I don't suppose," Charlotte ventured coolly, "we could hope that you've also seen him in a suit and tie, cooing at babies, or plotting to build a business empire?"

Maddie saw in the answer both a way to set Charlotte back on her heels and to turn the focus of the attention away from herself. "Rivlin's not interested in building empires and he's horribly uncomfortable in a suit. It went out the train window not long after we left St. Louis. As for babies, he keeps his distance unless he doesn't have a choice. He holds them very carefully and gives them back the first chance he gets."

Their stunned expressions were exactly what she'd hoped for. "I should probably tell you about the baby that came into our care, shouldn't I?" They nodded in unison and not even Charlotte could pretend indifference. Maddie smiled and gathered them into the palm of her hand.

THIRTEEN DOWN, ONE TO GO, Rivlin told himself as the front door finally closed behind his departing kinsman. Two hours—the longest he'd been without Maddie at his side since she'd come into his life—had been an eternity and the ache to hold her had become physically painful. If his mother suggested that the three of them retire to the drawing room for more conversation, he'd be reduced to begging for mercy. He looked over at Maddie, who stood at the base of the stairs, her hands clasped demurely in front of her, the perfect picture of patience and acquiescence. He could just say to hell with decorum and his mother's sensibilities, sweep Maddie up into his arms, and carry her away. He glanced back in his mother's direction, judging the distance and figuring just how quickly he'd have to move.

She cleared her throat softly and gave him one of her infamous "don't you dare" looks just before she turned to Maddie and said, "It's been a very long day and you must be tired from your travels and all the family activity."

Agree, Maddie, darlin'. Tell her you're flat-out exhausted.

Before Maddie could utter a word, his mother turned to him and added, "I instructed that the Rose Room be prepared for Miss Rutledge. Stevens has already taken her bag up. Will you see that she's settled comfortably?"

Bless you, Mother! "I believe I can manage

that," he replied, keeping his face a mask of nonchalance and offering Maddie his arm. She accepted it and even as she was thanking his mother for her hospitality and expressing wishes for a pleasant night, he started her up the steps. He heard his mother move to the base of the stairway, could feel her watching them. There was no need to look back; he knew that she was still wearing that special look of hers meant to keep him in line.

He managed to restrain himself all the way to the top of the stairs, around the corner, and halfway down the hall. There he stopped, opened a door, and guided Maddie over the threshold. She halted two paces in and looked back over her shoulder at him, her brow arched and a smile tipping up the corners of her mouth.

"I presumed that the Rose Room would have rose wallpaper."

He closed the door and locked it. "It does."

Laughing, she stepped into his open arms and twined her arms around his neck. "Perhaps we ought to exercise just a little bit of common sense."

She felt so good pressed against him; he felt whole and centered and wonderfully alive. "Maddie, darlin'," he drawled, pulling the pins from her hair, "what you do to my common sense ought to be a crime."

"Punishable by?"

He brushed his lips over hers, saying, "I think maybe I'd better show you."

HE'D GOTTEN A BIT of sated sleep, but his mind had refused to grant him a true respite. Rivlin dressed and wandered back down to the study. Two glasses of brandy and an hour of wearing a path in his mother's Aubusson rug had produced no more answers than he'd had the moment he'd awakened.

It was tempting to say to hell with it all and make a run for South America. He could find some way to support them and they'd eventually learn to speak Spanish. And it would be damn difficult for the U.S. Marshal Service to track them down. But there was a steep price to be paid for the safety. Once they left, they could never come back. No one could come see them without the risk of leading a lawman to them. Rivlin sighed.

If they weren't going to run, then they had to stand and fight. That posed a whole different set of questions, a whole different set of problems. In the course of discussing options earlier that evening, it had come to him that, despite his declaration otherwise, Maddie needed to be with him when confronting Harker. She was part and parcel of the whole thing.

The question of where to confront Harker had been pretty much decided over brandy and cigars. The train station was the only logical choice. But how to actually go about it remained up in the air. They were to meet again in the morning and hammer out the precise details of how to lay their trap.

Assuming that all went well—that they survived and Harker was no longer a danger . . . Rivlin closed his eyes. Then they faced getting the arrest warrants rescinded, returning to Leavenworth so Maddie could testify, and then securing a second trial for her. Not that Will or Maddie thought there was a snowball's chance in hell of winning her freedom. As usual, thinking about the prospects of Maddie back in prison brought him full circle. South America wouldn't be all that bad. There were worse fates.

But deep down inside he knew what the future held. They weren't going to run. Harker was going to be either in prison or dead. There was a satisfaction to be had in that certainty. But the other . . . He was going to lose Maddie. Circumstances would make him keep his first promise to Seth; his life would be hollow and empty. Rivlin looked down at his brandy and smiled ruefully. In all the years since that night, he was going to, for the first time, truly pay the price for his misjudgment. There was justice in it. Nothing had ever hurt like this did, but he deserved it, he'd earned it. The only thing to do was accept it and bear up to it as best he could. Maybe, if God were benevolent, Harker would put him out of his misery.

Rivlin frowned. If he died, Maddie would be all alone in the world. He was all she had, the only one who cared what happened to her. Not that that would make any difference to her existence once she went back to prison. Not that his caring would be enough to sustain her through the eighteen years looming ahead of her.

A soft sound from the doorway started him from his dark thoughts. He looked up, hoping to see Maddie. "Mother," he said brightly, trying to hide his disappointment. "What are you doing up?"

"Old people sleep very little, Rivlin," she answered, advancing into the room. "I think it's God's way of making sure we get everything done before we go. What are you doing up at this hour?"

"Thinking."

"About Maddie?" she asked softly, pouring herself a sherry.

He'd thought about little else since the second she'd vaulted down those stairs at Fort Larned. His world had come to revolve around her. "Mother," he began, studying his brandy again, "have you ever made a promise that you later wished you hadn't?"

"Everyone has," she countered quietly. "I think that's the nature of promises, Rivlin. What promise have you made that you've come to regret? Was it to Maddie? Or to another woman?"

"There hasn't been any other woman. Only Maddie. The promise was to Seth."

Her silence caught his attention and it wasn't until he looked up to meet her gaze that she replied, "Seth is dead, sweetheart. He can't hold you to any promises you made him."

Rivlin snorted and threw the remaining brandy down his throat. "I hold myself to it."

"Because the promise concerns something important or because you feel guilty?"

The answer came easily. "Guilty."

"And Maddie makes you forget that sometimes, doesn't she?" She didn't wait for him to admit it. "Good," she declared. "You've grieved long enough, Rivlin. We're all human and we all make mistakes we regret with all our heart. But the greatest tragedy is in letting them so consume us that we don't see the even greater mistakes we make in atoning for them."

"What about honor and keeping your word?" he posed.

"Honor is commendable, son. But all too often I've seen men cling to honor as a way to avoid making difficult decisions. As for keeping your word . . . Promises to the living mean more than those made to the dead."

"Maybe. I'll think on it," he said, not because he

intended to, but because it was a way out of a conversation that wasn't going to make any difference.

"Sometimes it's best not to think," she said gently. "Sometimes you should listen to your heart."

Rivlin chuckled and held up his empty glass in salute. "You and Myra."

Her brow inched upward. "And who is Myra?"

He mentally edited his reply down to the most fundamental truth. "Myra's the closest Maddie's ever had to a mother. Myra pretty much told me the same thing you just did about thinking. She said it got in the way."

His mother nodded and sipped at her sherry. After a long moment, she gently asked, "Rivlin, do you love Maddie?"

"Myra asked me that question, too," he answered, thinking that Myra and his mother would make a formidable pair. It was a damn good thing the two of them would never meet.

"And how did you answer?"

"I told her I didn't."

"And how are you going to answer me?" his mother pressed.

"I'm not." Rivlin put his glass back on the liquor cabinet. "I'm going back to bed."

"You mean you're going back to Maddie," she corrected, chuckling. "I'm well aware that you countermanded my orders to have your bags taken to separate rooms."

"All things considered, Mother," he said over his shoulder as he headed toward the door, "propriety isn't very important. Good night."

"Son, may I share an observation?"

He stopped on the threshold to the hall and, with a sigh of resignation, turned back. It was all the acceptance she seemed to need.

"This evening when the ladies retired to the drawing room, Maddie made the statement that she knew she wasn't the woman any of us would have chosen for you. She's quite correct. We wouldn't have chosen Maddie. And we would have been very wrong. You complement each other well."

It took a moment for the importance of the last words to sink in. "Thank you, Mother."

"Good night, Rivlin."

He nodded and went on his way, wishing with all his heart that his world was simple enough that a future with Maddie could be had with only his mother's approval.

Chapter Twenty-One

There was, Maddie decided, nothing better than waking to the feel of Rivlin's arms around her and the warmth of his skin against hers. She smiled, remembering the first morning she'd come from sleep to find herself cradled so protectively. The woman who'd blustered and cried propriety now lay naked against the same man, her head cradled on his shoulder, her arm across his chest and her leg drawn over his thighs. How far that woman had come, how happy that woman was. She snuggled closer and Rivlin's arms gently tightened around her.

"Are you awake?" he whispered, trailing a hand slowly over the curve of her shoulder.

"Pleasantly so." Maddie pressed a kiss to his chest. "Good morning, Rivlin."

"Mornin', darlin'." Against her cheek, she felt and heard his heartbeat quicken. "Maddie," he said, still stroking her shoulder, "what do you think of South America?"

Her heart instantly matched the cadence of his. "In what regard?" she asked warily.

"As a place to live."

Her stomach went cold. "It's very far away," she answered, trying to think of a way to kindly put an end to his fruitless hopes.

"Would you consider it, Maddie?"

"Well," she said, managing a dry chuckle, "it would certainly be a strategic retreat on a grand scale."

"I don't think it could be considered a strategic retreat, Maddie. It would be running."

"And hiding forever." There was no choice but to face the matter square on. Letting him hope would be cruel. Maddie shifted so that she balanced on her elbow and met his gaze. Such a handsome man he was, his hair tousled from sleep, his skin bronzed from the sun and shadowed with a night's beard. The amber flecks in his dark eyes were bright with anticipation and a bittersweet ache bloomed deep in her chest. If only she could let him pour his hope into her until the reality of her world was forever and always washed away.

"Rivlin, you have a family and a home and a future that's yours to make of it what you will," she said, trying to wrap a brave smile around words that were more regretful than adamant. "Throwing it all away for me . . ." She shook her head. "I can't let you do that. I'm very, very flattered that the thought of doing so has occurred to you, but please don't allow nobility to get in the way of your good judgment. We've known from the first day how our time together has to end."

"But—"

"No, Rivlin," she interrupted, putting her fingertips against his lips. "The answer is and always will be no."

He turned his head away from her touch, asking, "Why won't you even think about it?"

"We've had this conversation before," she said gently, her heart aching. "Please listen to me this time. What I want and what I can have are two different things, Rivlin. I think spending forever with you would be as close as I could get to heaven on earth, but I can't have it and I won't try to cheat my way into it."

"Cheat?" he repeated, clearly both wounded and befuddled.

"The only way I can have a life outside of prison is to steal all of your tomorrows." She felt him draw a breath and she went on before he could speak. "Yes, I know. It's your choice to give them up for me. But there will come a day, Rivlin, when you look at me and wish you hadn't surrendered them."

"You can't know that I'll come to regret it."

It was as certain as the sunrise and the sunset. "And then there's the promise you made to Seth," she said softly. "Have you made your peace with him?"

"That's gotten complicated," he admitted, frowning as he studied the ceiling over their bed. "I've realized that I made Seth only half the promise I should have that night."

"Harker," she supplied. He nodded and she pressed for more. "And what happens when justice has been dispensed to your satisfaction, Rivlin? Can you take back the tomorrows you promised not to have? Can you do that and not feel guilty?"

He exhaled long and hard. "Yes, I think so," he answered, still not looking at her.

"What if you can't?"

"So," he drawled, a sardonic smile touching the corners of his mouth, "it would be easier for both of us to walk away now, to give up rather than risk failing."

God, how she wanted to try, how she wanted with all her heart to believe that they could steal happiness. "I didn't say it was going to be easy," she whispered sadly. "But it's what we have to do."

His gaze came to meet hers. "You could be acquitted in your retrial."

And someday pigs might fly. "Then we'll see what's possible when that day comes," she offered, managing a smile. "Until then, though, let's just get through today and what it brings us."

"You always do that," he observed quietly. "You refuse to look past what's right in front of you."

"That's because what's right in front of me is all there is. And as long as we're together, that's all you'll ever have, too. I wish I could make you understand and accept that."

For a long moment he was silent, then he reached up and ran his fingers through her hair. He watched as he let the dark strands fall over her shoulder and softly asked, "Why don't you ever see yourself—the life you want—as being worth a fight, Maddie?"

"Because losing hope hurts worse than any beating."

He blinked at the simple, blunt honesty. His hand fell away and his gaze went back to the ceiling. "And you always lose."

She heard the sadness, the resignation in his voice. There was some consolation in it; in it was the possibility of his having at last recognized the foundation on which her world had been built. He hadn't heeded her warnings soon enough, though. When the end came he was going to have regrets. He'd allowed himself to dream. Maddie silently sighed, silently offered up a prayer that the matter with Harker would be resolved as soon as possible. When that was done, her struggle against hoping and wanting would be done, too. The effort to keep herself from tumbling into Rivlin's dreams was exhausting.

Maddie shifted again, sliding atop him. The movement brought his attention back to her and she smiled as she leaned forward to kiss his chin. "Is there a reasonable hope that I could talk you into making love to me this morning?"

He smiled in return, settling her hips more closely against his. "Don't for a minute think that I don't understand how you use your body to distract me, darlin'."

"Do you mind?" she asked, knowing the answer, feeling his body responding to hers.

"Only right at first," he admitted, cradling her face in his hands and gently drawing her lips to his, "and then I tend to forget all about it."

Oh, she understood so well. The taste of him, the scent and the feel of him were such heady elixirs. The world beyond them ceased to matter. Yesterdays melted away. Tomorrows didn't exist. There was only Rivlin and the breathless revelry of sensation. Everything was right. She was whole, incapable of wanting more than the moments she had. And in the sweet haze of completion, she lay atop him, wrapped in his arms, her body weak, her heart silently whispering, *I love you, Rivlin,* as she drifted around the edges of a sated slumber.

Knuckles rapped hard against the door to their

room. Maddie started upright, tearing herself from Rivlin's embrace, even as Emily called from the other side, "You have precisely thirty seconds to make yourselves decent and then we're coming in!"

Her pulse racing, Maddie bolted out of the bed and scooped her chemise and pantalets from the floor.

Rivlin followed on her heels, barking, "Don't you dare!" at the door as he, too, scrambled for his clothes.

Maddie was already pulling the chemise over her head when Anne called out happily, "Oh, dare we will!"

"You've got twenty-eight seconds left," Emily chimed. "Use them, baby brother."

"Goddammit, Emily!" he bellowed, flopping back on the bed to shove both legs into his pants at once. "I'm going to tell Mother!"

"Go right ahead," his sister countered. "We can live without dessert for a week."

"Personally, I could go two weeks without," Liz contributed. "It would do me good."

"Seventeen," Anne announced. "Tick, tick, tick. Now it's fifteen, Riv."

"This is my room and you'll stay the hell out of it unless I invite you in!" he declared as he found his shirt and Maddie managed to get her trembling fingers to tie the waist of her pantalets.

"Well, if you had put Maddie in the Rose Room like you were supposed to," Emily offered, "you wouldn't be in the awkward position of rushing around looking for your pants, baby brother."

"Ten and a half," Liz reminded. "You'd better hurry."

Maddie scrambled back under the bedcovers,

her panic easing enough that she could see the situation in a different light. She grinned, watching Rivlin scowl and ram his arms into his shirtsleeves. As he headed across the room, he looked back over his shoulder to say darkly, "Be thankful you don't have sisters." He flung open the door, faced his sisters, growled, "I'll get you for this," and then instantly backed up in the face of their united advance.

Maddie hid her grin behind her hand and tried not to choke on her laughter.

"Good morning, Maddie!" Liz declared, leading the petticoated brigade past Rivlin. "We brought you a breakfast tray."

"The men are downstairs in the dining room waiting for you to make an appearance," Anne said without looking back at her silently fuming brother. "Rob Baker's here, too. Button your shirt and tuck the tail in."

He'd no more than reached for a button and its companion hole when Emily came at him. "Here are your boots," she said, thrusting them into Rivlin's chest as Liz settled the bed tray across Maddie's lap.

Anne made the next assault on him. "And here's your gun belt. Now go away and let us take care of Maddie."

He stood there, blindly trying to get a grip on his boots and his gun belt, his eyes narrowed as he looked quickly between his sisters. "What are you all planning?"

Liz answered, her smile impish. "We like to think of it as going shopping."

"You're not taking Maddie out of this house," Rivlin declared, taking a step forward. "Do I make myself clear?"

Emily's hands went to her hips as she met him

toe to toe. "We're not brainless ninnies, thank you very much. We're raiding storage trunks and by the time we're done, Maddie's going to have a new wardrobe. I brought Isabella with me this morning."

Maddie watched the tension in his shoulders ease. The look of boyish befuddlement on his face was so sweetly endearing that she wanted to laugh, wanted to go to him and wrap her arms around him and tell him how very much she loved him in that moment.

And then Charlotte, with Mary in her wake, swept into the room, saying, "Kindly get out of our way."

Rivlin instantly sidestepped out of his eldest sister's determined path, meeting Maddie's gaze. The corners of his mouth twitched despite an obvious effort to maintain his offended demeanor. "You won't think this is so damned amusing by the time they're through with you."

She suspected he was right but knew that there was no escaping her temporary fate. Maddie simply shrugged, grinned, and picked up her coffee cup. He laughed silently, dumped his belongings into the chair by the door, and began to button his shirt.

"Will says he'll need Maddie for a formal deposition later," Char informed them all as she opened a set of draperies. Midmorning sunlight flooded the room. "He thinks it might be an hour or more."

"Which is, of course, an eternity to the male mind," Mary observed, pulling open the other set of draperies.

"Long enough to build Rome," Emily quipped.

"Where's Martha?" Rivlin asked sarcastically as he shoved his shirttail into his pants. Only the lower buttons had been done. He reached for his gun belt. "Didn't you bring her along, too?"

Emily provided the answer. "She's in the main dressing room with Isabella, getting things ready."

"Eat fast, Maddie," Liz instructed. "We have a lot to accomplish and not nearly enough time." She turned, her hands on her hips, and frowned at her brother. "What are you doing still standing there?"

"I'm going!" he retorted. "Just let me get my damn boots on first." He snatched them out of the seat of the chair, his gaze catching Maddie's as he did. He slowly froze, a boot in each hand, and cocked a brow. "What?"

Her face ached from smiling and there was nothing to do except be honest. "You're so adorable all ruffled and puffed."

With a half-strangled groan, he turned on his heel, tucked one boot beneath his arm, grabbed the doorknob on his way past, and departed with a wall-shaking report. Maddie laughed outright.

Emily grinned at the door. "Mother will have his ears for that. If there's one thing she can't abide, it's slamming doors."

"Well done, Maddie," Charlotte offered with a wide smile and a conspiratorial wink. "I do believe you have what it takes to be a Kilpatrick woman."

Maddie blinked in shock. What had happened to the dour and disapproving Charlotte of last night? She glanced at Mary and saw what could only be acceptance in the other woman's smile. Why the sudden change? Maddie wondered. She sought time to ponder in fiddling with her eggs and asking, "Who's Isabella?"

"My housekeeper," Emily explained. "She was the wardrobe mistress when we all lived at home. I took her with me when I married. I assure you that she hasn't lost a single one of her seamstress skills."

"She can do absolutely miraculous things

with no more than a pair of scissors, a needle, and thread," Liz expanded. "You'll be impressed, Maddie."

Anne held up a strip of cloth and whalebone, asking, "Is this your only corset, Maddie?"

Hoping no one would comment on the obvious absence of the laces, Maddie answered, "One's quite sufficient."

"Nonsense," Mary offered with a dismissive wave of her hand. "And no offense, Maddie, but this one's really rather uninspiring. I can think of at least a half dozen we have in storage that are ever so much prettier."

"The more lace, the more breathless men get, you know," Anne observed.

"And appreciative," Liz added, wiggling a brow meaningfully.

"Well," Charlotte snorted, "*that* goes without saying."

"And don't even attempt to tell us Rivlin is different in that respect," Emily chided playfully. "What did he do with the laces? Burn them?"

Oh, God. "They're here somewhere," Maddie said as heat flooded her cheeks. Rivlin was right, they were going to run her through the mill.

"Where's your dressing robe, Maddie?" Anne asked, turning slowly about and surveying the room. "I don't see it anywhere."

"I don't have one."

Mary rolled her eyes. "I suppose Rivlin didn't consider it necessary."

"Men have no conception of what constitutes a proper wardrobe," Char pronounced. "It's most fortunate that you have us at your disposal, Maddie."

"And speaking of disposal," Emily said, stepping

orward to take the breakfast tray. "It looks as hough you've finished your breakfast. Out of that bed. It's time to be on with our foray into the many deep and dark cedar-lined closets of Spring House."

Charlotte flicked the covers back. Liz extended her hands. And Maddie surrendered herself to the indomitable will of the Kilpatrick women.

RIVLIN STOMPED INTO THE DINING ROOM, his boots still in hand, glowering at the assemblage. Only Rob Baker, Cincinnati's chief of police, and Adam were spared.

"Jesus," Everett chortled. "You look like a man running for his life."

"You all might have at least *tried* to gain some control over your wives," he declared, dropping into a chair to pull on his boots. "I'd've really appreciated it."

"You can take a run at it, if you'd like," Albert offered, grinning. "But we'll bet you a million dollars that you'll be no more successful at it than we've been."

Accepting the truth of it, Rivlin swore softly and then rose to his feet, saying, "I didn't expect to see you *all* this morning." He extended his right hand, adding, "Rob, it's been a long time. Nice to see you again. Wish it were under better circumstances."

"I'll second the sentiment," Rob said, accepting the offered hand. He grinned in a boyish way. "But I couldn't resist. If I can bring in Harker on attempted murder charges, I can write my ticket for wherever I want to go." He winked. "Might even be considered for state attorney general when Lee's elected governor. Never can tell."

John cleared his throat softly. "I had a visitor waiting for me at the plant this morning, a very pretty young man out of Senator Harker's Illinois office. Seems the senator is hoping that I may know of your whereabouts and that I'll relay a message for him."

"You have my attention, John. Please continue."

"Harker wants to meet with you when he comes into Cincinnati this evening on the seven-thirteen. He's proposing to discuss terms."

"Discuss terms?" Rivlin repeated. "He's offering us a chance to blackmail him forever? And he expects us to believe he's sincere?" Rivlin chuckled darkly. "It boggles the mind, doesn't it?"

Lawrence joined the conversation, saying quietly, "My people report that he is indeed on the seven-thirteen."

Albert pulled his watch out of his pocket, flicked open the cover, and said, "Which will put him in town less than ten hours from now."

"And we're down to the brass tacks of it all," Rivlin observed, helping himself to the food on the sideboard. Over his shoulder he asked, "Did anyone think to bring a map of the train station?"

With a flourish and a big grin, Lawrence took a neatly tied roll of paper from the other sideboard. The table was cleared of dishes and decorations and the map unrolled. John was pinning the corners down with crystal salt and pepper shakers as Rivlin took his meal and joined the others around the table. He stood with Adam, Everett, Will, and Albert on one side. Leander, Rob, John, and Lawrence stood on the other side.

"The seven-thirteen always comes into terminal two," Lawrence said, pointing to the map. "As one of the older platforms, it's narrow enough empty, but when you add the crowds, it's a shoulder-to-shoulder jostle."

Rivlin saw the scene in his mind's eye. "With no room to maneuver," he observed. "And too many people in the way and at risk. So much for meeting Harker as he steps down from the car."

"Back here is out of the way," Rob Baker said, leaning forward to indicate an area outside the station. "You could send him a telegram, specifying this as the meeting place. There's only one way in and one way out."

"There's always a mountain of packing crates back there, too," Lawrence added, stuffing his hands in his pockets and rocking back on his heels as he considered the map with knitted brows. "We could secrete ourselves among them and no one would ever know we were there."

Rivlin mentally played the sequence of necessary events and shook his head. "He's not stupid; he won't walk into such an obvious trap. We'll have to make the meeting inside the station and in a place he'd choose."

"You can't be serious," Albert snorted. He indicated the map with a sweep of his hand. "It's a huge friggin' station, Riv. Allow Harker to choose the place and you won't have a chance to control the situation when you walk into it."

"I didn't say we were going to let him choose," Rivlin countered. He smiled. "We're going to herd him."

Albert cocked a brow and said dryly, "I'll remind you that men and cattle are two vastly different animals."

"Not really," Leander offered with a chagrined smile from the other side of the table. "Politics is based on the reality of men feeling most comfortable following and that they'll happily take the course of least disruptive change. It requires less thinking and less effort."

Albert scowled. "That's a pretty damn dismal view of the public."

"I didn't craft the nature of the game," Lee rejoined. "I simply play it by the givens."

"Well, don't expect me to blindly vote for you when you run for governor. I'll not be a complacent cow led to the polls."

"Fine, don't," Lee countered with a shrug and a certain smugness about his smile. "But you'll be the only one who doesn't."

"If you two don't mind," Will said, using his judge's tone. "May we get back to the matter at hand?" Albert *harumphed*, Lee looked innocent, and Will folded his arms across his chest, saying, "All right, Riv. Just how is it that you think you can herd Harker to where you want him?"

Setting his plate aside and focusing his attention on the map of the station, Rivlin mused aloud, "He'll want to meet us where there'll be as little chance for interruption or discovery as possible. He doesn't want this botched a fourth time and he doesn't want any witnesses to our deaths. We close down his options until he's left with just one place that will do. He won't have any choice but to accept it."

"And how do you propose to limit him?" Albert queried. "Without, of course, him being aware that he's being herded along like a stupid political cow."

Lee chuckled. "For a railroad man, you're remarkably idealistic, Albert. I never guessed."

Albert opened his mouth to retort, but Will picked up a salt shaker and rapped it hard against the tabletop. "Gentlemen, we'll come to order," he declared, looking between the two. Again they managed some semblance of contrition and again Will took the reins of the conversation. "Riv, despite the inflammatory phrasing, it's a relevant question. How do you intend to move Harker to the place of our choosing?"

Rivlin trailed a fingertip over the map as he explained, "The central portion of the terminal obviously doesn't meet Harker's needs; too many people. Some of these platforms are going to be busy with normal arrivals and departures so we don't have to worry about those areas, either." He looked up and swept the gazes of his kinsmen, saying, "All but one of the platforms that are usually deserted at that time of the night are going to be occupied by Lawrence's people moving cargo and such. The one we leave alone is the one Harker will have to choose."

Albert grinned. "Simple and yet brilliant."

"Simple, yes," Rivlin agreed, "but hardly brilliant. All you have to be is just a little bit smarter than the cow." He didn't give Lee and Albert an opportunity to fall back into their own exchange. He pointed to the place Rob Baker had indicated earlier. "Lawrence, those crates you suggested to use for cover in the alley—"

"Will work just as well for the purpose on our deserted platform," Lawrence finished with a crisp nod. "I'll have them in place." He leaned forward and pointed to the map. "These three platforms aren't used at night. Which of them would you prefer be left open to Harker?"

"The middle one of them," Rivlin quickly decided. "If we have gunplay, then the platforms on either side won't be those being used by passengers."

The chief of police instantly stiffened. "Are you expecting to have to use firearms?"

Telling himself that it was a legitimate concern

didn't do much to ease Rivlin's irritation; it was still a naive question. He cocked a brow and managed what he hoped looked like a good-natured smile. "Do you think that Harker's plan is to talk us to death? I'm wearing my sidearm, Rob."

Rob winced, glanced around at the other men, and then asked, "I need to know, Riv . . . Do you intend to kill Harker?"

His heart skipped a beat. Did he? He acutely felt the others' attention on him. "I'll do whatever I have to in order to protect Maddie and myself," he answered, certain of that much. "If Harker doesn't leave me any other choice . . . Yes, Rob, I'll kill him."

"Purely in self-defense," Rob clarified.

"For no other reason," Rivlin answered, forcing a degree of conviction into his voice that he didn't feel.

Rob fidgeted with the edge of the map, his eyes narrowed as he considered Rivlin. Will moved to the end of the table saying, "Judge Corbett has agreed to be there as an impartial witness to the meeting. I'll be there as well. Rob, you'll be there in your official capacity, of course. Everett, you'll handle the transcription of the conversation?"

Everett sighed, and though nodding, said, "I'd like to express one more time—and before it's too late—my reservations about Maddie being there. If anything should go wrong and she were injured, my conscience couldn't bear it."

"Maddie's in my custody and I can't let her out of my sight," Rivlin countered.

Everett snorted. "Having Maddie with you has little to do with her being a federal prisoner and we all know it."

There was no way out of the corner Everett had backed him into without being honest. "Having a choice of two targets forces a man to make a decision, Everett. Decisions require hesitation and in that hesitation comes opportunity to take it away from him. Maddie and I have done this before, out on the plains."

Everett's eyes widened. He sputtered for a moment and then asked incredulously, "You're planning to deliberately put her in jeopardy?"

"I'm not going to let anything happen to her."

"And what if something happens to you and you aren't able to protect her?" Everett instantly countered.

"Then I expect all of you to step forward and do so."

Adam laid his hand on Rivlin's shoulder. "You can count on me, Uncle Riv. I'll lay down my life for her if it comes to that."

God, Rivlin silently mused, had he ever been so full of idealism and gallantry? Yeah, he answered himself, he had. Long, long ago. Before he'd gone off to the war and met men like John Harker. An idea sprang up in his mind, fully formed and crystalline. "Adam," he began, studying his nephew's face, the face that was so much like his own had been at that age. "Would you be interested in pulling the tiger's tail for me?"

Eagerness lit up Adam's eyes and Rivlin smiled in rueful recognition of a young man's appetite for risk. "I want you standing on the platform so that you're the first thing Harker sees as he steps down out of his car. I want him blinded by memories and willing to follow without thinking. You'll stay well out of his reach, of course, but you'll lead him to the rest of us."

"I can do that," Adam replied, his features hardening with understanding. "How will I know him?"

"Private car," Rivlin supplied. "He's a very

dapper man, dressed in the height of fashion. Gray hair and huge muttonchop sideburns. As tall as your Uncle Will but a bit heavier. Mostly you'll know by the glint in his eyes when he catches sight of you. Your skin will crawl."

Adam nodded, his chin hard and his lips thinned. "I'll find him."

"I hope you can understand that I can be with you all only in spirit tonight," Leander said quietly. "If the Republican party were ever to find out that I participated in the embarrassment of bringing Harker down . . ."

Albert finished dryly, "You'd be reduced to following along, mooing at the moon with the slow-witted herd of common men."

"Well, Albert," the politician replied dryly, "I don't hear you promising to be on the platform for the grand moment."

Albert jerked his brocade vest down over his girth. "Anne's giving a dinner party tonight for some of my business associates. Invitations went out weeks ago and I can't very well not be there." He turned away from any observation Lee might have been about to make and said, "Riv, if you need transport for you and Maddie to Leavenworth, my cars are at your immediate disposal. You have only to ask."

"Thank you, Albert. I'll let you know."

Lawrence said quietly, "I take it then that you're still considering my offer for passage to South America?"

Rivlin stared down at the map of the station. Could Maddie be convinced to go? Not likely. But then it might be best not to give her a choice. "If something happens to me," he said slowly, "I want

Maddie taken out of the country. Can you find
omeone to escort her and see her situated? Someone
rustworthy?" He met Lawrence's gaze. His brother-
n-law blinked in stunned disbelief. "Can you do
hat for her?" Rivlin pressed. "For me?"

"If it comes to that, Riv," Lawrence said
olemnly. "I'll take her there myself."

"Thank you." He looked next to his brother
nd then to the family legal expert. "John, Will, my
ortion of the company profits is to go to support
Maddie. You'll see that the legal work is done and
hat she's financially taken care of?"

Both men nodded without hesitation. Will
nitted his brows for a second and then said, "I'll
eed to draft a simple document for you to sign."
He sat and reached for his valise, saying as he ex-
racted a sheaf of paper and a traveling inkwell,
It'll only take a minute—I can do it now before
we settle in for the depositions—and we can all wit-
ess it."

"Good. I don't want any loose ends." He
lanced around the table, noting the grim resolution
hat tightened the faces of every man present and
wondered if they were still heartened at his return.
Probably not, he decided. "Lawrence," he said with
half-smile, "you seem to have drawn the bulk of
he responsibility in this whole mess. I'm sorry, but
amn grateful for your help."

"Couldn't do any less, Riv."

"All right, gentlemen," Rivlin declared, suddenly
wanting the session over. "Let's make sure we all
ave the same plan in our minds. Harker's due in on
he seven-thirteen. We'll assume the train will be on
ime unless Lawrence's people notify us otherwise.
He'll have the platform ready well before then.

Adam will meet Harker as he gets off the train and lead him to Maddie and me."

Albert pulled his watch from his vest, opened the cover, and, studying the face, said, "I'll use my contacts with the B and O to be sure that the train isn't late." He snapped it closed and pocketed it, adding, "I'll feel better about all of this if the timetable isn't waffling on you."

"Much obliged, Albert. Given that, I think everyone should be in their places by at least six forty-five this evening. Maddie and I will arrive just before Harker does."

"And if Harker doesn't want to gloat before he tries to kill you?" Everett posed. "What then, Riv? What if there isn't any conversation to witness or transcribe?"

"Then we'll just have to hope I'm a better shot than he is."

"Jesus Christ. There's too damn much left to chance with this plan."

God, he'd never thought it would be Everett who'd turn into the nervous Nellie. "Well, if you'd like," Rivlin countered, laying his hand on the burly man's shoulder, "we can invite him to the newspaper office for a chat, but I don't think he'll accept."

"I'll have men in place and prepared to intervene if necessary," Rob Baker promised. "But we all need to understand that if the Marshal Service discovers what we're about and sticks their fat hands into the pie, there isn't going to be a damn thing I or my men will be able to do to muscle them out. Federal supersedes local. Be careful and keep your wits about you, Riv. They suspect you're in town."

"Do they suspect we're here at Spring House?" Rivlin asked.

"Not that I've heard, but then I'm not exactly

privy to their every thought. I think it would be wise to make this our last meeting before tonight, though. The less coming and going you all do and especially in and out of here, the better."

There were nods all around as Rivlin mentally made plans for getting himself and Maddie out of Spring House and into town without being seen.

"Done," Will pronounced, rising to his feet and handing Rivlin a single sheet of paper. "Read it and, if it says what you want it to say, sign on the line above your printed name."

Rivlin scanned, noting the words he needed to see. As he reached for the pen Will offered, Lawrence said, "I need to be getting on with my tasks. If no one has any objections. . . ."

Amid the murmurs of consent, Rivlin extended his hand. "Thank you, Lawrence. For everything."

"It's an honor and a privilege, Riv. I'll see you at the station tonight."

Leander, Albert, and Rob Baker took their leaves as Rivlin signed the document Will had prepared. As Everett and John and Adam took turns affixing their names as witnesses, Will drew a Bible from his valise, saying, "Adam, I'll pay you five dollars if you'd be brave enough to find the ladies and tell Maddie that I need her down here to give her deposition."

Adam grinned and without a word strode off in the direction of the stairs.

"Too young and confident to know any better," John observed as he watched his son go. "Sometimes I worry about that boy."

"He'll be all right," Rivlin offered, remembering. The blissful ignorance of youth was in many ways a cushion to the blows life dealt from time to time. You learned the lessons you needed to, the pain that came with them only dull aches in your memories. It was when you lost that naïveté that the lessons cut like knives. Suddenly Rivlin felt old and tired and wanted nothing more than to lie down with Maddie in his arms.

Chapter Twenty-Two

SHE'D LOST COUNT of the number of times she'd been positioned in front of the full-length mirror and buttoned into a dress by one of Rivlin's sisters. Emily was taking her turn at the honor this time while the others chattered about possibilities. Isabella ruthlessly attacked another pile of cloth, and a maid rolled a food- and tea-laden cart into the huge dressing room.

Maddie silently sighed and sought momentary refuge in her thoughts. It had been such a very long morning—multiple simultaneous conversations punctuated by laughter, intense cooperation, and almost frenetic activity that had left her feeling like a prized porcelain doll. And to think that she'd once told Rivlin that she'd rather go back to prison than face his family. She would have to tell him how very thankful she was for the chance he'd given her to see what being a part of a family was like—exhausting and exhilarating, frustrating and yet so comforting, too. She would miss the Kilpatricks and the whirlwind when she left them. There would be happy memories of the time she'd spent here.

And a new understanding of just how profoundly, achingly empty her life was, she realized with a start. She hadn't seen the danger in allowing herself to be drawn into the circle. She hadn't imagined that it would be anything like it was.

"Why the sad look?" Emily asked.

Maddie blinked and met Emily's gaze in the mirror. If any of Rivlin's sisters would understand her regrets, it would be this one. But they weren't alone and the others . . . Maddie focused her vision on the mirror and the reflection of herself in the third of the dresses Isabella had redesigned and fitted for her. This one was a trained violet brocade with the overskirt lined in mauve silk and gathered up by huge mauve grosgrain bows low on each hip. The neckline was square and dangerously low.

"I'm thinking," Maddie answered, slowly smiling in the hope that Emily would believe her, "that if I drop something, it will have to be forfeited. Bending over, no matter how carefully, will lead to a most embarrassing spill." She gestured at the pile of dresses which had been cannibalized in the process of creating her wardrobe. "Surely we can find some laces or ruffles or ribbons to make the neckline a bit more practical."

Emily grinned and smoothed the shoulders of the gown. "We're not interested in practical, Maddie. We're striving for breathtakingly inspirational."

"Amethysts and pearls, I believe," Charlotte said, coming to Maddie's side and squinting at her reflection. She whirled about and walked away, exclaiming,

"And I happened to have brought along the perfect necklace and ear bobs."

Maddie wondered, yet again, just where the Kilpatrick women thought she was going to wear all of the finery they were gathering for her. Now it was amethysts and pearls.

"I remember this set," Emily declared as Charlotte opened a black satin box and handed her a heavy wide band of gold encrusted with stones and pearls. "Papa gave them to you on your eighteenth birthday." As she passed them around Maddie's neck and fastened the clasp, she added, "You should wear your hair up like this all the time, Maddie. You have a lovely neck line."

Having a lovely line isn't something you want guards to notice.

"Oh, those look ever so much better on you than they ever did on me," Charlotte decreed, nodding crisply. "Consider them yours, Maddie."

The Sgt. Murphys of the world would love to see such a thing drop into a property box. "I couldn't possibly accept them," Maddie countered. "They were a gift from your father."

Charlotte adjusted the way the necklace draped while saying, "I've reached the age when a woman doesn't draw attention to her wattling chin and I'm not going to wear them, Maddie. I have only sons and I want you to have them."

Where *had* the Charlotte of last night gone?

Emily chuckled and, as though reading her mind, said, "She's decided there's more to be gained in trying to win you over than fight you. Be gracious."

Gracious *and* honest. "I appreciate the offer, Charlotte, I truly do, but the minute the situation with Harker is resolved, I'm going to be on my way to Leavenworth and then back to prison. If I accepted your generous gift, they'd be confiscated and quite likely stolen. It would be such a senseless loss."

Charlotte blinked as though she'd quite forgotten the circumstances that had brought Maddie into the Kilpatrick household. Emily looked first distressed and then determined.

"Rivlin isn't about to let you go back to prison," Liz stated, calmly pouring tea. "Lawrence told me that he's offered to arrange passage to South America for you and Riv."

In the mirror, Maddie saw Mother Kilpatrick start and knew that she, unlike her daughters, fully understood the cost of such a course.

"I've refused to consider it," Maddie announced, turning to face the matriarch directly. "I know that once Rivlin leaves, he can never come home again." She looked at the others, briefly meeting each gaze as she added, "None of you could come to see him without the risk of leading the authorities to him. It's a sacrifice that I can't ask of him or any of you. Being a part of a family is more precious than all the jewels in the world."

"Don't worry, Maddie," Charlotte said softly. "Will told me you have grounds for appealing your conviction. You'll receive a new trial and be set free."

And Rivlin had said he didn't fit in his family. Perhaps, in some respects, he didn't. But when it came to blind, boundless hope and optimism, he was a Kilpatrick to the marrow. There was no fighting it, of course. She could argue rationally until she turned blue, but she wasn't going to have any more success in making them see the certainty of her future than she'd had in making Rivlin see it. "We'll hope for the best," Maddie said, accepting a cup of tea from Liz with a gracious smile.

"Good afternoon, ladies."

They turned as one to the door. Adam's smile faltered just a bit before he added, "I've been sent for Miss Rutledge. Uncle Will's ready to take her deposition."

"Your Uncle Will can just wait," Liz declared, setting down the teapot and gliding toward her nephew. She slipped her arm around his and drew him forward. "Tell us what they decided to do about Senator Harker."

His eyes widened, he swallowed hard, and dragged his feet. He'd been navigated to the tea cart before he managed to find the wherewithal to say, "It's nothing very complicated or dangerous, Aunt Liz. You'd think it was boring."

"Hardly," Anne scoffed. "We want to know. And, quite frankly, as the wives and sisters in this affair, we have every right to know."

"And Maddie has more right than any of us," Emily chimed in, her hands on her hips. "She's going to the station with your Uncle Rivlin, isn't she?"

"Yes, Aunt Emily, she is," he hurriedly supplied. Then he started, glanced at the door, and swallowed yet again. "But I think it should be Uncle Rivlin who—"

"Adam?" Mother Kilpatrick said softly.

Standing close enough that she could have easily touched him, Maddie heard Adam's quiet groan. She barely contained her smile as he closed his eyes and tilted his face toward the ceiling as though pleading for divine rescue.

"Yes, Grandmother?"

"Sit down."

He groaned again, then opened his eyes, sighed, and murmured a contrite, "Yes, ma'am," before stepping around the cart and dropping dejectedly onto the sofa beside his grandmother.

"Thank you," she said, regal in victory. "Now, please tell us what the men of this family have concocted as a plan for ending Senator Harker's nefarious ambitions. Spare no details or suffer the questions."

Adam relayed what Maddie suspected were only the barest bones of the plan. She listened, her amusement snuffed out in realizing that embellishment, however detailed, wouldn't alter the basic weaknesses of it. When Adam declared the telling done and began to rise, Maddie put her hand on his shoulder and stayed him. "You're not done, Adam," she declared. "What happens if Senator Harker doesn't feel like talking before he shoots us?"

"Uncle Everett asked the same question," he answered. "Uncle Riv said that you two can work a diversion of some sort to distract Harker long enough for Uncle Riv to shoot him first."

Anne made a sound somewhere between a squeak and a snarl. "And what if Rivlin *doesn't* manage to shoot him first?"

Maddie's stomach dropped to her feet. Adam sat up straight and squared his shoulders. "Then I'm to do whatever I must to protect Miss Rutledge so that she can be taken out of the country safely."

Why would she care where she went if something happened to Rivlin? She blindly set her teacup on the cart. No, this plan would never do. She'd have to make Rivlin understand that such risks weren't acceptable, that they had to find a safer way to accomplish Harker's downfall.

"Out of the country?" she heard Mother Kilpatrick say.

"Uncle Riv said that if anything happened to him, he wants Uncle Lawrence to see that Miss Rutledge gets passage to South America. He doesn't want her to go back to prison. He's afraid that she'll die there."

But he was willing to blithely plan the aftermath of *his* death in the Cincinnati train station? She stared at Adam, stunned.

"Not to worry, Miss Rutledge," Adam went on. "Uncle Lawrence said he'd escort you there personally. Uncle Will drafted a paper that Uncle Rivlin and Father both signed so you'll have the income from Uncle Rivlin's half of the munitions works to live on. You'll be quite all right."

Quite all right? Rivlin would be dead and she'd be quite all right? Quite all right because she wasn't in prison and because she had money? She'd never be right again. Going back to prison she could accept; it was endurable. There was a chance that she would see Rivlin from time to time; the gates of a fort would swing open and she'd watch him ride through. There would be comfort in knowing that the sunlight that came through her windows was the same sunlight that touched Rivlin's shoulders and warmed his skin. But to see the gates open and know that no matter how long she waited or how hard she hoped . . . To see the sunlight and know that Rivlin was buried six feet under the cold, hard earth . . . She couldn't live with that. She had no choice but to change the way he intended to deal with Harker.

"We shouldn't keep Will waiting any longer," Maddie announced, gathering her skirt in her hands and heading toward the door.

"Maddie?" Mother Kilpatrick called after her. She paused and the older woman said, "It isn't Senator Harker who poses the greatest danger. It's Rivlin himself."

Maddie slowly turned back. It hurt to put the truth into words. "Yes, ma'am, I know. It's his sense of obligation to Seth. All the plans, all the risks, are for Seth." Understanding came as a sudden, crystalline, numbing whole. *So that Rivlin can finally make peace with his friend. And with himself.* Her knees weakened and she locked them, swallowed back tears, and lifted her chin.

"He has a sense of obligation to you as well," Mother Kilpatrick advised. "I hope you'll use that to our advantage."

Overwhelmed, her heart and mind battered, Maddie could only nod, accept Adam's arm, and allow herself to be led downstairs.

THE SESSION WITH WILL completed, Maddie stood at the window in Rivlin's room, watching the wind blow brittle leaves across the lawn. She breathed deep the cool air coming off the windowpanes and faced the truth. There were no reasoned arguments that could change Rivlin's planned course. Logic and rationality had no bearing; he was acting from the heart. He needed to find his peace and she couldn't deny him the right to reach for it. He might well feel obligations to her, but they weren't as important as those he felt to Seth. It was as it should be. Tears welled high in her throat.

Accept, Maddie. Just as you've always done, accept and adapt. The future isn't yours to shape or control. Endure and go on.

The sound of the door opening brought an end

to her struggle. Looking over her shoulder, she watched him enter the room, her heart full. Such a good man he was. So handsome and strong and confident. She loved him with all her heart. Losing him . . .

He closed the door and paused, studying her. "Are you all right, Maddie?"

Her heart lurched and she looked back out over the lawn as she sorted through the jumble of her emotions. Soft footfalls on the carpet. He stopped behind her, resting his hands on her shoulders and tucking her head under his chin. She nestled back into the hard warmth of his body, comforted by his strength.

"It's past noon," he said softly, his voice vibrating through her. "Would you like some lunch? We could eat and work out the details of the diversion we might need."

Maddie turned beneath his hands, finding his lips with hers and sliding her arms around his neck. As always, he understood what she wanted, what she needed from him in that instant. Maddie closed her eyes and reveled in it, in the fierce tenderness that was the hallmark of Rivlin's seductions. The last wispy tendrils of doubt and fear evaporated as he carried her to his bed, the shadows of tonight and tomorrow brushed aside by the sweet, heady promise of loving Rivlin now.

RIVLIN DREW HER CLOSER as the carriage rolled through the streets of Cincinnati. She'd been pensive all afternoon, preoccupied by all that she imagined could go wrong, but especially so after they'd discussed a possible diversion and he'd given her the small revolver to hide in the folds of her dress. Even distractions had failed to brighten her outlook. Emily had brought her one of the redesigned dresses to wear for the evening—a royal blue affair with a matching *paletot* that made Maddie's eyes look bluer than the sky—but she'd managed only polite conversation with Emily and tight smiles for Rivlin's compliments. Nothing had made any difference and so he'd resorted to simply holding her. It seemed to comfort her in a way that words couldn't.

She'd be better when it was over, he told himself. She'd give him a smile that reached her eyes and came from her heart and everything would be all right again. And whether she liked it or not, the minute Rob Baker led Harker away, they were going to be on their way to somewhere, anywhere, in South America. They could argue about the wisdom of it all the way to Tierra del Fuego if that's where they ended up. He'd figure out everything else along the way. But, by God, when they got off the boat they were going to be together. His mother was right; Seth was dead and promises to the living meant more.

The carriage rolled to a stop, shifted as Stevens and Lawrence's man came down from the box, and then stilled just before the door was opened for them. Rivlin went first, then assisted Maddie out and presented her with his arm. Her step faltered as they crossed through the great arch of the central entrance.

Adam stood alone just inside, clearly waiting for them, his eyes dark with frustration and concern. Rivlin silently swore, but deliberately kept his tone light and easy as he said, "I presume there's a wrinkle."

"Uncle Lor's people report that he's not on the

seven-thirteen anymore. They don't know where the hell he's gone."

"Where'd he get off?"

"They don't know that either. Uncle Lor's rolling heads as we speak."

That didn't help them much at this point. Rivlin squinted into the distance, seeing past the terminal and the scurrying throngs and into his memories. What was Harker thinking? How was he coming at them? "Where's your father, uncles, and the others?"

"Where they're supposed to be," Adam answered crisply. "Just in case we can still pull this off according to plan."

It would take a goddamned miracle for that to happen, but he couldn't say so with Maddie standing at his side. Her breathing was already too shallow for his liking. "Go to your father, Adam. And stay there," Rivlin instructed. "We've been derailed for the moment. Everyone's to hold tight. We'll pick up the pieces we can, when we can, and go from there."

"But what if you can't get him to the platform where everyone is?"

Rivlin glanced around the station, noting the large numbers of teamsters moving crates and baggage. "Lawrence has men in place. One of them will come and tell you if we can't herd Harker as we planned. Everyone will have to come to us. Now go, Adam."

He watched his nephew stride away and disappear through the doorways of the deserted platform. Maddie's hand tightened on his arm and he turned his head to smile at her. Covering her hand with his, he said softly, "It will be fine, Maddie. We'll find him and it'll go just as we planned from there on out. Just have faith."

She drew a deep breath and gave him another one of those tremulous smiles as she straightened her shoulders. She touched the tip of her tongue to her lower lip and then, as though she were afraid of losing her courage, said quickly, "In case something goes terribly wrong, I want you to know that I love you."

He stopped breathing, his heart hammering wildly. "I thought you said you weren't going to let that happen."

"Yeah, well," she whispered, tears welling in her eyes as she looked up at him, "common sense and good intentions got trampled along the way." She took another deep breath and hurried to add, "I don't expect any declaration from you, Rivlin. How I feel doesn't obligate you in any way."

"Maddie, sweet darlin'," he whispered. He froze at the hard nudge in the center of his lower back. The color drained from Maddie's face.

"Good evening."

He knew both the voice and that the game had begun. "Harker," he said quietly, tightening his grip on Maddie's trembling hand. She looked up at him, her eyes huge and dark. *Trust me, darlin'. It'll work yet.* "You seem to have caught a faster train."

"A carriage actually," Harker provided. "It shortened my trip by the better part of an hour. A pity in a way, though. The boy . . . Is he your son, Kilpatrick?"

"My nephew," Rivlin replied, his gut twisting. "And he knows to kill you if you get within an arm's distance."

Harker laughed dryly. "I've selected an appropriate place to talk. You'll join me, won't you?" He pressed the muzzle deeper into Rivlin's back. "Please turn and exit the station. Turn right once you're outside and then proceed around the far corner. And try to look as though you haven't a care in the world while you do. I'd prefer not to have to put a bullet in the lady's back too soon. There would be so many questions."

Maddie's chin came up a notch as Rivlin turned her around and guided her in the direction Harker had indicated. As they passed through the doors and into the light of the half-moon, she moistened her lips and said with haughty poise, "You should know that we haven't come here alone, Senator. Rivlin's kinsmen are well aware of our meeting."

"Indeed. But they're all gathered behind the crates so artfully arranged on platform five, well out of my way and well beyond offering you any assistance."

He and Maddie were on their own. His mind raced. They were going to be exactly where Rob Baker had first proposed the meeting be staged. But he'd counted on Harker staying on the train, on Harker behaving predictably. In the old days he would have. The son of a bitch had apparently learned some new slithering tricks in the years since their last meeting. Rivlin cursed himself for not having considered that possibility.

They rounded the corner of the station as instructed and Harker immediately said, "Put your hands up, Kilpatrick, up where you won't be tempted to reach for your revolver. Go past those crates, to the first set of tracks, and then turn around."

Rivlin lifted his hands midway to his shoulders and silently swore. There was cunning in Harker's logic. Behind the station, gunshots would echo off into the night rather than into it. Bodies lying in the dark alongside the tracks wouldn't be found nearly as quickly as bodies lying on a platform. They passed the crates and Rivlin glared at them, wishing he'd had the foresight to have some of his kinsmen hidden there just in case something went awry. Hindsight was always so much keener, he silently groused. God give Maddie the courage and strength to play her part. It was their best hope of staying alive.

When they reached the tracks, Rivlin turned, putting his body between Maddie and Harker. "We understand that you want to discuss terms. What are you proposing?"

"Step back into the patch of light, if you would. And I want the woman out from behind you. I want to see her hands up in the air as well."

Maddie clenched her teeth as she obeyed, backing with Rivlin into the soft light spilling from the tunnel-like opening at the end of the platform. Harker remained in the shadowed moonlight, his face eerily masked. So far, not one damn thing had gone as planned. They needed time for the others to get word of their whereabouts and come to their rescue. "I have a name," she said with all the regal poise of Mother Kilpatrick. "It's Madeline Marie Rutledge. You have to know it or you couldn't have tried so intently to have me killed."

Harker's teeth glimmered in the moonlight and his gray muttonchop sideburns seemed to slide up his face. Irritated by his smugness, she said, "But I suppose I shouldn't hold that against you. If you hadn't tried to kill me, I would have never known how dangerous I am to you and your grand ambitions."

"Well, well," Harker said brightly. "Don't we

have an inflated sense of our own self-importance." His eyes glittered. "You're nothing more than an annoying loose end, Miss Rutledge. Tom Foley's dead and so's Jacob Evans. You can testify to witnessing their meetings, but, for all the court knows, it's a barefaced lie. There can be no corroboration."

"Sam and Bill were at a meeting once," she countered. "Odds are that they attended meetings on a regular basis. I'm sure they'll tell what they know."

He barely shrugged. "The testimony of two drunks trying to save their own skin. I hardly think they'll stack very well against a man of my public reputation."

"Which won't be worth a tinker's damn when I get through with it," Rivlin said quietly. "The world is going to know what you did to Seth Hoskins."

Harker stepped forward, his eyes narrowed into slits as his upper lips curled back into an ugly snarl. A heavily oiled strand of hair fell out of place to flop over his brow. "You, Kilpatrick, are more than an annoying loose end," he said. "That's why you have to die. Dying with Miss Rutledge at your side has always been just a minor part of my plan. It would have been much more convenient if the two of you had cooperated by dying out on the prairie, but since you didn't . . ."

He paused to push the strand of hair back into place, drew a deep breath, and then smiled serenely. "As they say, a sign of genius is the ability to not only adapt to changing circumstances, but to make the new situation even more advantageous. Before, I would have had only a private satisfaction in knowing you were dead. Now I can have both the pleasure of pulling the trigger myself and the public accolades. I'll claim that I stumbled across a pair of fugitives and that, unfortunately, my civic attempt to see justice done ended tragically."

"And you think people will swallow a coincidence that big?" Rivlin drawled.

"The public loves a good story. They won't look past the surface. I haven't gotten where I am by luck alone. I could shoot Grant himself and get away with it if I have a good story to explain it all."

Her heart thundering, Maddie said, "Killing us isn't going to solve your problems, Senator. We've already told Everett Broadman the whole story. If something happens to us, he's prepared to print it." She paused for the effect, then added carefully, "On the other hand, if we can come to some sort of amicable terms, he's willing to forget what he's heard."

"A very predictable course," Harker said dryly. "But you see, all that Broadman would be printing is the story of a convicted murderess and the marshal who went rogue for the chance to slide under her skirt. Add to that Broadman's vested interest in preserving the family reputation and his known association with Greeley and all you have is a desperate attempt to soil the reputation of an esteemed public servant and political opponent. There'll be a brief tempest, of course. There always is. But it will blow over."

"I've also given a sworn deposition to federal judge William Sanderson," she countered. "Once that's filed, my physical presence in Leavenworth isn't necessary in terms of the testimony I have to give. If something happens to us, Will makes it an official document of the court."

Harker shrugged, his smile confident, the muzzle of the revolver pointed at Rivlin's chest. "Sanderson has a vested interest, too. I'll deal with him the same way I'll deal with Broadman. Do you think I've gotten as far as I have by allowing people like you and Kilpatrick to get in my way? You're by no means the first to think of opposing me and you certainly won't be the first to die for your folly."

Rivlin responded, "I assume you're speaking of Tom Foley and your aide, Jacob Evans."

Harker's laugh was soft and mirthless. "Poor Tom had the uncommon stupidity to threaten to reveal the details of our business dealings and had to be dealt with appropriately. Evans suggested that we disassociate and I happily obliged him. But I assure you, they weren't the first to misjudge me."

"More accurately, to misjudge the blackness of your ambition," Maddie observed.

"I'll make an excellent president, don't you think?"

"General Grant will never give you his endorsement," Rivlin countered. "He'd just as soon spit on you as see you."

The muzzle of the revolver inched upward as Harker snapped, "No thanks to your high-and-mighty, above-the-muck-rich-boy morality and a penchant for tattling. You and pretty little Seth Hoskins. I should have taken you down a few pegs, too. Made *you* beg for mercy and squeal like a little pig into the gag."

Bedside her, Rivlin tensed and snarled low in his throat. Maddie desperately seized the moment. She cried out, pressed a hand to her face, and let her legs crumple beneath her. Even as she fell, she fumbled for the weapon tucked in the folds of her skirt. Two shots exploded, the sound vibrating through her, twisting her heart. Gasping, she rolled onto her side, the butt of the revolver clenched tight in both hands and pointed in the direction of Harker.

Above her, Rivlin stood square and unflinching,

his arm steady as he pointed his gun at Harker and growled, "Drop it or I'll kill you, you goddamned son of a bitch."

Maddie allowed herself only a second to sag with relief, then quickly took in the rest of the situation. Harker still held his gun, but only barely so. His right arm hung limply at his side, a dark, thin line running from under his shirt cuff and down across the back of his hand. As Maddie watched, he slowly reached across himself and took the gun into his left hand.

"Don't!" Rivlin commanded. "Drop it."

"Cincinnati Police! Everyone drop their weapons! Now!"

Putting the small handgun aside, Maddie scrambled to her feet and turned to look over her shoulder. Behind them, a man stood just off the end of the platform, his gun drawn and pointed squarely at Harker.

Dear God, may the others be with him and may they have heard Harker's confessions! Trembling and gasping to breathe, Maddie brought her attention back to the standoff between Rivlin and Harker. Both stood frozen, Rivlin's revolver held steady and strong, Harker's weapon at his side and without a target.

Harker smiled, then called out, "I've captured two fugitives wanted by federal authorities. You've arrived just in time, constable."

"I'm Rob Baker, chief of Cincinnati Police. Put down your weapon, Senator, and submit to arrest."

"And the charge against me?" Harker asked dismissively.

"One count of conspiracy to murder in the first degree—Tom Foley," Will supplied as he, Everett, Adam, Lawrence, John, and another man stepped from the seclusion of the station wall. "One of murder in the first degree—Evans; and two counts of attempted murder in the first degree—Maddie and Rivlin."

"That's Judge Sanderson," Rivlin said quietly.

Will added, "With me as an impartial witness to this exchange is a fellow judge, the Honorable Franklin Corbett."

Everett stepped forward. As usual, his words boomed. "And I can assure you the scandal won't blow over on this, Hark, ol' boy."

They'd been there! They'd heard! "That's Everett Broadman," Maddie said, her pulse skittering with pure relief. "He took down every word of our conversation and noted the witnesses present to it. It will be the front-page story in tomorrow morning's paper. It's over, Senator Harker. You're caught."

Harker's eyes glittered as his gaze darted between her and Rivlin. "A trap inside a trap," he snarled. "Very neatly done, Kilpatrick. We appear to have considerably underestimated each other."

Rivlin recognized the intention the instant Harker shifted the gun in his hand. For a heartbeat he considered intervening, considered exacting his own justice. And then it was too late. Maddie screamed, her first careening into the second as Rivlin reached for her and Harker's head exploded into clumpy wads amidst a silvery red mist.

He was vaguely aware of Harker's body hitting the ground at their feet, vaguely aware of holstering his sidearm, of the confusion and angry voices erupting around him. He held Maddie to him tightly, her violent shudders slamming through him, her sobs hammering hard against his chest.

"Get her the hell out of here!" Everett yelled.

Rob was scrambling forward, gesturing wildly toward the platform. "For God's sakes, go! Take her through there and get my men out here!"

"Close your eyes and don't look, Maddie," he crooned, turning her in his arms and propelling her away from Harker's body and toward the soft light of the platform. "It'll be all right, darlin'. It'll be all right."

People rushed past them in the other direction, scurrying like excited rats to see what they could. Rob's men. Lawrence's men. Travelers, male and female. Rivlin threaded their way through the tide, holding Maddie close in the circle of his arm and making their way toward the central area of the station. Ahead of them a porter overturned a cart, spilling baggage across the marble floor. Rivlin pivoted, seeking the quickest way around the obstacle.

There was a sudden cold pressure at the base of his right ear. He froze. The ratcheting of the hammer came in the same heartbeat that a voice said low and softly, "United States Marshal. Hands in the air, Kilpatrick. Slow and easy."

He did as he was told even as the bumbling porter wheeled around and tore Maddie from his side. She gasped and cried out, looked back at him, her eyes huge and full of tears. The porter clamped his arm around her waist and yanked her from her feet to haul her out of Rivlin's reach.

"She won't fight you!" Rivlin cried, instinctively starting forward. "Don't hurt—"

A cry tore Maddie's throat as the butt of the gun came down at that base of Rivlin's skull. He crumpled to the marble floor, her heart and soul collapsing with him. The sight of him being cuffed was awash in fiery tears and his name came on a ragged sob as she was dragged away.

Chapter Twenty-Three

HE CAME TO in the transport wagon, his head splitting with pain, his gut heaving. He lay on his side on the floor of it, his arms pulled behind his back, the cold metal of iron cuffs tightly encircling his wrists. A shuffling sound came from the darkness around him and he grasped at hope.

"Maddie," he groaned, trying to sit up. The pain in his head wouldn't let him move. His stomach roiled.

"She's not here."

Rivlin recognized the voice—the same man who had pressed the muzzle to his ear and then cracked his skull. Oh, God. Where was Maddie? Was she all right? With every second that passed the odds of getting her back grew more remote. Rivlin fought back a gag. "Where have you taken her?"

"I wouldn't worry about what happens to Rutledge. You've problems enough of your own."

"Call them back," Rivlin moaned desperately. "We can explain. Give us a chance."

The man laughed dryly. "You're out of luck, Kilpatrick."

His stomach lurched upward and there was no fighting it down. The violence of it sent waves of red and then white pain pounding through his brain. Blackness offered him an escape in its wake and he surrendered to the merciful void, knowing that for the moment there was nothing he could do, that his and Maddie's fates were in the hands of his kinsmen.

MADDIE SAT NUMBLY between the two burly men, vaguely hearing the clack of the wheels against the rails. Her wrists were in irons again. Her ankles were also shackled. The other occupants of the train car stared and whispered, but it didn't matter. The marshals had said they were taking her back to Leavenworth to testify, that Rivlin would be dealt with harshly for having let her lead him astray, that she would never see him again. They didn't know Harker was dead. They didn't know the story of why she and Rivlin had traveled the road they had. All they knew, all that they cared about, were that warrants had been issued for her and Rivlin's arrests and they'd seen the task done.

Maddie closed her eyes. It was done, over. Her time with Rivlin had come to the end she'd always known it would. But seeing it coming and enduring it . . . She swallowed back her tears, reminding herself that she'd already shown the marshals more weakness than was wise. They weren't Rivlin Kilpatrick. If you acted like easy prey . . .

Holding her own didn't matter any more than

he stares and whispers, she realized. She didn't care what happened, didn't care what awaited her down the tracks. Rivlin had come into her life and made it worth living. Now he was gone and all that she had left was endless time, the tattered remnants of her heart, and the aching emptiness of her soul.

It hurt so badly, too deep to bear. Maybe if she simply closed down her mind and went to sleep, the pain would have eased when she awoke. Not that she cared if she ever did, she admitted, welcoming the bone-deep lethargy stealing over her. Without Rivlin, nothing mattered.

THEY'D HAD THE FORESIGHT to toss him into a bare cell. With nothing to throw, nothing to smash, he was left to pace and angrily bellow at no one. His head throbbed and his stomach pounded furiously, but they were inconsequential distractions. Where was Maddie? Was she all right? Had they hurt her? Had they cuffed her hands behind her? It frightened her to give up that measure of control. They wouldn't understand that and they'd force her. Had she fought them and been wrestled to the ground and into submission?

Rivlin grabbed the bars to the cell door and, once again, tried to shake it open by sheer force of will. He had to get out of here. Why the hell was he still here? Where were his brothers-in-law? Had any of them even noticed that he and Maddie were missing? Had they even begun to wonder where they were? How long had it been?

How far could they have taken Maddie by now? How long would it take him to find her? He saw her in his mind's eye, looking up at him in the train station and with a tremulous smile telling him that she loved him. She hadn't meant for it to happen, she'd said. Her feelings didn't obligate him, she'd said.

Rivlin clung to the cold metal of the bars as the fullness of truth and understanding washed over him, refusing to be ignored and denied any longer. His knees gave out and he sank to the cold stone floor, overwhelmed by all that he'd had and lost. He hadn't meant for it to happen, either. He hadn't wanted to love her, had known that she was right and that only heartbreak would come of it. He'd kept her by his side, telling himself that it was because he understood her and no one else would protect her. He'd seen it as his professional duty and then as a matter of conscience. But it had been more than that, so very much more. He'd loved her from almost the beginning. He'd loved her when Myra had asked him if he did and he'd denied it. He'd loved her even more when his mother had asked him of his feelings and he'd walked away without answering.

And when he'd looked down into Maddie's eyes in the station, he'd known that she was wrong, that he *was* obligated to her. He just hadn't understood why and where it had come from until now. It wasn't Maddie's heart that bound him to her, it was his own heart that needed her. He loved her, hard and deep and forever. And he hadn't told her.

Maddie had been torn from his arms not knowing that she held his heart in her hands. She was facing the future and thinking . . . Rivlin choked back an anguished sob. He hadn't told her and she thought she was alone again. She didn't know that he'd move heaven and earth to get her back. She didn't know that he'd spend every last penny of the

Kilpatrick fortune and consume the lives of his kinsmen to have her in his arms again. He'd call in every chip owed him, swallow every bit of his pride to beg and plead for favors he didn't deserve.

He grabbed the bars and hauled himself to his feet. "Let me out of here!" he bellowed at the dim light at the end of the long hall. "Let me out or I'll bring this place down around your ears stone by goddamned stone!"

He yelled until his voice wouldn't carry any further than the bars in front of his face. The frustration of no response was added to all his others and he paced the width of the cell with angry strides, furiously sorting through all of his options, ticking through the merits and drawbacks of each, searching for the solution that would get him Maddie back fast and forever. There was only one way to go, he decided. It was a gamble, and there'd be a hefty price to pay for it, but Maddie was worth it all.

He had no idea how long he paced, how long he organized the series of actions he needed to take, how many times he turned the necessary words over in his mind. It felt like an eternity. He heard the jangle of keys and met the guard at the cell door, tamping down the urge to punch the man's teeth down his throat. All that mattered was getting the hell out of here and setting his plans in motion. The door opened and he pushed past the guard, leaving the man reeling in his wake as he stormed down the hall toward the open door at the end of it.

Everett stepped forward to hand him his gun belt the instant he came into the room. "Sorry it took so long," his brother-in-law hastily said. "We didn't know you'd been arrested until Stevens came back to the house without you and we set out looking.

Corbett ordered your release based on your and Maddie's depositions."

"Where's Maddie?" Rivlin demanded, quickly strapping the gun belt around his hips.

"We don't know precisely," Will admitted, handing him his Stetson. "She's not here in Cincinnati. No one in the Marshal Service is talking to us. You're not exactly their favorite officer right now."

"As if I cared what the hell they think of me," Rivlin growled, heading for the door. He heard Will and Everett come after him.

They'd reached the sidewalk when Will caught him by the arm and hauled him to a stop. "I think it's safe to assume that the marshals are taking Maddie out to Leavenworth to testify. I wired ahead to have an attorney waiting to meet them at the station in Kansas City. His only task is to stand between Maddie and everyone else. I have another attorney filing the appeal paperwork in the original jurisdiction. It should be in the court record by noon today. It's only a matter of time before it's granted."

Rivlin pulled his arm from Will's grip. "Much obliged for the effort, Will," he said. "But I'm not wasting time on a goddamned appeal. Maddie doesn't have time."

Everett held up his hands as though the gesture could calm him. "She knows you'll come after her, Riv."

Maddie didn't know anything of the sort. "Find her, Everett," he commanded, his heart pounding, precious seconds ticking away in his mind. "Find her and get word to her. Tell her she's got to hope. She's got to believe in me." He turned on his heel and strode away, certain that Everett would see it done.

"Where the hell are you going?"

"I'll wire you as soon as I can," he called back over his shoulder. "Find Maddie!"

THE TRIP FROM CINCINNATI to St. Louis had passed in a foggy blur. So had the miles between St. Louis and Kansas City. The transfers at each station had been slow and torturous, marked by the mincing steps the leg irons forced her to take and the scandalized stares of her fellow travelers. Maddie settled into the seat between her guards and sighed quietly. Only one more station to negotiate and then her traveling would be done for a time. She looked around, noting the few passengers boarding the car that would take them from Kansas City to Leavenworth. Perhaps, with the many open seats, the marshals would move away from her just a bit. She was so tired of being pinned between them. Being close to them wasn't at all like the feeling she got in being close to Rivlin. There had been comfort in Rivlin's touch, a sense of being safe and cherished. With these men—who steadfastly refused to tell her so much as their names—there was only the sense of being a prisoner.

Maddie shifted, trying to find a position which would ease the ache in her lower back. She couldn't and sought distraction in watching a woman lead a dark-haired little girl to a seat in the middle of the car. Maddie thought of Grace and wondered if Dr. Fabrique had been able to find her a home yet. Every child needed a home, a family, to be loved. If only she were able to give Grace those things. Saddened, Maddie deliberately went back to watching the other passengers file aboard.

A rather short man in a dark business suit and bowler hat came down the aisle, carrying a leather valise before him, the afternoon light reflecting off his thick spectacles as he moved steadily toward the rear of the car.

His gaze met hers and, knowing that she'd been caught in the impropriety of staring, Maddie smiled apologetically before shifting her gaze to the window and the activity on the platform outside.

"Gentlemen, I am Seymour Biggers, attorney at law," she heard the man say with more decisiveness than the look of him had suggested was likely. "I have been retained by Judge William Sanderson to serve as legal counsel for Miss Madeline Rutledge."

Maddie focused her full attention on him. Will had hired an attorney for her? Her heart raced. Maybe he knew something about Rivlin and what was happening to him.

"I'm assuming," said one of her guards, "that somewhere in all those fancy words is something you want."

Seymour Biggers cocked a brow and said coolly. "I'd like to speak to my client."

"So speak," the second guard said.

"Privately."

The first marshal snorted and pointed to the empty seat opposite them. "You can sit down there and talk or you can go away. The prisoner is not leaving our sight."

Biggers considered the option for a half-second, then sat. Pushing his glasses up the bridge of his nose, he laid the valise beside him on the seat, then faced Maddie, his manner suggesting that he was going to pretend that the guards were not there. "Have you been harmed in any way, Miss Rutledge?"

"No. I've been treated well," she answered honestly. All things considered, it could have been much worse than it had been.

"Are you in need of anything?"

To hear Rivlin's voice. To see his smile and the way the corners of his eyes crinkle. To brush the hair from his collar. To be safe and warm in his arms again. Maddie shook her head.

"Have you ever been represented by counsel, Miss Rutledge? Are you aware of the role I am to fulfill?"

Maddie shook her head again, remembering the sound of Rivlin's laughter and how he'd sewn new buttons on her shirt that first day.

"I will accompany you to Leavenworth and remain there until you are released from your obligations to the court. I will be present and advise you of your rights and responsibilities when you are questioned by the prosecutors prior to the delivery of your testimony in the formal proceedings. I will also be present in court and will intervene in your behalf should an attempt be made to compromise your constitutional rights."

"Thank you," Maddie said softly, knowing that he'd paused for her to say something and not willing to admit that she hadn't been paying all that much attention to what he'd said. She gently closed the door on her memories.

"I am also to serve as a conduit of communication between yourself and various parties," he went on. "Both the prosecutorial team and the defense attorneys will confer with me prior to making any requests of you. I intend to strenuously negotiate for concessions in exchange for your cooperation. You are to say nothing, do nothing without my presence and consent. Do you understand?"

"Yes."

"Do you have any questions so far?"

Maddie swallowed and moistened her lips. "When Judge Sanderson hired you, did he happen to say anything about Rivlin Kilpatrick? Do you know if Rivlin's all right?"

Biggers reached into the breast of his jacket and both her guards shifted as they reached for their revolvers. "Only a telegram, gentlemen," the attorney quickly assured them, freezing until they settled back in the seat. He slowly produced the folded piece of paper and handed it to Maddie, saying, "It was delivered into my care while I was waiting your arrival in Kansas City."

Maddie opened it and read.

> RIVLIN RELEASED. STOP. SAYS YOU MUST HOPE, MUST BELIEVE IN HIM. STOP. HE LOVES YOU, MADDIE. STOP. EVERETT.

She read it again. And then a third time, trailing her fingers over the words. Rivlin loved her? Her heart swelled and she blinked back tears. God, how desperately she wanted it to be true. The request that she hope and believe in Rivlin she knew to be from his own lips. How many times had he said those very words to her? Believing in him was easy. She trusted him to the center of her soul. But love . . . It would be safer to see those words as evidence of nothing more than Everett's wishful thinking. And hope . . . Maddie touched the words again.

How many times had she tried to explain to Rivlin the price of hoping? How many times had he asked her how she could live without it? He'd gone through their time together with his vision so firmly focused on tomorrow, hoping and believing that they could triumph over their circumstances.

She'd tried so hard to make him understand that it was an impossible dream, to protect him from the pain of losing it. Damn Rivlin and his hardheadedness. Even now he refused to give up, he still held to hope. Why? Why wouldn't he see the futility of it?

The answer came softly, but with crystalline clarity. Rivlin believed she was worth the risk to his heart. He wouldn't give up because he thought fighting for tomorrow was worth the struggle. He wanted them to be together. All that he asked of her was that she be willing to hope with him, to hold his dream as her own and trust him to make it real for them. It was such a simple, monumental request—made out of faith, hope, and, yes, love. Tears welled in her eyes and spilled over her lashes.

"What is it, Miss Rutledge?" Biggers asked, leaning forward, offering her his linen handkerchief.

She took it from him, dried her eyes, and lifted her chin to smile at him. "An unexpected shift in the foundation of my life, Mr. Biggers. I'll be fine now."

Biggers considered her for a moment, then reached over and opened his valise to remove a sheaf of paper and several well-sharpened pens. "I was advised in Judge Sanderson's telegram of yesterday that he has initiated the process of appeal of your conviction in the Oklahoma Territory," he explained, pulling his valise onto his lap and using it for a desk. "He is certain that a retrial will be ordered and I am to assist in the preliminary preparation for that eventuality. To that end, I will need to ascertain the facts of the case and the particulars of your previous trial and defense."

It was Rivlin's plan, had always been his intention. She had to believe it would work. Maddie took a deep breath. "I was sent to Tahlequah in the Oklahoma Territory to serve the Baptist Mission there," she began.

THE DOORS OPENED and a thick blue cloud of cigar smoke rolled out toward him. The secretary wordlessly motioned him forward and, his hat in hand, Rivlin strode into the lion's den. Poker chips clicked on the green felt tabletop as he came to a stop and waited for permission to speak.

"You look like hammered hell, Kilpatrick."

Yeah, he probably did, his haircut notwithstanding. He hadn't slept in days. His head still throbbed and struck white hot if he turned his neck just right. "Life's gotten a bit complicated recently. I need a favor, sir. You can name your price for it."

More poker chips hit the table. "You must want it badly."

"Yes, sir."

"Well, sit down, have a drink, play a couple of hands, and give me a report. Start with the Harker mess you got yourself involved in."

Rivlin sat and started with the day he'd ridden through the gates of Fort Larned.

Chapter Twenty-Four

MADDIE WATCHED THE DUST MOTES dance in the beam of light passing through the window bars. They were wild today, which meant the world beyond her cell was windy and dry. The air inside the stone square was always chilly, but today it had a keener edge to it than it had had in the days before. How many days? she wondered. She thought back, counting by the only meeting she'd been allowed with Seymour Biggers, the one time she'd been shackled and hauled out to meet with the other attorneys, and the various meals that had been brought to her. Eight. It had been eight days since she'd arrived at Fort Leavenworth.

She smiled ruefully. She'd learned a great deal about the law in the last week, the foremost lesson being that nothing happened without discussing it near to death first. The second lesson had been that concessions were hard to come by. She didn't have a doubt in her mind that Mr. Biggers was a formidable negotiator. But, by all indications, so were the other lawyers involved in the trial. The only benefit she'd seen of Biggers's efforts was the removal of her leg irons. While it was certainly nice to be able to pace her cell with something approximating a normal stride, it only took three to cross the width of it, two to cover the distance between the door and the bed. As a use of her time, it wasn't a noteworthy activity.

Maddie passed her hand through the stream of light, sending the motes into an even wilder swirl. Today was supposed to be the day she went to court and told them all what they'd brought her here to say. She'd been brought a clean wool skirt, a chambray shirt, and a bucket of hot water and a cake of lye soap just a while ago. Maddie ran her hand over the rough blue cloth of her skirt, remembering the feel of the foulard and satin costume Rivlin had bought her in Wichita. What had become of it, she didn't know. A matron had stripped her out of it within minutes of her arrival at the fort. Maddie chuckled quietly. The woman had acted as though taking the corset away was a greatly debilitating punishment. Maddie had let her have it and the illusion.

Illusions. . . . Maddie sighed, rose from the edge of the bed, and stepped into the beam of light. Where was Rivlin? Eight days. It only took three and a half days, maybe four, to get from Cincinnati to Leavenworth. Was he here already and she just didn't know it? Or had he remembered his pledge to Seth and—

Maddie resolutely refused to allow the doubt to develop any further. Her hope was a fragile thing. It crumbled easily and took great effort to put back together again. Lifting her face into the sunlight, she closed her eyes and remembered being out on the prairie, riding with Rivlin, Grace in her arms. Maddie smiled. No matter what happened on the road ahead, the one behind her held good memories. She'd been right to take the chance of loving Rivlin Kilpatrick.

IT WAS JUST PAST NOON when Maddie swore to the same oath that Will had administered in Mother Kilpatrick's dining room and then took her seat in the witness box. The newspaper article she'd read in Mike Meagher's office had led her to expect a packed courtroom and, if not an atmosphere of high tension, then at least a bit of drama. It was anything but dramatic, however, and the only tension seemed to be in waiting to discover if the lead prosecuting attorney was really asleep.

She looked around the courtroom, expecting to at least see Seymour Biggers in the pewlike seating. He wasn't there. In fact, no one was there, not a single reporter or even a disinterested spectator looking for a quiet place to nap. The only occupants of the room were the six members of the respective legal teams, the three defendants—George Foley, Sam Lane, and Bill Collins—and the judge, the bailiff, the court reporter, the twelve acutely bored members of the jury, and herself.

The defense attorney didn't bother to stand up. He simply looked at her and said, "Miss Rutledge, would you please tell the court how you know the defendant, Sam Lane."

Maddie dutifully provided the information and answered what few questions the man asked for in terms of clarification. None of the prosecutors said anything. When the shallow subject of Sam had been fully plumbed, she was asked the same question concerning Bill Collins and then, in turn, George Foley.

"Now that we've established the basis of your original association with the defendants," the defense attorney said, smiling, "please tell the court, Miss Rutledge, why you are sitting in the witness box in wrist irons."

Seymour Biggers had warned her of the certainty of this tactic. He'd described it as "an attempt to discredit the witness and thus impugn the testimony." She knew that, in plain talk, the man was trying to paint her as a liar. It rankled. "I suspect it could be for any number of reasons," Maddie answered. "I wasn't provided an explanation."

He picked up a feather quill from the table and using the tip to clean under his fingernails, asked, "Are you a federal prisoner?"

"Yes."

"For what crime have you been imprisoned, Miss Rutledge?"

"Murder."

"And who sat on the bench at the trial in which you were convicted?"

"George Foley."

He looked up as though stunned by a sudden realization. "The *same* George Foley who is a defendant in this proceeding?"

"Yes."

"Would you say that you're somewhat pleased by the opportunity to testify against him? To turn the tables on him, so to speak."

She considered him and then the three men whom she'd been summoned to testify against. They all watched her with confident smirks. And suddenly she was done being nice and pleasant and docile about all of it. "To be perfectly frank, Mr. Defense

Attorney," she said coolly, "I don't care what happens to George Foley. Or to Sam or Bill, for that matter. I didn't ask to be brought here and I didn't search out the prosecutors to tell them what I know of what went on in Tahlequah. Is there satisfaction in testifying against the three of them? Yes, there is. They're small men with sticky fingers and no consciences."

There was murmuring in the jury box and poorly muffled chuckles from the prosecutors' table. "Speaking of being brought here, Miss Rutledge," the defense attorney said hastily and gruffly. "Is it true that you escaped custody?"

"No, it is not."

"Really?" he asked, leaning forward to glare at her. "Then how is it that you were apprehended by the U.S. Marshals in Cincinnati? Weren't you imprisoned at Fort Larned? How did you end up in Cincinnati if you weren't escaping?"

She knew what he wanted her to say, what he expected her to say. Hell would freeze before she'd drag Rivlin's name into this. And she'd make this man damn sorry he'd even thought to try the strategy.

"Oh," she declared softly, as though some great light had dawned in her simple brain. "You want to hear the story of how George and Sam and Bill—and poor dead Tom Foley—were involved with Senator Harker in stealing all the money from the agency. Why didn't you just say so?"

He blinked, then quickly waved his hand and said, "That will be all, Miss Rutledge. No further questions."

The prosecuting attorney rose from his seat and crossed over to the witness box. He smiled at her and said, "I'd like to hear the story of Senator

Harker's involvement in this whole affair. Would you please tell it, Miss Rutledge?"

The defense attorney vaulted to his feet to protest, claiming that Senator Harker's tragic suicide made any testimony as to his involvement inadmissible since the senator couldn't refute it. The judge agreed with him before the prosecutor could counter the argument. The ruling didn't seem to rattle him in the least. He looked at her, cocked a brow, and said, "Then, if you would, Miss Rutledge, please tell the court the circumstances under which you traveled to Cincinnati."

She did and by the midway point, the jurors were leaning forward in their seats, their attention riveted on her. The prosecutor returned to his seat and smiled as Maddie continued with the tale. The defense attorney tried twice to object to the telling and on the third attempt to interrupt and derail her, the judge ordered him not to try again.

When she was finished, the prosecutor thanked her, said he had no further questions, and turned her over to the defense attorney in case he did. He didn't. He simply waved his hand dismissively while looking out the window of the courtroom. George and Sam and Bill were no longer smirking. There was a long moment of silence and then Judge Abbott picked up his gavel, smacked it sharply on his desktop, and declared, "The court will take a ten-minute recess. The jury will retire and then the bailiff will escort the prisoner to my chambers."

Long seconds ticked slowly past as Maddie watched the jury file from their box and out the door; watched the attorneys and George, Sam, and Bill exit through yet another door. The bailiff closed it behind them, then crossed to the witness box and took her upper arm in hand. Maddie allowed herself to be led out the back door of the courtroom and down a short, dark hallway. She couldn't imagine that they would need her to say another word in court and so she braced herself for the certain sight of marshals who would accept her custody from Abbott and take her to wherever she was to be imprisoned next. She wondered if they would send her back to Fort Larned and if Rosie was still there.

The bailiff guided her across the threshold and into the judge's office. Abbott stood behind his desk, glowering at the army officer standing on the other side of it. They *were* sending her back to Larned, Maddie thought, her gaze skimming over the man in the blue uniform. He'd traveled hard; his coat and trousers were badly wrinkled and dusty, his hat brim coated with a fine gray powder. She breathed deeply and frowned. No scent of horse. He'd come by train? Probably. The careless way he'd tucked his yellow kid gloves through his belt said he was impatient. He probably wasn't any happier about having to escort a female prisoner than Rivlin had been.

She looked him over again, noting the short dark hair barely visible between the brim of his hat and the collar of his jacket. Rivlin's had been long enough that it had curled over his collar and invited her to touch. It had been so wonderfully warm and silky between her fingers. Maddie looked lower, mentally measuring. Her breath caught at the familiar length of leg and width of shoulder. *Rivlin? In military uniform?*

He turned at the sound and her heart thrilled at the sight of him. He hadn't slept in days and the deep shadow on his chin and jaw said he hadn't paused long enough to shave in the better part of a week. He was tired and travel-worn, but he was there; he'd come after her as he'd promised.

She started forward, wanting only to be in his arms again. The bailiff tightened his grip on her upper arm and hauled her backward toward the door through which they'd entered. She stumbled, trying to stay on her feet, never taking her eyes off Rivlin.

Rivlin's hand went to the butt of his revolver as he said through clenched, bared teeth, "Let go of her. *Now!*"

Judge Abbott stepped around the desk, saying, "You may remove the prisoner's irons, bailiff," as he placed himself squarely between her and Rivlin. "Miss Rutledge," the judge said with crisp coolness as the bailiff hurriedly opened the locks, "you will advise this court of your planned whereabouts and present yourself in a timely manner should further testimony be required of you. Do you understand?"

"Yes, sir," she replied as the cuffs fell away. The bailiff again took her arm firmly in hand.

"Major Kilpatrick," Abbott said, turning to face Rivlin, "if you ever appear before my bench in a legal matter, you may be assured that I will remember the manner in which you have invaded my office."

Saying, "And if I ever see you outside of court, you won't be able to eat anything but pudding for the rest of your life," Rivlin stepped around him and started across the room, his jaw set and his eyes hard with determination. The bailiff quickly released her and stepped away as he bore down on him.

Her mind raced as fast as her feet as Rivlin caught her hand in his and led her out another door and down the hall. Had Abbott put her in his custody? Why were Abbott and Rivlin at odds? Rivlin took her out yet another door and into the deserted central foyer of the courthouse. He stopped, slammed the door closed behind them, and then pulled her into his arms.

"Hello, darlin'," he said, looking down at her, a wide smile spreading over his face. "I love you."

The questions were swept away in the flood tide of her happiness. His heart hammered against the palms of her hands and his smile warmed her to the center of her soul. "I love you, too," she declared, twining her arms around his neck and drinking in the sight of him, reveling in the feel of his body against her own again. "And I've missed you so much."

The amber lights in his eyes sparkled. He reached up with one hand and pushed his blue felt hat back on his head. "Show me how much."

Days of weariness and frustration and worry were washed away at the touch of her lips. She was his world and everything had come right. He was alive again: mind, body, and soul. Rivlin gathered her closer, surrendering awareness of everything that existed beyond the wonder of her love, beyond the coiling hunger she always stirred in him. He kissed her in return, tasting her deeply, aching with the need to love her, to devour her and lose himself forever in her.

"Jesus," he whispered, laying a trail of fiery kisses to her ear. "I won't ever have enough of you, Maddie. Never."

She clung to him, trembling, her breathing ragged, and gasped softly, "How long do we have together this time, Rivlin?"

He started, realizing that in his desperation to hold her, to taste her again, he'd assumed that she'd figured out what had happened. He eased back to look into her beautiful blue eyes and was suddenly glad that Abbott hadn't told her as he'd promised he would. Telling her himself was worth the wait. "You're free, Maddie," he said softly, his heart pounding. "By presidential pardon, five days ago. It's carved in stone, no one can take it away from you. No one can ever put you back in prison. You can go wherever you like, do whatever you want with your life."

"President Grant?" she asked incredulously. "But how does he know anything about me? Why would he care?"

"I went to see him. Right after Everett and Will sprung me from jail. I asked the general for a favor and threw myself on his mercy to get it."

Her gaze dropped to his chest. Her hand followed it and she fingered the lapel of his coat. "And this is his price?"

Rivlin put his fingertips under her chin and gently tilted her face up. "I'd have given him any damn thing he asked for, Maddie. He needs decent field commanders and I need you. It was a fair bargain. The only hitch in the whole thing is that my command's in Santa Fe and we have less than two weeks to get there."

"We?" she repeated, hope blooming and surging so wildly that she couldn't breathe.

He trailed his fingertips over her lips. "Marry me, Maddie," he said with gentle earnestness. "Please."

Oh, dear God. It was all her heart had ever wanted, more than she'd ever dreamed she could have. To be Rivlin's wife . . . To be the mother of his children . . . She tried to speak, but couldn't make a sound.

"If you don't marry me," he pressed gently, his eyes twinkling, "there's going to be a whole bunch of disappointed people in Wichita. My entire family's waiting there for us. Myra's got a wedding dress for you."

The mental image shocked her past speechlessness. "Your mother and Myra?" she whispered. "Together?"

"Yeah, I know," he admitted, grinning. "I don't like to think of it, either. We'll just keep our distance and leave town as fast as we can." His grin turned wicked as he added, "And speaking of leaving . . ." He gently pulled her arms from around him and brought her right hand around to lie on his left forearm. "I'm of a mind to make up for some lost time, darlin', but I'm not about to make love to you in the courthouse foyer. I want you in a bed with no interruptions."

"Do you have some particular place in mind?" she asked, walking along at his side, blissfully uncaring where they went as long as they were together.

He slid her a sideways glance. His smile was quirked. "Did I mention that we have Lawrence's private car at our disposal?"

"I remember that car quite fondly," she admitted, smiling as they left the courthouse behind and made their way toward the train station.

"Just so you know, darlin' . . . Consider it a fair warning. You can climb aboard that car as Maddie Rutledge, but I'm not letting you out of it until you've agreed to become Maddie Kilpatrick."

"Maddie Kilpatrick," she said softly, finding it not only easy to say, but comfortable. It felt like it fit her, like it was meant to be her name. *Maddie Kilpatrick.*

"Do you like the sound of it as much as I do?" he asked.

"I like it very much."

He drew her to a stop. "Do you like it enough to wear it for all the todays and tomorrows of your life?"

Tomorrows. . . . He was offering her what he'd pledged to never have for himself. Had he found his peace with Seth in confronting Harker? Could he face the future without looking back with guilt? Her heart whispered that he could. There was a certainty about him that hadn't been there before now, a kind of acceptance and resolution that made him seem more . . . more planted. But she needed to know for sure. Maddie touched his cheek and gently asked, "Are the tomorrows only mine, Rivlin? Have you taken yours back from Seth?"

He caught her hand gently in his and brought it to his lips. He pressed a lingering kiss into her palm, then threaded his fingers through hers. "I'll always regret what happened," he answered quietly, "but I don't want regret to be all there is to my life. I don't want to be alone anymore. I want to be happy, Maddie. I want a family and a home of my own. I want to spend every day of the rest of my life with you. Denying myself those things isn't going to change the past, isn't going to bring Seth back."

His fingers tightened around hers. "Since the day you came into my life, I haven't looked at a single tomorrow without seeing you at my side. I love you and I'll love you and cherish you and protect you until the day I die. That promise means far more than the one I made Seth. It's the one I'll live by if you'll have me for your husband."

Maddie's heart swelled and tears of happiness tightened her throat. "I love you, Rivlin Kilpatrick. I'd be honored to share your name and your life. Today, tomorrow, always."

There would be a wedding and formal words spoken before family and friends, but as Rivlin's arms came around her, Maddie knew that the vows of their hearts had already been spoken. Against all odds, they were one, heart and soul, together forever.

Epilogue

MADDIE SAT IN THE MIDDLE of the luxurious feather bed in a rented palatial room on the second floor of the palatial Empire House Hotel, Grace sleeping in her arms. She stroked the soft cheek and breathed deep the sweet scent of baby. The last two minutes had been the longest stretch of daylight silence she'd experienced since yesterday morning when she and Rivlin had arrived and the clamoring circle of family and friends had closed around them. Maddie closed her eyes and smiled. Had Myra and Mother Kilpatrick been generals, the war wouldn't have lasted more than a month. How they'd managed to so quickly form an alliance remained a mystery. Maddie hadn't been allowed to get a word in edgewise to ask.

As though summoned by her thoughts, the door opened and Myra came in, the embodiment of a refined lady in a circumspect day dress. "You'd think," Myra said, dropping onto a velvet-upholstered chair, "that with all that family of Rivlin's, there'd be at least one unattached male."

"Adam's supposed to be in on this afternoon's train," Maddie offered in the way of hope. "He's eighteen and looks very much like Rivlin."

Myra smiled and shook her head. "I picked a helluva time to retire, you know that, Maddie? Now it wouldn't be anything but cradle robbing."

"You've retired?"

Myra shrugged. "Well, I'd been thinking about going respectable for some time and Rivlin's telegram about your pardon and his family coming here shoved me off the fence. I sold the house to Helen on payments and moved my belongings to this side of the river."

Maddie considered all the questions she wanted to ask and decided that the most pressing concerned preserving Myra's new life. "Does Mother Kilpatrick have any inkling of how you made your living?"

"Inkling?" Myra laughed softly. "Maddie, honey, in the first place this is a small town and it would be only a matter of time before she heard the tales. And in the second place, you know me well enough to know that I can't pussyfoot around the truth. When she asked, I flat-out told her."

Maddie was ever so grateful for having missed that conversation.

"I could have knocked her over with a feather," Myra went on with a flick of her fingers and a grin. She sobered to add, "But I've got to hand it to her. Katherine Kilpatrick is nothing if not determined to do whatever it takes to make Rivlin happy. And since I'm just as determined to see that you're happy . . . Well, it's the basis of a working partnership. And, amazingly enough, in the course of putting together this wedding, we've discovered that we're really more alike than we are different."

Grace stirred in Maddie's arms. Watching the infant scrub her cheek with a tiny fist, Maddie said softly, "I'm glad Dr. Fabrique hasn't been nearly as efficient in finding Grace a home as you and Mother Kilpatrick have been in arranging the details of the wedding. It's so soothing to hold her and watch her sleep."

"Speaking of Mother Kilpatrick," Myra said, pushing herself out of the chair and quickly heading for the door. She opened it, her finger pressed to her lips, to admit Rivlin's mother.

Mother Kilpatrick smiled at Maddie and then at Grace as she stripped her gloves from her hands and quietly said, "I was *finally* able to make arrangements with the band. They assure me they'll play a suitable selection of songs for a reception." She removed her hat and laid it on the bureau as she added, "I stopped by the dress shop on my way back to check on the progress of the alterations. We are so very fortunate that you long ago decided to diversify your holdings, Myra. I can't begin to imagine how we would have been able to find Maddie a suitable trousseau on such short notice if you didn't own both a dry-goods establishment and a millinery shop."

Maddie looked at Myra. A dry-goods store and a millinery shop?

"Well," Myra answered, taking her seat again, "you know what they say about putting all your eggs in one basket. Have I mentioned that I'm considering the purchase of a promising millinery establishment in Santa Fe?"

"Oh?" Mother Kilpatrick seated herself in a chair beside Myra.

Myra nodded. "I noticed an advertisement in the *Eagle* just yesterday morning. The price is certainly attractive and the terms are quite agreeable."

"And it would allow you to visit Maddie and Rivlin from time to time."

Myra grinned and patted a curl at the side of her head. "Quite clever of me, don't you think?"

"You are a woman of amazing resources, Myra Florence."

"As are you, Katherine Kilpatrick," Myra rejoined with apparent sincerity. "I can't remember ever seeing the staff of the Empire House attend to their duties as precisely as they have this last week. It requires great skill to manage people so flawlessly. Perhaps you should consider a future as a hotelier. I think you'd be very good at it."

"Did you happen to notice any newspaper advertisements for such establishments in Santa Fe?"

"No. But if you're seriously considering doing something like that, perhaps you should think about staying on in Wichita for a while after the wedding. We could make inquiries of the lady selling the millinery store in Santa Fe. She might know about a suitable property."

"I'll have to give the idea some thought."

Maddie looked between the two women, amazed at how well they led each other down the road they'd both obviously decided to travel. Smiling, Maddie decided that she'd been wrong earlier. If Myra and Mother Kilpatrick had been generals, the war wouldn't have lasted any longer than a week, at the outside.

There was a knock on the door, but before anyone could move to answer it, it opened and Rivlin poked his head around the edge. His gaze met Maddie's and he grinned as he stepped across the threshold and came across the room. She hadn't seen nearly enough of him since they'd arrived in Wichita. The sight of him in military uniform still startled her, but it was the light in his eyes and the warmth of his smile that made her heart race.

"Rivlin, sweetheart," his mother said. "Do come in."

"Perhaps another time," he said, reaching the side of the bed and leaning over to brush a kiss over Maddie's lips. He drew back with a wink and carefully took Grace from her arms as he added, "I know that you're up to your chins in hammering out life and death details, but I was wondering if I might borrow Maddie and the baby for a little while."

"A short while," his mother admonished as he helped Maddie climb from the bed. "In thirty minutes we have to meet with the hotel manager concerning the dinner menu."

"And then we have the final fitting for the wedding gown right after that," Myra contributed as Maddie let Rivlin guide her out of the room.

The instant he pulled the door closed behind them, Rivlin slipped his arm around her shoulders and gently drew her close for a proper kiss. Grace, held securely in the crook of his left arm, kicked her feet in sleepy protest of the close quarters and they laughingly parted. His arm still around her shoulder, Rivlin eased her away from the door and down the hall.

"Your mother and Myra are planning to buy businesses in Santa Fe so they have an excuse to come visit us often," Maddie said as they went.

"Are they planning to travel together?"

"It wouldn't surprise me if it came down to that. The two of them together are . . ." She shook her head and chuckled.

He laughed softly. "Formidable?"

"And absolutely unstoppable," she rejoined, slipping her arm around his waist. Smiling up at him, she asked, "How have you managed to stay out of their clutches?"

"I've been busy with important business of my own."

Something in his tone . . . Maddie drew them to a halt and arched a brow in silent question.

"I've been getting your wedding present squared away." Rivlin grinned. "Well, it's not your *official* wedding present. Mother insisted that there be the traditional strand of pearls delivered just before the ceremony tomorrow morning. Try to act surprised when it arrives, all right?"

"I don't need pearls," Maddie countered, "but if it'll make your mother happy, I promise to ooh and aah appropriately. And you should try to look deliriously pleased about the gold cuff links Myra insisted that I give you."

"I'll do my best," he assured her. With Grace still tucked along one arm, he opened just enough of his jacket buttons to allow him to reach inside. He produced a folded piece of paper and handed it to her, saying softly, "This is your unofficial wedding present, Maddie. It's what *I* want to give you, what I want to give *us*."

Maddie opened the document and read. She got no further than the third line before she gasped. She looked up at Rivlin in stunned disbelief. He watched her, his eyes dark and gentle and adoring. "Grace is ours?" she asked, hoping she hadn't misunderstood.

"All we have to do is sign the papers," he replied, drawing her closer. "She'll be Grace Kilpatrick."

Her heart swelling with unbridled happiness, Maddie rose to her toes and pressed kisses over his face. "Thank you for loving me, Rivlin," she joyously declared. "Thank you for giving me far more than I ever dreamed I could have."

Rivlin captured her lips with his own, then, mindful of waking Grace, slowly eased back to smile at the woman who had so thoroughly claimed his heart. "We're going to have to work on that dreaming of yours, darlin'," he said softly. "I enjoy the giving too much to even think about stopping."

"What shall I hope for next?" she asked, her eyes bright with excitement and her smile wide.

The door opened down the hallway and Myra poked her head around the jamb.

"Escape," he supplied with a chuckle as he took her hand in his and headed for the stairs.

About the Author

LESLIE LAFOY grew up loving to read and living to write. A former high-school history teacher and department chair, she made the difficult decision to leave academia in 1996 to follow her dream of writing full-time. When not made utterly oblivious to the real world by her current work in progress, she dabbles at being a domestic goddess, and gives credible performances as a hockey wife, a Little League mom, and a cub scout den leader. A fourth generation Kansan, she lives on ten windswept acres of prairie with her husband and son, a Shetland sheepdog, and Sammy the cat.